MW00987380

Those Summer Nights

Also by Mandy Baggot:

Those Summer Nights

Mandy Baggot

bookouture

Published by Bookouture

An imprint of StoryFire Ltd.
23 Sussex Road, Ickenham, UB10 8PN
United Kingdom

www.bookouture.com

ISBN: 978-1-78681-026-7
eBook ISBN: 978-1-78681-025-0

ONE

Southampton, England

'I've bought something.'

Imogen Charlton's breath caught in her throat, and her hand, under strain from a Gut Buster Breakfast Special, started to tilt forward. Baked beans swam their way to the edge of the plate. Her brother Harry's statement had the café noises fading away. Local radio playing the latest from Olly Murs, banter from the truckers, fierce sizzling from the griddle in the kitchen and Old Joe's bronchial cough – it all slipped into the distance as her brain caught up with the three-word sentence.

Steadying the plate, she looked her brother in the eye. It was a bloody boat. She knew it. A *speed*boat. Some hideously expensive Sunseeker he'd got for a *bargain* price from someone at the pub. She scrutinised him closer, wondering if she stared hard enough she might be able to see details of the purchase written on his face. How much money he'd thrown away. How many horsepower and what colour – the listing on eBay when it was confirmed a dud and not good for anything but parts.

'Aren't you going to ask me what it is?' Harry asked in a sing-song tone.

Imogen came to, looking at the plate of sausage, bacon, egg and those watery beans on a slide. She tightened her grip on the china and brushed past Harry, heading for table five. Harry was hot on her heels like an eager, untrained puppy. If he started to pant they really were in trouble. Panting had happened before, just prior to him telling her he had bought a trailer tent.

'Here we are, Brian, sorry about the delay.' Imogen slid the plate onto the Formica table near the window in front of their resident hairy biker.

'Out of Daddies here, darlin'.' Brian held up the empty bottle of brown sauce.

Imogen smiled at her customer. 'Can't have a fry-up without Daddies. I'll be right back.' She about-turned, pushing stray strands of her blonde hair back into place and heading off to the kitchen.

Out of the corner of her eye she saw Harry's smile drop. 'Why do I get the distinct impression I'm being ignored?' he asked, crossing his arms over his chest and looking affronted.

Imogen turned back to him, feeling bad. The sparkle in Harry's blue eyes was fading, his floppy blond hair slightly losing its bounce. She wiped her hands down the front of her apron and forced an upbeat look. She was betting, if it wasn't a boat, it was something in bulk. She still had a hundred bottles of antifreeze 'capable of thawing Antarctica' in her garage.

Harry's smile was back and Imogen braced herself. *Not a boat. Not a boat.*

'I've bought a restaurant.'

Be a boat. Be a boat. Her first urge was to thump Harry squarely in the chest to stop him saying anything else. He couldn't be serious. It would be something else. A joke. Or maybe it was Lego. Yes, wasn't he constructing something serious with Tristan? They'd done the Millennium Falcon and everything in between. Now maybe it was time for a building-brick Harvester.

'Lovely,' she said, swiping up two finished mugs from table two. 'How many hours is that going to take to complete?'

Harry blew out a breath, his arms folding behind his head, hands on the back of his skull. 'Wow, I don't know.' His abdomen expanded as he bent his torso back. 'I mean, you can't tell everything that's involved from the pictures.'

Imogen nodded. 'And the instructions are always pretty useless too.'

She watched Harry's brow furrow. 'Well, I have had a couple of really detailed emails.'

'From Lego?'

'What?' Harry laughed.

Imogen grabbed a bottle of Daddies sauce from table two and held it tight in both hands. It *wasn't* Lego. He'd said the word 'restaurant' and he really *meant* 'restaurant'.

'Like this place?' Imogen asked, waving the sauce bottle to highlight the tables and chairs and people eating their way to heart disease.

'Oh no,' Harry said, shaking his head. 'Not like this place.'

What did that mean? She didn't know what to say next. Brian's waving became frenzied and Imogen rushed over to table five and handed over the sauce with a quick apology.

Coming back she took Harry by his plaid shirt-covered arm and tugged him over to the serving hatch where more orders were waiting for her. The scent of deep-frying wafted through the opening as she pulled a white slip off the door.

'Harry,' she begged. 'The other week you said you were thinking of starting a local club for fans of *Castle*.'

'I might still do that.' He looked sheepish. 'Maybe in the winter.'

Imogen shook her head. 'You *can't* have bought a restaurant.'

'Why not?' Harry asked, folding his arms across his chest again and looking close to defiant.

'Because when people go down the pub they go for a drink...
maybe a packet of crisps, or pork scratchings on a particularly
rough day. And if they buy something from a dodgy bloke in a
hoody it's pirate DVDs or miracle anti-ageing face cream that
turns out to be relabelled Swarfega.'

'Who said I bought it down the pub?'

'Harry, tell me what you've done,' Imogen ordered, picking
up two plates of scrambled eggs.

'I *have* told you.' Harry grinned again. 'I've bought a restaurant.'

This was bad. He sounded genuinely serious. How could that
be? She'd only spoken to him two days ago. They'd visited their
mum, Grace. Imogen had brought two Jill Mansell books and
the latest copy of Bella and Harry had brought pickled onion
Monster Munch and ate them all himself. She knew, in between
their mum's talk about the weather – too hot one day, too cold
the next – there had been no indication Harry was about to
purchase a catering business.

Imogen deposited the scrambled eggs on table six and headed back to the hatch for the accompanying drinks.

'Tell me it's another sandwich van.'

Harry laughed, his eyes crinkling at the corners. 'Why would
I want another sandwich van? Sandwiches are old school now.'

Shit. 'Why would you want a restaurant?' she responded,
moving forward, stepping over Mrs Green's bag of knitting in
the walkway.

'Because I need another job, Immy and...' Harry began, following her.

Imogen looked over her shoulder at him as she delivered the
coffees. He'd got Mrs Green's pale lemon three-ply wool stuck in
the Velcro straps of his trainers.

'And...' Harry started again.

'Harry, just stop walking!' She'd raised her voice just as the radio went quiet and forced a smile. 'Please, just stop before you become part of a matinee jacket for Baby George-slash-Georgina.'

Harry glanced down at his feet and the wool caught up in his shoes. 'Oh dear. Sorry,' he said, bending down to unravel himself.

'Harry, don't. Just…' Imogen sighed. 'I'm really busy. Just spit it out. Tell me about this restaurant in very short sentences.'

Harry stood up, a grin back on his face. 'I've bought it.'

Imogen kept quiet, hoping she could sort this out, help him go back on the deal.

'And I want you to run it with me.'

Double shit.

'And you're going to love this part the best!'

She felt sick.

'It's in Corfu! In Greece!'

Fuck. She was officially screwed.

TWO

Southampton, England

'It's got so much space. There's a separate function room out the back and a large flat above. It's right on the beach. I mean, the view is to die for and in the summer it's going to be packed with holidaymakers. It's perfect.' Harry grinned before shovelling in another mouthful of chips. 'And it's Corfu! It's where Janie and I had our first foreign holiday together and three more after that before the children arrived. I can still smell those lemons on the trees and taste the *ouzo*.'

Harry had come back after the lunch rush and Imogen was huddled over a tuna jacket potato she had no intention of eating, looking at the restaurant details. The price said ninety-nine thousand Euro and underneath was the word 'Acharavi' – presumably the place in Corfu this disaster was situated. The building looked far from *her* definition of perfect. With its roof resembling a pile of tiles a three-year-old had scattered randomly, smashed front windows and graffiti in the Greek alphabet on the outside walls, it looked like something from a warzone, not this appealing summer bistro Harry was describing. There was only one explanation. He was manic. He had to be suffering again and she had missed the signs. She needed to get him to his doctor. Depression was a heavy beast and, when things were at their worst, the whole family had gone through it with him. And he was talking about Janie as if everything was fine. He had never accepted the separation and Imogen wasn't sure what their current position was.

'Harry,' Imogen said softly. 'You haven't paid any money out yet, have you?'

He laughed then, eyes shining like a happy Minion. 'Of course I have. The deal's done. I've been working on this for weeks.'

Had she really taken her eye so far off the ball? 'You… you didn't say anything,' she croaked, her head starting to throb.

'No, of course I didn't,' Harry said, gulping at his glass of Coke.

'Well, why not?'

'Because you would have said I was crazy and tried to stop me.'

'Yes!' Imogen exclaimed. 'Yes, I would have and that's exactly *why* you should have told me!' She put her hands into her hair, clenching clumps into her fists.

'Why are you angry?' Harry asked, eyes wide, hair rumpled, a blob of ketchup on his shirt, looking a bit like a rejected toy at a jumble sale.

'I'm angry because this is another one of your fads, Harry.'

'Fads?'

'Impulses… ridiculous urges… mad ideas.' She sighed. 'Are you getting the picture?'

'I don't know what you're talking about.' Harry sat back in his seat now, arms folding across his chest.

'Harry, a couple of months ago you told me you were thinking of being a cox for the next GB Olympic rowing team.'

'It was just a loose idea. I do have some experience in that area.'

'Then it was being a rep selling pet food.' That had been a disaster. He had constantly smelled of liver and he had lost more money than he'd made.

Harry sat forward, pointing his finger at Imogen. 'Now, that was a good idea. If I hadn't had to buy so much product up front that could have worked out well.'

Imogen shook her head. 'This restaurant. It's a mad idea, Harry.'

There was no point going softly softly. Her brother needed to hear the facts. How could he possibly buy a dilapidated building in Corfu, let alone think he was going to run it as a profitable business? You didn't need to be an expert in international finance to know that Greece was going through a sticky patch.

'Why's it a mad idea?'

'Because…' Imogen picked up the details and shook them in the air. 'Look at it! It looks like it belongs to someone with an ASBO.'

'It's just been slightly neglected, that's all.'

'*Slightly* neglected?! The weeds have almost formed a privet hedge.'

Imogen watched as Harry picked at a thread on the leg of his jeans. This sort of behaviour, coupled with his refusal to deal with his depression, was why his marriage was on the verge of collapse. Harry and Janie were on a break. Originally intended to be a few weeks it had so far been almost four months.

For over a year Harry had been unsettled, up and down more than a trapeze artist, making steady employment and being completely present in a relationship akin to trying to run up Kilimanjaro in six-inch heels. Son Tristan and daughter Olivia were Harry's first priority, but they were having to adjust to their father not living with them and it wasn't doing them any good. Imogen swallowed. Now there seemed to be a restaurant too. 'What about Tristan and Olivia?'

Harry looked up, his eyes quizzical.

'If you head off to Corfu you'll hardly see them,' she added.

Harry sat up straighter. 'This is what's going to bring us all back together.' He smiled. 'Janie loves Corfu. We were in love in Corfu. Think of it, Immy. Olivia would love the beach and Tristan and I could go hiking like we used to.' Harry reached for the property details on the table and picked them up. 'This place, it doesn't look like much now, but I know we can make it work.' He turned his full attention to her. 'You and me, working together, making a go of a restaurant.'

He really meant it. Harry thought he was going to be the next Hugh Fearnley-Whittingstall, spending the summer ankle deep in crushed grapes for wine or boiling up arse of local goat to create an aromatic jus.

'You've got the skills and I had the money.' He laughed. 'I can see us cooking up a storm in the kitchen while our customers sit back and relax, their eyes on the sea view.'

'Harry, I work in a transport café. It isn't haute cuisine.'

'You used to do haute cuisine though.' He grinned, then sang. 'Watch me whip, watch me flambé.' He waved a hand in the air. 'And you're doing that exam now. Business and stuff.'

'It's an NVQ.' And the truth was, she was struggling with it.

Her career path when she had left school had been to complete a business studies and hotelier diploma. Working in the hotel industry had been a long held dream ever since their father had brought her souvenirs – conch shells, a necklace made of pebbles – and a pen from every different hotel he'd stayed at when he'd travelled for work. Those glossy ballpoints and his stories about the tropical heat of Malaysia and sands of Australia had filled her with ambition and longing to see more of the world – until the day he hadn't come home. Her grief had killed every single dream and she'd run headlong into marriage with the first man she'd fallen for and planted her feet firmly on English ground.

Ten GCSEs, a finalised divorce and those knick-knacks collecting dust were all she had to show for her twenty-eight years. Study was so much harder now and coming home to hit the books after a full day on her feet at the café just wasn't working. All she craved was something she hadn't served up during the day – usually pizza – and a couple of glasses of wine. Her days of taking time to perfect a little Spanish tapas or a rich tagine had been swamped by real life and the need to meet mortgage payments. The only reason she was struggling on with the course was because she had found out about the Wyatt Hotel Group's Leadership and Development programme. After several chardonnays and a few too many slices of pepperoni, she had filled in the online form to apply. White wine had helped her write truthful and confident-sounding responses to the questions and she'd ended the page with a heartfelt soliloquy about her interest in the hotel industry because of her late father's travels. The next day, seeing the automated response saying her application had been received, she immediately regretted being so naïve. Re-reading the page made it clear the hotel group wanted graduates, not her and her basic ability to keep Mrs Green happy with a toasted teacake.

'I'm a waitress, Harry,' she reminded him.

'You do a mean paella.' He blinked his blond eyelashes at her and pouted. 'And what about when you cooked for me and Janie when she was trying to seduce those clients? Salmon mousse, steak and ale pie and a brandy snap basket that could have been put on display.'

'None of that is remotely Greek.'

'Who says we have to open a *Greek* restaurant?'

'It's in Greece. I think that's a pretty big clue.'

'Which means they have hundreds of tavernas. We could do something different. Fish and chips… or tapas.' He nodded at Imogen. 'You know how to do tapas, don't you?'

'I usually just open a packet from Tesco these days.' She shook her head. 'And you can't just go over to Greece and start stamping the Union Jack over everything, Harry.'

In truth her mouth was watering over the thought of Greek food. There was a lovely place not far from her house that was as authentic as you could get in England. Greek scenes in oils on the walls, candlelight, pretty tablecloths and dish after dish of treats – the salty sourness of the feta cheese on hot, fresh bread, the smooth, creamy texture of the *taramasalata*, the succulent aubergine in the *moussaka* and the tangy, sweet lemon of the drizzle cake for pudding. She could almost taste it.

'I knew you wouldn't take this seriously,' Harry said, his tone cross.

'I am. Really, you have no idea how serious I think this is.'

Harry reached over the table and took her hand in his. 'Just picture the scene, Immy. You and me, our own business, in Greece. The sun, the sea, the Soltan Once for my fair skin.' He laughed. 'A new start for the both of us.' He paused. 'I just know Corfu could make us both happy.'

The excitement and hope in his voice stabbed at Imogen's heart. As much as she wanted to grab him and shake him to his senses she couldn't crush this dream to death today. She would just have to hope another grand, ridiculous plan was going to come along before Harry booked the plane tickets. Did she know anyone, anyone at all, who was selling a boat?

She smiled and patted Harry's hand. 'We'll see.'

Harry grinned. 'That's as good as a yes, then.'

THREE

Rethymnon, Crete, Greece

Panos Dimitriou couldn't believe what he was hearing. He held the telephone away from his ear and moved his eyes to the scene outside his balcony windows. It was a beautiful summer day, a light, warm breeze shifting the translucent gauze hanging over the ajar French doors. There was the Greek coastline, a cruise ship moving sedately across the water, sun glinting from the caps of latent waves. He took a breath, hoping it would extinguish the burning fire pit in his belly.

'Pano, you cannot be angry about this,' his grandmother, Elpida spoke down the phone line.

Oh, he could be angry. No, angry didn't cover it at all, he was *furious*. How had this happened? The last time he'd visited his grandmother she hadn't said anything about selling the family restaurant. He knew she had been struggling, had employed a manager but this… this had come right out of the blue. And where was her family loyalty? As that last thought rode through his bones it jarred a little. He adjusted his position in his leather chair and pressed the phone closer to his ear.

'It's over a year since I've seen you,' Elpida continued.

Panos let out a snort of disagreement. 'It's not a year.'

'It was Easter, *last* year.' She sighed. 'We had such a wonderful time. Throwing pots from the top of the house like we did when you were small.'

Was it a year ago? Something stabbed his conscience like a mosquito needling its victim. He had been *extraordinarily* busy. The past six months had been full on. He'd clinched deal after deal, travelling all over Greece, sprinkling much needed employment everywhere he could… and making a small fortune. He looked at the gold watch on his wrist. He was no longer the son of the man who lost everything. He was the man *with* everything. And that was how it would stay.

'… and we made *baklava* and you ate so much you were sick.'

He shook his head. '*You* made *baklava*, *yiayia*.' Sentimentality quickly killed. How could she talk about tradition and missing him when she had sold the family business?

'So, when are you coming to visit?' Elpida asked with all the finesse of someone who was used to being in charge.

'As soon as you tell me I can take over the restaurant.' There was little point beating around the bush. The thought someone else was going to make a fortune on a project that should be his was scratching his innards.

'You never had any intention of taking it over,' she snapped in response. 'If I thought you had I would not have sold this.'

'*Yiayia*…'

'Pfft! Don't *yiayia* me, Pano. I know what you would do to the restaurant.' She puffed out a breath. 'You'd bring a bulldozer onto the beach and knock it down, along with every other business around it.' She breathed in. 'And then you'd cover it in steel and mirrors and let people hardly more than children drink so much *ouzo* they take off all their clothes in public.'

He shook his head. She had never understood what he did. Even after all his father had put the family through, Elpida still didn't know why he had to be a success.

'Your father… he would not have done this.'

It was a low blow to the gut. 'My father literally threw his life away.' He tightened his grip on the receiver. 'And I do not wish to discuss it.'

'Have you called your mother? Your stepfather was nominated for an award.'

Panos knew that. His stepfather John's nomination for a prestigious English business award had been all over the financial news. And he hated it. It was almost as if his mother, Sophia, had picked a second husband who came with a guarantee of success after being burned the first time. Each reminder of John's brilliant business endeavours was like salt being rubbed into sore wounds. And no matter how hard he fought it, he always felt like he was proving himself to cancel out his father's bad deeds. And sometimes more than that. Sometimes, usually alone – frequently with a bottle of Metaxa brandy – it felt like he had to be the man his father had wanted but failed to be – the man John was.

'Did you tell *her* you had sold the restaurant?' he bit back.

There was another intake of breath before a pause. 'She was the one who suggested this.'

He clamped his eyes shut as visions of his mother fought their way into his mind. Her long, red hair, the warm smile.

'I am not getting any younger, Pano,' Elpida continued.

He opened his eyes. 'Which is why you should have sold the restaurant to me.'

'Pfft! And let it become one of those bars you build? In Acharavi?' She blew out a breath. 'Never.' A spate of coughing ensued.

'You are still smoking!' Panos exclaimed. 'I knew it!' He thumped his free hand on the desk and got to his feet.

'What do you care? I never hear from you. I never see you. What do you care if I smoke? What do you care if I collapse right now and never breathe again?'

'*Yiayia,* that is not true.' He walked toward the balcony doors, pausing at the threshold as the warmth began to prickle through the sleeves of his cotton shirt.

'What is true is that I am glad to be rid of the restaurant. There was nothing there for me anymore. It wasn't the place I remember. The people are all gone and the memories went with them. I have no care for dwelling in the past. I only have time for those willing to share some time with me.' She paused. 'Who knows how long I have left?'

He pushed outside, stepping into the Cretan sun, making for the stone wall of the balcony overlooking the town. He raised his face to the sky, letting the heat hit his olive-skinned cheeks as he tried to think of what to say. He loved his grandmother, but he still didn't understand why she had done this. If she didn't want to remember the past why was she so opposed to embracing the future and his reinvention business? And why had she sold out to someone else? Surely whoever had bought it was going to have the same idea as him. It couldn't be profitable as a little local restaurant in these times. It needed to be flashy, something special to attract hordes of tourists rather than just a few couples or families still craving quaint and rustic. Redevelopment was the only sensible option.

'I'm coming home,' he stated.

The words almost choked him. That wasn't what he'd planned to say. Did he really need to go back to Corfu? There were plenty of other projects requiring his attention. He didn't want the family business. Maybe he should just let it go. *Lose out. Miss opportunity.* He gritted his teeth. No, he couldn't let it lie. And he was damned if he was going to let someone walk in and steal it from him.

'I'll make up the spare room,' Elpida answered. 'Your cousin Risto will be so pleased to see you.'

He could tell she was smiling.

FOUR

Botley Lane, Southampton, England

Imogen had been forced to cook today. Mary had called in sick, so after the breakfast rush Imogen had raided the store cupboard and got to work on something a little different for the lunch-time crowd. The goat's cheese and caramelised onion tart and mixed red berry pie hadn't outsold the jacket potatoes but she'd received plenty of compliments. Luckily no one had seemed to notice the pastry wasn't homemade. Pastry was her nemesis.

Juggling the leftovers, Imogen pressed the doorbell of her mum's home. She was hoping Harry had already left to take Tristan to Scouts. She wanted her mum to herself to tell her all about this restaurant in Corfu.

The door opened a crack and one blue eye appeared just above the gold-coloured security chain.

'Mum, it's me,' Imogen announced. 'I forgot my key.'

The eye seemed to refocus like a darts player staring out the bullseye before finally a hand reached up and unlatched the chain. The door opened and there was her mum, wavy blonde hair not brushed, wearing a Marks and Spencer dressing gown and poodle-head slippers on her feet.

'What time is it?' Grace asked.

'It's half past six, Mum. Aren't you feeling very well?' Imogen asked as she entered the hallway.

'I'm fine. Why?' Grace snapped.

'No reason. I just… You're wearing your dressing gown already,' Imogen said.

'So? I haven't been out today. It isn't a crime, you know, to wear comfortable clothes. It's not like I've got a garden party at Buckingham Palace to go to or… anywhere to go to with April.'

At the mention of her much-loved neighbour and best friend a sob escaped Grace's lips. And that was where the problem lay, with the lack of hair brushing and getting dressed. April had filled the gap Glen's death had left. Grace and April had been two widows together, taking trips to the garden centre, coach tours to the bulb fields of Holland and the war graves of France. Inseparable bosom buddies, until cancer had claimed April just last month. Now it was like Grace had been widowed all over again.

Imogen put the food down on the wooden console table that held the digital analogue-style phone, the flip-up address book and a wooden ashtray Harry had made in Year 9.

'Oh, Mum, come here,' Imogen said, gathering her mum into an embrace. 'What would April say if she could see you like this?'

Grace sniffed hard. 'She'd tell me off. She always hated this dressing gown.'

'So you know that staying cooped up in here isn't doing you any good.'

'I don't want it to do me good,' Grace retorted.

'Don't say that, Mum. I mean, I know how much you loved April but you've got me and Harry… and Janie and the children,' Imogen said.

'Who I never see any more because Janie won't come over.'

Imogen swallowed. She did have a point. Harry and Janie's separation had changed things for all of them. Before the couple's split there had been Sunday lunches, all around the table like when her dad had been alive. April had been part of that too. They'd all eaten their own bodyweight in chicken and taken it in turns to urge Tristan to eat his carrots. Since April had passed Grace had refused to leave the house, even for bingo.

'Listen,' Imogen began, letting her mum go and turning to the small table. 'I've got a tart and some pie here. Why don't I warm it up and make some tea and we can have a chat.'

'I'm not hungry,' Grace answered, folding her arms across her chest.

'It's goat's cheese and caramelised onion,' Imogen tempted, holding the cling film-wrapped parcel closer to her mum's face.

Grace closed her eyes in defiance.

'It will go to waste if you don't eat it. You know how April felt about waste. She'd rather have stuffed herself sick with roast potatoes than see one go in the bin.'

Grace's eyes slowly opened, then dropped down to the platter. 'Just a very small piece.'

Imogen poured tea from a pot her dad had brought back from Singapore. The house was still full of so many memories of him. Harry had had their parents' wedding photo blown up into a sixteen inch by twelve canvas for Grace's sixtieth birthday and it sat over the wooden mantle above the fireplace. Across the shelves were ornaments and reminders of Glen's life and travels: a miniature barrel of whisky from a trip to Edinburgh, a silver piskie on a rock from Cornwall, ornate Portuguese plates. She turned her attention back to her mum.

'So, Mum, has Harry said anything to you about Corfu?' she asked.

'Corfu?' Grace said between chomps. 'Corfu in Greece?'

'Yes,' Imogen said. 'Corfu in Greece.'

'No. Why? Should he have?'

Imogen steeled herself as her mother stopped eating and set those blue eyes on her.

'What's going on, Imogen?'

'I don't really know,' Imogen sighed. 'But... Harry says he's bought a restaurant in Corfu.'

She met Grace's eyes as the ticking of the clock on the wall – an original cuckoo piece her dad had brought back from Switzerland – overrode everything else.

Grace seemed to grow out of the dressing gown, her untamed hair widening as she straightened her back. 'What!'

Caught between being concerned about what Grace was going to say next and being pleased her mum was showing an emotion other than despondency, Imogen opted for spearing a piece of tart with her fork.

'He's bought a restaurant!' Grace exclaimed. 'In Greece?! Oh, Imogen, is this like the sandwich van?'

Imogen swallowed. Harry's first venture into catering was infamous. He'd bought a van, filled it with sandwiches and taken it around building sites and offices. By the time he'd hit the heat of midday in August and the refrigeration unit had packed up, the tuna and chicken were well past their best. When everyone fell ill and it made the local paper it was Imogen who had to dispose of the evidence and sell the van on Gumtree.

'Or is it depression again?' Grace asked, hands going to her mouth, looking like shock was about to set in. 'It's that, isn't it? It's the side of it that makes him feel he can conquer the world. The bit before he comes crashing back down to Earth and rocks in a corner.'

Imogen swallowed, remembering a particularly bad episode when Harry had forgotten to pick the children up from school. It was a couple of months after the accident at work and everyone thought he was slowly recovering. Physically he was getting better, mentally it had stirred a lot of things up.

'I don't know. I thought that too but—'

'But, why would someone thinking straight, someone who used to be an aircraft engineer, buy a restaurant in another country?'

'I'm pretty sure he's done it to try and win Janie back.' She sighed. 'It's been months now and I think he thinks he needs a bold move, something big, to get her attention and... to prove himself.'

'Whatever happened to buying flowers or chocolates and saying you're sorry?' Grace tutted, shaking her head. 'You need to sort this out, Imogen. He listens to you.'

'I'm not sure he does.'

'And you need to speak to Janie,' Grace went on, shifting in her chair and reaching for the belt of her dressing gown to tighten the fastening. 'They may not be together at the moment but buying restaurants and moving to the other side of Europe isn't the route to go down if he wants a chance of making things right again. Surely you can see that.'

All Imogen saw was that her brother was Red Bull happy. Seduced by the chance of a new life in another country, battling for his family, wanting her to help him... and here in front of her was her mother – worried and still in her dressing gown from the night before.

'April would say "you need to take him in hand, Grace".'

Imogen reached across the table and placed her hand over her mum's. 'Mum, don't get upset. I'll talk to him and I'll talk to Janie. I promise.'

She squeezed Grace's hand and said a silent prayer that this restaurant transaction was somehow reversible.

FIVE

Forsyth Road, Southampton, England

Imogen sat in her silver Fiesta outside the red-bricked, semi-detached home, torn between looking at the property details in her hand and the lights on behind the net curtains.

The restaurant became more dilapidated with each glance. It was taunting her now; the broken windows looked more broken and she was sure the weeds had grown in height since that morning. At the very corner of the photo, only just visible if she squinted, was the shape of a small creature she'd convinced herself was a rat. She closed her eyes and took a deep breath. This was nothing that couldn't be fixed. She would help steady the ship, steer Harry down the right path. Things could be a lot worse. She was in control here and, any day, maybe, if they didn't have many other applicants, or if all the other emails went into spam, she could get a response about her dream job. A little frisson sparked through her.

Imogen stepped out of the car. It was a warm July evening and in the dusky sky the sun was just beginning its descent. She walked up the path and stood facing the forest-green front door of her brother's home. The home he hadn't been living in for months. Imogen hadn't visited for a couple of weeks now and guilt rumbled through her. When the separation had first happened – after she had had Harry sleeping in her spare room and drowning his sorrows in banana Nesquik – she was torn between making contact and not. It was Harry and Janie's relationship not hers. She didn't want to appear to be interfering but didn't want to look disinterested either. She also didn't want to lose touch with the children. She loved Olivia and Tristan so much. Caught between a rock and a hard place she'd called Janie as soon as Harry had decamped to Grace's. She'd had Janie and the children over for dinner – herby lamb burgers with a beetroot mayo she'd made herself and Häagen Dazs for pudding – and Janie had appeared almost as sad as Harry. But Imogen hadn't given her opinion, or advice, she'd just been there. And, no matter what, she was going to carry on being there for the sister-in-law she loved. They just needed to tackle Situation Corfu first.

She pressed the doorbell with conviction. She heard foot-steps. Two sets? More? Imogen pulled the sleeve of her shirt up, checking the time on her watch. Was Tristan back from Scouts? Was Harry there? Holding her breath, she waited.

Finally, after what seemed like aeons, the door swung back and there was Janie, and seven-year-old Olivia at her mother's side. Her niece's curly blonde hair bounced as she jigged about, brandishing a wooden spoon. Imogen smiled at her. 'Gosh, you're armed.'

Olivia grinned. 'Hi, Auntie Imogen. We're making cakes for the fete at school tomorrow. Do you want to come and help?'

Imogen smiled. 'What sort? Battenburg? Angel?'

Olivia giggled. 'Chocolate.'

'My favourite.'

Janie didn't look any different to the last time Imogen had seen her. Her hair was immaculate in a sleek, mahogany bob, she had a blue-and-white-striped apron on over a work suit and high-wedged shoes still on her feet.

'Help me lick the bowl out?' Olivia suggested, her tongue lolling onto the spoon.

Janie opened the door a little wider and took a half step back. 'You've already licked the bowl out,' she said to Olivia. 'Maybe Auntie Imogen would prefer a coffee.'

'I'll make it. I need to practice for my Brownie badge.' Olivia made an about turn and skidded up the laminate floor towards the kitchen.

Janie let out a sigh as Imogen stepped up into the house. 'What's he done this time?'

Imogen gave her a watery smile. 'Is it that obvious?'

'I know the look you're wearing, Imogen. It's one I perfected over ten years.'

Suddenly she noticed how tired her sister-in-law looked. It couldn't be easy managing two children and her job on her own. Maybe Imogen should have pitched in to help more, but she'd been too busy managing the fall-out with Harry. He'd almost made an investment in BitCoin the day after he'd moved out.

'Oh God.' Janie's hands went to her mouth as Imogen closed the front door behind her. 'It isn't your mum, is it? Has something happened? I know she hasn't been too well.'

'No... no, she's fine.' Imogen swallowed. 'Well... still grieving for April and not getting dressed but... nothing else.'

'So it *is* Harry.' Janie's voice was back to sounding harassed as she led the way down the hall towards the kitchen. The radio was on, playing an upbeat summer pop tune, and Olivia was shrugging her shoulders in time to the beat, knelt up on a stool, waiting for the boiling kettle. Janie steadied her daughter's shoulders.

'Yes, it's Harry,' Imogen answered. She wriggled her handbag off from across her body and put it down on the granite-topped island. She sighed. 'He's bought something.'

'Oh shit.' Janie whipped her head around. 'It's not a boat, is it?'

'No it's… much worse.' She swallowed, the photos of the Corfiot restaurant already burnt into her retinas. 'It's a restaurant.'

'Daddy's bought a restaurant?! That's so cool!' Olivia piped up, face covered in chocolate icing, boiling hot kettle swinging from her hand. Janie made a grab for it, steadying it over the mug.

'Concentrate on the hot drinks, darling,' Janie advised before hitching her head towards the living room.

Imogen got the message. She stepped through the double doors that separated the lounge from the kitchen–diner and plumped for Harry's leather chair in the corner. Well, what *had been* Harry's chair. She started to lower into it then stopped where she stood.

Janie closed the doors, then turned, wringing her hands like she was about to receive fatal news or be ejected from *The X-Factor*.

'It isn't good, Janie,' Imogen started. 'The restaurant is in Corfu.'

'Corfu!' Janie's hands went to her hair. 'You've got to be kidding.'

Imogen shook her head. 'No, unfortunately I'm not. I spoke to the agent today. It's been months in the making. He had to get a Greek bank account and a tax number, a lawyer and a notary to make the purchase and he did it all without telling me… and I assume without telling you, from the expression you're wearing.'

Janie looked like she might cry and Imogen considered going over to her, giving her some sort of hug of consolation. She stayed where she was though, feeling just a little uncomfortable.

'Why has he done this? I mean Corfu… OK, it's where we had some of our best holidays together before we had the children.' She tutted. 'And we joked about calling Tristan Spiros once… but this is walking away, isn't it? From me and the children and our marriage.' Janie put her hands to her head.

'No,' Imogen said. 'That isn't what it is.'

Imogen didn't want to be here telling Janie this but it would be just like Harry to bluster in when he was collecting the children and announce he was leaving for Corfu like he was just off to do a weekly shop at Aldi. Her brother delivering the news in a blasé way would have been far worse. Apocalyptic, probably.

A long breath left Janie's lips. 'I know you and Grace think I gave up on him…'

'What? No!' Imogen exclaimed. 'We don't think that at all!'

'But I have to think of the children, and Harry… when he's having a down episode is… just… soul destroying.' Janie raised her eyes to Imogen's. 'I have to feel confident that he's getting better and that what we have is strong.'

'I know,' Imogen said. She slipped her hands into the pockets of her jeans. 'I understand completely and so does Mum.'

Janie sighed and her body dropped down to the leather settee. 'And now he's gone and bought a restaurant in Corfu.'

Imogen nodded. 'Yes.'

Watching Janie close her eyes and shake her head, Imogen moved across the room and plumped down next to her sister-in-law. 'I don't think it's his illness, Janie, he's always been like this, ever since we were young. You've heard all the stories.' She sniffed. 'Although he did have some moderate success charging friends to come to a disco in a tent in the back of our garden once.'

Janie turned in her seat, facing Imogen. 'Do you want me to talk to him about it? We're on good terms at the moment, well, you know what Harry's like, I'm not sure he takes anything seriously. I could…'

'No, Janie, I didn't come here to ask you that, I just…' She clasped her hands together in her lap. 'I just wanted you to know, and to know I'm going to do my best to sort this out. The compensation money he got from the accident should be better spent. For the children.'

'Imogen…'

'I think he thinks he's done a good thing but, at the moment, in my mind, he's thrown nearly one hundred thousand Euro down the drain.'

'What are you going to do?' Janie asked.

'I'm going to go with him to Corfu and make him see, with that ramshackle excuse for a restaurant right there in front of him, that he'd have been better off investing in…' Her eyes went to Olivia, who had appeared in the doorway and was hanging on every word. 'One Direction nesting dolls.'

SIX

Southampton, England

'So I thought we'd leave the day after tomorrow.'

Harry's words were slightly muffled by the mouthful of homemade pasta he was munching. If there was one thing that would make Harry stop for five minutes it was food.

'Harry, about the restaurant…'

His head shot out of the bowl straightaway. 'Has your passport expired?'

'No, it isn't that.'

'Phew! I was panicking for a minute there because I booked the tickets. I got a great price on a flash mob online.'

'Flash sale,' Imogen corrected, as she began to imagine air hostesses performing dance moves to Sia.

'It's an early morning flight but I'll book us a taxi to Luton,' Harry continued.

'Harry, Mum's worried about you and so am I. This has all come so out of the blue.'

'Not really. You know a new project has been on my mind for a while. I can't do a–' he made quotation marks in the air '–*normal* job very well, so I have to think outside the box as they say.'

'I know that, but Corfu…' She left the sentence open, not really knowing what else to say.

'You're going to love it, Immy. Janie loved it. Little tavernas along the beach, green mountains and great people.'

'But, Harry, having a holiday somewhere is a bit different to buying a business you've had no experience in.'

'That's why I've got you. With your culinary experience and your NVQ.' Harry grinned.

'I spoke to Janie,' she admitted.

Harry put down his fork then sat back in his chair, steepling his fingers together and bringing the triangle shape to his mouth. 'What did she say?' he whispered.

His tone had tears springing to her eyes. What she said next was going to be make or break. She could see just how much this adventure meant to him and all she had done so far was jump up and down and crush everything like a recycling maniac trying to fit everything into the weekly black box collection.

Imogen swallowed before forcing out a smile. 'She said she remembered your holidays there.'

'I told you, didn't I? I knew she would.' He smiled, his eyes moving to the window and her view of the Brooks Plant Hire unit as if he was admiring the forklifts and diggers.

Imogen's heart was breaking. He was putting so much on himself and now she felt equally burdened because he was relying on her to make it happen too. Maybe she should have acknowledged how serious this separation could be for all of them. How was Grace going to cope if 'the break' became permanent? Their mum had already lost so much. She smiled at Harry. Tristan, Olivia and Janie were Harry's world and now he appeared to be hanging all their futures on a restaurant in Greece.

'I have two weeks' holiday I can take,' Imogen said to him. 'After that we'll have to play it by ear.'

'Yes!' Harry exclaimed, knocking the pasta bowl with his elbow. 'You wait, Immy, you're going to love it.'

Harry had left her with a Greek phrasebook and an AA travel guide from his very first trip to Corfu – the one he was still re-playing as if it were a collection of scenes from an Oscar-worthy romantic motion picture.

Curled up on the sofa, a glass of chardonnay on a side table next to her, Imogen perused both books, her finger clicking on and off a bright turquoise pen that stated in gold letters it was from the Hotel Palma Real in Varadero, Cuba. She now knew the words for 'wine' and 'where are the toilets'. Basically a native. However, Harry was expecting her to know the Greek for words like 'flambé' and 'julienne'. She wasn't even sure she still had those skills.

She had to admit that Corfu did look beautiful though. The capital city was packed full of history, two forts – old and new – and more mixed architecture than you could shake some marble at. Coves of white pebbles, golden beaches and a seemingly endless cerulean sea. These facts were what the stress-ravaged, holiday-hungry looked for when booking a package with Travel Republic or Holiday Hypermarket. But they only came when the sun was shining and why would they come to Harry's restaurant when there were already authentic Greeks serving authentic Greek cuisine and they were just two Brits trying their best?

Imogen put the books down, got up, and walked over to the windowsill, with the view of the unit of Medwell's Blinds, stopping only to pick up the palm-sized stone her dad had brought home from Mexico. A piece of foundation from an ancient Inca temple. When she was twelve she had believed him; now she wasn't so sure. There had to be a law against p   r
But, to her, the most important thing was h
to find it, even if it was in a tourist shop. Jus
never forgot.

She squeezed the pebble in her hand until the cold stone made her skin ache. Her dad would want her to help Harry. And, despite all her plans for the hotel industry, she had only ventured abroad once and it hadn't been Greece. Maybe it was time to stop holding on to the past and take off her safety belt. Harry was throwing everything at something new with hardly a second thought. What did she have to lose by joining him?

SEVEN

Ioannis Kapodistrias Airport, Corfu, Greece

The heat hit Imogen as soon as they disembarked the Easyjet flight. Her skin prickled at the twenty-plus temperature as she and Harry walked from the plane to the waiting bus.

'We're here,' Harry stated. 'In Corfu.' There had been a smile on his face ever since they'd boarded. In fact he had grinned the entire flight, even when the baby seated on her mother's lap next to him had thrown half the contents of a snack box at him.

'Yes,' Imogen answered, clinging onto her handbag as she powerwalked toward the bus.

'Wooo,' Harry said, flapping a hand in front of his face. 'Hot, isn't it?'

'Yes,' she answered. She would think of something else to say soon. Hopefully in Greek. She had taken the non-worrying time on the plane to look at the phrase book. She could now add 'good morning' and 'unleaded petrol' to her repertoire. She stepped up onto the bus.

'Hello,' Harry greeted an elderly woman sat in one of the few seats. He put his rucksack down on the floor and straddled it before choosing a pole to hold on to. He smiled at the woman. 'Have you been to Corfu before?'

'Oh yes, dear. We've been coming here every year since our honeymoon. Haven't we, Bill?' The woman nudged the man next to her, leaning on his two sticks.

'1965,' he stated, nodding.

'Gosh, congratulations.'

'Is this your wife?' the woman asked, her eyes going to Imogen.

'No,' Imogen said quickly. 'I'm his sister.'

'This is Imogen's first time in Corfu,' Harry informed them.

'Is it, love? Well, you're in for a treat.' The woman adjusted herself in the seat as the bus doors closed and the engine revved up. 'Where are you staying? North? South? Somewhere in between?'

Imogen watched Harry's grin widen, his blond hair flopping over his forehead as the bus moved across the tarmac. 'The north,' he said. 'Acharavi.' He waited a beat. 'We've bought a restaurant.'

She swallowed heavily, the taste of the in-flight *croque monsieur* repeating on her. Harry saying the words out loud to other people made the situation hit home. Here they were, a thousand miles from England, in charge of a rundown restaurant.

'Did you hear that, Bill?' The woman elbowed her husband a second time. 'These two have bought a restaurant. Ooo, that's so lovely. Isn't it lovely, Bill? We had a pub… Well, it was a few years ago now and it wasn't anywhere exotic like Corfu, it was in…'

'Bromsgrove, 1980,' Bill answered.

'I can't wait,' Harry stated, another beaming smile stretching his lips. 'I'm still high on the summer of 2000.'

The bus came to a halt and Imogen looked out of the window at the small terminal. They had travelled less than a hundred metres. The doors opened at a paved slope leading indoors.

'Always makes me laugh, that bus ride,' the woman said, getting to her feet. 'All that palaver for a few feet even I could walk. Still, I suppose it's something to do with health and safety.' She shook her head. 'What did we do before health and safety?'

Imogen's eyes shot to Harry. A lack of health and safety had been the cause of the accident that had led to him being unable to carry on with his career. He had fallen from the aeroplane he was working on in the hangar and shattered his hip, an event that ultimately contributed to his depression. The sad times had started with the death of their father and Harry had never seemed to come out of it as well as anyone else. It always seemed to be loitering in the background ready to step in when life proved difficult.

Harry grinned again. 'I'm guessing we weren't healthy or safe.'

Imogen blew out a breath and followed Harry down the step and out onto the tarmac again.

'I tied a woggle round it,' Harry announced. They were standing at the carousel in arrivals watching luggage appear in front of them. Buggies, car seats, a leather holdall with the zip undone, all rotated around waiting for their owners to claim them.

'What?' Imogen asked, her eyes going to her brother.

'Tristan had a spare neckerchief and I tied it onto my case with a woggle so I could find it easier.' Harry stopped talking and pointed. 'See! There it is!'

Imogen looked in the direction Harry was pointing to see his already extremely noticeable bright green case slipping down the rubber-clad incline to join the rotation party, a Scout's scarf flying from its handle.

She watched Harry rush over to fetch his luggage, kicking the edge of a metal trolley in his hurry. Unlike Harry she was in no rush. In fact she needed every second to work out how this was all going to go down when they got to Acharavi. What sort of a town name was that anyway? It sounded like a hot curry.

As she hauled her case from the carousel she noticed Harry had found the elderly couple from the bus again. He was animated, his hands in the air. Imogen let out a breath. She could imagine every word he was saying. This restaurant, in his eyes, was only a few days away from being awarded its first Michelin star. Setting her luggage down, she pulled it along the floor to join him.

'…we're going to be doing traditional Greek food with a British twist. So if you like fish and chips, you're going to love fish and chips with *taramasalata*,' Harry stated.

'Ooo,' the woman said. 'Is that the pink stuff made of fish eggs?'

'I think so,' Harry said. 'My sister's the food buff.'

Imogen smiled. 'I've tried to tell my brother that traditional Greek is the way to go. I'm sure, coming here for so many years, you have your favourite dishes.'

'Well,' Betty began. 'I am partial to chicken *souvlaki*. And I like to have a good squeeze of lemon all over it.'

Imogen could almost smell the meat, herbs and citrus. 'Have you tried squeezing a lime over it?' she suggested.

'Ooo, no dear, I haven't.'

'Can you cook that?' Harry asked, looking at Imogen, eyes hopeful.

'Even you could cook that, Harry,' she answered.

'Lea Bridge Road, London, 1976. That's where I had my best chicken *souvlaki*,' Bill told them.

'See, Harry,' Imogen said, nudging his arm. 'Greek food, not English.' She smiled at the couple. 'We ought to go. We need to pick up the hire car. It was nice to meet you both.'

'Yes, it was very nice to meet you, Betty and Bill, and if you're in the Acharavi area do drop into "TO",' Harry said.

'Two?' Betty looked puzzled. 'There are two restaurants?'

'Maybe I should have said "toe".' Harry shook his head.

'Toe? As in... part of your foot?'

'Have a lovely, lovely holiday,' Imogen said, tightening her grip on Harry's arm and tugging him towards the sliding doors out of the airport.

'Maybe the name needs a rethink,' Harry mused. 'It was supposed to be 'T' for Tristan and 'O' for Olivia but I didn't realise it would be so hard to say... or translate.'

'To be honest I think the name of the restaurant is the least of our worries.' She scrutinised the signs for the hire car companies. 'Now, please, just tell me you didn't book a Cinquecento.'

EIGHT

Ioannis Kapodistrias Airport, Corfu, Greece

It had only been a short hop in his private plane across other Greek islands, but Panos was tired. He hadn't slept properly since his phone call with his grandmother. And then there had been the Rhea situation.

As he exited the airport, manoeuvring his black case on four wheels, he remembered Rhea's face when he said he was leaving and their relationship was over. She'd brought her hand to her perfectly styled hair, bracelets jangling, her plump lips down-turned and thrown down the magazine she was reading. Then she'd prowled like a cat on heat around the villa in one of her barely-there sarongs over a tiny bikini, following him as he packed, crying, begging, as if he owed her further explanation. He felt he didn't. She knew the score. Despite letting her have free rein at the villa for the two months he'd spent in Crete, she wasn't his girlfriend, would never be. She was a friend of a friend, the ideal companion for the type of businessman he was. Two months was the longest he had stayed somewhere in the past five years and Rhea's reaction to his leaving only made ending the liaison easier. She had got too clingy, expecting things he wasn't able to give. He'd left her packing the items she'd gradually moved in when she thought he wasn't looking. He wouldn't make that mistake again.

Panos stepped out of the airport, through the sliding doors and onto the tiled concrete, the sun sprawling its rays across his face. He drew his sunglasses from his shirt pocket. Slipping them onto his face, he swept a hand back through his dark hair. *He was home.* He took in a breath, a deep lungful of the air that was so unique here: dust, the scent of pine, fumes from the rank of coaches parked opposite, heat. The sentiment welled up inside him and quickly he hardened his body to it, narrowing his eyes at the mountains like they were a curse. This island was not a part of him anymore. He needed to remember that.

As Panos made his way over towards the line of taxi-drivers waiting for a fare, his mobile phone began to trill. Picking his case up, he lifted it over the yellow-painted kerb, then dropped it back down before reaching into the pocket of his trousers. He pulled out the phone and checked the display. It was Manilos from his office.

'Dimitriou,' Panos answered.

'I've been trying to contact you for an hour,' came the frantic response.

This didn't sound good. There had been none of Manilos' usual prelude. No 'Good afternoon, Mr Dimitriou', no talking between mouthfuls of lunch.

'I've just touched down.' Panos beckoned a taxi-driver.

A sound of annoyance at the other end of the line suggested this wasn't what his employee wanted to hear. Now his interest was piqued.

'You're really in Corfu?' Manilos asked.

Panos' eyes went back across the road to the grey-panelled airport building, its name in large yellow Greek letters along the front. There were scooters and cars parked up in front of it, workers idling on benches for their break, reps with clipboards waiting for holidaymakers, all seeking the shade of the overhang. 'Yes, I am really in Corfu.'

Manilos sighed. 'Then we have a real problem.' He paused. 'The Asp deal has collapsed.'

It was like someone had thrown a bucket of ice-cold water over him. The beads of perspiration on his back suddenly turned chill. This couldn't be happening. He closed his eyes and refocussed before opening them again. 'This had better not be a joke.'

'Would I make a joke about something this big?'

Panos gritted his teeth. 'What the hell happened?'

'He changed his mind,' Manilos said.

'Just like that?' His tone gave away all the exasperation he felt. He needed to rein it back. He didn't lose control.

'There has been some local resistance and—'

'Manilos, there is always local resistance. It is par for the course. I spoke with Asp personally about this.'

'I know, but—'

'Have you told him we can send people to deal with situations like this?'

'I have.'

'Did you tell him if he doesn't go through with *this* deal there will be no second offer in months or years to come?'

'Of course.' Manilos sighed. 'I told him everything.'

'Did you...' He stopped. He didn't really want to know any more if the next answer was also a negative.

'I offered him a hundred thousand Euro more,' Manilos confirmed.

'Shit!' Panos exclaimed. He kicked the ground, his foot coming off worse than the concrete. He leant back against the metal barrier separating the taxi rank from the coaches waiting for tourists. This was serious. If Asp hadn't backed down at the offer of extra money the deal really was as good as lost. He needed to make a decision. This deal was huge – a row of properties on Kos, in a prime beachfront location. He'd worked hard for three months putting things in place to ensure the outcome swung his way. And here he was, a plane ride away when things had gone south.

'What do you want me to do?' Manilos asked down the line.

What should he do? Panos' instincts were to head into the airport again and get his private jet to take him to Kos. But Elpida's voice was in his ear and there was that squirming in his gut that was telling him even his presence in Kos wasn't going to win this deal back. Asp had been uncertain from the very beginning, as had the tenants of the properties. He thought he'd done enough to convince them his way was the only logical conclusion, but he was also astute enough to know community relationships were still held in high regard. The tight-knit village had obviously closed ranks. He looked across at the hire car parking lot, differently coloured flags fluttering in the warm breeze. Well, those businesses might survive another summer, but when the winter came and tourists went home, the financial crisis, coupled with the influx of migrants, would just about finish them off. And when Asp came crawling back for help he would have great pleasure in saying no. One chance was all you got with Panos Dimitriou, everyone knew that. He knew exactly what he was going to do.

'Do nothing, Manilos,' he stated. 'Let it go.'

'Let it go?' Manilos repeated like he was speaking another language.

'That's what I said.'

'But—'

'You cannot win them all, my friend,' Panos stated. He didn't believe this. But Kos was one thing, he was damned if he was going to let it happen with Corfu. He wasn't going by cab. He was going to hire a car. Because he didn't care how long it took, he wasn't just going to get the family restaurant back, he was going to own the whole strip.

NINE

En route to Acharavi, Corfu

Imogen might have studied the guidebook on the flight but perhaps she should have looked closer at the map or, to narrow it down a little further, the geography. Corfu was a lot more mountainous than she'd realised and the roads left a lot to be desired. Despite his previous holidays, Harry was doing a pitiful job at navigating and it had been up to her to traverse the terrain in a Nissan Micra that sounded like it was going to expire at any second. And now, as they crawled around another hairpin bend, she felt a bit sick. The only thing that was lightening her mood was the beauty outside. Judas trees covered in candyfloss-pink blossom swayed on each side of the ravine.

'I think I'm going to have to pull over,' she said as all colour faded from her face.

'We're almost there,' Harry answered, shaking the phone showing the sat-nav and bending his head to stare at it in greater detail.

'You said that twenty minutes ago, Harry.' She was feeling hot now and she pressed a button to open the window.

'Don't do that. We'll turn the air-conditioning up.' Harry reached forward to the grey plastic dials on the dashboard.

'I thought you said it burns fuel like a Chinese lantern scalds gazebos.'

'But if you're hot—'

'I want this to be over.' She swallowed, gripping the steering wheel to negotiate another death-defying curve in the road.

'Really?' Harry turned his head to look out of the passenger window. 'I've been enjoying the scenery.' He filled his chest with a breath as if he was sucking in fresh air rather than the air-conditioning. 'It's just like I remember it. So green… and beautiful.'

Imogen dared to shift her eyes from the grey concrete road to the flora and fauna surrounding them. Tall pines pillared up from the rugged drops to their left and right, bushes budded with vibrant flowers of purple and yellow and gnarly olive trees had black netting at their roots waiting for their fruit to fall. Her gaze went further, a few hundred feet below and ahead, to the azure sea, flat, still, a length of taupe beach in front of it. For once Harry was right. It was a landscape to behold. If she forgot about the restaurant element she could relax enough to imagine cooling cocktails and fruit sweeter, fresher and juicier than anything you could get your hands on back home.

'We're really not far,' Harry stated, his voice bringing Imogen back to the task at hand. 'It's just past Roda, which should be the next place we come to. I don't know why Google Maps isn't talking to me.'

Google Maps probably felt the same way Imogen did. She focussed back on the road as the terrain began to flatten out a little. She sucked in a breath. She needed to give Harry a chance and stop panicking before she really knew what she was dealing with. It might not be as bad as everyone thought.

'Take a left here,' Harry said.

'Are you sure?' Imogen asked, flicking on the indicator. It had been another half hour since Harry's 'we're really not far' comment. She was sticky in places she didn't even know she had places and she was sure her left forearm was being burnt through the glass. The 'road' Harry was wanting her to turn down looked nothing more than an ungraded track. It was concrete – just – but there were potholes like giant black Oreos in the middle of it.

'Are you sure, Harry?' she repeated.

'Yes… I think so.'

They rounded another bend and that's when it came into view. Imogen couldn't stop the gasp escaping her lips. Straight ahead of them, only a few metres away, was the sea. An almost indescribable turquoise blue, gently stretching away from a sand and white-pebbled beach.

'Beautiful, isn't it?' Harry said, his words wrapped up with emotion as the car rolled to a stop.

Imogen couldn't disagree. It was like an oasis after the tortuous drive, a sliver of peace and tranquillity laid down before them. A mosquito landing on her arm brought her out of her thoughts and she shook her wrist before it could settle and bite.

'How far is the restaurant, Harry?' She eased the car forward.

'Turn right here,' he replied as Imogen turned the steering wheel in accordance with his instructions. 'And it's just… here.'

Imogen pulled the car up and turned off the engine, her eyes going to the property on their right. She swallowed. The weeds hit her first. Spiky, evil-looking green fronds protruded from the perimeter of the building and she had to squint and focus hard to even see the rest of the property. Remnants of chairs and tables stood outside, broken and upturned, under what must have been a pergola in years gone by. Dark, withered vines hung from the metal construction that was nothing more than rust and neglect.

Harry had got out of the car and he stepped up into the outside eating area that resembled the scene of an IED blast. The building looked ripe for demolition and, although Harry was fond of *DIY SOS*, she wasn't sure either of them had the skills to even know where to begin.

'Come on, Immy! Come and look!'

But then again. Harry was projecting more enthusiasm than Mary Berry over millefeuilles. Imogen opened the door and stepped out of the car, her feet crunching on the stones at the edge of the beach. Maybe this was what had really seduced her brother. She breathed in hard, letting the salt water and driftwood scent invade her body as she looked out to sea. She might have been bewitched looking at photos of this. The sound of the water rushing over the fine shingle on the sand, the light breeze whipping past her ears, the hot sun warming her skin and that view – the endless azure blue running up to the mountains the guidebook had told her was Albania.

'Immy! Come on!' Harry called again.

She moved onto the square of concrete covered in twines of greenery that shouldn't have been there. It was like Sleeping Beauty's castle, except the castle was a two-storey stucco skeleton of a building, and there was no dashing prince. And there was the *pièce de résistance*: those two broken windows that made up the entire frontage, meaning unrestricted access to any would-be robber, if adequately equipped with super-strength weed-killer. Just how long had this place been abandoned? She wondered how much of the inside her brother had seen before he signed on the virtual dotted line.

Harry held up a terracotta pot. 'I've got the key!'

Great! Broken panes of glass and the key kept under a pot right outside.

Imogen took a deep breath and batted a flying beetle away from her face. She had to think positive. The inside couldn't possibly be as bleak as the outside, could it?

TEN

Elpida Dimitriou's home, Agios Martinos, Corfu

Panos had hired the most expensive car the company at the air-port had at its disposal. The sleek, black Mercedes circled around the familiar twists and turns of his island like it was following a path ingrained in its make-up. From its secret coves and beaches to the rugged terrain en route to the highest peak of Pantokra-tor and all the remote tracks, farmland, olive groves and fruit orchards in between – Corfu was a jewel. He sighed, turning the vehicle around another bend towards Agios Martinos. He remembered every stretch of this particular road. The dense trees either side of the highway – pines, bush scrub, twisted and warped olives – the purple geraniums and lupins, the tiny yel-low flowered crosswort.

He slowed the car down as it rounded the final loop then pulled it to a stop. He let his breath fill up his lungs as he gazed into the thicket just in front of him. It was still there. The same fraying blue rope, haphazardly tied around a branch of what his grandmother had always said was the oldest olive tree in Agios Martinos. Below the rope was a splintered plank of wood, a swing, shifting gently with the heat. How many hours had he spent here? His legs shooting up into the air, touching the higher boughs of the tree, body prostrate, back arching, work-ing to send the swing as high into orbit as possible. He could almost feel the wind through his hair now as he pictured the scene, the warmth of the sun on his face and laughter. Him, his cousin Risto, and children from the village. His eyes went further up the tree, midway on the trunk, and he smiled. Their treehouse, the rough wooden shelter that had kept them from the heat, sheltered them from thunder and provided the perfect hiding place when chores needed to be done. They'd played cards for *drachma* and sent toy cars speeding off the platform into the wood below. *His father had built the treehouse.* Visions of the lithe man, hanging from the tree, nailing planks of wood together, planing rough sections with his hands, asking Panos to pass him screwdrivers, rope, a spirit level. Simple pleasures. Time and love spent creating the hideout.

Instantly the happiness fell away. Panos swallowed. He knew he wasn't the only teenager in the world to have had to cope with a marriage breakdown. But when it had ended in his father's death rather than a divorce it was like God had run in and grabbed everything all at once. His mother's happiness. Their money to get by. Their home. His father. Again, his mother came to mind. Her endless nights of tears, his inability to provide consolation, his father's harsh words to everyone. He shook himself. He hadn't come here to rake over old ground but to show the island that the Dimitriou name meant success again. His father may have failed to adapt to modern business but he had learned to thrive on the pace, the invigorating ruthlessness of it all. He restarted the engine and continued up the steep hill until the house came into view.

Like the play area of his youth the house was unchanged. The biscuit-coloured brick of the two-storey villa was just the same as it had been when he'd left at seventeen. His heart thumping against his ribs told him exactly how it felt to be back. He was anxious, feeling none of the usual business bravado he was so used to practising. Like it or not, this was affecting him deeply.

Which was probably why, up until now, his trips back to Corfu had always taken place on neutral ground. He'd stay at a soulless hotel and his grandmother and relatives would come to a restaurant of his choosing. A couple of hours, the bill on his credit card and he would leave for the next big deal away from this island.

He parked the car and looked up at the villa again. Dark green shutters were closed over the windows shading the inside from the intense daytime heat and the window boxes were in full bloom. A fiesta of pink and white bougainvillea and lilac clematis budded from the sills, and urns of the same sat upon the front patio area. It seemed his grandmother might be too old to manage a restaurant full time but obviously her gardening wasn't suffering. Another pot of flowers sat in the middle of the old round stone table on the patio.

Panos stepped out onto the paving. Coming from the air-conditioned vehicle, the temperature outside hit him straightaway. The buzz of the cicadas invaded every sense and he started to roll up his shirt sleeves, looking towards the front door and wondering who was going to break first. He tucked the shirt sleeves in at his elbows and let out a breath. His grandmother was even more stubborn than him and she had done nothing to deserve his disdain. On the contrary, she was the only constant he'd had when things began to fall apart.

His gaze shifted to the left, to the patch of grass and pair of trees in front of the house, next to the driveway. A man sat on his grandparents' seat between the olives, swigging from a bottle of water, his eyes on the view across the trees. Who was this? So carefree about sitting on his grandparents' seat? Panos strode across the grass, his hands clenched into fists at his side.

'Who are you? What are you doing here?' His voice came out like an angry bark and the dark-haired young man jumped to his feet, dropping the bottle to the ground.

'I—'

'I asked you a question. What are you doing here?' He narrowed his eyes at the man dressed in dungaree overalls, who looked no more than eighteen.

'Pano!' Elpida's voice screamed from the house. 'For the love of Zeus will you leave Nico alone?'

Panos' gaze went from the man to his grandmother. She was hanging out of one of the windows at the top of the house, waving a handkerchief in the air. 'He's the gardener!'

Of course he was. Panos cleared his throat and hurriedly extended a hand to the worker. 'Panos Dimitriou,' he introduced. 'I apologise. I didn't realise my grandmother had hired a gardener.'

'It is OK,' the man answered, accepting the offered hand and shaking it. 'Mrs Dimitriou does not like to have help. I offered to take care of the garden and she cooks for my mother.'

Panos shook his head. That sounded exactly like Elpida. Perfectly capable of paying for a gardener but preferring an old-fashioned bartering system. Unless… perhaps selling the restaurant hadn't been about it being too much for her. Maybe the financial crisis had hit her too.

He turned back to the house and waved a hand at his grandmother.

'Come into the house! I have cooked *kleftiko*!' Elpida called.

The fragrance of the lamb, rosemary and bay leaves weakened Panos as he stepped over the threshold, a hard reminder of what he'd distanced himself from. The aromatic authentic Greek dish was kicking him where it hurt even more than the memories of playing on the olive tree swing as a boy or his grandmother's unchanged home. He looked around the kitchen, trying to spot anything he didn't recognise. There was the range – a copper-bottomed pot bubbling away, a fresh sheaf of lavender over the brick surround – the large circular moon clock slow as usual. As in the rest of Greece you never knew quite what the time was here. He wasn't even sure why his *yiayia* had the clock.

'Pano!' Elpida greeted. 'Come here, let me look at you!'

Panos turned and met with the grandmother he allegedly hadn't seen for a year. He smiled but inside his stomach twisted. Despite the neatly set, dyed blonde hair slightly streaked with silver, the bright pink silk scarf at her neck and the large glasses on her nose, Elpida was starting to look her age. Dressed in a tight-fitting knee-length orange dress, Nike trainers on her feet, the woman smiled. She was only five feet tall, still slim, but perhaps lacking the outward strength she'd always exhibited. Now it looked as though her formidable nature was the only thing keeping her standing. He adjusted quickly and opened his arms to her. '*Yiayia*, you're looking well.'

She snorted and withdrew as quickly as she had met his embrace. 'Pfft! You are not.' She pointed a finger. 'You are too thin.'

'You have been saying this to me since I was five.'

'And it is still true! Look at you!'

Elpida had made it sound like he was on the verge of famine. There was still colour in her cheeks and those eyes that saw everything, externally and internally. He smiled.

'How much do I have to eat before you'll sell me the restaurant?'

It was meant to be a joke. An ice breaker. But the way her dark eyes blackened and her lips formed a scowl he knew immediately he'd said the wrong thing.

She pointed her finger again. 'I tell you the restaurant is sold! Do you not believe me?'

'Yes, but—'

'But nothing. There is no conversation to be had about the restaurant anymore.' She reached to the counter for a packet of cigarettes and held onto them like they were a comfort blanket. Her eyes dropped to the packet. 'You wish for me not to smoke. Stop making me want to smoke.' She threw the cigarettes down again.

'I—' Panos started.

'You will eat *kleftiko* and then we are going out. We are meeting Risto.' Elpida grabbed an oven glove and pulled open the cooker door, releasing the meaty aromas. 'He has missed you.'

He swallowed. He should have kept in better touch with his cousin. They had been brought up like brothers since Risto's parents had both been killed in a car accident. He hadn't spoken to him in so long.

'Risto needs a little help.'

'From me?'

'Is there someone else in my kitchen?' She waved a tea towel in the air. 'Yes, you!'

'Is he in some sort of trouble?'

'We will discuss this with alcohol, but all in good time.' She pulled a large casserole pot out of the oven. 'Come and eat!'

ELEVEN

The restaurant, Acharavi beachfront

Imogen almost wanted to cry. The shambolic state of the outside of the property was nothing compared to the inside which looked like someone had driven a tank through it. Everything was either coated with dust or was broken – or both – and that was just the main room. The kitchen looked like it shouldn't be entered without a hazmat suit. She'd held her nose before opening the fridge room and almost vomited when she found mouldy potatoes with roots a foot long protruding from one of the cupboards.

The second floor was completely empty apart from carcasses of dead critters liberally spread across the tiles. There was a bathroom at one end, with a shower designed for people of Barbie and Ken proportions and a toilet with a basin resembling the bottom of a coffee cup. Now, with the dirty curtains parted, she stared out of the filthy glass window at the sea, hoping it would soothe her aching soul and provide some much needed inspiration. Or provoke a siren song to a TV home make-over team. Outside, on the beach, her legs stretched out on a lounger – that's where she wanted to be. Eyes closed, drifting into a half-sleep, a half-litre of something alcoholic on a table next to her, listening to the lull of the sea…

'It's brilliant, isn't it?'

Imogen drew in a breath. Unless Harry had found a lifetime's supply of Cillit Bang in a cupboard there was nothing to be happy about. She let go of the curtain and tried to ignore the shower of dust that caught the ray of sunlight flooding through the glass.

'I know it's only one big room and the bathroom up here, but that's alright, isn't it? I mean we can manage until we can get some partitioning put in. And Olivia and Tristan will love it. They'll think it's like camping out.' He paused. 'And then, when things are going well here, we could maybe look at getting a little house to live in.'

'Harry,' Imogen started, the word catching in her throat. 'There aren't any beds.'

'It's all in hand.' Harry had acquired a broom from some-where and was sweeping it across the terracotta floor, sending up plumes of thick dust that were seeping into Imogen's mouth.

'What does that mean?' She put her hands on her hips and focussed her blue eyes on him. Suddenly the dust dried her throat up and she forced out a cough. When was the last time she'd had a drink? She looked to the limescale-tarnished hand basin in the bathroom, a green coating around the tap. Could you drink the water in Greece?

'It means that I packed sleeping bags in my luggage.'

Imogen blinked in astonishment. She didn't know what surprised her more. That Harry thought sleeping on the floor in this sty of an 'apartment' was acceptable, or that he managed to pack clothes, toiletries *and* two sleeping bags in a luggage allowance of twenty kilos.

'Harry,' she began. 'I think we need to sit down…' She looked around for chairs that weren't there. 'Somewhere… as in not here… and talk about this.'

'I agree,' he replied, still sweeping. Now the dust was like a fog between them and Harry was becoming fuzzy round the edges.

'You do.'

He nodded. 'Of course! We need to work out a schedule.'

'A schedule.'

'Yep. Everything works better with a schedule. So we need a date to work towards.'

She cleared her throat. 'A date for…' She deliberately left the end of the sentence open, feeling a little like she was teetering on the edge of Beachy Head.

Harry grinned. 'The grand opening.'

Beachy Head wasn't enough of a drop; now she was freefalling off the Shard. She steeled herself. It was OK. Because this was day one. They'd just arrived. She had plenty of time to get him to realise no amount of cleaning would make this a place where people wanted to eat. She swallowed. 'I see… So your plan is to take a week or so to clean it up and open it… as a restaurant?'

Harry stopped brushing and leant his weight on the broom as he looked at her. 'Are you alright, Immy?'

Suddenly reality was kicking in. It was only a few days ago she'd been told she was going to be head chef at a restaurant a thousand miles from home that looked like it had held a Hell's Angels party. She croaked out an affirmative. 'Yes.'

'I know I dropped this on you but there was a good reason for that,' Harry continued.

'You told me,' Imogen replied. 'You knew I would talk you out of it.'

'*Try* to talk me out of it, I said.' Harry sighed. 'I wanted to prove to you… prove to everyone that I could rejuvenate…' Harry shook his head. 'No, that isn't the word. Reinvigorate…'

Harry moved his head as if trying to dislodge a blockage that was there. Imogen remained quiet, watching the specks of dust dance in the air between them. She watched him lean backwards and take a deep breath of the musty air.

'I wanted to prove to everyone and prove to myself that I could make something happen,' he said finally. 'I know how things have been with me being ill and—'

'Oh, Harry…'

'No, Immy, please. I'm not a child.'

'I know that, I just want to help you…' She hesitated before she continued. 'Help you work things out. With Janie, Olivia and Tristan.'

'Then help me with this,' Harry said, his blue eyes wide and pleading.

'Harry, I really don't know the first thing about running a restaurant,' Imogen said.

'You've worked in one for years.'

'I know, but that was cooking the odd pan of fried eggs and microwaving baked potatoes. It wasn't marinating or blanching, I haven't done that for so long.' And he was going to expect pastry, she just knew it.

'But you can learn it again… and so can I.' He grinned. 'It might be like bike riding. Once learned, never forgotten.'

'It's in Greece, Harry. You can't expect us to live here. Is that what you thought would happen?'

'For the summer, maybe? I'm not sure how busy this area is in the winter but I do know there are a lot of ex-pats who live here. They'll want food in the winter.'

'Well, what about permits? I don't know much about Greece but I do know they love their red tape when it comes to things like this. They don't just let you open a restaurant willy-nilly.'

'I've got some of them. I need to meet with the fire guy to go through what kit we need and get the music licence from someone called Helios,' Harry responded. 'Then there's a business licence. I need to sort out that one.'

She hadn't been expecting that. It seemed her brother was far more organised than anyone had given him credit for.

'I've thought about this, Immy. I told you. I've been planning this for weeks. It's just what I need.' He inhaled air like it was sweet mountain dew. 'A fresh start. I can show Janie I'm still the man she fell in love with and seduce her with Greek treats that are going to have her remembering the time I took her up the monastery.'

She nodded quickly, hoping 'monastery' wasn't a euphemism.

She watched Harry's smile widen. 'I know something we need more than beds,' he said. 'Let's get some wine and toast our new venture!'

'Our new venture,' Imogen spoke with a little uncertainty. Feeling like a trapped third class passenger on the *Titanic*, she forced a smile. She could do this. She just had to keep them both afloat. The trouble was, if things got rougher, she couldn't imagine who was going to arrive with a lifeboat.

TWELVE

Tomas' Taverna, Acharavi beachfront

This definitely felt better. Imogen and Harry had walked along the beach road then back, stopping at the bar next to the restaurant. Now, with her body elongated on a large well-cushioned chair, Imogen almost felt relaxed. If she closed her eyes she could just about pretend she was here on holiday and not the project manager of a Greek crisis. As the sound of the sea slushing back and forth over the shingle at the water's edge lulled her close to slumber she recalled the last time she'd been on holiday abroad.

Daniel had booked them what he had called 'a second honeymoon'. A week in picturesque Cape Verde. She had looked at the brochure – the turquoise waters, the white sandy beaches, the couples snorkelling with multi-coloured tropical fish and turtles – and thought he was really trying. This was what their relationship needed. An injection of alone time without the constant drone of the forty-seven-inch television. How wrong she had been. The television in their gorgeous lily-filled suite with a swim-up pool was slightly smaller and only had German channels but it was switched on the second after Daniel turned the key in the door. Couple time was a quickie before breakfast and her day consisted of getting intimate with her Kindle and the cocktail list while Daniel exerted himself taking part in every activity available – volleyball, tennis, wakeboarding. Looking back now, perhaps she should have done something, told him how she felt. You couldn't demand attention one minute and ignore someone the next. He wanted her there with him all the time just so she wasn't anywhere else. It was quietly controlling and she wished she'd realised it sooner. It said a lot that on that holiday she'd never even taken one of the hotel pens.

'This is the life, isn't it?'

Harry's voice broke through her thoughts and she opened her eyes, shielding her vision from the sun to look across at him. He had his eyes shut too, his face turned up to the sky. Imogen looked, taking in every line and crease in her brother's face. He had been through so much. It had been hard enough for both of them growing up in a one-parent family, but what had happened afterwards – Harry's accident and his depression and the separation from Janie – didn't seem fair. Her soft, sweet, Harry had had to shoulder so much, it was understandable he wanted to claim back his life, be in control.

Harry opened his eyes then and that smile was on his face again. She couldn't deny he looked far more relaxed than she'd seen him recently.

'Just think, Immy. Our restaurant could be just like this one in a few days' time.'

Days. Had he really said *days*? She sat up, pulling down the t-shirt that had started to stick to her body, and looked around the taverna they were sitting in. It was traditionally Greek with lots of wooden tables inside. Each had a slim bottle of olive oil and vinegar and a paper sheet clipped over its burgundy cotton tablecloth. Outside, under a vine-covered pergola with grapes just starting to sprout, were less formal chairs and tables next to pots of palms and flowers. All of it was surrounded by a low whitewashed wall on which sat plastic terracotta planters filled with white, pink and purple geraniums.

Imogen reached for her wine glass and picked it up quickly, bringing it to her lips. She wished she'd ordered a carafe… maybe with a side of *Kalamata* olives and a garlic dip.

'I think we should take the rest of today to make plans and tomorrow we can really get stuck in to it.' Harry took a sip of his beer. 'I've got a skip coming first thing… well, you know, a Greek 'first thing'. Might be here by tea time.' He grinned.

'I'm going to order some food,' she stated, flipping open the brown plastic book on the table.

'Good idea,' Harry said. 'Let's see what they have.'

There weren't just words but pictures. Photos that made her mouth water and her stomach start begging. Platters of *meze* stared back at her. Shiny black and green olives slick with oil, nestled next to fat hunks of feta and halloumi, fleshy, scarlet tomatoes and thick chunks of cucumber. An earthenware pot of meats and vegetables was labelled *stifado* and she could almost taste it.

'I'm going to have some *souvlaki*,' Harry announced. 'The chicken on skewers. Like the woman said at the airport, we can easily do that in our restaurant, can't we? What did you say we should squeeze on it?'

'Lime,' Imogen answered.

She looked to the sea. It was idyllic. The trees at the water's edge, the white stones and soft sand, the blue, gently shifting sea, the hyacinth sky and the mountain backdrop all made for one picture-postcard view. She watched two swimmers bobbing up and down in the water a few metres out before a black, expensive-looking car parked up outside the restaurant and blocked out everything. She sat forward. putting the menu back on the table. 'I'll have the *stifado*.'

She watched as the driver got out and immediately moved around to the passenger side. Tall, slim, black hair swept back from his face, he was dressed in business trousers and a white shirt with the sleeves rolled up to the elbows. Imogen watched as the man opened the passenger door and a tiny older woman in a bright orange dress got out and batted the man on the arm, speaking quickly and loudly in Greek.

'Uh-oh. Looks like a domestic,' Harry said, turning to look. 'When Janie looks at me like that I know I'm in trouble.'

'Sshh!' Imogen hissed, still watching. As the pair made their way up the steps into the restaurant, Imogen turned away, making a grab for her wine glass and knocking it clean off the table, where it fell to the tiles with a smash.

At the sound and the debris in front of them, the man and the little woman stopped walking and with heated cheeks Imogen dropped to the floor and began picking up the larger pieces of glass.

'What are you doing? Are you out of your mind?'

The deep, Greek-accented voice was close to her ear and she felt the heat from his breath before she noticed the glass shard puncture the skin of her palm. Now it hurt and blood was starting to trickle down her hand.

'*Yiayia*,' he addressed the small woman. 'Ask Tomas to get something to clear this up.' He stood up, taking her hand with him. 'And the first aid kit.'

'Are you alright, Immy?' Harry was out of his chair and standing next to her but all Imogen could focus on was the man holding her hand. He had olive skin, the darkest of brown eyes and a strong jawline specked with stubble. It wasn't the need for food that was kicking her insides into action now.

'I'm fine,' she said to Harry. She kept her eyes on the man with his fingers touching hers and then addressed him. 'Honestly, I'm fine. It's just a scratch.'

He snorted. 'If it were fine I would not have asked for the first aid kit.'

She wasn't sure she liked his tone. 'I can manage,' she stated firmly. 'I don't need a first aid kit, just a serviette.' She turned her head to her brother. 'Harry, pass me a napkin.'

The man shook his head. 'Why are you English so stubborn?'

'Why are you Greeks so sure you know how to manage everything?' She let out an irritated sigh. 'I'm sure that's at the crux of the financial crisis.'

Imogen's face instantly flamed in shame. Why had she said that? It was completely uncalled for and she had no excuse apart from being unused to and a little uneasy about someone trying to tell her what to do.

For a brief moment, as the man's eyes darkened further still, she thought he was going to smash another glass in fury at her comment. But then he smiled and let go of her hand.

'I apologise,' he said, taking a step back. 'I will leave you to your stiff upper lip and constant clock-watching.'

She swallowed. The very first local she'd spoken to and she'd insulted him. When he was trying to help her.

'Immy, let me have a look at it,' Harry suggested.

She watched the man turn his back on her and she took a step forward.

'Excuse me,' she called.

He turned back to her enquiringly.

'Thank you, for trying to help.' She paused. 'I'm sorry I was rude. It's my first day here and to be really honest, the drive from the airport has exhausted me more than a trek across the Andes.'

His mouth shifted from a firm line into a half smile. This was better. She stuck out her hand – the injured one – and quickly took it back, extending the other one instead.

'I'm Imogen Charlton,' she said.

He regarded her left hand until finally he took it in his and gave it a firm shake.

'Hello.' Harry's voice broke in. 'I'm Harry Charlton.' He offered his hand to the Greek. 'It's a pleasure to meet you.'

The man was still holding her hand, his eyes fixed on hers and she wasn't sure he'd even heard Harry speak. She flexed her fingers and he released his hold, quickly moving his hand to grasp Harry's.

'Dimitriou,' he said. 'Panos Dimitriou.' He shook Harry's hand.

'Do you live here? In Acharavi?' Harry continued, as bright as ever.

The man shook his head. 'No.'

'That's a shame,' Harry said. 'We've just moved here.'

Imogen jumped in. 'For a few weeks…'

Harry looked at her defiantly. 'For the summer.'

'I have the first aid kit.' The little woman was back with a white box bearing the Red Cross logo that looked as if it hadn't been opened since the eighties.

'Thank you,' Imogen said. 'But we're OK now.' She picked a napkin off the table and pressed it to her wound.

'My name is Elpida,' she said. 'And this is Pano, my grandson.'

'It's nice to meet you,' Imogen said.

'I've just bought a restaurant,' Harry announced.

'Oh, my congratulations! That is wonderful for you!' Elpida grabbed Harry into a fierce embrace that had him wobbling on his feet.

'Thank you. We're really looking forward to getting stuck in to the renovation work,' Harry said, extricating himself. 'We're going to reopen in a week.'

'What?!' Imogen couldn't help the word expelling from her mouth like a blast from a category five hurricane. 'A week!'

Harry waved a hand in the air like he was trying to quieten her. It only served to irritate her more and she grabbed hold of his arm. 'Harry... A week!'

'I think that's wonderful news,' Elpida said, smiling.

'Where is it?' The question came from Panos. 'In Acharavi?'

Harry nodded and pointed to the restaurant, the weeds gently moving in the breeze. 'Yes, just next door actually. The property right there on the corner.'

Imogen heard the sharp intake of breath from the tall, dark-haired man but his expression gave away nothing.

A loud squeal from Elpida broke the air. 'I do not believe it!' the woman exclaimed. 'You are the new owners of my old restaurant! This is amazing!'

'What?' Harry said, confused.

'I sell this to you,' Elpida said in simple terms. 'This used to belong to my family.'

'I... well... what a lovely coincidence,' Harry said, all grins. 'Isn't it, Immy?'

Imogen was still looking at Panos, who was now scrutinising Harry like he was a noisy cicada he wanted to crush. Despite his rushing to her aid over the wine glass, *this* was not demeanour akin to the fine Greek hospitality she'd read about.

'Well, it was a pleasure, but we should...' Panos held out his arm, indicating the interior of the restaurant.

'It was lovely to meet you both,' Elpida said, taking a step closer to Imogen. 'What is your name, my darling?' She took Imogen's uninjured hand.

'Imogen.'

'Well, Imogen, you need anything, anything at all, then you come and see me.'

She nodded. 'I will.'

'I am not far,' Elpida added. 'Just a few kilometres up there.' She pointed to the sky. 'Agios Martinos.'

'OK,' Imogen said. 'Thank you.'

'*Yiayia*,' Panos said a little sharply.

'Pfft! Anyone would think we are in a rush for something, Pano! Where are your manners?'

Imogen looked to Panos Dimitriou and his dark eyes met her gaze, holding it in what seemed like a challenge. Perhaps her stupid remarks about the economy hadn't been repaired by her apology.

'See you again, I hope,' Harry said, waving a hand as the two natives departed. 'You should come for dinner when we open!'

'Harry,' Imogen hissed. 'Stop it.'

Panos and Elpida made their way into the restaurant and Imogen watched as the waiters hugged and kissed them both like great friends.

'Why should I stop? Wouldn't it be nice? To have our first customers be the people who used to own the restaurant?' Harry picked up his beer glass and swilled down the contents.

'I'm not sure it would,' Imogen snapped. 'And I'm definitely sure that that place is going to be nowhere near ready to open in a week! Mum and Janie think it's the biggest mistake you've ever made and I think... Well, I know why you're doing it but... I think maybe you're taking on too much.'

'Immy—'

'No, Harry, don't, please. I'm... I'm going for a walk.' She picked up her handbag. 'I'm going to try and find somewhere that sells milk and tea bags and then I guess I'll meet you back at... Baghdad. There, how's that for a name for the restaurant?' She stopped talking, tears pricking her eyes.

THIRTEEN

Tomas' Taverna, Acharavi beachfront

The view from the taverna hadn't changed at all. Even the old beach shelters were still there, their rattan a little weathered and faded from the winter rain but standing stoic. Panos watched Corfu life go by – mopeds, holidaymakers laden with beach bags, children in swimwear cleaning their sandy feet underneath the shower.

Tomas and his mother had embraced Panos like he was a long-lost relative. When he was small he had come here with his parents on Saturday nights to share *meze*. There had been friends, local families all sitting together enjoying traditional music, swapping stories, laughter, dancing. It all seemed like a century ago.

Now he was looking at the drinks menu but not really seeing anything. His brain was churning up the conversation with the English couple who had bought the restaurant, *his* restaurant. Who did they think they were? Taking his inheritance from under his nose, conning his grandmother into parting with it. He'd wanted to say something right there and then, get mad, tell them they were out of line, but something had told him to wait.

'Pano, your cousin is here!'

Elpida's voice sliced through his thoughts and he looked up to see his cousin, Risto, next to him.

There was the boy he had spent the whole of his childhood with. He was sure it had been less than a year since they had seen each other but Risto looked different somehow. His dark curly head of hair was just the same but he was thinner, his skin wan. Finally he slid the wood and rattan chair backwards and got to his feet.

'Risto,' he said, embracing him, both hands slapping his back.

'Pano.'

Panos held his cousin away and regarded him again. Risto would always be the boy who had swung on the olive tree next to him. Then it struck him. Risto was wearing trousers and a smart white shirt not dissimilar to his, although obviously a poorer quality of cloth. Panos couldn't remember Risto ever wearing anything but jeans or shorts unless there was a wedding.

'You are going somewhere?' Panos asked, pulling at the sleeve of his cousin's shirt.

Risto shifted away, looking a little embarrassed. He shook his head. 'No.'

'Pfft!' Elpida said. 'Why does there have to be a reason for Risto to wear something smart?'

'Because before he was always covered in mud from working the fields,' Panos remarked.

The faces around him sobered instantaneously. Panos' eyes went from Risto to Elpida and back again before he eventually sank to his seat and reached for the jug of water on the table, pouring himself a glass. 'What's going on?' he asked.

Risto moved to a chair next to Elpida and, as he sat down, Panos saw the woman pat her younger grandson's hand.

'Is anyone going to tell me?' Panos asked impatiently.

'We will order some strong drinks before we start talking,' Elpida said, removing her packet of cigarettes from her handbag.

'It wasn't my fault, Pano,' Risto began, his eyes dropping to the tablecloth.

'Risto, wait,' Elpida insisted. She put a cigarette into her mouth and lit it up, inhaling hard.

Panos shook his head. 'What is this, *yiayia*? Some other shock to drop on me, like the restaurant you sold to an English couple?'

'Aren't they lovely?' Elpida answered, blowing a cloud of smoke up into the air. 'Very pretty girl, wasn't she?'

Panos shook his head and wet his lips. The woman's beauty hadn't been lost on him but neither had her sharp reply to his offer of help. And she had his restaurant. She and her husband were going to develop it right in front of his eyes.

He cleared his throat and put a hand in the air, beckoning a waiter. 'Spiros, some *retsina* here please?'

Thirty minutes or so later the *retsina* had coated his throat with its sap-like qualities and he was ready to about turn and head back to the airport. This was not what he had come for. He had come to get back the restaurant and make plans to purchase every other eatery along the sand he could get his hands on.

'Say something, Pano, please,' Risto begged.

He toyed with his glass, running his finger around the rim, eyes fixed on the honey-coloured liquid inside. He didn't know what to say. He thought the Greek crisis was something that had only really affected the mainland, Athens. To think that it was touching this island – his own family – that Risto hadn't worked for almost a year. He could feel two sets of eyes burning holes into the top of his head. Why had Elpida not given him a head's up about this on the phone?

'The boy needs our help.'

'Well, *yiayia,* the first question I have is, why isn't he your gardener?'

He regarded them both. His grandmother puffing on her second cigarette, his cousin looking lost.

'We tried this. Risto does not know the difference between plants and weeds,' Elpida stated.

Panos shook his head. 'Bar work?'

'I try this, Pano,' Risto replied forlornly. 'The last person in is always the first person out when business slides again.'

'Well, we all know I had to leave the island to find success.'

'Pfft! We are not talking about success, Pano. We are just talking about earning enough money to live!'

Her words kicked him. Here he was in his tailored suit, opposite his cousin who, he was told, had barely two Euro to rub together.

'I am trying to do the same for Risto as I did for you,' Elpida stated firmly. 'I gave you everything I could spare to start your new life.'

His fingers reached for the serviette close to hand and he pulled it into his fist, clenching it up.

'Risto lost his job on the farm when the crisis hit. He's been out of work ever since. I wanted to tell you this before but Risto would not let me.'

He watched Elpida sit forward and stab her cigarette out in the ashtray. She pushed her glasses up her nose and sat a little further forward in her chair. 'He needs guidance, Pano. Help from his cousin.'

'It is OK. It does not matter. I should not have come.' Risto got to his feet, his shirt untucking from his trousers as he moved.

'Sit down, Risto!' Elpida ordered.

'You want me to guide him?! Guide him where? How?' Panos asked, throwing the contents of his wine glass down his throat.

'*Yiayia* thought you might be able to give me a job.'

This was why Elpida had berated him on the phone for not keeping better contact with the family. She was hinting at wanting him to give his cousin a way out of Corfu. His grandmother might have given him the airfare to escape but he owed the rest of his success to himself.

Risto's dark curly head was hanging so far down it was almost touching the placemat on the table. What was he doing? What was there to think about? Risto was his family. He loved him. He hadn't been there for him.

'I'm sorry,' he said in low tones. 'I just did not know any of this. It is a shock.'

'Sit up straight, Risto,' Elpida snapped. 'And stop looking like you have no backbone.'

Risto snapped his head back up and adjusted his posture.

'You are a Dimitriou,' Elpida continued. 'You are both Dimitrious and, as the surviving elder of this family, I want to bash your heads together.'

Panos remained quiet, looking to his cousin.

'Now, we need to work something out together. Pano, there must be something within your organisation that Risto can do. Awful, bright, metallic bars he can advertise with flyers or posters, yes? Or phone calls he can make?' She turned to Risto then. 'You still have your moped, yes?'

'Yes, of course.'

Elpida clapped her hands together. 'Good. Pano?'

He nodded his head slowly as a plan began to formulate. Smiling, he replied. 'OK, Risto, yes. I have something coming up that might be ideal.'

FOURTEEN

Acharavi beachfront

The man who gave Imogen directions to the high street was called Spiros. As was the man who sold her a doughnut as she came off the beach. *And* the man who ran the first shop she came to on the main road. It had taken her fifteen minutes to stomp from the beachfront to the town centre, navigating potholes, a loose goat and a van full of fish. She thought they were all having some Greek joke with her about the name, until Spiros the shopkeeper told her it was tradition to call your firstborn son after the island's saint, Spyridon. Spiros the shopkeeper had a dog she'd patted and had given her grocery essentials for free, despite her insistence otherwise, and a plaster for her hand.

There were shops all along the main street of Acharavi selling a multitude of touristy items – coloured friendship bracelets and slap bands stating *I Love Corfu* as well as beaded keyrings, baseball hats and postcards. A boutique claiming to stock the latest fashions was next to a jewellery shop and there were numerous bars and eateries both sides of what looked like a roundabout in the middle of the road.

Now, provisions dropped off and Harry avoided, she was changed into her swimsuit, the sun relentless in its role to scorch her like the top of a crème brûlée. She sucked in a breath of humid air and removed her t-shirt, dropping it to the beach. Then she ran, racing through the sand, puffs spiralling up around her as she headed for the surf. Her soles went from dry powder to wet paste and once she was thigh-high in the warm sea she stopped, digging her toes into the moistness and relishing the relief. Looking up, she took in the ocean she was standing in, water sparkling like a beach scene from *Hawaii Five-0,* two small boats just visible on the horizon and the breathtaking rise and fall of the craggy mountains of Albania.

A piece of pure bliss amongst all the chaos, she launched herself forward, running into the waves then diving head-first until she was completely submerged. Cooling, body-quenching water flashed over her skin and the sea-salt and sunshine smell wrapped around her senses. She swam out a little further, hands gliding through the turquoise water, heat on her shoulders. This was better. This was more than the guidebook had offered up. This was a sensory experience like no other.

Imogen laid back in the water, letting the gentle waves support her as she tipped her head skywards. She shouldn't have snapped at Harry. He had bought the restaurant after all, without help, without any hitches that she knew about. She kicked her legs, letting the water soak into her hair, her stomach flat against the surface of the sea. She would apologise, just as soon as the Ionian water had finished soothing the journey out of her.

Coming out of the water and back onto the sand, Imogen picked up her t-shirt, towelling herself down with it and slipping her sandals back on.

She stepped back onto the road, heading for the restaurant. A few metres away she stopped. There, right next to Harry's property, was a square parcel of land she hadn't noticed earlier. It looked odd simply because the grass was lush and green and cut short, like it had been tended, not left to grow Triffids like the restaurant. And it was flat. She was discovering not a great deal of Corfu was flat.

Then she caught sight of a man at the edge of the beach, his business shoes imbedded in the white stones. It was him. The Greek from the taverna. What puzzled her more was the fact he wasn't gazing out at the view, he was staring at the restaurant. *Harry's* restaurant.

Her sandals crunched on the stones on the road and the man's gaze fell on her. That jet-black hair, followed by broad shoulders hinting at a muscular torso and, the skin that was visible, a warm teak. As he looked at her, the deep, dark eyes connecting with hers, she shivered, becoming acutely aware she was wearing very little. And he seemed to be taking in that fact. She gripped onto her t-shirt, pressing it to her damp skin.

'Hello,' she said, deciding to hurriedly put her t-shirt on.

'*Kalispera*,' Panos replied. 'Your hand… It is OK?' He took his hands from his pockets and moved towards her.

She stopped walking. 'Yes, it's fine,' Imogen said. 'But picking up broken glass probably wasn't the wisest move I've ever made.'

'I agree,' he stated, halting beside her. 'So, you have been for a swim.'

She swallowed. His eyes were definitely appraising her and the t-shirt was clinging to every curve she possessed. 'Yes, it was lovely. It's been so hot today.'

He nodded, his dark eyes still heavy on her.

'In August it is hotter,' he replied. 'So you are going to re-open the restaurant soon, yes? In a week?'

'That seems to be the plan,' Imogen responded. She wasn't about to tell him her reservations. Harry had apparently walked into the situation with open eyes. Besides, he and his grandmother were probably, quite rightly, rubbing their hands together at being a hundred thousand Euro better off without the dead weight of something that looked like a war zone.

'You are not sure?'

Had he noted her earlier shock at Harry's suggestion of opening in a week? She didn't want him and his grandmother to know neither of them knew anything about running an eatery or that the idea was making her feel a little bit sick – and not in the *Urban Dictionary* way.

'Oh, no, I'm sure… very sure.' She swallowed. 'Harry's very keen.'

'And you are "keen" too?'

'Yes of course.' What was this? Twenty questions? His dark eyes were observing her closely. She dipped her head out of the sunlight and put a hand on her forehead to shield her eyes.

He nodded then. 'Good.' He pulled in a breath. 'Good for you.'

'This was your only restaurant?' she found herself asking.

He smiled. 'This was not *my* restaurant.' He paused a beat before continuing. 'This belonged to my grandmother. But she… decided it was no longer for her.'

'I see.' She took her hand away from her forehead and pushed a stray damp stand of hair back behind her ear. 'So you don't have a whole chain of restaurants all over Corfu?'

He shook his head. 'No, well, that is…' He wet his lips. 'I'm in a slightly different line of work. You could still call it the hospitality industry. I currently live in Crete.'

'Currently. Wow. That makes it sound like you travel the world.' Her mind drifted to her father and the far-flung places he visited in the name of Egyptian cotton.

'Europe, for the most part.' He smiled. 'But here you are, *currently* living in Corfu.'

'Yes,' she answered. 'Apparently I am.'

'So, did you choose here for the Metaxa brandy or the plate smashing?'

She laughed. 'I'm hoping to try both of those.'

'Do not forget to tell your first diners that plates should not be smashed on every night,' he said, smiling at her.

'I'll remember that.'

Imogen watched him scuff the sole of his shoe against the concrete. It should have made her feel uneasy, here, alone, in a foreign country with a man she didn't know, but her stomach was telling her his presence was exciting her a little. Maybe it was both.

'Looking at the place, you might need a little help, yes?' Panos said.

'Help?'

'If you are to open this soon?'

She nodded her head automatically.

'Then you are going to need more than two pairs of hands,' he stated.

'Well… yes, maybe but…'

She stopped talking, not knowing what to say next. Her heart was hammering on her insides ordering her to tell this man she wasn't quite sure about the plan, but her pride and loyalty to her brother was telling her something completely different.

'There is something wrong?'

'It's just all very new,' she answered, stumbling a little over the sentence.

'You have not worked in a restaurant before?' he quizzed.

She shook her head. 'No, that is, I have… just not quite like this.' A heavy sigh escaped her lips.

Something inside Panos shifted. He could see her doubt in this project. It was written over every inch of her. Although, for some reason, his body seemed more interested in looking at her in that swimsuit, barely covered by her t-shirt. Not much was hidden by the cotton. Her breasts, her hour-glass figure...

'It used to be *the* place to come,' he spoke, his eyes moving back to the restaurant frontage.

'Did it?' Imogen turned around, moving beside him to look too.

'A long time ago. When my grandmother and grandfather both worked here. The restaurant was their life. My grandfather would fish for the catch of the day and my grandmother would always tell him nothing was big enough or small enough or right for the recipe she had in mind.' He smiled. 'I can still remember them "debating". And my grandmother, she would chase him onto the beach with the biggest pot in the kitchen swinging from her hand.' He shook his head. 'All of this while our customers' danced *sirtaki* and ate *meze* to the sound of the *bouzouki*.' He drew a breath, and cleared his throat. He needed to remember what his remit was here. 'After my grandfather died... well, it hasn't been the same for many years. People, they find new places to go and look for more than just eating. Entertainment, music, free wi-fi...' His eyes appraised her expression. 'I am sorry. What am I saying? I do not mean this cannot be popular again, of course! I am sure—'

'It's OK. You don't have to soft-soap things for me. I know the country has fallen on hard times and it's going to take a lot of work.'

'Your husband fell in love with Corfu like he fell in love with you, huh?' He nudged her elbow and smiled. 'It was a romantic decision, not a business one?'

She stiffened and stared back at him. 'My husband?'

Her expression made him feel like he had said something insulting. Was it because he had made contact with her? Instinctively he pushed his hands back into the pockets of his trousers.

Then, all at once, her demeanour changed again and she let out a laugh.

'Oh, I'm sorry, you thought Harry was my husband.' She shook her head. 'No, Harry… He's my brother.'

'Your husband is not here?' Now it was he who was confused.

'I don't have one of those anymore.'

He'd been thrown for a moment but now he could see his way in. She was single. *He* was single. If he could stop spilling ancient history to her and keep his eyes from wandering, this was going to be child's play. The trick was to *seem* attracted to her, not to actually *be* attracted to her. In a few days, after he had charmed her, after she had realised what an impossible challenge this place was going to be, she would be begging him to take it from her.

'If I'm truly honest, Mr Dimitriou, right now, if someone came along and offered me half the money Harry paid for the damn restaurant I'd bite their hand off.'

He rocked back a little on his shoes.

'How about exactly *what* he paid for it?' The words were out of his mouth before he had a chance to stop them.

'What?' She looked completely bewildered.

He wet his lips. 'The restaurant. How about I pay your brother exactly what he paid?' His heart was racing as his eyes searched hers for a tell.

She wasn't saying anything. That was a start. She hadn't rejected it straightaway. He kept as still as his frenzied insides would let him, studying her expression, waiting for her to make a reply.

He watched her take a breath.

'Unfortunately, it isn't mine to sell.' She lifted the bag in her hand a little. 'It's my brother's enterprise and he's very keen to make a proper go of it.'

'But it is a lot of work, no? All these weeds and the broken windows and… I can only imagine what the inside is like.'

'Just imagine a news report about bombings in Syria.' She straightened her expression. 'And, if you don't think the restaurant can be popular again, why would you want it?'

He swallowed. She was smart… and he didn't have an answer ready that he was willing to share.

'My offer still stands despite its condition.' He wet his lips, his eyes holding hers.

'It's very generous, Mr Dimitriou… for something that cannot be a success. Is there a Greek fortune hidden under the foundations?'

He smiled. 'Not that I know of, but if you come across any doubloons I'd be very interested.'

She took a step back, trying to dry her thighs with the bottom of her t-shirt. 'I will let my brother know of your interest but once he sets his heart on something…'

'Likewise,' he replied. He held out his hand. 'It's Panos,' he stated. 'You must call me Panos.'

She took his hand. 'Imogen.'

'I remember,' he responded, enjoying the softness of her skin on his. He broke the connection. 'So tomorrow, I send my cousin to work here with you. His name is Risto.'

'What? No… we haven't worked through staffing budgets yet…' She stopped talking briefly to sweep the hair off her face. Her cheeks were reddening. 'I'm not sure we can afford to pay anyone at the moment.'

He shrugged his shoulders. 'Risto needs something. He is between jobs. He will work for bread and *tzatziki* and something to drink. *Non*-alcoholic.' He smiled. 'And later, if you decide to sell the restaurant to me, it will be in a much better state of repair.'

'Mr Dimitriou... Panos... I can't...'

'Please, it is my gift to you,' he stated. 'To welcome you to Corfu and... well, really, very honestly, you will be doing me a service no matter how things turn out.'

'I—'

'Risto is a hard worker. I am sure he can do anything you want him to do. He will be here at eight.' He gave her one last smile before turning left and walking back up the road. The next phase of his plan would start in the morning.

FIFTEEN

The restaurant, Acharavi beachfront

Imogen couldn't quite believe what was happening. Had she really just been given someone to work for free? And why did Panos Dimitriou want to buy the restaurant when his grandmother had only just sold it? She stopped in the doorway of the upstairs apartment and looked down at a floor scattered in pieces of A4 paper. Each one was covered in frenzied writing. *Harry's* frenzied writing. And there he was, curled up on one side of the room between a broken chair and an empty cardboard box. He looked like someone bedding down in a squat.

She stopped just in front of him. He was sound asleep, his eyes tight shut, sandy hair tousled, a sleeping bag half over his body. Her eyes moved to the writing on some pages stuck to the wall. There were several pages, Sellotaped into place on the ancient floral wallpaper. She stepped towards them, trying to read what was noted down.

> *Name – something Greek or English or Greeklish?*
> *Menu – what does Immy cook best? What does Mum*
> *cook best? What do Olivia and Tristan like best? Janie*
> *liked moussaka.*
> *Food – what? Where from?*
> *Vegetarians – what? Where from?*
> *Vegans – ?*

Fire man – fire kit, hose, extinguisher, what else?
Music licence – band for opening night?
Business licence – put more money in Greek bank account
Opening night – when?
Skip man – chase if not here by midday
Plants – revive dead ones? Buy new ones? Plastic?

There were reams and reams of questions and hardly any answers. While she had been throwing her toys out of the pram looking for the very English stress relief of tea and milk then swimming, Harry had been throwing the contents of his mind down in ink.

Her brother was exhausted from the trip but in the morning she knew he was going to wake up ready to throw himself into this restaurant and give it everything he had. A feeling of pride rolled over her like one of the waves in the sea. He had worked hard to get this place, kept it to himself, wanted to be capable. It was a shambles now but Harry saw the potential and she should be seeing *his* potential and having a little faith. She moved to the side of the room facing out over the sea and tugged open a pair of windows.

Looking out onto a darkening scene she watched the setting sun, a giant glowing orb slowly disappearing from sight, the sky around it turning shades of pink and orange. Imogen leaned on the windowsill, stretching to the right and observing the lights of the town. Strings of bulbs – gold, green and blue – to her far right on neighbouring tavernas, the faint noise of Greek music and joviality on the breeze. It felt like a whole world away from this dusty, barren room. She tried to imagine the little Greek lady, Panos' grandmother, running around the restaurant after her husband with a saucepan while full tables of diners ate fresh fish of the day and Greek delicacies. Harry would probably make her crazy enough to do the saucepan chasing at some point.

She leant back in, slapping at a mosquito on her arm, and checked her watch. It would be just after seven in the evening in the UK. She needed to update her mum and Janie.

With tea made using an old-fashioned steel kettle on the electric hob and a half-empty bottle of *ouzo* she'd found in a cupboard, Imogen sat on an unbroken chair and waited for her call to the UK to connect.

'Tristan Charlton, who is speaking please?'

Imogen couldn't help smiling. 'Well, hello, Tristan Charlton, this is your Auntie Imogen speaking.'

'Auntie Imogen!' Tristan shouted in response. ''livia, it's Auntie Imogen. Are you in Greece? Mummy said you're in Greece with Dad. Are you? Are you really?'

She laughed. 'Yes, I really am and your dad is asleep already. It's past nine o'clock here.'

'He texted me earlier. He said the restaurant is really cool. Is it really cool?'

Imogen curled her fingers around the chipped glass she had found to pour the *ouzo* into. 'It's really…' There were so many words she wanted to say other than 'cool'. She smiled to herself. 'It's right by the beach.' That wasn't a lie and the beach was pretty spectacular.

'Right by it?! That *is* cool,' Tristan answered.

'Is Mummy there, Tristan?'

'Yes, she's making lots of arm movements so I think she wants to talk to you. See ya, wouldn't wanna be ya!' And he was gone. There was a pause and then…

'It's a bloody disaster zone, isn't it?' Janie's voice greeted. 'I'm imagining those photos you showed me, but doubly worse, like *World War Z*.'

'The flight was on time, no turbulence and I had the best *sti-fado* I've ever had at a lovely little taverna.' Imogen downed the shot of *ouzo* and closed her eyes. Her sister-in-law was panicking but a degree of panicking was good. It meant she still cared what Harry was doing. That she hopefully still cared for him.

'You're drinking, aren't you? It's that bad, you're drinking just thinking about it.' Janie sniffed. 'Are you there? Are you looking at the devastation and wondering what the fuck is... duck, I said duck, children, what the duck is going on?'

'It's going to be OK, Janie. I promise. And I promise it isn't *World War Z*.'

'*Mad Max*?'

'No, it's...'

'*Sharknado*?'

'Janie, calm down.'

'I can't calm down. You're on the other side of Europe, Harry's spent a fortune on a money pit and Grace is...'

At the mention of her mother's name Imogen gripped the *ouzo* glass tighter. 'Is Mum OK? Was she dressed?'

'Sorry... I didn't mean to worry you. We went to see her on the way back from school and... well, I haven't seen her for a while and...'

Janie didn't need to say any more. Nothing seemed to get her mum animated – until she'd dropped Harry's restaurant news on her. She swallowed, putting the glass down and picking up the tea cup without a handle.

'She had a dressing gown on. And she asked if you'd taken Harry in hand yet,' Janie finished. 'She was catching up on *Pol-dark*.'

Imogen let out a sigh. 'She's doing something I guess.'

'Is Harry there?' Janie asked.

'He's asleep.'

'I had a thought… you know… because this restaurant idea is so mental. Is he taking his medication?'

'I'll check in the morning. He's been fine today.'

'So,' Janie said. 'Tell me. Apart from the hideous run-down restaurant, what's Corfu like in 2016? It must have changed since I visited it last.'

Imogen focussed on what was in front of her. A star-filled sky and the sound of the waves as they spurted rhythmically forth, shaking the stones on the shore. She watched the fronds of a nearby palm shifting in the light wind. 'It's lovely,' she answered finally, meaning it. 'If things were different, then…'

'Then?'

'Then I'd definitely consider it for a holiday destination.'

Imogen closed her eyes as tension took hold again. If only this *could* be a holiday. How different would she be feeling right now? What would she be doing? Seeking out the music drifting across the beach? Dancing until her feet got sore? Maybe she would still be on the beach with Panos…

But she was here now, committed to helping Harry set up a restaurant to win back Janie. But what if they could achieve neither of those things? There were no guarantees about any of it. And she had a life back in England to maintain. The possibility that the Wyatt Group might reply to her application…

'Do you think you're going to be able to persuade him to sell it on?'

She held the phone a little tighter to her ear. What was the right thing to say to someone so many miles away? What did she really think after half a glass of this disgusting aperitif? She couldn't tell Janie about Panos' offer. Janie would probably find his contact details and accept the offer on Harry's behalf before the sun set.

'We'll see,' she answered, slugging back the rest of the drink and wincing as it burned her insides. She started to cough violently.

'What *are* you drinking?'

'I don't know,' Imogen answered, shaking her head as the alcohol flooded her system. 'I found it in a cupboard under the sink.'

'Bloody hell, Imogen, are you sure it isn't cleaning fluid?'

'I'm sure,' she answered. 'Cleaning fluid would probably taste a whole lot better than this.'

SIXTEEN

Elpida Dimitriou's home, Agios Martinos

The sound of a garden strimmer roaring into action had Panos shutting the lid of his laptop and simultaneously getting up from his seat, coffee cup swinging from his hand.

'What is wrong with that boy?' he asked his grandmother, who was sitting at the breakfast bar reading a thick hardback book.

'What time is this to start work?' He put the cup down on the worktop, tension in his shoulders. The restaurant was on his mind but he couldn't shake the image of Imogen Charlton, coming off the beach in her swimsuit, sparkles of water speckling her skin…

'Speaks the man who has been working since five a.m.' Elpida said without looking up.

'That is different. That is quiet work, not waking up the entire village.'

Elpida raised her head, pushing her glasses up her nose and directing her gaze at him. 'You did not sleep,' she stated. 'That is why you are being like this.'

He took a breath and calmed himself. 'I just have some documents to look through and it isn't being aided by the gardener.' He leant against the work top and put his finger and thumb to the bridge of his nose. He was starting to get a headache. Despite what he had said to Manilos on the phone, he was not going to let the Asp deal go if there was still a sliver of a chance. But the man hadn't replied to his email last night and there was nothing this morning either. He now had to wait until it was a civilised – not too eager – time to call him.

'I saw you talking to Tomas yesterday,' Elpida remarked, turning over her book.

He closed his eyes. He knew Elpida had noticed him taking Tomas to one side before they left. He'd wanted to test the water, to know if the owner of one of the most popular restaurants on the strip was willing to embrace new opportunity. At first he was greeted with resistance where the restauranteur would dig in his heels and flatly refuse to continue the conversation, but, as soon as he mentioned the sum of money he had in mind, he saw the alteration in the man's attitude. He would fold. Panos was sure of it. And once the other owners folded too, he would be well on the way to his reinvention of the Acharavi seafront. His contact on the council would see to the rest. But his grandmother didn't need to know that.

'Yes, I was asking him about the family, getting up to date on the news of the town.'

Elpida looked less than convinced. 'And what news of the town did he give you?'

Panos smiled. 'He told me you had employed a gardener.'

'Pfft! That is not news of the town and I don't see what is wrong with helping Nico and his mother.' Elpida reached for her cigarettes, hurriedly opening the packet up.

'Please, *yiayia*, must you smoke?' He hated the habit and when he had heard her coughing like a car unable to start last night he knew it was taking its toll on her lungs.

'Yes, I must smoke,' she answered, flicking her lighter and igniting the end of the cigarette. He watched her inhale deeply before holding the breath then exhaling a grey-blue cloud that polluted the kitchen air. 'Smoking is my one pleasure these days. I will give up when I have great-grandchildren, so…'

Panos shook his head. She always brought this up. Continuing the family line was on him and Risto and she never let Panos forget it.

'Then you will be smoking for a long time,' he stated.

'Pfft! So there is still no one special in your life?'

It irked him the way she said it and he thought about Rhea. He didn't consider her to be someone special. The time they had spent together had been in bed. As agreeable as that had been it didn't come under the category of 'special'. He swallowed. There had been a time when he had thought his parents' relationship was special. Up until those last few years, they had appeared so deeply in love, behaving almost like newlyweds. His father would always hold his mother's hand, whisper in her ear, gaze at her like she was his whole world. And they would always dance. It didn't matter where they were – at home, at a neighbour's house or a restaurant – the sound of *bouzouki* music would have Christos pulling Sophia into his arms and holding her close. He rolled up the lead for his computer.

'Have you called your mother? Have you told her you are here?' Elpida continued, thankfully not waiting for an answer.

'What is this? It feels like an interrogation.'

'She worries about you, Pano.'

'I thought you were the one worrying about me. Which is it?'

'We both worry.'

'She has John,' Panos answered. He hadn't really meant the sentence to come out as hard and self-centred as it had sounded.

'What sort of answer is that?'

He had no reply.

'Please, call your mother, that is all I ask,' she said.

'*Yiayia*—' he began.

'I don't want to fight with you, Pano. I've never wanted to fight with you… but I will if I have to.'

He held her gaze until he had to look away. How could making million-Euro deals be easier than a conversation with his grandmother?

'You will be back for dinner tonight. I have some friends coming over. I am cooking. Drinks will start at seven.' She shook a finger at him. 'Don't be late.'

It was futile to try to refuse.

SEVENTEEN

The restaurant, Acharavi beachfront

Imogen's mouth felt like someone had been sharpening pencils into it. She opened and shut it, looking up at the ceiling and slowly remembering where she was. She reached down to scratch an itch on her leg and shifted into a sitting position, looking around the room for Harry. The two windows she'd opened last night to let some much-needed air into the building were now sending early morning heat into the room and suddenly it wasn't just the one spot on her leg that itched, it was everything. She pulled the sleeping bag off her body, almost too scared to look. What was there made her scream out loud. Her entire lower half was covered in ugly red welches. How had this happened?

Harry burst through the door, dust and debris all over his face, like someone had coated his cheeks in flour. 'Immy? Are you alright?'

Imogen let out a frustrated noise as she scrambled to her feet. Both legs were on fire. She stamped her bare soles on the tiles and glared at Harry. 'Look at me! Look *at* me!'

'What's happened?' Harry moved closer, bending to inspect her. 'Have you got an allergy?'

'No! They're bloody bites aren't they?! From God knows what! Fleas from all the dust and grime in this place, or mosquitoes!' Imogen screwed her face up, trying to ignore the itch and heat.

Harry stood up, his head turning left. 'Did you leave the windows open all night?' He looked puzzled. 'I definitely shut them before I went to sleep.'

'Well… the whole place was like an oven. I had to let some air in somehow!'

She watched her brother march over to the windows and pull them shut. 'That will be it then. Corfu is well known for its mosquitoes, Immy. I thought you read the guidebook.'

'I did… but it was all stunning scenery and flora and fauna and—'

'Ah-ha!' Harry said, pointing an accusing finger. 'And that's why the mosquitoes love it so much. Lots of vegetation.'

'Tell me there's a cure.'

'I've got some bite cream,' Harry answered. His eyes went from her legs to her face. 'Just let me find it before you look in the mirror.'

'What?' Imogen's hands went to her face and straightaway the itch spread. 'You have got to be kidding me? Where's the mirror?'

'It's not too bad, well, not from one side,' Harry began. 'The cream will bring the redness down.'

'Get me a bloody mirror now!'

It was official. Imogen looked like a government advertisement about the dangers of not being vaccinated against measles. She had no idea you were supposed to close every window, douse yourself and the entire room in jungle-strength insect repellent to achieve a bite-free good night's sleep. Now, she was drenched in sweat from sweeping and clearing broken furniture in already thirty-degree heat in preparation for the skip's arrival… some time.

The outside area didn't look much different except the broken chairs and tables were piled to one side. She leant on her broom and wiped a forearm over her brow.

'*Kalimera*,' a soft male voice greeted.

Imogen looked up to see a Greek man in his twenties standing in the entrance of the restaurant, dressed in jeans and a plain red t-shirt covered in paint. He had a mop of dark curly hair and large brown eyes that gave him a child-like quality. This had to be the cousin Panos Dimitriou had offered to help.

'Hello, you must be…' What had Panos said his name was?

'Risto,' the young man introduced himself.

'Hello! Calamari!' Harry greeted, bursting out onto the terrace, hair flopping with every stride. 'It's very good of you to help. Very generous.'

Imogen thought about Panos' offer to buy the restaurant. She hadn't told Harry about that and she really didn't know why. She cleared her throat and addressed Risto.

'So, we're just clearing everything to one side out here and in the main room. Broken things, of which there are many,' Imogen said.

Risto nodded. 'Yes, I see.' He looked at the brush Imogen was holding. 'You have another of these?'

'I'll find something,' Harry said. 'Then we can get this place looking more like the restaurant I dreamed about last night.'

EIGHTEEN

The restaurant, Acharavi beachfront

Wearing sun cream, bite cream and insect repellent, sweat trickling down her back, hair plastered to her red, blotchy face, Imogen stopped sweeping, stepped back and took in her last couple of hours of handiwork. Thanks to Harry and Risto putting all the rubbish and broken furniture in the skip, salvaging what could be repaired and generally shifting everything from the front terrace, it now looked… almost good.

She leaned against the broom handle and looked hard around the open air terrace. With everything clean and bare apart from the thicket of weeds around the perimeter, it looked so different to the wreck they'd encountered yesterday. The tiles on the floor were actually made up of tiny pebbles – some brown, some white and orange – and she had an idea that when she mopped the area they were going to shine. Even the plants in the wall planters seemed to have perked up a little. Or maybe that was just her feeling exhausted and going cross-eyed. A look left to the sand and the glistening sea every few minutes had kept her going. She'd imagined the perspiration that was putting the twenty-four hour promise of her Sure deodorant to the test was that fresh, cool water on her skin from yesterday. Perhaps she'd take another dip later, after the meeting Harry had scheduled to discuss menus.

'*Kalimera!* Hello!'

At the sound of the voice Imogen turned her head. It was Elpida Dimitriou, dressed for a cocktail party in a bright, figure-hugging floral dress but with black trainers on her feet. She was holding a brown paper carrier bag in each hand.

'Hello,' Imogen greeted, leaning the broom up against the wall and brushing her palms together to remove any dust.

'Argh!' Elpida exclaimed. 'What has happened to you? You look like someone from horror film!'

Imogen nodded. 'Thank you, I'm taking that as a compliment because I thought I actually looked much worse than that.'

'These are bites?' Elpida asked. She planted the bags on the floor, and before Imogen could move the woman had slapped her hands on both her cheeks, examining the damage.

'Apparently so,' she sighed. 'Stupidly, I didn't know Corfu was twinned with the Congo.'

'I have something for this,' Elpida said, stepping back and picking up her bags. 'We will fix it.' She strode towards the door of the building and Imogen hastily followed.

'That's very kind of you but I got some cream and some spray and—' Imogen said.

'What is this?!' Elpida exclaimed, looking into the main room, eyes bulbous, shock written on her face.

'What is what?' Imogen stood beside the woman, trying to see what there was amongst the destruction that was causing this reaction. The chairs and tables that could be fixed were stacked to one side, it was only the other half that was still filled with all manner of rubbish from the kitchen and upper room.

'This!' Elpida stated. 'This holy horror of destruction!'

'Um…' Imogen didn't really know what to say. This used to be this woman's restaurant. Surely she would know the state she had left it in.

The woman was shaking her head now. 'This cannot be. How has this happened?' She turned back to Imogen. 'This is how this is when you get here?'

'We've cleared a lot out this morning,' Imogen answered.

'This was not how I left things. This is terrible! What must you think of me?' There were tears gathering at the corner of the woman's eyes. 'The weeds, they grow so fast in this weather, I will get Nico to fix this. But this… I had a manager, the last few months the restaurant was open. I cannot believe he—'

'It's all right,' Imogen found herself saying. 'It isn't your fault.'

'And your Harry, he buy this like this!' Elpida exclaimed. 'Is he crazy?!'

'Yes.' Imogen nodded. 'Yes, he is.'

'Well, this is not right. Not right at all. I will fix it.' Elpida began striding through the building, stopping each time she had to navigate the debris in her way.

'Wait, Mrs Dimitriou, you don't have to do that,' Imogen said, hurrying after her and hurdling two plastic buckets in her bid to catch up.

'Pfft! I say I will fix it and I will fix it.' Elpida stopped walking when she saw the further mess in the back room. 'For the love of Zeus! There is more!'

'We wanted to get the front area clear before we started on this,' Imogen said, scratching her legs as the bites heated up again.

'I will make phone calls,' Elpida told her seriously. 'But first we fix your face. Come!'

Elpida had cut a lemon in half and smeared it all over her face. Now the woman was crushing garlic into a paste Imogen was supposed to apply to the affected areas before she went to bed that night. Sat on a wonky stool in the kitchen, she realised she was exhausted.

'Where did you say Harry has gone?' Elpida asked, savaging a fresh loaf of bread with a blunt knife.

'Well, Risto said he knew someone with a van and they were going to a hotel who are getting rid of some of their tables and chairs.'

Elpida waved the knife in the air and stared at Imogen. 'Risto? Risto Dimitriou? My grandson?'

'Yes, I…' Imogen cleared her throat. 'Your other grandson offered us his services.' She hoped this was acceptable to the woman brandishing the bread knife.

Elpida put down the knife and leant on the countertop, both palms on the granite surface like it was bearing her weight. 'He did, did he?'

'Should I not have accepted? When he said it was free I thought it was too good to be true, but—'

Elpida shook her head. 'That boy!' she cursed.

Imogen frowned, wondering if she meant Panos or Risto.

'Panos has so much to give but he chooses to chase the dream his father had,' Elpida said. 'Of course, he does not realise this. He thinks he is doing the exact opposite.'

Imogen recalled the tall, dark-haired man with the soulful eyes standing beside the beach and looking at the restaurant with half a life story written on his face. She also remembered the taut forearms and the way the espresso eyes had held hers.

'Some people live other people's lives, don't they? Always doing something that isn't in their own soul,' Elpida announced. 'But not you and your Harry, huh?' She smiled.

Imogen felt sick and the lemon smell emanating from her face was making things worse. What was in her soul apart from her family? A forgotten love of cooking? A dream about working for a hotel company? Worldwide destinations and a suitcase full of trinkets and pens? Or serving bacon and beans in Southampton and looking after her mum?

'Working here will be good for Risto,' Elpida stated. 'He is a good boy who has fallen on hard times…' She paused. 'I don't know why I tell you all this. You do not want to hear these old stories from an old lady.'

'No, don't be silly.'

The back door slammed and Harry and Risto appeared, covered in dust and sweating profusely.

'We're back!' Harry announced. 'Got twenty tables in the back of the van and they're perfect.' He put his hands into his hair, shaking flakes of sand and shavings onto the floor.

'Pfft! Risto! You know better than to come into a kitchen covered in grease! Out!' Elpida ordered, turning to face the man and making shooing motions with her hands. 'Out!'

Both men backed away. Imogen looked at her brother, juice running down her face, palms up as she shrugged her shoulders.

'You can come back in when you have dusted yourselves down and then I will start to work on this kitchen,' Elpida said, following the men as if to make sure they were going to leave. 'Lunch will be five minutes.'

'Mrs Dimitriou—' Imogen began.

'Elpida,' the woman corrected.

'Sorry, Elpida.' She wet her lips then screwed up her eyes as the lemon tainted her tongue. 'You really don't have to do this, you know.'

'Do what? Make this meal?'

'No… I… well, maybe. I mean, not that it isn't all appreciated, but we don't want to put you out,' Imogen tried to explain.

'Put me out?' Elpida asked, her face creasing with misunderstanding.

'Sorry, what I mean is, you don't have to do this for us. Cleaning and clearing up.'

'Pfft!' she snorted. 'What is wrong with young people today? Always refusing help. Look at this place!' Elpida waved the knife outwards, indicating the mess the kitchen was in.

Imogen hadn't even opened all the cupboards and drawers yet and wasn't keen on finding out what was inside. She had visions of blue cheese being far mouldier than it should be and out-of-date tinned items.

'We work together to fix the kitchen,' Elpida stated, placing heavy slabs of white crusty bread on a platter. 'I call people to help with the restaurant area. Then tonight you and your Harry must come to dinner.'

'Oh, really, we couldn't and…' Imogen's stomach lurched at the invitation despite her immediate refusal. This woman was knocking together a divine-looking *tzatziki* right in front of her eyes. She could only imagine what Greek delights would be served up for a dinner party. Perhaps she could pick up some recipe tips.

'Please,' Elpida continued. 'I have some friends coming and it will be a good chance for you to meet people from the town.'

'Well, in that case…' Imogen smiled, her skin straining beneath the lemon juice and the tautness of her bites.

Elpida dropped her fork into the bowl and clapped her hands in delight. 'Good!' Her smile dropped as she surveyed Imogen closely. 'But I think we will need something else on that face or my guests might think you have disease.'

Now she didn't know whether to laugh or cry.

NINETEEN

Versus Club, Acharavi

Panos was shaking so much he needed the hit of the *ouzo* he was holding in his glass. Sat outside the bar on Acharavi high street he tried to focus on the comings and goings of the town – the scooters, the holidaymakers carrying buckets, spades and bottles of water, the locals trying to find somewhere to park – but all he could hear were Asp's words in his head. Words that could harm him and his business. His gut instinct had been to react. To get straight off the phone from Asp and make another call, but he'd stopped himself from doing that, instead heading to the bar. And he'd done nothing else since, except stare at the alcohol in his glass and wonder what to do next.

His mother came to mind. Was Elpida right? Had it been months since he had spoken to her? He had been so busy and he told himself she was bound to be wrapped up in whatever John was doing. Or were both of those convenient excuses? A thought was niggling him that he wasn't quite on top of his game right now. But did he really feel he needed to be before he spoke to his own mother?

He slipped a hand into the pocket of his trousers and drew out his mobile phone. He could make it quick, say he was just about to go into another meeting... he'd just ask her how she was and say he was fine... say he was good... better than good, then end the call.

He tossed the phone onto the table and drank the *ouzo* back in one gulp. He couldn't do it and it was all his bloody father's fault. Even dead he was directing things. Panos put the glass down on the table and sat back in the cream canvas-backed chair, shading his head under the large palm tree in the bar's courtyard. The Corfu weather was so different to Crete. Crete was arid, desert-like in both its climate and its countryside. He always thought of Corfu as that little bit sweeter. The green hills, beautiful coves and picture-perfect scenes. As he focussed on the sea, just visible down one of the roads that led to the beach, he noticed her.

Across the street was the woman from the restaurant that should belong to him. *Imogen.* She was wearing very short denim shorts and a white t-shirt, her blonde hair scraped back from her face in a ponytail, flip-flops on her feet. Panos sat forward, narrowing his eyes to get a clearer view. She was making her way along the road, shielding her eyes from the sun, one hand on the strap of a bright yellow handbag. He took in her lean torso and those endless legs. A shard of lust hit him in the gut *and* a little lower. He swallowed. This was a good thing. It would be much easier to woo her if his body was agreeable to the idea. And *that's* what he had to do today. He needed to regroup before acting on information from Asp. Paving the way to a development in Acharavi would go a long way to restoring his acumen.

'Pano.'

Risto stood beside him.

'There's a problem?' Panos asked, ushering his cousin into the adjacent chair. 'You are working hard at the restaurant?'

'Yes.' Risto wiped the sweat from his brow with his forearm.

Panos leaned forward and grabbed a napkin from the steel holder on the table and handed it to him.

Risto smiled. 'I know the woman is not quite happy about the restaurant.'

'I know this already,' Panos said. 'She told me this herself.' He sighed. 'What else?'

'They are working hard to make this right. I do not think they will want to sell.'

Panos blew out a breath and wished his glass was full again. 'You would like a drink?' he asked his cousin.

'How long must I work at the restaurant?' Risto replied. 'I want to work with you.'

'Patience, Risto, you *are* working with me.'

'But I… could help you with other things. With *your* business.'

Panos saw the eagerness and hope in Risto's eyes. What real future did Risto have here in Acharavi, where tradition still ruled the day? What feel for modern business was Risto ever going to get if he stayed on this island?

'That restaurant is going to *be* my business,' Panos stated. 'What you are doing there is very important.'

'I know but… there is something else,' Risto admitted. He dropped his eyes to his lap.

'What?'

'*Yiayia* is there.'

Panos gritted his teeth. 'What do you mean she is there?'

'At the restaurant. She arrive, she make lunch, she clean kitchen … she has only just left to go and make food for her dinner party tonight.' Risto swallowed. 'She is helping them.'

That was the very last thing he needed.

'She has invited them to the dinner party tonight,' Risto added.

'What?'

'The Mr Harry and Imogen,' Risto clarified.

Panos nodded as thoughts flooded his mind. He would make sure he was seated next to Imogen, start the charm offensive. She had said it wasn't her decision to make, but he had a feeling that wasn't the case.

'Good work,' he said to Risto, patting the man on the arm before drawing his wallet from his trousers. 'Now, more drinks, yes?'

From its position on the table his mobile phone began to ring. It was Tomas. He let it ring.

'Are you going to answer it?' Risto asked.

He nodded, counting in his head until it had trilled five times. He snatched it up.

'Dimitriou.' Slowly, a smile crossed his face. 'I am so pleased to hear that, Tomas. Of course we can meet.'

Perhaps today was not going to be a complete wash-out after all.

TWENTY

The restaurant, Acharavi beachfront

The lunch had been out of this world. Creamy sour yoghurt with cucumber and fresh mint on thick hunks of bread. She'd almost forgotten how good Greek food was. Afterwards, Elpida had insisted on spreading the smelly garlic paste on the blemishes. Apparently it was another Greek remedy for soothing ailments. Personally, Imogen thought it was a placebo: you were so distracted by the smell you worried less about the bites. But it was nice, being taken care of, and with a few careful dabs of concealer, she didn't think the bites were that noticeable.

'Ta da!' Harry announced, coming out of the bathroom and into the main apartment.

She observed him, her mouth opening in shock and surprise. 'You're wearing a tuxedo. You brought two sleeping bags and a tuxedo in your luggage?'

Harry smiled. 'Well, I was in the Scouts like Tristan.'

She immediately felt underdressed in her peach cotton knee-length dress.

'What's wrong?' Harry asked.

'Nothing, I just… feel a lot less cocktail bar than you.'

Harry laughed then. 'I didn't put this on for anyone else. I hardly get to wear it now I'm not working for Norton Aerospace.' He nodded to himself. 'We used to have quite some parties there.'

'Yes, you did,' Imogen agreed. 'I had to pick you up from some very odd places after those parties.'

'The police station,' Harry said, grinning.

'Blackpool Tower was the strangest location. Tied to a donkey,' Imogen reminded him.

'Milo.'

'You remember the donkey's name? That's impressive.'

'No.' Harry shook his head. 'It was Milo's stag night.'

'In London.'

'Yes, well, you know how the boys got carried away.' He pulled at the lapels of his jacket. 'So, will I do?'

Imogen smiled. He was buoyant. The most buoyant she had seen him in such a long time.

'You look very handsome,' she answered. 'So will *I* do? Bites and eau de something-you'd-eat?' She put her hands on her hips and adopted a confident pose, her hair swishing in its high ponytail.

For a split second Harry looked sad. 'Janie always wore perfume that came in a funny-shaped bottle.'

'Well, I have perfume on too, but it isn't working on the edible remedies Elpida plastered all over me.'

'I spoke to Janie earlier,' Harry stated. 'She asked if I was having a relapse.'

Imogen closed her eyes. She had hoped Janie would hold in her concerns and leave dealing with the situation to her. 'She cares about you, Harry, that's all. And that's what you want, isn't it? Her caring is a good thing, a positive thing. Coming to Corfu was a bit of a shock for us all, that's all.'

Harry snapped his head forward, his eyes locking with Imogen's. 'I don't regret buying the restaurant,' he stated. 'Not for one minute. And after all the work we've done today… I can see so much potential for us, Immy.'

She knew he could. The excitement and sense of achievement was just pouring out of him. She thought about Panos Dimitriou's offer for the restaurant. She should really tell him. She opened her mouth to speak.

'I know you're excited too,' Harry continued. 'I saw you getting all Nigella over those recipes we looked at today.' He grinned. 'Lamb shanks and fresh figs.'

It was true. The internet had provided them with a wealth of information and inspiration. She had enjoyed thinking about the possibilities but still wasn't confident of her ability.

'We'd better go,' she said, eager to change the subject. 'Have you called a taxi or are we taking the car?'

Harry shook his head. 'Neither. Terry, that's the man with the van, he said we can borrow it for a couple of weeks while we're moving things about. I need to get used to driving it. I'm going to take us in that.'

Suddenly Imogen felt sick. 'You are?'

He nodded. 'Might be a good job you aren't too dressed up and smell of garlic. Terry uses it for fish.'

TWENTY-ONE

Elpida Dimitriou's home, Agios Martinos

'This is nice, isn't it?' Harry remarked, slamming the door closed and looking up at the property.

Yes, it was nice. It was more than nice, it was Greek-style palatial. The beautiful stone, the shutters at the windows, the flourishing window boxes. It looked just like something Jasmine Harman would show an escaping couple from the UK if they had a mammoth budget on *A Place in the Sun*. Her eyes went to the sleek Mercedes they'd parked alongside. Panos' car. Dark, attractive, polished… just like the man himself. Someone cleared their throat in a rather obvious manner and Imogen swung around, cheeks flaming, as Panos stood at the threshold of the house.

'Hello,' Harry greeted, thrusting his hand out.

'Good evening,' Panos replied. 'It is nice to meet you again.'

Imogen stepped towards him, her hand outstretched. 'Hello.'

'Good evening, Imogen,' he responded, ignoring her hand, instead drawing his face level with hers and kissing her on both cheeks in turn. He stepped away, looking a little taken aback, his fingers at his lips.

'Gosh, I'm sorry,' Imogen stated. 'I got bitten… by mosquitoes and your grandmother, she…'

He held his long, olive fingers under his nose then sucked the tip of his index finger. Her stomach dipped as a small smile formed on his lips.

'Lemon and garlic,' he said, nodding. 'She did this to me all the time when I was younger.' He smiled. 'Come in, please.'

Suddenly it struck her all she was carrying was her yellow handbag. They hadn't brought anything. No chocolates or wine. She felt like the worst guest ever.

'Here we are, Panos,' Harry said, pulling a bottle of red wine out from under his tuxedo jacket. 'I don't know if it's any good but I suppose when we drink it we'll find out.'

Panos took the bottle, looked at the label, then moved his eyes back to rest on Imogen. 'Full-bodied,' he said, nodding. 'A hint of spice and excellent… with white meat.' He tipped his head a little. 'I look forward to enjoying it.'

He was flirting with her. And how did it make her feel if he was? Intimidated? A little excited? She couldn't be sure.

'Ah! You are here! Excellent!' Elpida appeared, hands in the air, an apron over a black sequinned dress, platforms on her feet that added at least six inches to her height.

'Thank you so much for inviting us,' Harry stated. 'And for all your help today with the boys.'

'I wish to embrace you, Harry, but my hands are covered with aubergine.' Elpida wiped them on her apron. 'Pano, make Harry and Imogen some drinks.' She screwed up her face. 'Where is Risto?'

'He is setting the table like you asked,' Panos responded. There was that smile again, directed straight at her. She was glad Harry was driving.

'Who else is coming tonight?' Imogen asked, heading towards the open-plan kitchen and Elpida.

'Just one other couple and my good friend, Cooky,' Elpida responded.

'As her name suggests, Cooky, is a little kooky,' Panos told them.

'I tell you before! That is not why she has this name,' El-pida exclaimed. 'She work at the bakery with her father. You can guess what it is she made there.'

'Cookies?' Harry asked.

'Exactly,' Elpida announced. 'Now, all of you, shoo! Pano, get drinks and take our guests outside.'

The entertaining space at the rear of Elpida's property was like a little piece of show-garden heaven. A large decked area decorated with cream and toffee-coloured urns full of trail-ing flowers and miniature ferns were dotted around the space that led down to another, bigger paved area. On this patio Risto was putting the finishing touches to a long wooden dining table. As Imogen made her way across the cobble-stone slabs she admired the pretty beige-and-light-blue-striped tablecloth with matching napkins in sparkling wine glasses, polished silverware and two cream glass lanterns, a pillar candle glowing in each. Around her, golden fairy lights had been hung from the boughs of the fruit trees that created an avenue onto a grassy channel that boasted spectacular sea views at its end.

'Wow!' The exclamation came from Harry and it was by no means an exaggeration. The outside area was nothing short of beautiful. Everything about this garden was special. The view, the elegant table setting, the scent of citrus, jasmine and laven-der in the air.

A buzz from a mosquito-like creature snapped Imogen back from her reverie. She shook her head to encourage it to flee.

'On a clear day you can see the houses in Albania.'

Panos' voice was close to her ear and the deep vibrations of his tone, plus the musky scent of his cologne, caused her to shiver. She turned her body and offered him a quick smile. 'It's a beautiful garden.'

He was standing so close she found it hard to concentrate. The muscular outline of his upper arms visible through his shirt, the cotton brushing over an athletic frame…

Imogen cleared her throat, wishing she had a glass to hold. She curled her fingers around the handbag on her shoulder.

'Risto, you did some great work today,' Harry greeted, holding his hand out to the younger man.

'Oh, this is nothing,' Risto answered, bowing his head a little as he took Harry's offering.

'The restaurant is looking better, yes?' Panos asked them both. He plucked a bottle of wine from the container on the table and began to fill a glass.

'Yes, it is,' Harry enthused. 'Already it's starting to look like I dreamed it would.'

'That is good,' Panos answered, looking once again to Imogen.

She knew what he was waiting for. He was waiting for Harry to say something about his offer, or for her to admit the offer hadn't been put forward. Instead she turned a little and watched her brother. His face was lit up like the Las Vegas strip – bright, vibrant, glowing like a dozen neon signs. So much enthusiasm, drive and passion. And, as she watched him sipping at his drink, standing tall in this foreign country, a Corfu business owner, she was flooded with pride. Seeing Harry this way filled her with pure joy.

'It is a lot of work though,' Panos continued. 'Not just to clear but to make good again.' He looked directly at Imogen. 'You wish for white wine? I am sorry, I do not ask.'

He had the most amazing eyelashes over those dark eyes and that rich olive skin that had tried to soothe her injured hand the other day. It was a second before she realised she hadn't answered his question. 'White's fine, thank you,' she replied.

Panos held out the glass to her and as she accepted it, their fingers connected and her breath caught in her throat. Although she knew nothing about the man, as he held her gaze she silently cursed her susceptibility to his good looks. Drawing her hand away, she put the glass to her lips and focussed on the stunning views.

Panos felt confused. The attraction he felt towards Imogen was interesting yet completely ill-placed and it was causing him unnecessary distraction. She was beautiful, even with the mosquito marks on her face, this natural English woman in a dress he was trying his best to see through. But tonight, after wine, good food and his smooth tongue, he would get on with setting out his proposal. This didn't have to be complicated. He was a businessman and the transaction was simple. He would offer them more money to give the restaurant to him and they could be on a plane back to England in the morning. Tomas was selling him his taverna. He had agreed a price and had arranged for his lawyer to draft the papers. It was the first property under his control on the strip and it wouldn't be the last. Dimitriou Enterprises was coming home.

'*Kalispera!*' The deep Greek tones were bellowed like the foghorn of a ship and Panos didn't need to look to know that his grandmother's best friend, Cooky, had arrived.

'Where is the new blood?' Cooky exclaimed. 'Hello, darling! Aren't you a handsome one?'

Panos grimaced as Cooky pressed her well-lipsticked lips to Harry's, then moved to greet Imogen. The woman was as tall as Elpida was small – a little and large combination that had worked for over fifty years. She was wearing a gold sequinned dress that left little to the imagination, her curls of dyed red hair bouncing on the décolletage of her ample bosom.

'I am Cooky!' she announced, taking Imogen's hand and kissing the top of it. 'Risto! Where is my drink?'

Panos stepped forward, plucking the bottle of white wine from the cooler again. 'Good evening, Cooky. You are looking very beautiful tonight.'

Cooky grimaced, looking him up and down from his leather shoes to his dark hair. 'You are here alone?' she announced as more of a statement than a question. 'You are not married?'

He smiled. 'You propose to me... again?'

She had asked him this question so many times. Her face remained expressionless for a good five seconds and then she had the good nature to laugh and launch herself into his arms.

'How are you, my beautiful boy? It is so long since we have seen you!' She stepped back, turning towards Harry and Imogen. 'He hides away on another island making his millions and doesn't remember where he came from.'

Panos gritted his teeth and tried to hold on to his smile. Cooky knew far too much about his past, courtesy of his grandmother.

'Millions?' Harry remarked.

Panos waved a hand. 'Cooky likes to exaggerate,' he said quickly.

'You don't have millions by now? What are you doing all the work for if not to make millions?'

He took a step towards the decked area. 'Excuse me, I think the other guests are here.'

TWENTY-TWO

Panos couldn't fault his grandmother's cooking but he wished she hadn't invited Roger and Ann. From what he remembered, they were British ex-pats who had lived in Agios Martinos for what must be five years now. He had only met them once and that had been enough. He was certain he had heard the exact same speedboat stories the last time he'd dined with them. He refilled his glass with wine and took a healthy swig. His eyes found Risto. He was concerned about his cousin, who had hardly eaten any food and was drinking far too much. Now he looked like he could hardly keep his eyes open. Was it wrong of him to make him be his eyes and ears in the restaurant with Harry and Imogen?

'Risto!' he called. He watched his cousin rock in his seat and force his eyes wider open. 'Could you get some more wine from the cellar?'

'Pfft!' Elpida interrupted. 'There is no need for you to go to the cellar, Risto. There is more wine in the kitchen,'

'More for me!' Cooky piped up. 'And Imogen's glass is almost empty. How about you, Ann?'

The mouse-like Englishwoman held her glass up and nodded, pushing her round glasses up her nose.

'I never say no,' Roger piped up.

Risto stood up, holding onto Harry's chair to retain his balance. 'I will bring some more.'

Panos got to his feet. 'I think I will help him.' He nodded at the guests. 'Excuse me.'

As soon as they were out of sight Panos grabbed him by the shirt sleeve. 'What is wrong with you? You barely eat, you drink too much.' He narrowed his eyes at him. 'You have an alcohol problem? Is that why you have not found work?'

'No!' Risto exclaimed, shaking his head.

'Then what?'

'I do not like what I have to do today,' he admitted. 'I find it hard.'

'What? Clearing up in the restaurant?'

'No! You know!' Risto said, eyes wide.

Panos sucked in a breath before responding. 'We cannot speak about this here.' He looked back at the table of guests to ensure they were fully engaged.

'They are nice people,' Risto said, dropping his eyes to the ground. 'I like them and *yiayia* likes them. I start to feel bad. If *yiayia* finds out…'

Panos shook his head and sunk his hands into the pockets of his trousers. 'I think *yiayia* would be more concerned about your drinking right now.'

He looked at Risto, seeing the boy he had shared his childhood with. All his cousin wanted was a job and he had given him something that challenged his Corfiot amiable nature.

'Risto,' he continued. 'Do you want to help me in my business?'

'Yes, of course, Pano.'

'Then please, Risto, keep your drinking under control and help me with this.' His mind drifted to the Asp deal. That was an exception. One blip. He had Tomas' Taverna now and he would have more.

'What I propose for the restaurant is going to give you and the residents of Acharavi something to celebrate. You want this, don't you?' Panos continued. 'More villagers with work. More tourists coming to the island?'

'Of course.'

'Then where is the problem?' Panos turned to look at his dining companions. He would make his second offer tonight and he had little doubt he'd be holding the keys to the restaurant by tomorrow afternoon.

Imogen took another mouthful of wine and enjoyed its warmth. It was idyllic here in Elpida's garden, the lights in the trees and the candles on the table providing a soft glow, listening to the cicadas' song, Roger's stories of the sea – OK they were a little boring – Cooky's loud laugh and Elpida's playful banter with her friend. Her eyes went to Harry. He hadn't stopped smiling all night and had shared conversation with everyone at the table. Like the old Harry.

She put down her glass and reached for her napkin to wipe her lips. A fig tart with vanilla cream had just about finished her off and now her stomach was full to bursting. There was no doubt Elpida was an amazing cook. The stronger flavours hadn't overpowered the subtle, everything had complemented each other, each dish offering something a little different for the palate. If she could become half as good for Harry she'd be pleased. She stopped her thinking. Did that mean she was really doing this? Really going to help her brother open the restaurant?

'So, Imogen,' Roger began, unfastening a button at the top of his collar, his round face as burgundy as the wine he was drinking. 'Owning a restaurant, eh? Is that a long held dream?'

She hesitated, shielding her lips with a napkin.

'Shall I answer this one, Immy?' Harry chipped in. 'It's actually *my* dream.' He beamed, sitting forward a little in his chair. 'Quite a new dream if I'm honest.'

'You visited Corfu and fell in love with it, like all people from UK,' Cooky said, swigging back her drink, putting the glass down and pulling at the neckline of her dress.

'That's what Ann and I did,' Roger said.

'Actually, I haven't visited Corfu for quite a while. But I did have some amazing holidays here. But it's Imogen's first visit to the island,' Harry informed them.

'You've never been here before,' Ann said, shocked. 'And you've bought a restaurant?'

'Well, *I* haven't bought it,' she clarified. 'Harry has.'

'I did a lot of research on the internet and the estate agent was ever so helpful.'

Imogen's attention went to Panos, who was making his way across the decking holding a bottle of wine in each hand. The man was an archetypal Greek god. He strode, head held high, a dark wave of hair curling slightly over tanned skin. She watched him as he approached.

His shoulder brushed hers as he sat and he spoke low. 'You enjoyed your dessert?'

'Yes, it was lovely.'

'You are OK?' he asked, his eyes meeting hers.

There was that deliciously warm sensation again overriding the dance of the figs. Perhaps she should run with it if it stopped her being sick.

She nodded again. 'Yes, I'm fine,' she replied, blushing faintly.

'You have not told your brother about my offer,' he stated simply.

'No.'

'Why not?'

Those eyes were burning into hers, making her heart speed up. What did she say? That she'd seen today how happy the restaurant was making her brother and her earlier reservations had been somewhat relieved? That she wanted to try and make the project work?

'Because I haven't seen him this happy in years,' she answered truthfully.

'Imogen,' Elpida called.

Quickly she turned her attention away from Panos.

'You and your Harry are going to open the restaurant next week!' She cleared her throat. 'We need to toast this! To...' Elpida paused, her hand still held high. 'What is going to be the name?'

'Well,' Harry began. 'What do you think of... Halloumi?'

Imogen balked. What?! The figs were now eating their way through her stomach lining and keeping a controlled smile on her face was taking every scrap of energy she had. After all this talk of Greeklish food, chips and *taramasalata* he was going to name his dream restaurant after a cheese. She wished he'd mentioned it to her first. She could have told him what a mad idea it was. She forced a smile.

'I thought it sounded welcoming. It's foody and Greeky and it has the letters of mine and Immy's names in,' Harry concluded.

Elpida shot out of her seat, the chair scraping across the cobbles. 'I think it's wonderful! Absolutely wonderful!' She cleared her throat loudly, her eyes roaming over her guests. 'To Halloumi!' she toasted.

Imogen watched everyone looking at each other, as if wondering what to do, but seemingly knowing there was only one thing they *could* do. She was juggling the words in her throat, each syllable scratching its way out. 'To Halloumi,' she croaked. Then she put the glass down, got up and headed indoors.

TWENTY-THREE

If Imogen had been a smoker she would have been lighting up and puffing away by now, but instead she stood outside the front of the house pacing in the dark. The only light came from the moon until she paced too close to a motion sensor and the porch light flicked on. The minute she started to feel confident about things, Harry put a spanner in the works. It was like taking one step forward and two steps back. Harry's new-found love of life and this project to open the restaurant and get his family back together was admirable and she wanted to be all in, but then he did silly things. He borrowed a fish van and named the place Halloumi. What was she going to tell Grace and Janie when she was wavering so badly? They were relying on her to end this and get Harry's money back. And the offer was right there in front of her. But…

'Imogen.'

She knew who was speaking before Panos came into focus.

'I'm fine,' she said, quickly smiling. She couldn't let this man know how desperate she felt. 'Just need a minute.'

'You would like a glass of water?' he offered, stepping close.

'No, thank you. We should get going soon. It's been a long day and…' Her breath was coming thick and fast like an asthmatic about to have an attack.

'Slowly,' Panos said softly. 'Breathe slowly.'

She felt like a prize idiot. She shouldn't need instructions on how to breathe. She stood still, the air still clogging up her windpipe. She felt Panos put a strong hand on her shoulder and she leant into the touch.

'You think your brother is crazy,' he stated. 'To think he can open the restaurant in a week. To name it after cheese?'

She shook her head. She was not admitting this to anyone who wasn't immediate family.

'Remember, Imogen, I can make this go away,' he whispered.

The statement made her breath catch and her eyes widen. She observed the strong, full-lipped mouth, the firm jaw and the onyx eyes. There was something there, something dancing in the air between them like there had been earlier and yesterday on the beach. He moved his hand from her shoulder and placed it on her waist, drawing her closer.

She met with a solid wall of muscle, the heat from his skin transcending the fabric of her dress. His fingers drew away a section of hair that had escaped from her ponytail, the tips brushing the surface of her cheek.

'Sell me the restaurant, Imogen,' he said lightly, lowering his head towards her.

For a moment she didn't react. The sentence hit her gradually, each word slowly being understood as his face neared hers.

'I will give you two hundred thousand Euro for the restaurant,' Panos whispered. She shifted back then, trying to read his expression.

'You really want the restaurant, don't you?' she said.

He nodded. 'I really want the restaurant.'

'Why?' Imogen asked.

Panos was holding on to so many emotions and each one was scrabbling up on top of the other like a game of *Jenga* that could topple at any second. He wanted to hand her the cash right now, get his Acharavi project accelerating.

'Because your family has just sold the restaurant,' Imogen reminded him. 'To my brother.'

God, she was attractive. He hadn't meant to hold her like he had but she'd looked so vulnerable.

'I know,' he began. 'But my grandmother should not have done that.'

He watched her put her hands on her hips and adopt a stance of attack. 'Why not?'

'Because it should be mine,' he admitted bluntly.

'Well, Harry needs it to save his marriage.'

The two statements hung there together, words confronting each other like they were. Imogen's clear blue eyes were moist and set defiantly on him. This was all too intense.

'The offer is two hundred thousand Euro,' Panos repeated.

She didn't reply, the only sound Cooky's faint laughter and the buzz of bugs surrounding the property. Panos held his breath, stomach tight, watching her for any sign of response.

'Please…' God, he didn't want to beg, but this was not going as easily as expected. 'The offer is a good one. All I ask is that you think of it.'

'Did you not hear what I said?' she asked.

'This is business,' he replied. 'It should not be about family relationships.'

She toyed with a strand of her hair. 'And why is it you want to run a restaurant when you have a million-Euro business elsewhere?'

He couldn't give her an answer.

She took her hands from her hips and took a step forward. 'I'm going to forget we had this conversation.'

'Please,' he said, his hand grabbing her arm. 'Please, Imogen, you must… You *will* think about it.'

He knew he had gone too far and removed his hand quickly, watching as her expression hardened.

'I did think about it – last night and this morning. And then something changed. I saw my brother light up. Every crease and line disappear from his face… because of this restaurant.' She swallowed. 'Yes, he might have chosen a ridiculous name for it but he's fallen for it and I'll do anything to keep him being this happy.' She took a breath. 'I am *fiercely* protective over my family and I don't appreciate anyone thinking they can tell me what to do.'

He felt like he'd been punched. There was fire in her words and flashes of defiance in her eyes. She may not have wanted this restaurant to begin with, but she wanted it now. She was loyal and she could fight. He had misjudged this. This was not going to be easy. She was anything but a pushover.

'Please tell Risto his help won't be required tomorrow.' She shifted past him. 'Excuse me, I think it's time Harry and I went home.'

He sidestepped out of her path and watched her power towards the house, anger obvious in every single step.

TWENTY-FOUR

Terry's fish van, en route to Halloumi, Acharavi

'Can't you drive a bit faster?' Imogen asked. She knew the roads were winding but this one looked almost as good as the A36 at home and Harry was barely reaching twenty mph. She just wanted to get back down the mountain.

'I'm still learning the van technique and what's the rush?' he asked. 'You shouldn't rush in Greece. It's against the law I think.'

'You're not Greek,' Imogen reminded him.

'Not yet,' Harry said, with a smile.

Imogen let out a breath. This was all Panos. Panos and his bewitching eyes. Panos and his offer to buy the restaurant. She needed to tell Harry.

'Is it the bites? Aren't you feeling well?' Harry asked, crawling around another corner at the speed of an ill slug.

'Panos Dimitriou wants to buy the restaurant from you.'

There, it was out. If anything, the surprise might kick-start Harry's driving. She looked out of the window at the undulating mountainside as they navigated their way to lower ground. It was pitch black here, no street lamps, just darkness and the outlines of thick trees, a few pinpricks of light just visible in clusters through the olive groves. She suddenly realised Harry hadn't said anything and turned towards him. Her brother's eyes were fixed on the road, his position unmoved, hands still on the large steering wheel.

'He's offered two hundred thousand Euro,' she added, sucking in a breath.

'I did like what Elpida did with the roast potatoes, didn't you?' Harry remarked. 'Rosemary and garlic, wasn't it?'

'Did you hear what I said?'

'Yes, Panos Dimitriou wants to buy Halloumi from me for two hundred thousand Euro.'

'When you showed me the property details… well, if someone had offered us a way out then, I would have said give it to them,' Imogen stated. 'I would have said take the money and run and you could have… bought a boat… two boats… in England… or anywhere.'

She pulled her yellow handbag to her body and took comfort in it like it was a favourite cushion. Harry was quiet again and all she could hear was the engine of the van and the soft tone of a *bouzouki* coming from the radio.

'And that's what Mum and Janie want me to do. Get you to sell the restaurant on and go back home.'

'Is that what you said to Panos?' Harry asked, eyes still on the road as they rounded another corner.

'Of course it wasn't what I said to him!'

'Well, what *did* you say to him?'

'I said it wasn't my property to sell, it was yours and I said…' She paused. 'I said no one tells me what to do. And I told him I had never seen you so happy,' she concluded.

Harry laughed. 'Oh, Immy, I knew this would happen.'

She looked at him, saw the smile still on his face. 'Knew what would happen?'

'You'd fall in love with Halloumi.'

She was still struggling to know why her brother had named the restaurant after a cheese.

'I'm not *in love* with it,' she said quickly. 'But I can see how hard you've worked to achieve this and what it means to you.'

Harry pulled the van to the kerb outside the restaurant and turned off the engine. He faced Imogen.

'Immy, I know you weren't sold on the idea at first but I'm so pleased you're here with me.' He sighed. 'Buying this restaurant, it was about me acknowledging that things were wrong in my life and taking steps to make a change. I know the depression isn't going to completely go away for good. And I've come to terms with that. But what I can't accept is the thought that my life can't be good again.'

'No one's ever said that.'

'I think it's why Janie and the children are still living without me and I don't blame her,' Harry said. 'Some days *I* don't even like living with me.'

'Harry…'

'No, it's true and that's OK.' He nodded. 'There's lots of ups and downs. It's been difficult for all of us.'

Imogen swallowed, trying in vain to hold on to the tears. 'I know.'

'So, Immy, when I bought this restaurant it wasn't a mistake. It was me taking a leap, proving my life's still my own, investing in my future and my children's future and achieving something.' He paused. 'Not for anyone else, not because I thought it was right… Just because I wanted to make a positive change.' He cleared his throat. 'And if Janie sees enough of the man she fell in love with before, well, who knows?'

Imogen nodded as the first tears escaped.

'But, as much as I love that you're here, it was wrong of me to expect you to drop everything and come to Corfu with me.'

'Don't, Harry,' Imogen begged, her heart being squeezed by the emotion in the van. 'I just… this is so alien to me and…'

'It's alien to me too.' He smiled. 'And I like that. Who would have thought I'd be able to negotiate a deal for tables and chairs in Greek?'

She couldn't help but smile and reached over to pat his hand.

'I forced you into it, I know that.' He swallowed. 'But this time it wasn't because I needed your help, Immy. It was because I *wanted* you to share it with me.'

Of course it was. And she had assumed Harry was being needy. What a disloyal sister she was.

'Hey, don't cry,' Harry said, reaching for her hand and squeezing it. 'I don't want you to think that I forgot about Mum for a second or Janie and Olivia and Tristan. This is about creating a better life for all of them. Imagine Olivia and Tristan on the beach here,' Harry said, his eyes shifting to the black of the night, the sparkling lights of Albania across the water. 'And Mum... once she gets over April passing, I'm hoping she'll come out here too.'

He was right. Completely right. He was striking out and forging ahead, not acting without thinking. It was courageous and admirable.

'If you want to head back home on the next plane, Immy, I totally understand,' Harry told her.

She gave him a watery smile and squeezed his hand. 'I have two weeks if you want it, remember?' she said. 'And I am a dab hand with a paintbrush and roller.' She smiled. 'And I'm really hoping Elpida can help me master some Greek cooking.'

'Not Greeklish?' Harry asked.

'We can do a lot better than chips and *taramasalata*, Harry.'

'You know... Panos could have offered me a million Euro for the restaurant... I still wouldn't have taken it.'

'I know.'

But she also remembered the fire in the man's eyes and the heat in her belly. Her body had belied her words. She had wanted to get close to this man whose arrogance oozed from every pore. She shuddered.

'I've fired Risto,' Imogen stated, pulling at the handle and swinging the van door open. She stepped out onto the road and breathed in the balmy night air.

'But why?' Harry slid out of the van too and closed the driver's door.

'After Panos Dimitriou's offer of intention…' She wet her lips. 'I just think if we need extra help then we should pay for it.'

'You're right,' Harry agreed. 'He's a good worker. I'll offer to pay him the going rate.'

'No… I didn't mean that,' she said quickly. 'I just don't trust Panos,' Imogen admitted, shivering.

Harry put the key in the door and unlocked it. 'Well, it's a shame, because I like Risto.' He strode into the main room, reaching for the light switch.

Imogen stepped in and her sandals slipped on something on the floor. She regained her balance, looking at the shiny card that had slipped across the tiles. Bending down she plucked it off the floor and looked at it. It was a business card: 'Dimitriou Enterprises' and an address in Crete, embossed in gold.

'What is it?' Harry asked, leaning closer to get a look.

'It's Panos Dimitriou,' Imogen said. 'Obviously a reminder of his intention.'

'Well, a flashy business card doesn't change anything for me,' Harry said.

Imogen nodded. 'No, I know.' She pocketed the card. Who was the man behind those intense espresso-coloured eyes? She shivered. Only time would tell.

TWENTY-FIVE

Elpida Dimitriou's home, Agios Martinos

A steaming cafetiere was thumped down on the kitchen table in front of Panos. He was sitting, dressed for business despite the morning heat, a sheet of projections open on his laptop. If only he had actually been reading them. Despite every business distraction he had thrown at himself since he'd woken, his mind was still on Imogen. And not the fact she had rejected his offer for the restaurant, but her long blonde hair shifting in the humid night and how her body had felt pressed against his under a silvery moon. Shifting the computer slightly, he earned another snort from his grandmother.

'Why would you do this?'

The accusation flew through the air with no foreword or extra information. His hackles raised instinctively.

'I invite friends for dinner, Pano. I want to have a nice night, to welcome Harry and Imogen to Corfu and you... you...' Elpida pointed her index finger as she shot out the words like machine gun fire. She halted only for a quick breath. 'What do you think you are doing offering to buy the restaurant back from them? I thought I made myself very clear on the telephone to you. I do not want to own the restaurant.'

So Imogen had told his grandmother what he had said to her last night. Had she visited in person? Early? Before he was awake? He had to remind himself, he was here for business and business alone. He had had an email from his lawyer this morning about the Tomas' Taverna deal.

'And I made it clear you should have sold this to me.'

'Don't make me smoke, Pano, I am trying to cut down.' Elpida toyed with her wedding ring. 'They are good people, trying to make a living, start a new life…'

'And what about me, huh? Your grandson. Don't I deserve to make a living? Begin a new life?'

He had sounded almost sentimental there and sentimentality didn't win deals.

'Is that what you want, Pano?' Elpida asked. 'A new life? Here? In Acharavi?' There was hope in her eyes.

Would it be better to play along? Nausea flooded his gut. He wasn't going to lie to his grandmother. That was something his father would have tried to do.

And straightaway there was one of the images he'd tried to forget. His father, dark hair tousled, swarthy skin creased and reddened, clothes crumpled, smelling of alcohol and filth, stood in this very kitchen spitting venom at Elpida. He'd screamed and shouted until his voice was hoarse and then he'd cried. Through a crack in the doorway Panos had watched his father get on his hands and knees and beg Elpida to give him money.

'Did she come here?' The question was out of his lips before he knew it.

'What?' Elpida asked. 'Who?'

'Imogen.'

'Pfft!' Elpida exclaimed, turning around and reaching for her cigarette packet on the worktop. She flipped open the top and gazed at the contents. 'It would not surprise me if she never comes here again!'

Panos frowned. If Imogen hadn't been here then how did Elpida know about the offer? He nodded then. *Risto*. Risto also knew about his plan for the whole Acharavi seafront.

'What else did Risto tell you?' Panos asked, getting to his feet and picking his tailored jacket up from the back of the chair.

Elpida narrowed her eyes, pulling a lone cigarette from the pack. 'What else is there to tell me?'

He nodded then, slipping his arms into the jacket, a smile on his face. 'You interrogated him.'

'Don't be stupid,' Elpida snapped.

'What did you do, *yiayia*? Tie him to a chair and threaten him with the homemade fig wine from 2001?'

She held the cigarette to her nose and inhaled. 'I wanted to know why the guests I had invited into my home wanted to run away faster than Pheidippides.'

'And you assumed this was because of something I'd done?' He began to collate his papers. 'Perhaps, as we were sat outside, the mosquitoes were becoming a problem for Imogen. Maybe they were eating the other half of her they hadn't already feasted on.'

'Risto told me everything. He tell me you hope to get information about their finances, their strengths and weaknesses, in order to make them sell the restaurant to you. Risto was to be a spy like in James Bond, reporting everything to you and telling them stories about the restaurant's past hardship and making them want to go home.'

Panos tried not to let anything show on his face. This did not matter. He wasn't giving up on the offer just yet. He was meeting with two other bar owners on the strip today and once he had convinced them both to sell he might not need the property on the corner anyway.

'Where is Risto?' Panos asked, snapping his laptop closed.

'Risto has gone to apologise and offer his services to Harry and Imogen under *my* employ.' Elpida reached for her lighter.

'*Yiayia*, please,' Panos stated. 'You say you want nothing to do with the restaurant yet you are going to pay Risto to help these people?' He threw his hands up in exasperation.

'I never said I do not want anything to do with the restaurant.' She flicked the lighter at the end of the cigarette and sucked hard. Blowing out a thick cloud of blue–grey smoke she responded, 'I said I did not want to *own* it.'

He shook his head hard.

'And I am disappointed in you, Pano,' she added.

He tucked his laptop under his arm and picked the car keys off the table. 'Well then… like father, like son,' he stated, his face set.

He waited just long enough to see sadness coat his grandmother's expression and then, flooded with guilt, he turned and left.

TWENTY-SIX

Halloumi, Acharavi beachfront

The sun was already hot. Imogen sat on the sand, listening to the early morning sound of the sea. Here, looking into the water, surf like hundreds of pearl droplets scurrying up the beach towards her, it was peaceful. She watched a large cruise ship appear in the right-hand side of the ocean. Like a floating hotel it was slipping through the waves taking its passengers away from the Greek island to a brand new destination. And here she was, in a brand new location herself, with Harry embracing each morning with gusto.

Sitting here, her fingers stirring up the grains of soft sand, the sea whispering on the shore, she could feel it too. *Possibility.* The restaurant was a blank canvas. The bare walls, dust and crumbling plaster weren't devastation, they were just signs that a reinvention was needed. If Harry was willing to try then so was she. There was nothing to lose and everything to gain. Two weeks in the sun, dusting off her cooking skills and supporting her brother. The best of fresh, Greek food and a restaurant full of happy diners just like Panos had described. Her mobile erupted from inside her bag. She slipped her hand inside and drew it out. *Janie.*

'Hello,' she said.

'Please tell me you're packing your bags and Harry's given up the idea,' Janie said.

Imogen shut her eyes. 'Hi, Janie.'

'Well?'

'No, not quite yet.'

'What does that mean?'

'It means it's still a work in progress.' That wasn't a lie.

'I've looked at it, you know, the black hole of Calcutta.'

Imogen swallowed. 'It's a bit different to the photos now.'

'It's still on Rightmove,' Janie continued. 'If it's still on Rightmove there must be a chance it can go back on the market, right?'

Imogen understood. This was the same shock she'd gone through. And Janie wasn't here. Janie was back in the UK. Far away and panicking.

'Tell me, are those windows still broken? Or haven't you been able to get to them because of that hedge of weeds?' Janie let out a breath. 'I feel sick at the thought of you being there, going through all this with Harry… If it wasn't for the children I…'

'It's OK,' Imogen said, her eyes on two birds pecking at the sand about a metre away from her.

'It's bloody not though, is it? And what is he doing there while you're trying to persuade him to give it up and come home?'

'Janie…' She braced herself. 'It actually isn't as bad as we thought.'

'What do you mean?'

'Well, Harry and I, we've been working on the restaurant since we got here. And it's clean now, with some lovely traditional features…'

'Are you still there?' Janie checked. 'I thought you said something about traditional features rather than bag packing.'

'Listen, I know we all thought Harry had jumped into something bad but Janie, I'm not sure he has.' She looked back out to sea, the water so inviting, almost calling to her to come back in. 'Harry's so happy here and… I checked this morning. He's taking his medication.'

'Oh, thank God for that. I had visions of him there, steam coming out of his ears, writing shopping lists and ordering menus and… what about the new furniture he bought online? Have you managed to cancel it?'

Cancelling an order the restaurant now badly needed wasn't on her priority list any more. After her talk with Harry last night, surrounded by the scent of sardines and squid, her priority was re-learning how to cook gourmet Greek food.

'Did you hear what I said, Janie?' Imogen asked. 'Harry's really happy and he's working ever so hard.'

'But it's a fad, isn't it? Like the sandwich van and the club for fans of *Castle* he told Tristan he was setting up.'

'No, it isn't like that. I promise.' Imogen rested her eyes on the cerulean water. 'He's committed to this project. More committed than I've seen him before.'

There was silence from the other end of the phone until… 'Really?'

'Yes, Janie, really.'

'Well, I hope you're right because he's been going for it with the kids. It's been excited emoji after excited emoji – the cake one and the chicken leg one – and hundreds and hundreds of cat faces with hearts for eyes!' Janie finally drew breath. 'He's building them up with talk of them coming over in the summer holidays and… I don't know what to say.'

'He *is* excited,' Imogen admitted. 'All the time.'

'Well, that isn't natural. No one is excited *all* the bloody time unless there's something wrong with them.'

'Janie, he's really, truly the most happy I've seen him since the accident.'

She knew Janie was concerned about the children. She didn't want them being promised things that might not happen. And she understood that. But what Harry really needed was a little faith.

'I want him to be happy, of course I do. But I'd rather it was here, not in Greece doing something he isn't equipped for.' Janie paused. 'You agree, Imogen, don't you?'

The birds pecking in the sand in front of her were starting to fight with each other over a sandworm. She let out a breath.

'Janie, I'm going to call you back,' Imogen said, getting to her feet.

'What? Why? What's going on?'

'I'm going to call Mum. Speak soon!' She didn't give Janie a chance to say anything else. About to get up, her phone bleeped at the arrival of an email. She settled back down on the sand. Pressing into her inbox she saw the message. It was from the Wyatt Hotel Group. Her mouth dried up and her heart began racing as she pressed on the bold type. Another automated reply. They were thanking her again for her application but due to the number of applicants it would take some time to review them all individually. She swallowed. That was good, wasn't it? It wasn't an out-and-out rejection. They were looking at her. She was still in with a chance.

She put the phone in her bag and, brushing the sand from her clothes, she got up, heading back up the beach towards the restaurant.

TWENTY-SEVEN

Halloumi, Acharavi beachfront

Imogen had picked up a flagon of bottled water from Spiros the shopkeeper and heard a couple of ladies chatting in Greek, the only recognisable words being 'Tomas' Taverna'. When she had asked Spiros about this he had said Tomas was retiring and the restaurant was going to be closing. Less competition for Harry's restaurant – she couldn't bring herself to call it Halloumi yet – had to be a good thing. She almost felt excited along with nervous. She would throw herself into this project with Harry and hopefully it would take her mind off the the Wyatt Group email.

She'd practically bounced back up the terrace, the Corfu heat on her body, heading for the kitchen and the Greek recipes she'd perused online. She would make a list of the core ingredients they needed for the store cupboard and refresh herself with the dishes Harry had liked the sound of when they'd discussed it. As she beat up eggs, chopped aubergine, tomatoes and cheese, adding in a pinch of salt and pepper, and throwing in small pieces of a basil plant she'd found in a pot at the back of the restaurant she started to feel the anxiety lift from her shoulders. This could really, actually work.

For the *saganaki* she just needed to coat Greek cheese in flour and fry it in olive oil. It wasn't Jean-Christophe Novelli standard yet but it was a start. Her first flavours of Greece in Greece.

Her eyes went to the window that looked out over the side aspect of the property. There was sea and sand from every viewpoint in this place. Mixing up the omelette ingredients and breathing in, she caught sight of Tomas' Taverna and beyond, hanging baskets of flowers and terracotta urns spilling with colour.

'*Kalimera*, Imogen.'

Imogen turned from her beating to greet the woman as she came in.

'*Kalimera*, Elpida.'

'You are making!' the Greek woman exclaimed.

'Just some omelettes and a *saganaki* for lunch.'

'It smells wonderful.' Elpida came closer, lowering her nose over the bowl and inhaling hard.

Imogen smiled at her enthusiasm and turned on the cast-iron pan on the hob.

'Imogen, I must apologise,' Elpida said, bending down and lifting up two large sacks to the countertop. 'For Pano and Risto and the offer for the restaurant at a dinner party I invite you to. Pfft!'

Her mind went instantly to Panos, not to the part where he had insisted it was only a matter of time before he got his hands on the restaurant, but to the bit where her body had been melded to his in the humid night outside Elpida's home. She swallowed and gave the eggy mixture an extra harsh flick with the fork.

'Panos is very keen to buy the restaurant back,' Imogen said. 'When we came home last night he had pushed his business card through the door.'

Elpida began to pat the front of her dress, her forehead creasing. 'Where are my cigarettes? That boy will kill me! I am smoking more now he is home than when he is not.'

'But Harry likes Risto,' Imogen said. 'He's spoken to him this morning, sorted things out. We want him to keep helping us, but *we're* going to pay him, Elpida, so there's no confusion. Harry's made it very clear that the restaurant isn't for sale, so no amount of reporting back to Panos on our position is going to do any good.'

Elpida nodded, still patting her way around her body. 'He is a good boy at heart. A hard worker.'

Imogen tipped the contents of the bowl into the pan, the mixture immediately sizzling and bubbling until she turned down the heat. Next she drizzled another pan in olive oil and began to coat slabs of cheese in flour for the *saganaki*.

Elpida picked up a finger of aubergine and held it like a cigarette. 'You and your Harry, you are exactly what I dream for this place.' Her eyes went around the kitchen as if she were reliving every memory. 'The very last thing I want is for Pano to rip down the walls and put up all his metal and loud music and flashing lights.' Elpida flexed her palms as if she were simulating strobes.

'His what?' Imogen questioned.

'His monstrostitties… is that the right word? The nightclubs and racing cars. Young people who do not know any better, all drinking like sailors, all wearing little clothes,' Elpida stated.

'I don't understand,' Imogen said. A bitter, uncomfortable feeling was starting to bubble in her gut. The sputtering from the pans grew louder.

'Pano,' Elpida said. 'He run Dimitriou Enterprises. He go to towns all over Greece and put in these awful places.' She threw her arms up. 'He is very successful, he make lots and lots of money but at what cost, huh? Where is his loyalty to the people of Greece and their traditions? Why does money have to come before everything else with him?'

Imogen felt a veil lift from her eyes, revealing crystal-clear clarity. *That's* why Panos wanted the restaurant. Not to replicate Greek summer nights of old and the memories of his grandparents, *bouzouki* music in the air and fresh fish on the griddle. He wanted to tear it down. To destroy it. To rip up Harry's dream and replace it with a nightclub and whatever else Elpida was talking about. She pursed her lips, not hearing the words as Elpida continued to speak of Panos' business.

'Where is he now?' she asked.

'Who? Pano?' Elpida replied, sucking on the piece of aubergine.

'Yes, Pano,' she said. She lowered the heat in the pan and slipped a hand into the pocket of her shorts, her fingers touching the pointed edges of the business card.

'I do not know,' the woman answered. 'He is always in meetings so I think he—'

'He isn't at the house?' Her eyes searched the kitchen, looking for something.

'No. You are OK? You look a little flushed,' Elpida said. 'Is it the bites? Do you need more of my special remedy?'

'No,' Imogen said bluntly. 'I... just need to pop out for something.'

TWENTY-EIGHT

Avalon Bar, Acharavi beachfront

Panos had led negotiations successfully for years. It was what he did. It was *all* he did and it was usually as natural as drawing breath. This time, though, as he sat on a high stool at the bar of Avalon, he was nervous. He gripped his glass of *ouzo* and water and let his eyes roam. The bar was actually the busiest he had ever seen it. There were locals, a few he recognised, at the couple of tables closest to his seat at the bar, then the rest of the floor space was filled with families, couples, all with drinks *and* food. Just outside, a man was refreshing the paintwork on the wooden struts, coating it a bright white to cover the flakes of last season. *Refurbishment. Renewal.* It didn't bode well for his conversation with the owner. He took a breath. But he *had* got hold of Tomas' Taverna. He could lead with that. Make Lafi open to the idea of retirement like the business owner next door.

He let his eyes move to the scene through the open side of the bar that faced the beach. It was another glorious, hot day. On the sand were people lying prostrate on loungers, a couple playing bat and ball, energetic youngsters digging giant holes and making castles with buckets. All around was enjoyment, excitement, relaxation. That's what Corfu had been to him when he was younger. A magical island full of hope and promise. The world was his oyster, he never wanted for anything, he had a loving family, a stable existence… and then the façade had crumbled.

He watched a woman and her son on a lounger on the sand. The boy of about five was having sun lotion rubbed into his shoulders. The mother's long hair kept slipping forward, getting coated in the sun cream. Panos watched them both laughing as the woman stretched forward then proceeded to tie her hair up in a loose bunch. *His mother had started tying up her hair.* He swallowed, turning and directing his gaze into his drink. Another memory spiked his mind. His mother's long red hair, brushed until it shined then left loose and flowing each day. And back then, that's when things had changed. His father's other women had come on the scene and his mother had given up, become resigned. His hand went around the glass, gripping it hard. But she had survived. And now she had John. Successful John.

'Panos, I am so sorry.' Lafi approached looking flustered. 'It is a good time, no?'

He nodded quickly. 'Yes, it is very good. Lots of customers.'

'The best start to the season for a long, long time,' Lafi said, smiling. 'Give me one more minute.'

Joy was written all over the owner's face. Panos felt a stab of guilt, but only for a moment. Lafi would be better off without this taverna. Being so busy wasn't typical. He drew a breath in as Lafi deposited plates full of Greek *meze* to a table of customers. He took a swig of the *ouzo*. His heart was pumping. Elpida's face this morning came to mind. *Disappointment. Sadness.*

The slam of a car door drew his attention to the road in front of the beach. A small grey vehicle had pulled up outside and its occupant was getting out, her eyes scanning everything in front of her. *Imogen.* Dressed in those cut-off jeans and a salmon-coloured t-shirt, her hair a tangle of blonde tendrils, he couldn't help but look. She marched up the road, her head turning to the beach, then back again to the bars along the beachfront. It was like she was looking for something… or someone. He shook his head. It wouldn't be him. She had made her stance on the restaurant quite clear. With eyes burning with resistance she had made her point so severely he had wondered just how badly her husband had treated her. Not that her personal life was any of his business.

Panos turned his attention back to Lafi, who was now balancing platters up his entire forearm and heading for a table at the front of the bar. Busy wasn't necessarily a good thing at Lafi's time of life. He finished his drink and cleared his throat, unbuttoning the top button on his shirt and looking out at the sea. And then Imogen was there, right outside Avalon, her eyes on his Mercedes. He watched her dip her head, trying to look from the bright light outside into the shade of the bar. It took only a second for their vision to connect and he felt it hard.

There he was! Sat at a bar, the top of his shirt undone, his hair tousled, looking like he didn't have a care in the world. She could feel her cheeks were crimson already. She raised a hand and waved first, before turning her palm towards her and beckoning him. Was he going to come? She held her breath, her eyes not leaving his as she backed up to the Nissan Micra.

He was moving. Striding with confidence, or perhaps arrogance, down the walkway between the tables.

She smiled, watching him amble off the bar's terrace, navigating the promotional neon chalk-written blackboards outside, before his feet met the tarmac of the road.

Adrenaline and the heat meant her t-shirt was starting to cling. She kept her gaze on him as he stopped still, no more than a few inches away. She maintained her anger, determined not to become distracted. She was furious – and not attracted to him in the slightest. She swallowed, realising they were just staring at each other and she had a loud and clear message to deliver.

'*Kalimera*, Mr Dimitriou,' she greeted.

'*Kalimera*, Imogen.'

'So, I'm glad I caught up with you,' she began, wetting her lips that felt as dry as sand.

'You are?' he replied.

She nodded. 'Yes.' She cleared her throat. When she left Halloumi she was being driven by a crimson fog, like a Spanish bull ready to do battle with the *matador*. Now she was feeling ever-so-slightly nervous.

She grounded her feet, hoping it would fuel her fire again. 'I wanted to be clear about the restaurant… and your offer.' She slipped the business card from her pocket and held it up. 'Thank you for the calling card.'

She saw his demeanour alter a little. A flicker of something crossed his features before he had a chance to keep it in check.

'You have thought about my offer?' he purred.

Imogen smiled. 'Oh yes.' She leant forward a little, putting her body a half inch closer to very personal space. 'I've thought about it long…' She paused. 'And hard.'

A smile played on his lips then, his eyes matching hers as he closed the gap between them a few centimetres more. 'This is what I was wanting to hear.'

They were now so close, if she breathed out too hard their bodies were going to become one. The thought of having Panos pressed against her again was tempting. At a very base level, he was the archetypal Greek Adonis. But underneath the obvious sex appeal was one ruthless individual who would stop at nothing to get what he wanted, Imogen knew that now.

'I told you last night,' she breathed. 'That I'm very protective over my family.'

'I understand this,' he responded. He was looking at her closely, perhaps trying to read her expression.

She could feel the heat of his breath as he leaned ever closer. Did he think he could just blink those ridiculously long eyelashes at her and she'd swoon into his arms? Last night was one thing, today she had his number.

She broke the connection, snapping her head up and stamping her feet into the concrete. 'Then understand this, Mr Dimitriou!' She flicked the business card at him, watching it catch him in the chest. 'Offering to buy the restaurant not once but twice was bad enough, and planting an employee in our midst was definitely underhand, but, to push it further with your business card is not appreciated. Give up!' Her breath came thick and fast. 'The restaurant is not for sale!'

He continued to stand there, cool, unaffected, just looking back at her. And then, for a nanosecond her attention was diverted to the man in overalls painting the outside of the restaurant. She watched him put down his pot and pick up a bottle of water, wiping the sweat from his brow with his forearm.

'I can have the papers drawn up today,' Panos told her.

'Read my lips. The-restaurant-is-not-for-sale.'

He shrugged. 'Tell Harry I will come by after my meeting here.'

It was the final straw. In one swift move she picked up the painter's pot, launched the contents at him, and watched the white emulsion coat Panos from head to foot. And all the while, as the paint slopped, Panos didn't move.

'Is that clear enough?' she shouted, desperate for a response.

She hadn't expected this. She had expected flailing and shouting and cursing her to the Greek gods, but Panos was just standing there like being doused in paint was the most natural thing in the world.

Finally, he shifted. Bringing his arms up, he put both hands to his face. His fingers met the emulsion and he clawed two handfuls of the substance and then, it hit her. Spatters of paint slapped her cheeks and her t-shirt, then more of her, as she watched Panos flicking the liquid from his body straight at her.

She turned her body away and tried to shield her face. 'Stop it!'

'You don't like it?' Panos scraped more of the paint from his clothes and flicked it at her.

She screamed again as another stream of paint hit her face. She pulled the hem of her t-shirt up and rubbed her cheeks with it. 'Elpida told me what you do for a business!' she yelled. 'You're one of those property developers who destroys small towns for their own gain. You lie your way into other people's trust and profit from their misfortune. You break communities and you... you suck the soul out of everything.'

His cheeks, underneath the thick, white paste, flamed at her words. Was that what his grandmother had told her? He increased his pace, scooping off another palm full of paint and flicking it at Imogen.

'That is not true,' he retorted.

'Stop it!' Imogen exclaimed, breaking into a jog. She stepped off the road and onto the sand, where her pace slowed as her flip-flops failed to compete with the terrain.

'You are the one making a war with paint! All because I am trying to help you!' He grabbed her then, his soaking wet white hand clamping down on her forearm. It was all oozing down from his every part, globules of alabaster pigment sullying the sand as he moved along it.

'Don't touch me!' Imogen exclaimed, still trying to escape up the beach.

'Don't touch you?! You embarrass me in front of the village, throw this stuff all over me! What do you expect me to do? I am here to do business. I have bought Tomas' Taverna and I will be buying Avalon too! It's only a matter of time before you are begging for me at Halloumi.' He tugged her towards him until their bodies were touching. 'Now is the time to change your mind!'

'Never!'

'Are you quite sure about that?'

'You're making me wet!'

Her choice of words had his whole body reacting. His core tightened as he tried to maintain some sort of control. What was it with this woman? She had attacked him in the street and still he wanted to… what? What exactly did he want to do?

She was looking directly at him now, still backing away over the sand and tugging at his arm, her blonde hair falling over her face, covered in specks of white. He wanted to reach out and brush those loose, straw-like strands away, touch a fingertip to her jaw and…

Before he could think further he was falling forward. There was nothing he could do to stop himself, and he landed right on top of Imogen.

Grains of the shoreline flew up into the air around them and Imogen let out a gasp. Panos Dimitriou was on top of her! And although he looked like a human Flump – without the pink bits – he was still ridiculously attractive.

Paint from his body was seeping onto her clothes, drips slipped from his neck onto hers and the sand was sticking to them both. She knew she ought to move, but the only thing she seemed to be able to focus on was his heartbeat echoing through her chest and the visible throb at the base of his neck.

She stilled further as he raised a hand, paint spiralling down from his wrist as he cupped the side of her face. The delicate trace of his fingertips felt like the most expensive silk gently trailing over her skin. Those full lips were mere centimetres away from hers. The sun was warming her exposed skin, his closeness heating up everything else. It was almost surreal. She just had to let it happen…

She snapped herself forward, almost knocking heads with him as he fell to her left and down onto the sand. What was she thinking? *Again!* This was not the message she was supposed to be conveying. How was he supposed to take her outrage seriously if she kept wanting to kiss him?

She got up, hands furiously brushing paint and sand from her clothes. It was a wasted effort. She was like a dirty salmon-and-white-spotted Dalmatian.

'Imogen…' Panos began, standing himself and making no effort to rid himself of the mess he was in.

She shook her head. 'No. I said what I came to say and I want you to stay away from the restaurant.'

She turned away from him and, with her head held high, she began a march back towards the roadside, a small piece of driftwood caught up in her hair.

TWENTY-NINE

Halloumi, Acharavi beachfront

'Harry,' she breathed. 'We need to find out who owns that piece of land next to here.'

Imogen pointed in the direction of the manicured patch of land adjoining Halloumi as paint dripped from her face, down onto her t-shirt and onto the partially cleaned floor.

'Ai! What has happened to you?!' Elpida exclaimed.

'Imogen? What's going on?' Harry asked.

'Elpida, Panos has bought Tomas' Taverna and he's going to buy the Avalon restaurant too. There's only that patch of land in between those restaurants and Halloumi. If he gets that too, he could build one of his nightclub things right next to our restaurant.'

Elpida shook her head. 'No, I do not believe it. This cannot be true.'

'It is true. He told me himself.'

'And he threw paint over you!' Harry exclaimed.

'No,' Imogen said. 'I actually threw paint over him but... we need to find out who owns that land... quickly.'

Elpida took Imogen's arm and pulled her into the restaurant building. 'Come, my car is out the back. We will get you cleaned up.'

'Harry, I'm sorry,' Imogen said as she moved with Elpida's pace. 'I left our car up the road.'

Elpida Dimitriou's home, Agios Martinos

'I really should be helping Harry, Elpida. We need to do everything we can to get the restaurant open and get it successful before Panos… Will he really knock everything down? Is that really what he does?'

She let herself be steered through Elpida's front door and into the kitchen. She still had paint and sand in her hair and on her clothes and a growing concern that her brother's dream was about to be flattened like an irritating cicada sitting somewhere it shouldn't.

'Yes, it is what he does,' Elpida answered, moving to the line of olive wood cupboards on the farthest wall. 'But I really did not think when he got back here that he would keep pursuing this. Acharavi is part of our family, our traditions.' She sighed. 'This is what happened with my son, Christos, Pano's father. He was divided. Between family and traditions and modern business. It does not mix well.' Elpida stood on tip-toes, reaching down packets from the highest shelf.

'I don't know what to do,' Imogen admitted. 'I thought maybe, with a lot of blood, sweat and tears, it could work. Now…' She shook her head, fear of demolition and development churning up her insides. 'Now I just don't know.'

'Pfft! *I* know,' Elpida said confidently, reaching down more packets and lining them up along the worktop.

'You do?' Imogen said, looking at her wide-eyed.

Elpida turned from her frenzied emptying of the cupboards and beamed at Imogen. 'We will make *baklava*!' she announced as if it was a solution to world peace.

'What? I can't make food now!' Imogen replied, throwing her hands up in the air. 'I haven't got time! I have to find the owner of the parcel of land next to the restaurant and beg him not to sell it… or sell it to me… so Panos can't ruin my brother's plans. How much is land in Corfu?'

'Stop!' Elpida ordered roughly. 'We make *baklava*,' Elpida repeated, softer. 'Repeat this, Imogen.' She closed her eyes and breathed like the leader of a meditation class. 'We make *baklava*.'

What was this? Some sort of Greek hypnotism? Imogen attempted to copy Elpida's long, lung-loosening breath. 'We make *baklava*…' She let the breath go.

'We will need this too,' Elpida announced. She grabbed at something nestled between two lower cupboards. As Elpida snapped it out, Imogen saw it was a small, collapsible stool. The woman leapt onto it and reached up onto the very top of the cabinet, fingertips just able to grab a thick, brown leather book. Dust came down along with the bound tome and Elpida started to cough.

'Are you alright?' Imogen asked, reaching out an arm to steady the woman's descent.

'Cutting down on smoking is doing nothing for my cough and everything to make me more miserable,' Elpida grumbled as she returned to ground level.

'Maybe I should take up smoking,' Imogen mused.

'No,' Elpida said. 'You will take up more Greek cooking instead.' She put the book to one side. 'Later I will show you my recipes but, for now, I will get the pastry ready and you will melt the butter.'

THIRTY

Imogen melted butter then crushed walnuts and pistachios. She spread the mixture onto the filo pastry-coated trays under her Greek teacher's supervision. If making *baklava* had been Elpida's idea of therapy then it was working.

'Good!' Elpida exclaimed. 'Now, very carefully we must put more layers of the pastry on top.'

Imogen looked at the wafer-thin pastry. It seemed like an impossible task. Pastry had always been her downfall. She hovered her fingers over it then slowly dropped them to the corners of the flat tracing paper-like substance.

'Be careful not to break it,' Elpida chipped in, leaning over Imogen.

The sound of an internal door closing and the fragrance of lemon, soap and something musky piqued Imogen's nose. She looked from the pastry to the door that led into the rest of the house just as Panos entered the room.

Showered and dressed in another pristine white shirt and dark trousers, his hair and skin still damp, Imogen tensed, her fingers pulling away and separating the pastry.

'Pfft! You must pay attention!' Elpida exclaimed. She then looked up at the slow clock above the range. 'Ai! I have to go!'

'Go?' Imogen stated. 'Go where? I thought we were making *baklava*. The kind that heals everything!'

'I have a pie to take to Nico's mother and biscuits for Mrs Rokas.' Elpida began to move dishes around, pulling forward foil-wrapped porcelain bowls.

'But, I'm not sure what I'm doing here,' Imogen said, her eyes going to her nut and butter-encrusted hands. 'I'm going to waste all these ingredients.'

'Pfft! No,' Elpida said, arms laden with items. 'Pano can help you.'

'What?' he barked.

Imogen watched him spin around from his laptop on the table, face like thunder yet still remarkably attractive. They were two people at war at the moment and she no more wanted to spend time in the kitchen with him than she wanted to invite Hannibal Lecter to Halloumi's opening night.

'Pano, you have been making *baklava* for years. Help Imogen,' Elpida ordered.

'*Yiayia*, I have work to do,' he responded.

'And I have deliveries to make,' Elpida replied quickly. 'Perhaps making something together will help settle differences, no?' She sniffed. 'And when I get back I expect perfect *baklava* and no blood on the floor.' Elpida scurried towards the kitchen door, plates piled high and her handbag swinging from her arm. 'And just in case you were wondering, when I say the blood on the floor, I mean meteorologically.'

'Metaphorically,' Imogen corrected.

'Pfft! No blood on my floor… or paint… or *baklava*… or anything,' Elpida threatened, narrowing her eyes at both of them. '*Antio!*' She waved a hand and was gone.

'So,' Panos said, draping the super-fine filo pastry over the second tray. 'Should we call a truce for the sake of the *baklava*?'

Her shoulders shrugged with a lack of conviction.

He took a breath. 'Whatever you might think, Imogen, this is not personal.'

'Of course it is!' she snapped.

'It is just business.'

'And what you're doing is going to impact on my brother's business.'

'He has no business yet. You have been here only a few days.'

'You have no idea what this means to Harry… or what Harry means to me.'

He looked directly at her then, saw the fire in her eyes had been replaced with something much rawer.

'Why don't you tell me?' he offered gently.

'Why? So you can dissect it and work out the best attack to make him change his mind and sell the restaurant to you?'

He smiled, shaking his head.

'Maybe you could tell me why you need to build a nightclub complex in Acharavi when you have Euro millions already?' she asked. 'My brother just wants to make a living and a new start for himself and his family.'

Why *was* it so important for him to build his next entertainment complex here? Was it because of that stupid hotel a few miles up the road haunting him like a spectre? Panos had to wonder.

He focussed his attention on the pastry, carefully easing it up off the board and placing it on top of the previous layer. He sighed. 'Corfu was where my father started his business,' he answered simply.

'So Dimitriou Enterprises is really your father's business?'

'No,' he said, selecting the next strip of pastry. He didn't need to look at her to know she would be wearing a confused expression. 'My father started Dimitriou *Hotels*. A very different business.'

'Hotels,' Imogen stated. 'So how many does he have?'

'None now. But when the business was doing well he had six.'

'What happened?' Imogen asked. 'Did he try to build one on Acharavi seafront?'

'No,' Panos stated. 'He died.'

He opened and shut his eyes and pretended to himself it was the cardamom in the nuts that was causing the stinging sensation. He pulled too quickly at the pastry and it split apart.

'I'm sorry,' Imogen said softly. 'I didn't know. Elpida said something about tradition and modern business not mixing but I didn't know your father had… Well, that he wasn't here anymore.'

He shrugged. 'It was a long time ago. Time moves on.'

Imogen picked up the long-handled spoon in the bowl of *baklava* filling and stirred the sweet nuts, lemon, sugar and butter around. 'If it's any consolation my father's dead too.'

He caught the edge to her voice and looked at her. 'I am sorry for your loss.'

'Like with your father, it was a long time ago. Not that that makes it any easier, does it? I guess it's possible my father might have stayed in one of your father's hotels once.' She paused. 'Although I don't have a pen.' She mixed the *baklava* ingredients again. 'My dad travelled a lot with his job. He sold linen… expensive linen, all over the world,' she said. 'He loved what he did. The only irony was he worked hard, travelled far, so we could go on holidays together.' She sighed. 'And we only just managed Spain before he died.'

She had no idea why she was telling him all this. Perhaps, after the email from the Wyatt Group, her dad was in her thoughts more than usual. She carried on stirring the mixture, getting the syrupy mix on her fingers.

'Your mother is alive?' Panos asked her.

'Yes, currently spending her time sitting in her dressing gown watching Gogglebox and Grantchester.'

'What?'

'She's a bit down at the moment. She recently lost a close friend and… I think when you get to that age and you're widowed, you start questioning your own mortality. I think she feels like everyone is leaving her,' Imogen said.

He nodded. 'We need some more mixture in here.' He indicated the baking tray on the counter in front of them.

'How about *your* mother?' Imogen asked, lifting the spoon again and depositing the sticky stuff into the container.

'She is fine,' Panos answered abruptly. 'She lives a lot of the time in England now. With her new husband.'

The way he had fired out the response told her his mother having a new husband wasn't something he particularly liked.

'He wins awards for business every week and makes his money taking over companies,' Panos continued.

'Oh, a bit like you?'

'No,' he responded tartly. 'Not like me.' He flattened out the nut mixture with the flat side of a knife. 'I work hard. Things do not just fall into my lap.'

'I'm glad you're realising that,' Imogen stated, a half smile on her face.

He sighed and put down the knife. 'Imogen, I want that restaurant.'

'You've made that quite clear.'

'So what do I have to do to make you give it to me?' He turned his body towards her, leaning slightly closer, his dark eyes capturing hers.

He was utterly, crazily gorgeous, but he wanted to take away something Harry had his heart set on. It was like wanting to get passionate with the Devil and she couldn't let it happen.

'There's nothing you can do,' she stated.

'Nothing?' he said again, leaning closer still.

She could smell dewy lemon and sweet syrup and she wasn't sure if it was coming from the *baklava* or him.

'Imogen. Don't make me beg.'

She edged slightly forward. 'For what?' she whispered, the words almost catching on her tongue.

The kitchen door banged open and Nico strode in, the strimmer in his hands. 'Mrs Dimitriou,' he began before looking. 'Oh, I am sorry…'

Panos sprung away, distancing himself and moving towards the gardener. 'What is the problem?'

'I have no fuel for the strimmer,' Nico said.

'There should be some in the shed,' Panos answered. 'I will go and look.'

Imogen watched him turn back towards her, but she was quicker, moving her body in full circle until she was back focussed on the *baklava*. She picked up the spoon and recommenced stirring. The next thing she heard was the door closing again.

THIRTY-ONE

Acharavi beachfront

'Hello, Mum,' Imogen greeted.

Her skin sparkling with droplets of sea water, the refreshing salt and sun lotion scent on her every part, Imogen had dropped her towel down onto one of the old wooden benches by the beach, drying her body off with the evening sun. The swim had been meant to clear her mind of the Panos situation but all she'd been able to do was think about how much he irritated her... before imagining what his lips would feel like on hers.

Panos hadn't returned to the kitchen after Nico's appearance with the garden tool. She had watched him, at first assisting the gardener with the strimmer, then pacing the grounds. Occasionally he had looked up to the house, for a while he had sat on the garden bench in the shade, looking at his phone but ultimately she knew he was avoiding being with her. She had just carried on making *baklava*, letting the sticky texture and the sweet, sugary smell override everything else. Eventually, Elpida had returned, taken trays from the oven, put more in and then she'd driven Imogen back to the restaurant where Harry and Risto were still dismantling the gazebo.

'Have you managed to get another buyer for the restaurant?' Grace asked. 'Janie says it's still on Rightmove.'

Imogen swallowed. What could she say? Just half an hour ago she had walked up to the craft shop on the main street and picked up some ornaments for the upper flat. They still didn't have beds but there was now a small table and chairs, a rug she had found in the back restaurant area she had beaten the life out of until it no longer produced noxious dust, and an olive wood bowl containing fruits Elpida had given her. She was finding everywhere she looked in this town there was something pretty or charming she wanted to hang on a wall or position on a window ledge. Despite everything going on, every day here seemed to be another moment filled with glorious sunshine, smiles and good mornings from the locals. The white pebbled beach, the sand on Almyros beach just a short walk away, the lazuline water on every coast. She could see why Harry and Janie had been enchanted by the island all those years ago… why Harry thought his future lay here.

'Mum…' she began.

'I'm worried sick here, Imogen. Have you heard about the Asian hornets?' Grace asked.

'What?'

'Asian hornets. They're invading,' Mum said. 'They're in France at the moment.'

'I don't think we have them in Greece but there are a lot of mosquitoes,' Imogen admitted.

'And they spread malaria,' Grace said. 'I've looked it up.'

'Have you?' Imogen asked. Looking something up involved her mother moving from the sofa and using her laptop. This, despite the content, was a step forward on the grieving process.

'Yes and there are snakes on Corfu too. About half a dozen different varieties and one, the nose-horned viper, is venomous.'

Imogen shivered and wondered whether it was quite as dangerous as the local property developer intent on poisoning the seafront. 'Well, Harry's restaurant is by the beach, Mum, and I haven't seen any snakes.'

'You need to tell him these things though, Imogen. He needs to realise that moving abroad isn't an option for him. He has responsibilities, Janie and the children, here in England.'

'He knows that, Mum. That's the whole reason he's here.' She stopped talking and set her eyes out to sea, the waves gently breaking at the beach edge. A man wearing a straw Trilby hat was making another trip along the sand, a basket swinging from each arm. Fresh fruit – apples, oranges, melon – were nested inside one of them and fresh, sugary doughnuts were inside the other. Harry had bought one of each earlier and had introduced himself to the Greek – Spiros – telling him about his plans for Halloumi. Harry knew he had responsibilities. He wanted Janie and the children back full time. Why wasn't moving abroad an option for him in her mum's mind?

'Harry's well here, Mum,' Imogen said. 'He's so much more like the old Harry.'

'Because he's on holiday,' Grace said. 'It's only been a few days, as soon as it starts raining and reality sets in he'll realise what a mistake he's made.' She sighed. '*You'll* make him realise.'

'He doesn't think it's a holiday,' Imogen insisted. 'He's been working since we got here. Clearing… cleaning… taking things down and putting things up… he's revelling in this project.'

'Is he?' Grace asked softly.

'Mum, he wants Janie and the children back so desperately.' Imogen let a breath go and looked to the mountains of Albania, the sky turning pink. 'They holidayed in Corfu… they drank *retsina* in the tavernas and held hands on the beach… He wants Janie to see him as the man he was then… as the man he knows he can be again.'

She heard a sob leave her mum and she clamped her lips together, stilling her own emotion. 'I think Dad would have understood,' she whispered. 'He always wanted us to be part of his travel adventures and we never really got the chance.' She dipped her hand into her yellow handbag, finding the small compartment at the back and clasping her fingers around the pen there. *Corinthia Palace Hotel and Spa, Malta.* 'Mum, this is Harry's travel adventure and so much more.'

She gripped the pen, the feel of the plastic grounding her thoughts. She really thought Harry could make this restaurant a reality now. There was just that small matter of Panos Dimitriou and his ambition to own the beachfront. And her attraction to him – she couldn't possibly tell her mum or Janie about that.

'Those hotels,' Grace said with another sigh. 'All that opulence and grandeur and we never got to see any of it.' She paused. 'Sheets for five star hotels and no-more-than-a-three-star wage. Makes it even more of a cheek that they've been phoning me.'

Imogen sat up straighter on the bench. 'Who's been calling you?'

'Some hotel group or other,' Grace said with a sniff. '"Is that Mrs Charlton? This is Lisa from hotel liaison" or something like that.'

Imogen held her breath. Could it be *the Wyatt Hotel Group*? She was sure she hadn't given a phone number, just her email, but could they have found Grace's contact in the directory and tried to call *her* there? Had they looked at her application now? Were they going to offer her an interview? A fizz of excitement rushed through her.

'What did they say exactly?' Imogen asked as calmly as possible. She hadn't told anyone about her application because she'd believed, in all likelihood, nothing was going to come of it. And, like Harry's restaurant, she was a little concerned about everyone else's opinion on it.

'I told you. Lisa… or Lorraine… or was it Lindsey? From hotel liaison,' Grace tutted. 'She was about to launch into that usual spiel, I could just tell, you know, about how I need to visit their hotel for a "spa rejuvenation day" which would all be free and then they would try and entice me into joining their "members club" where you can't even have a towel without putting down a mortgage on it.'

Imogen shook her head, trying to loosen her thoughts. Perhaps this was nothing. Her mum hadn't even said the caller had been from the Wyatt Group.

'What was the name of the hotel group?' Imogen couldn't resist asking. She moved her hand into the other section of her handbag and pulled out her phone. Maybe she had another email. She shot the screen down until a little wheel appeared at the top and started checking for new messages.

'No idea,' Grace replied. 'I didn't really listen. As soon as I got that feeling she was trying to sell me something I switched off. That's what April told me to do, you know.' There was another sniff. 'She could sense someone selling solar panels in seconds.'

Imogen watched her phone tell her there were no new emails and she dropped it back into her bag.

'I met April's great-niece yesterday,' Grace continued. 'Nice girl, hair in long plaits and wears those Army-type boots.'

'Doc Martens?' Imogen offered.

There was a pause. 'Martin Clunes doesn't wear boots like that,' Grace said. 'Not in the episodes I've watched.'

'Is she selling April's house?' Imogen asked, moving the subject on.

'I think so,' Grace answered. 'It's all in the hands of the solicitors now.'

'Listen, Mum, I've got to go now,' Imogen said, getting to her feet. 'I just wanted to make sure you were OK and to let you know that things here are… stabilising.'

'Stabilising?' Grace replied. 'What does that mean?'

'Well…' Imogen started. 'It just means that Harry and I are OK, we're working on getting the restaurant up together and…' What else could she tell Grace to ease her concerns? 'And… there's definitely no sign of Asian hornets.'

'It isn't funny, Imogen,' Grace said, her tone a little snippy. 'Huw Edwards was wearing a very serious face when he did his piece to camera.'

'Well, I promise I will keep a look out for them and, if I see one, I'll cover myself in garlic and hold up a cross.' She thought about Elpida's paste for bites.

'That's what you do to ward off vampires.'

'I'm glad you're feeling better, Mum.' She took a deep breath. 'Because… we're opening the restaurant next week.'

'What!'

'If you could break it to Janie gently,' she said hurriedly. 'Bye, Mum!'

THIRTY-TWO

Sunset Taverna, Mount Pantokrator

'Risto, straighten up your collar,' Elpida hissed.

Panos watched his cousin do as he was told, slipping his fingers beneath the shirt fabric and adjusting it. He didn't want to be here. Imogen and Harry were coming. Elpida had berated him about the Tomas' Taverna deal and his plans for Avalon until she had started coughing so much he thought he was going to have to call a doctor. He knew how she felt about his plans. He didn't want to cause her upset but he needed this. For so many reasons. His step-father John had been in the business news again that day. There was talk of his company buying out StoreCo. If it happened, it would be a big international coup and earlier Panos had found himself churning the information round in his head hoping desperately that the deal wouldn't come off. It was a large move on John's part and Panos had first-hand experience of what happened if someone stepped up and onwards too soon.

Elpida turned to face him. 'You still have some apologising to do.'

He held up his hands in defence. 'I do not know what you are talking about.'

Elpida narrowed her eyes as they stepped onto the terrace. 'The restaurant is not for sale. It is sold. Stop trying to buy this!' She wagged a finger.

He swallowed, trying to maintain a nonchalant expression.

'Imogen attacked me in the street.' He followed his cousin and grandmother to a large table at the edge of the terraced area. He had been surprised no one had commented on the smell of paint in the Mercedes. He'd organised a complete valet in an hour but the seats were still a little damp. 'The woman is crazy,' he added.

'Well, all I know is, I tell her what your business is and she comes back looking like an avalanche telling me you have bought Tomas' Taverna.' Elpida sighed.

'You have bought Tomas'?' Risto exclaimed, eyes bright.

'I am looking through the paperwork,' Panos confirmed.

'I do not know what is wrong with you, Pano.' Elpida stretched her arm out, highlighting the top-of-the-mountain scene in front of them. 'Here is home. And business should always come second to home.'

Panos let his eyes stray to the view beyond the terrace. Green firs, carobs and cypress trees stretched out as far as the eye could see, all leading down to the ocean, sparkling with the last few rays of sun. It was a view that caused emotion to flood his gut. This restaurant evoked so many memories for him. His mother and father together, holding hands, laughing, dancing to the traditional band as the sun dropped below the horizon and darkness fell. He had separated himself from all that. Happiness never lasted. It was forced and fickle. It didn't mean anything. Anyone who thought it did was living in the last century. To succeed you needed only self-belief. Faith was something that no one had in you but you.

He watched his grandmother pull out a wooden chair and sit down, dropping her patent leather handbag onto her knee.

'In my mind we have some making up to do,' she said, dropping her handbag to the floor. 'I sell this restaurant to Harry and it is left like an earthquake has happened. Pfft!' Elpida rolled her eyes.

Panos beckoned a waiter before sitting down next to his cousin. 'I thought you were making this right by working there?'

'Yes,' Risto said.

'Then what more making up is there to do?' Panos asked.

His grandmother pulled her cigarettes from her bag, setting the packet on the table. 'Did you know that they are sleeping on the floor?' Elpida said.

'Their business is none of my business.'

'No,' Elpida said. 'Your business is destroying things.'

'I am not my father,' Panos snapped. 'I am going to succeed where he could not. Why do you not want me to have this success?'

'Christo failed because he let business eat him up, Pano.'

Elpida's stare was like a laser slicing through his retinas. He straightened his back, lifting his body a little off the seat and turning to the waiter. 'Can I see the wine list please?'

'Pfft,' Elpida said. 'We will have a couple of bottles of house red.' She slipped a cigarette from the packet, put it in her mouth and lit it up.

He wanted to interject and tell his grandmother he didn't want what they always drank here. He needed to reschedule his meeting with Lafi as Imogen had ruined the last one by dousing him with paint.

'Ah,' Elpida said, standing up and resting her cigarette in the ashtray. 'They are here.'

Panos pretended to study the menu.

'The house red *is* good here, Pano,' Risto said, nudging his arm. 'And *yiayia* says she is paying.'

He ruffled his cousin's hair good-naturedly. 'Then we shall all drink as much as we can, no?'

Risto grinned.

Imogen hadn't been able to take her eyes off the view from the second they'd been led out to the terrace. The mountain fell away in a blanket of greenery, every shade imaginable. Dotted throughout the limbs of trees were sparks of colour – vibrant pink, purple and yellow flowers, their petals turned up towards the falling sun. And there, at the bottom of the incline, was the sparkling sea, rolling backwards and forwards in front of the rugged coastline of Albania. Corfu was beginning to cast a magical spell on her. Her hands back in mixing bowls, the sun and sea on her skin, the sweet, humid air…

'There they are,' Harry said, nudging Imogen's elbow.

She looked to the large wooden table at the edge of the balcony. 'You didn't say Panos was going to be here. You said Elpida was bringing her recipe book and we were going to try and finalise a menu.'

'I didn't know,' Harry stated. 'But maybe it's a good thing.'

She slowed her pace, ducking behind Harry as he navigated his way around terracotta urns spilling begonias and geraniums. She didn't trust Panos. There would always be that not-so-hidden agenda. And the fact he made her stomach twist with longing despite how inappropriate an object of affection he was.

'Come on,' Harry said, linking his arm with hers. 'You love food like I love food. Let's go and choose a menu for our restaurant.'

She looked to her brother then, taking in the light in his eyes, the playful smile, his hair springing about like an eager Afghan. She nodded and faced the table. With a metre of solid oak wood between her and Panos she was sure she could talk about *taramasalata* and olives without getting flustered.

THIRTY-THREE

Imogen sipped the delicious red wine while Elpida waxed lyrical about the benefits of avocado. 'So good for the skin.'

Imogen smiled. There had never been any need for avocados in the roadside café but she liked them. She'd made stuffed avocados with spicy kidney beans and feta for one of Daniel's work colleagues and his wife once. That was vaguely Greek. Perhaps she should suggest it.

Elpida flicked over another page of the thick brown leather book on the table in front of her.

'Fish was always our most popular dish,' Panos said suddenly.

Elpida raised her head from the dusty book to eye her grandson. Imogen put down her goblet.

'Was it?' Harry asked.

'Yes,' Imogen joined in. 'Was it... *really?*' She couldn't believe anything he said.

'You want to know about the local fish?' He fixed his eyes on her. 'Well, I can tell you, it is fresh... soft... melt-in-your-mouth flesh that dissolves on your tongue and... it is like you can never have enough.'

As Panos described the food he rolled each and every word with his tongue. She looked away and took hold of her goblet.

'Pano is right,' Elpida said. 'Fish dishes were our best sellers in the restaurant's finest days.' She paused, her eyes watching the sun's silent decline.

Imogen looked too. She had never seen such a perfect sunset. From their position on the side of the mountain the circle of light looked like a giant fiery wheel turning quickly now from a vibrant orange to a deep magenta. Diners began to gather at the metal railings, cameras on video mode, capturing the slow whisper of the sun's descent as it melted away inch by inch, slipping below the horizon. This was what she had to do for Harry, Janie and the children. Stop their family unit burning out and slipping away.

Tears pricked her eyes and she blinked them away quickly, turning back to the table and her almost empty goblet of wine. Seeing Panos watching her, she willed the emotion away.

'What a beautiful sight,' Harry announced with a loaded sigh.

'This is what brings all the customers here,' Elpida said. 'This is the very best place to watch the sunset from.'

'I proposed to my wife as the sun was setting,' Harry stated. 'Here in Corfu. Actually in Kassiopi.'

'Really!' Elpida exclaimed. 'That is wonderful! So romantic!'

He sighed. 'But we're not together anymore.'

Imogen swallowed the knot in her throat. 'It's just a trial separation though, isn't it?' she said quickly. She addressed the table. 'Harry has two children. Tristan and Olivia.'

'That is lovely,' Elpida announced. 'They will come here and they will fall in love with Corfu too.'

'I will get more drinks,' Risto said, shifting back his chair.

'No, Risto,' Panos said.

Panos had seen Imogen's eyes glaze as she watched the setting sun. Something had been brought to mind as she involved herself in the scene and it had caused her to tear up.

'*I* will get more drinks,' he stated, standing. 'Imogen, would you help me?'

She stayed in her seat, looking at Harry, as if she were searching for a reason to decline.

'Yes, Imogen, please go with him,' Elpida said. 'Make sure he gets the house wine, and Pano, order some *meze*.'

For once he was glad of his grandmother's intervention. He waited, watching Imogen until she rose from her seat. As she stood and pushed her chair into position he was given a chance to see just how the cut of her dress highlighted the length of her legs and the curve of her waist.

'Swordfish is a good choice,' he heard his grandmother say. 'It is a very meaty fish.'

'I'm thinking green beans, new potatoes and a mustard dressing,' Harry chirped up.

Panos let Imogen come around the table toward him before he led the way to the bar.

Leaning his weight against the rustic wood countertop he looked at her. Her cheeks were glowing from the red wine and she had self-consciously folded her arms across her chest.

'Your body language says that you do not trust me at all,' he stated, a small smile on his lips. 'What do you think I am going to do? Throw *meze* at you?'

'Of course I don't trust you. What do you expect?'

'I expect, given that I have apologised and you have half drowned me in paint, to be given a second chance.'

'A second chance at what?' she asked him. 'You're buying up property all around us. Harry's restaurant isn't going to have a chance if you move diggers in and start tearing up the beach.'

Those flyaway strands of gold were dancing around her jawline and his fingers itched to push them back. He called over the barman before digging his hands into the pockets of his trousers. He ordered in Greek and turned back to Imogen.

'Panos, I told you Harry's trying to save his marriage. He wants Corfu to be a new start. He hasn't been well and back in England people are quick to judge. He sees the restaurant as a lifeline. It isn't helping knowing you're trying to change everything around us when we've only just got here.'

'He is ill?' Panos questioned.

Imogen shook her head. 'No… not like that.'

'You do not have to tell me,' he said when Imogen failed to expand. 'It is none of my business.' But the fact remained he wanted to know.

'Harry had an accident at work.' She toyed with the edge of a lace doily on the countertop, twisting the thread in between her thumb and forefinger. 'He was working on a plane and the ladder wasn't secure and he fell off. He broke his hip badly and he was at home for months recovering. When he finally went back, nothing was the same and *he* wasn't the same. It all just spiralled from there.' She paused. 'He has depression and depression isn't something you can just fix. It takes time and patience and… maybe a restaurant in Corfu.'

He reached for one of the carafes of red wine brought by the barman and filled two tumblers.

'Drink,' he ordered, raising his glass to his lips. He took a large mouthful and turned his eyes on her. She held the glass with both hands and gulped at the liquid. A little found its way to the edge of her lips and she dabbed a finger at the excess. Why did he find that small motion so sexy?

'I apologise,' Panos said. 'For making things difficult for you.' He swallowed. Did he mean that?

She looked up at him. 'Thank you.'

Then he felt it again. That pull he'd felt on the beach today. He might have been covered from head to foot in paint but when he'd lain over her, looking down at her, he'd wanted to kiss her so desperately a fist of longing had thumped in his gut. Why did things have to be so complicated? He wanted the restaurant, this beachfront project and… he wanted her. But was it only because neither of them were straightforward?

She took another swig of the wine and leant back against the bar, her gaze on the diners on the terrace and the mountain backdrop. 'So, after Harry fell off the aeroplane he used to tell people he was a stuntman at parties for a while.' She smiled. 'He was an engineer… so, so, clever… not like me.'

He watched her. She was relaxing slightly, her shoulders loosening, her demeanour lightening.

'He always loved planes,' she continued. 'He used to annoy me so much when we were children – making models for hours on end, throwing polystyrene ones around the house. He said aviation was his destiny. He wrote that phrase on all his school books. Whereas I… I wrote *I heart Justin Timberlake*.' She laughed.

'He was your husband?' Panos asked.

She laughed again.

He was confused.

'Justin Timberlake's a pop star… *was* a pop star. Now he's famous for… being Justin Timberlake I guess.' She shrugged. 'I don't suppose he's that big in Greece.'

Panos' attention went to where the band were setting up on a small stage, a grape-vine-covered pergola over the top. He turned back to Imogen.

'If he does not play the *bouzouki* he is not really a musician in Greece.'

She laughed. 'Do you play the *bouzouki*?'

He shook his head. 'No.' He didn't wait for her to ask another question. 'So, Imogen, Harry's destiny is with this restaurant now? Not planes any longer?'

'He can't climb any more. He had to leave the job he loved and that didn't help anything. But even after everything he's been through, Harry's Harry, always with a glass half full, ever the optimist.'

'And you?' Panos asked.

'What about me?'

'How is your glass?'

He watched her look to her wineglass as if hoping the answer was going to be found amid the dark, berry-infused drink.

'I've been sharing Harry's glass for so long I'm not sure what mine looks like.'

He nodded, resting his body against the bar, his arm just touching hers.

'What about your glass, Pano?'

The use of his shortened name sent a delicious chill up his spine.

'My glass?' he said, considering the question as if his answer might hold the resolution to the Greek financial crisis.

'Yes,' she breathed. 'The very expensive one bought from the proceeds of all the village tavernas you've torn down.'

His elation was short-lived and he felt his cheeks rising in temperature. He deserved that. He was a successful businessman who put profit and deals above anything and everything. It was what he knew. It was safe. He should smile. Congratulate her on her repartee. But it wouldn't be the truth of what he felt.

'My glass is broken, Imogen,' he said eventually. 'And it's been broken for a very long time.'

THIRTY-FOUR

'What is this one?'

Harry popped another tit-bit of the *meze* into his mouth and closed his eyes as if trying to work out the flavours.

'That is *keftedes*,' Elpida answered. 'It is made with lamb, garlic, breadcrumbs, spices… very easy to make and delicious.'

'You've said every one of these recipes is easy to make,' Imogen said.

'It will be, Immy,' Harry said. 'She's a great cook, Elpida, just a bit out of practice.'

'It looks complicated,' Imogen protested.

'Pfft!' Elpida exclaimed. 'Pano could make this… In fact, Pano *has* made this. Like *baklava*. When he was a child he loved to cook.'

Imogen looked for the Greek who hadn't returned to the table since their drink at the bar. Her eyes found him. He was sat at another table with Risto, chatting to a Greek man and two very attractive women about her age. It irked her and she hated that.

'Do you think a choice of four starters is enough, Elpida?' Harry asked, picking up his pen and writing on his pad of paper.

She nodded. 'Yes, this is where I make mistake with my restaurant. You need very good dishes you can do very well. We make them individual to Halloumi so no one else on the beachfront has the exact same thing as you. And we make specials.' She narrowed her eyes. 'No one makes *keftedes* the way my grandmother used to make it.' She lowered her voice to a whisper. 'But you can.'

Harry beamed. 'What do you think, Immy?'

What did she think? At the moment she was worried they might be serving food in between pneumatic drilling and wrecking balls. She supposed the workers might want lunches and Greek beer. She looked to the platter. 'I liked this one.' She pointed at a triangle-shaped parcel of pastry. 'But I've never been very good with pastry.'

'Ah!' Elpida said. '*Spanakopitakia*. They make this here at Sunset with feta cheese and spinach.' She whispered even lower this time. 'For you I think we make this with halloumi, feta, spinach and a little garlic and rosemary.'

'I like the sound of that,' Harry said, making more notes.

Imogen watched one of the women with Panos get up out of her chair and drape an arm around his shoulders, leaning into him like it was the most natural action in the world.

'What do you think, Immy?' Harry asked again.

'What? Sorry… I didn't hear what you said.' She flushed. What was the matter with her? Why was she compelled to look at Panos Dimitriou? Because he was her nemesis or because he sent her feminine zones into a frenzy?

'I think we've got our starters. *Spanakopitakia, keftedes, saganaki* – because what you made for lunch the other day was delicious, Immy – and soup of the day. I think it's a nice mix,' Harry explained.

'And you have meat and vegetarian,' Elpida added.

A loud, excited laugh filtered over from the table Panos was sat at and Imogen couldn't help but look. The woman now had both arms around Panos, embracing him from behind as he sat back in his chair. She had a perfect figure and long dark curls.

'I do not like that man,' Elpida stated, her eyes following Imogen's line of vision.

'Who is he?' Imogen asked. The man looked like a cross between Buddha and Gio from the Go Compare adverts.

'That is Alejandro Kalas. He is on the *simvoulio* here. The council,' Elpida explained. 'Sometime he do a lot of good for the village. Other times he make a lot of money for himself.' She frowned. 'I can guess Panos will be speaking to him about his plans for loudy shouty disco party palace.'

'Are those his wives?' Harry asked, looking as well.

'No,' Elpida said shaking her head. 'They are his daughters. Cleo and Margot. Both of them spoilt little princesses who would not know a day of hard work if it came up and said "boo" in their faces.' Elpida sighed. 'There is his son, Vasilis. Now he is a good man. He run a boat company out of Kassiopi.'

'Would the councillor be a good man to get to the opening night of Halloumi though?' Harry suggested.

'I do not know if *good* man is the right word but yes, wherever he go there will be photo opportunity and newspaper reporter.'

'Perhaps Panos can introduce us,' Harry said.

'I would tread a little careful, Harry,' Elpida stated. 'Once you get into bed with a man like this there is no getting out of it again. And, I like to know who exactly is plumping my pillows.' She nodded, reaching for her wine goblet. 'And also with a man like that you never know which side of the mattress he is sleeping on.'

The bed analogy gnawed at Imogen as she watched Panos and the not-so-ugly sisters. Was that what he was doing now? Having apologised and asked about Harry was he back plotting and scheming? The monstrosity he intended to build would need council planning but if this Alejandro was corrupt like Elpida was suggesting, who was to say what he would push through? And who would really want to eat a quiet meal next to a throbbing nightclub?

A shiver ran through her as visions of Club 18-30 holiday-makers lunging onto Halloumi's terrace in a conga line came to mind, vomiting into plates of *spanakopitakia* while Harry rocked back and forth in a corner. She just couldn't let it happen. She stood up without saying a word and manoeuvred out from behind the table, making strides towards Panos, Risto and Alejandro and his family.

Every time there had been a break in the conversation Panos had looked for Imogen. *A broken glass.* Why had he confided in her like that?

He felt Cleo's arms go around his neck and wanted to shrug her off but her father was a useful man to know. They had already spoken on the phone about plans for an entertainment venue in the area. They both thought Acharavi could be better than it was.

He turned his head and came eye to eye with Imogen, stalking her way towards the table. She stopped a pace away, smiling and turning her head a little to greet each diner with a hello in turn. She didn't look to him. She looked directly at Alejandro.

'Good evening, Mr Kalas. My name is Imogen Charlton.' She extended a hand to the large Greek man.

Panos watched Alejandro move her delicate hand to his wide, greasy mouth, pressing a kiss to her skin. He could hardly bear to look.

Vasilis Kalas got to his feet and held out his hand to Imogen. 'It's a pleasure to meet you. You are from England, yes?'

Imogen smiled, moving her hand from father to son. 'Yes, I'm here with my brother. He's bought the old Dimitriou restaurant on the beachfront in Acharavi.'

'Oh, Pano, I thought you were going to make that place into one of your clubs!' Cleo squealed in a mix of excitement and disappointment, all the while pawing at his shoulders.

He didn't know what to say. Imogen was looking at him now, almost as if she were goading him to make a reply. She had told him exactly how much the restaurant meant to her brother and he was back in fifth gear with his plans.

'My congratulations,' Vasilis said. 'Welcome to the island.'

Vasilis' eyes were lingering a little too long on the scalloped neckline of Imogen's dress for Panos' liking. He sat up in his chair, shrugged off the hands of Cleo and opened his mouth to speak.

Imogen jumped in. 'Mr Kalas, I just wanted to assure you that the new restaurant is going to be a real credit to the beach-front. My brother and I have a long history with food... and he chose this area in particular because he's visited this part of the island several times before. It's the perfect mix of relax-ation, Greek tradition and, of course, peace and tranquillity.' She paused and turned her eyes to Panos. 'I know there are some people who think the area needs to liven up a bit...' She looked back to Alejandro. 'But Elpida Dimitriou tells me you're always a man who has the interests of the village at heart.' She smiled. 'We're looking forward to becoming part of the community and, with all this rumour of development, I just wanted to introduce myself and to say that... well, I re-ally want you to be a man who wouldn't mistake making quick Euro with better plans for long-term regeneration.' Her gaze locked with his.

The table fell silent and Panos just stared at her, her impas-sioned face stoic, her presence bigger than even the rotund councillor. She clasped her hands together in front of her. She had just warned a council member about his stance on development and she was standing there looking as innocent as Maria from the *Sound of Music.*

Vasilis started to clap and gestured to his sister, urging them to do the same. Within seconds they were all clapping and looking slightly bewildered.

'Hear, hear,' Vasilis announced, banging a fist on the table. 'Did you hear that, *pateras*?'

Alejandro looked stern, his fingers going to his thin, curled moustache, and turning the ends. Then Panos watched him grin and a belly laugh erupted from deep in his core.

He wagged a finger at Imogen. 'She is right,' he stated. 'She is absolutely right.' He picked up a wine glass and wafted it in the air. 'Only at today's meeting we talk of a new community market. It is wonderful,' he stated. 'Wonderful.'

Community market? What was this? Who needed a community market? There were shops and supermarkets down the whole main street of Acharavi. Panos reached for a goblet of wine and squeezed his hand around it. Imogen had done this for one reason and one reason only. To put a halt to his plans. To publically tell the councillor she would be opposing any development, that his grandmother would back her, that the village didn't want or need it. That making money was not a priority. But what did she know? She'd been here *days*. She didn't know what Acharavi needed. She didn't know how desperate things had been in Greece.

'What sort of community market?' Cleo asked, moving from behind Panos to sit down next to her father. 'Designer clothes from Corfu Town? Jewellery?'

He couldn't listen to this anymore. He was being thwarted at every turn by this Englishwoman, this foreigner who knew nothing about the island, who knew nothing about business, who... made him want to... He swallowed, his eyes moving over her as she chatted to Alejandro and Vasilis. The fact that she always angered him only heightened his desire. He could have any woman he wanted. What was it with her? Was it perhaps because she hadn't fallen at his feet? She spoke her mind. She had loyalty and deep-rooted values. She was beautiful.

Suddenly the lights on the terrace dimmed, allowing the candlelight from each glowing jar on every table to become the focus. Then spotlights picked out the musicians on the stage. Lute, guitar and *bouzouki* started to play.

'Imogen,' Vasilis called over the music. 'You would like to dance?'

'I… don't really know any Greek dancing,' she replied.

'I will teach you,' Vasilis replied.

'Risto, dance with me,' Cleo said, moving to tug at his arm.

'And me!' Margot added, standing up.

As Panos watched his cousin going off to dance, he felt an uncomfortable jealousy begin to spread over his body and he lifted himself up off the chair. A meaty hand met his arm and he stopped moving, turning his head to face Alejandro.

'I know you would like to talk to me about your entertainment complex,' the man began.

'Yes, I do,' he said quickly, adjusting his stance and getting his mind back in business mode. 'I have agreed a deal to buy Tomas' Taverna and I am meeting with Lafi from Avalon this week. I am confident both properties will be under my control very soon.'

Alejandro shook his head before splaying a hand out in front of him, indicating the people around them. 'I am not getting any younger, Pano. And as you get older you come to realise what is important in life.'

'Growth,' Panos interjected. 'Investment in the future.'

'Yes,' Alejandro agreed. 'But perhaps not in the way you mean. Not at the expense of history or tradition.'

Panos let out an exasperated sigh of discontent. 'You thought nothing of tradition when you let my father build the largest hotel on the island a few miles from here.'

'That was on wasteland, Pano. It did not meet with any resistance from the community. It didn't spoil anyone's view and would not make too much noise for residents,' he responded. 'And it was going to bring jobs to the area.' Alejandro poured some more wine into his goblet.

'My complex will bring jobs to the area,' Panos insisted. He took a breath. 'And I am not my father.'

'I know this. But you want to build your disco bar and carting track right on the beachfront.'

'It has to be there to capture the highest footfall. It is the obvious location.'

'Not for the people who live there.'

'It has worked well on Crete and Rhodes.'

'I could see this working in Kavos, Pano, not Acharavi.'

'It *has* to be Acharavi.'

'Why?'

It was a question he didn't want to answer because he knew it was nothing about business and all about the past. He didn't want to fail at a project in Acharavi like his father had. Alejandro was supposed to be his golden ticket to a yes from the council. He could see it in the man's eyes. All his plans were starting to crumble away in time to the Greek folk song playing in the background.

His gaze moved to the dancefloor where a few diners were already up, circling around the tiled floor to the moderate tempo. And there was Imogen, with Vasilis Kalas, hands together, moving slowly, bodies close. Her cheeks were as ruby red as the wine, a smile on her lips, her hips shifting in time to the thrum of the stringed instruments. He swallowed.

'How long are you staying on Corfu?' Alejandro asked him.
He shrugged. 'I do not know.'

'I like the idea of the community market. It is something different.' Alejandro drank some wine before continuing. 'It is not just about shop-holders taking their things onto stalls, it is about villagers making their hobbies and traditions a business.'

'I do not understand,' Panos replied.

'Take your grandmother,' Alejandro said. He leant back in his chair and looked over to where Elpida and Harry were sitting, still engrossed in the leather bound recipe book.

'Sometimes I wish someone would,' Panos said, sighing and sitting back in his chair.

'She does not have the restaurant any more but she still wants to bake. She bakes at every opportunity. For weddings, for babies' births, for every saint's day, for young Nico's mother who is house-bound, for anybody.' Alejandro laughed, shaking his head.

Panos watched his grandmother light up a cigarette, puffing plumes of blue smoke into the air, a smile on her face at something Harry had said to her. Did she still bake as much as that? Like she had when he was young? Her house had always been filled with the fragrance of Greek delicacies – feta-filled parcels, rich *moussaka*, honey-drenched *baklava*. What had happened to make her give up the restaurant? Was it just his grandfather's death and her age or was it something else? He hadn't hung around to find out. He had only cared about escaping the trappings of the small-minded area and carving out something bigger and better.

'Old Mrs Pelekas still makes those beautiful tablecloths at age eighty-six. Think of how much the tourists would like to buy these with almost all the profits going to the stallholder?' He sniffed. 'They could have a wonderful holiday and know they had contributed directly to the people that live and work here. People would not just be taking home a piece of Corfu in their suitcase, they would be taking a little piece in their hearts also.'

Panos swallowed, remembering Mrs Pelekas shouting at him as a boy when he'd chased her chickens around her garden as a dare. She'd scuffed him on the back of the head then coddled him to her breast and fed him *dolmades*. She'd looked eighty-six way back then.

'If you are staying for a while, I'm sure your project management and business expertise could be put to good use in a community market scheme,' Alejandro said.

He shook his head immediately. 'I have no idea what these are. In Crete there are fish, meat and vegetable markets, not pies and tablecloths. That's what tourist shops are for, no?' He rested his hands on the table, staring down the councillor. 'I want to build on the beachfront.'

Alejandro laughed. 'This is new, Pano… and it could be big business. If we are one of the first villages to do this we can attract artisans from all over Corfu.' He cleared his throat. 'Obviously priority will be given to local people, but when word spreads, so will interest. People will pay the town to rent a stall and keep eighty percent of their profits. It will be a win for everybody.'

The word 'community' was something he usually battled against, trying to win favour to bulldoze an area for his nightclub scheme. He didn't see how he could be part of this when it was in conflict with everything he had strived for at Dimitriou Enterprises.

'They started a community market in Arillas just last month. There is another one tomorrow.' Alejandro leant forward and topped up Panos' glass with wine. 'Why not take a look?'

He nodded his head. There was no point saying any more, Alejandro had switched off. Tomorrow he was going to speak to Lafi, get a contract secured to buy Avalon and then he would make enquiries as to who owned the square of land next to Halloumi. He was sure Alejandro would come round in time.

'Your father, he came to me once,' Alejandro spoke, gazing into the mid-distance. 'Just before he died.' He made the sign of the cross over his chest. 'He said the one regret he had was not spending more time with his family. Business can be like that. Sometimes we are blinkered. Can only see the goal like the bright light at the end of the tunnel.' He nodded his head. 'We all make so many mistakes, Pano and time goes on around us just the same.'

He didn't want to hear this. He bit the inside of his bottom lip and tried to tune out. His eyes moved back to the dancefloor and Imogen, spiralling under Vasilis' arm, her slender waist spinning in rhythm to the players on stage.

'Take a look at the community market,' Alejandro said again. 'I would be interested to hear what you think.'

Panos got to his feet with a brief nod. He was going to say his goodbyes to his grandmother, then he was going to leave. He turned onto the dancefloor just as the song came to a frenetic end.

Before he could take another step Imogen collided hard into him. She gasped, the breath flying from her on impact, and he quickly caught her, steadying her body and holding on tight as she tried to regain control of her feet.

There she was, in his arms, breathing ragged, her face flushed from the humidity of the night and the Greek dancing, those blue eyes looking up at him, spirals of soft, golden hair grazing her face, her hands gripping onto his arms. All he could do was look at her as the lights on stage diminished and there was nothing but candlelight, highlighting her beauty.

Slowly he lifted her back into a standing position, his eyes not leaving hers as she slipped her hands down his arms, fingers staying connected, tracing the fine hairs on his skin.

'Imogen,' Vasilis called. 'Another dance?'

He pulled back.

'Pano,' she said.

He walked away without reply.

THIRTY-FIVE

Halloumi, Acharavi beachfront

Imogen pressed send on the text message she'd just composed to Janie.

> *The restaurant is really coming together. It's stunning and I think you'd love it! We even have a menu! I really wish you could see it! Could you see it? Maybe bring the children? Xx*

She had attached a photo of the newly constructed pergola and the clean unbroken windows at the entrance she'd taken earlier that day, plus the stunning beach scene from the terrace. The beautiful view of an island Janie had holidayed on should prompt some interest from her sister-in-law.

It seemed to have taken far more than fifteen minutes to descend from the mountain back down to the beachfront of Acharavi and now her head was spinning from the red wine, her eyes slightly blurry. She refocussed on the entrance of the restaurant hoping the scene before her was to do with her alcohol content and not reality.

'Harry,' she called softly into the night as she slipped down out of Terry's fish van. 'Please tell me there aren't animals outside the restaurant.'

'What?' Harry replied.

Imogen stepped through the scrub onto the terrace and stood still, looking at the farmyard menagerie in front of her. There was a dark-furred goat, at least five chickens and half a dozen cats. They all seemed to turn together, licking, scratching or shaking their tail feathers. She blinked and blinked again. The goat bleated and shunted one of the chickens, which flew up into the air. There was a black cat, a white one with ginger patches, a tortoiseshell, one that looked just like Mog and another was a tiny, grey-and-black-striped kitten.

'Blimey,' Harry announced. 'How many are there and what are they all doing here?'

Imogen put her handbag down on one of the tables and took a step further forward. 'I'm hoping they aren't a live menu you've ordered.'

'No… no, I definitely ordered meat from a source Elpida recommended.'

Imogen shifted her feet as the kitten wound itself around her legs.

Harry jumped as the goat butted his backside. 'There's a field with goats just down the road, isn't there? There's probably chickens there too and—'

'Cats?' Imogen asked.

'They've probably escaped. A loose fence or no fence at all. It's a bit like that here, isn't it?'

Imogen stamped her feet as the kitten's rough tongue licked her shin. It scuttled away then settled, looking wide-eyed at her like Dreamworks' *Puss in Boots*.

'Well, what do we do?' she asked, scooping up the kitten and cradling it in her arms, rubbing its head with her fingers.

Harry scratched his head. 'I'm not really a fan of chickens. It's the beady eyes.'

'How far is this field?'

'Not far.'

'Right,' Imogen said. 'Help me get the goat in the van.'

'What?'

'Help me get the goat and all the cats in the van,' she repeated. 'I'll deal with the chickens. Here, Goaty McGoat Face!' She looked at Harry. 'What do goats eat apart from grass? Can we entice it with something?'

'We've got a whole cupboard full of avocado,' Harry offered.

Imogen made a grab for the goat's horns and tried to pull it towards the edge of the terrace. It dug in its hooves and looked mean.

'Gosh, Immy, don't upset it,' Harry said, eyes wide. 'Let me go and find some rope and I'll call Elpida, see if she knows the farmer.' He stopped for a minute, looking at his sister, her hands on the horns of the mammal. 'You have to laugh, Immy. We're like the Durrells right now,' he stated, grinning. 'Only in Greece, eh?'

'Hurry up or I might decide we *will* put them all on the menu,' she said through gritted teeth.

The goat shook its head, wrestling with Imogen's grip as it tried to free itself. The chickens began to squawk and Mog jumped up onto the table and stuck its head in her handbag as Harry went inside.

A beak pecked her leg and she let go of the goat, almost falling forward with the force. This rustic place full of nature and tradition was somehow becoming her crazy normality.

Stepping away from the animals she looked out onto the beach, hoping to breathe in some solace. A single iron streetlight was shedding a faint glow over the sand and the inky water beyond, the clear night sky lit with a thousand stars. She looked down at her feet as the kitten began to nibble her toes and when she raised her head they had company. Letting out a gasp of shock, she rocked backwards, almost colliding with the goat.

Panos stood at the restaurant entrance, the sleeves of his white shirt rolled up to the elbows, sleek, dark hair jutting over his forehead.

'Please tell me these animals have nothing to do with you,' Imogen demanded. 'That it isn't something else to discourage us and to sell you the restaurant.'

The goat bleated and Panos stepped up onto the terrace as if he hadn't heard her at all, taking long, purposeful strides, closing the distance between them.

'So, have you come for the goat or the chickens… or the cats?' she asked, slightly less self-assured as he neared.

'I have come for you,' he stated.

She swallowed, forgetting to breathe. The memories of him catching her as she slipped on the terrace of the Sunset Taverna and earlier, covered in paint in the sand then making *baklava*, held her still.

He was so close she could feel the heat of his breath on her cheeks. Those hypnotic dark eyes were drawing her nearer still, her body reacting like iron filings to a magnet.

'Why did you dance with Vasilis, Imogen?' Panos demanded.

His question threw her for a second.

'Wh-What?' she stuttered.

'Why did you dance with Vasilis Kalas?'

'Because,' she began. She swallowed, her eyes unable to look away from his. 'Because he asked me.'

'Immy, I've found some rope!' Harry called.

Panos grabbed her hand, pulling her off the terrace. Before she had a chance to draw breath he had pushed her up against a wide-trunked palm tree.

He was millimetres away, a hand on the bristly bark each side of her form. Whatever ridiculous under-thought notion this was, she couldn't fight it any longer. His mouth met hers and she pressed herself against him. Wrapping her arms around his neck, she whirled her fingers in the dark hair at his nape, deepening their kiss, needing to fall harder and heavier.

'Immy? Are you there?' Harry called.

She pulled her mouth away from Panos, gasping for air as his lips met the V at the base of her throat. What was she doing?

His strength pushed her back again, his lips meeting hers once more and delivering another dangerously sensual kiss to her mouth. The urge to carry on was so strong. But the knowledge that any second Harry was going to come looking for her won out.

'Stop,' she said, dragging her mouth away from his.

He slid back, breaking their connection, his eyes not leaving hers. The top button of his shirt had come undone and his breathing was laboured. Her eyes strayed briefly to the zip of his trousers and she bit her lip at the obvious intention she saw there.

'I have to go,' she whispered.

'I know,' he answered.

'This is crazy,' she breathed. 'We're completely at odds. You want to ruin our business. I can't be kissing someone who wants to ruin our business.'

'I don't want to ruin your business,' Panos replied.

'But, even if you don't have Halloumi, can't you see how your complex will change things? Not just for Harry's restaurant but for the whole village here?'

He put a finger to her lips. 'Please, Imogen, can we not separate things?'

'What? Like eggs?' She sighed. 'The yolk for one part, the white for something else?'

His breath was hot on her cheeks and she wanted to kiss him again, surrender to pure pleasure.

'Imogen?' It was Harry's voice again and she shuddered in a mix of thrill and fear.

'Come to Arillas with me tomorrow,' Panos said, his voice low.

'Where?' she whispered back.

'It is not far,' he answered. 'On the west coast of the island. Let us get out of Acharavi, put our differences aside,' he suggested. 'Focus on...' He picked up her hand, holding it in his. 'Focus on this.' He brushed his lips against her skin.

'I don't know,' she answered. In the real world it was a ridiculous idea. In this head-rush of a romantic bubble, it seemed like the best plan ever.

'I will pick you up at ten,' he responded, backing away from her.

'I said I didn't know.'

He smiled. '*I* know.'

'Immy! Where are you?!' Harry called, sounding anxious.

She watched Panos head off up the road out of sight, her heart pounding in her chest. Harry's touch on her arm made her leap in the air.

'What are you doing here?' her brother asked. 'Are you alright?'

Was she alright? Not really. She had just been kissed like never before. By the man who had blighted almost every moment of their time in Corfu so far. A man who wanted to see her tomorrow.

'You look tired,' Harry stated.

She wasn't tired, she was buzzing. Every tiny particle of her was jumping up and down and shouting for attention.

She jumped suddenly and looked down. The stripy kitten was weaving in and out of her legs again, looking up at her, almost grinning.

'The farmer's coming,' Harry said. 'I have to admit I like the cats a whole lot better than I like the goat and the chickens.' He picked the animal up and cradled it in his arms. 'What's your name then?' he asked. The cat meowed and rubbed its head against Harry's hands as it was petted.

'It has to be Spiros,' she replied, scratching under its chin and stepping up onto the terrace to retrieve her handbag from the table. She pulled her phone out, looking to Harry and the cat before dropping her eyes to the screen. There was a reply to her text.

Janie: I see the weeds are gone. Is the sea really that blue?

The message ended with an emoji of the Greek flag. This was positive. She quickly tapped out a reply.

The beach is to die for and so is the food. Tristan and Olivia would love it. Harry misses you all xx

Her gaze went to Harry again. He was cuddling the kitten and rubbing its belly, all the while smiling as the cat writhed in his arms and the chickens chased each other behind him. She had to ensure Janie saw that this project could work, that Harry wasn't throwing everything at it on a whim and that he was working towards a future with his family. If she managed that, it would be up to Harry to do the rest. She only hoped Panos hadn't moved any bulldozers in by then.

She hit 'send'.

THIRTY-SIX

Halloumi, Acharavi Beachfront

Imogen sat on the terrace of the restaurant looking at the patch of land that separated Halloumi from Avalon. It was strange. A perfectly good rectangular piece of ground no one seemed to be doing anything with apart from cutting the grass. Was it big enough to cut down on noise and distraction if Panos did build a nightclub next door? What would they do with it? Extend the restaurant terrace? They didn't really know what they were doing with what they had. And how much would it cost? If a restaurant could be obtained for just under a hundred thousand Euro then a piece of land couldn't be that expensive, could it?

She smiled at a woman passing by and waved her hand at her little girl who was kicking a small pink ball.

'*Kalimera*,' Imogen greeted.

'*Kalimera*,' the woman replied.

The little dark haired girl booted her ball and it shot off the road, rolling over onto the land next to Halloumi. Giggling, the girl trotted after it, running over the grass, curls bouncing as she bounded. Imogen straightened up. That's what it could be! A playground for children visiting the restaurant. It was big enough for a set of swings and a see-saw and maybe even a small playhouse. She really needed to find out who owned it.

Turning back to the beach she checked her watch. It was getting towards half past nine and she really didn't know what to do. Was Panos really going to turn up here at ten o' clock to take her somewhere she couldn't remember the name of on the other side of the island? And more importantly, if he *did* turn up, did she want to go? It seemed crazy to even think about spending time with a man who she considered to be at the crux of everything going wrong for her and Harry. But perhaps she should have thought harder about that last night, before he had pinned her against the palm tree and delivered a red hot kiss. Maybe this was her chance to discover more about him, find out just what sent his determination into overdrive.

Shivering, she hugged her hand around her cup of coffee, shifting in her chair. It was another picture-postcard morning.

'I'm not sure about the puddings,' Harry stated, rushing out. He sat down in the chair opposite, a piece of paper in his hand. 'I need to be sure before I get the menus printed.'

'What have we got on there at the moment?' Imogen asked, drawing her eyes away from the view. She remembered there was a fig tart she didn't have a figgy idea how to make and it had to be pastry, didn't it? Perhaps Elpida could give her more pastry lessons.

'A filo of fig… I really like the sound of that one. Elpida's going to make these for us to try later,' Harry said, grinning. 'Then we need to learn to make them ourselves.'

That was good. What wasn't good was the fact she hadn't heard from Janie after her text to her last night. Although she wasn't sure what she expected, she *had* expected something. She hadn't heard anything from the Wyatt Group either. She had chanced a call earlier, forgetting Greece was two hours ahead, and got the answerphone, but had been too apprehensive to leave any message. She didn't want to appear too eager. Maybe she would try later, when she'd practised the right thing to say in a professional, unhysterically excited way. Or perhaps she would just wait. Not push or tempt fate.

'Are you alright?' Harry asked. 'You're not still suffering from the wine last night are you? I'm not sure we'll be putting any of that on Halloumi's wine list.'

'Something lighter definitely,' she said, nodding her head. 'What other puddings?'

'Ice cream by the scoop,' Harry said. 'Greek style panna cotta with honey and a blackberry coulis and a white and dark chocolate roulade.'

For a brief moment she thought it sounded like the best pudding menu ever. Then she remembered she would be trying to cook it. She had made panna cotta before but it was years ago. BGD. Before Gino D'acampo.

'Don't forget *baklava*. It's pretty much a staple around here,' she said. Panos' hands in the mixing bowl came to mind. His olive skin, treating the filo pastry so delicately.

'You're right,' Harry replied.

A creaking came from above her head and her eyes went to the new pergola. 'Harry, is that safe?'

'I think so,' Harry answered. 'We tied it off to that palm tree until the final struts get put into position later today.'

The palm tree. Imogen swallowed as she remembered the night before. She could still feel that bristly bark in between her shoulder blades, Panos' hot mouth on hers. She looked at her watch again. She needed to say something to Harry if she really was going to disappear at ten o'clock.

'So, Immy, we need to get some cloths and candles and things for the tables. I thought you might like to do that. I think it needs a woman's touch.' He stopped, a look of panic in his eyes. 'I mean that in a completely non-sexist kind of way. I just wouldn't know where to start. Janie was always the one who made things nice in our house. And you've done such a great job with making the apartment look homely.'

Cloths and candles. They were bound to have those in the place Panos had suggested visiting. This was the excuse she was looking for. A legitimate reason for her to be out and about... if she decided to actually go with him. Because she was still caught between two versions of Panos – the one who was a ruthless property developer, set to break apart Harry's dream, and the one who was coated in Greek honey and she was doing unspeakable things with figs.

'Cloths and candles,' Harry repeated as if she hadn't heard him.

'You said that, Harry,' she said softly.

'I know, and you didn't answer.' He paused. 'And before you ask me... like Janie did the other day... yes, I am taking my tablets and I've got plenty to last me until I get signed up with a doctor here in Corfu.'

'I didn't say anything about your tablets,' she said.

'No but my shower gel was at a forty-five degree angle the other day. I'm guessing you felt the need to look.'

Now she felt truly awful. 'Sorry.'

'I'm not down at the moment, Immy. I'm happier than I've ever been. In a completely non bi-polar way.'

'I know,' she assured. 'Cloths and candles. I'll get on it today.'

'Sorry I am late.'

It was Risto's voice and he entered from the side of the terrace and joined them at the table. He looked slightly flustered, his face flushed and sweat already on his brow.

'I have flat tyre on my moped,' Risto announced. 'I have to walk here.'

'Oh no, that's a pain,' Harry stated.

'Yes, a pain,' Risto agreed. 'But I am here. What would you like me to do for today?'

'Well, I'm heading out…' Imogen started. 'For tablecloths and candles.'

'We need to put in the final struts of the pergola, then later you can help me with the shopping,' Harry said. 'We're going to fill Terry's van with ingredients for Halloumi's new menu.'

Out of the corner of her eyes Imogen saw the sleek, black Mercedes crawling along the road. She leapt up out of her chair. She didn't want Harry to know where she was going. Risto either. If Risto didn't know already.

'Right,' she stated. 'I'd better get a move on if I want to get the best tablecloths and candles Acharavi has ever seen.'

Both Harry and Risto were staring at her now. She swallowed, picking her bag up from the floor.

'So, I've got some cash and I've got my phone if you need to call me.' She began to back away across the terrace towards the exit, waving a hand. 'I'll send some photos,' she said.

She saw Risto look to Harry with confusion on his face before she turned and stepped down onto the road.

Panos had parked the car a little way away from the restaurant and turned up the air conditioning. It was already over thirty degrees and even he, accustomed to the climate, was feeling the heat. But was it really the outside temperature getting to him or the fact it was ten o'clock and there was every chance he was about to be stood up?

He took a breath and looked out across the sand, taking in a scene he was so familiar with. Sunbeds were filling up already – teenagers, young couples, families, all here for the same reason. To make the most of the sunshine and the long, unspoilt beach. *Unspoilt.* There was a lot to be said about that word. He wished his life had ended up being as unspoilt as the landscape every-thing had played out on. Maybe that was why he was intent on changing things, ripping away the goodness and replacing it with something fabricated yet profitable.

He tore his eyes away from Spiros the doughnut man, who was starting his rounds on the beach. The taste of those sugar-coated delights flooded his mouth along with the memories that went with them. He and Risto building speedboats in the sand. His mother reading, looking up from her book now and then and smiling as she watched them run, chasing each other through the surf. His father, building a castle with buckets of sand, decorating the turrets with weed, shells and driftwood, calling his mother *prigkipissa. Princess.*

Why had things gone so wrong? Why had Christos wanted the world for them when home would have been enough? He winced, his gut twisting. Before the ruination of his parents' marriage and his father's hotel chain he had loved this place just the way it was. Had his father's actions poisoned that feeling permanently? Or could there be an antidote?

Suddenly the door of the car opened and hot air swept in along with the delicious form of Imogen Charlton. He watched her drop down into the seat in another thigh-skimming summer dress, this time in light blue.

'Drive!' she announced like they were running from the law, ducking down into the leather seat. 'I don't think anyone saw you.'

He turned to her. 'This is a problem for you?'

'Yes! Of course it is! You're the enemy,' she reminded him.

'Then we will go,' Panos said. 'Before anyone can ask any-thing of either of us.'

'Is it far?' Imogen asked as he pulled the car away.

'About thirty minutes,' he replied. 'You are OK with roads in Corfu?'

'What does that mean? They can't all be like the ones from the airport, can they?'

He laughed. 'You should tighten your seatbelt.'

THIRTY-SEVEN

Arillas

Panos hadn't been wrong. The road to the other side of the island was *worse* than the run up from Corfu airport. Even in this elite vehicle she had been thrown from one side of the seat to the other as they traversed hills that required every bit of the driver's experience as well as car agility. However, despite having to hold on for dear life, the views had been spectacular.

Lush green farmland gave way to small villages all unique in their appearance – whitewashed and terracotta walls, wooden shutters in blue, white and sage. Tiled roofs, tin roofs, roofs with most of the bits missing, church bell towers and an explosion of blooms surrounding everything – red and purple bougainvillea, primrose and fuchsia.

Now they were meandering through a more populated area, like a smaller version of Acharavi but with the winding streets of a traditional village.

'No more mountains?' Imogen asked, sitting straight in her seat and taking in her surroundings.

'No more mountains,' he responded. 'We are almost there.'

And then he performed an emergency stop, sending Imogen shooting forward, her arms reaching out and bracing herself against the dashboard.

'Sorry,' he apologised. 'I was not expecting that.'

Just in front of where he had stopped the car a man was ushering half a dozen chickens across the road. *Chickens* again. Imogen shook her head and smiled.

The man waved a hand to them as he steered his flock to the other side but she could see the animals in the road weren't the only reason they'd had to halt. Right ahead of them were barriers and, in front of those and trickling down the street, as far as the eye could see, were little wooden stalls.

'This must be the community market,' Panos said, looking out of the windscreen.

'Is this what you've come here for? What Alejandro Kalas talked about last night?'

Panos let out a heavy sigh. 'If I am really honest, I do not know why I am here, Imogen.'

She swallowed heavily as she regarded his perfect profile.

He smiled then, lightening the moment. 'But I do know we should find somewhere to park the car,' he stated.

He had reversed the car back the way they'd come and parked it on the side of the road. Now they were walking down the street towards the bustling market.

He was wearing nicely fitting jeans and a blue t-shirt that showed off every perfect physical attribute he possessed. And he possessed plenty. She had never seen him dress in anything but a suit. He looked different, more relaxed now the leather shoes had been replaced with Vans. Perhaps their differences could be set aside for one day. If the two sides in World War One managed an amiable game of football together she could manage this.

'Have you been here before?' she asked, keeping pace beside him as the sun beat down on her shoulders.

'A long time ago,' he answered.

'For business or pleasure?'

'Both.'

'It's pretty,' she stated, her eyes going to the hanging baskets of flowers suspended from the porches of the houses and eateries they walked past. 'Traditional.'

'Yes,' he said, nodding. 'Tradition appears to still be important around here.'

'It *is* important though, isn't it?' Imogen said. 'Tradition is all about people's memories. And you have to admit... where would we be without memories?'

Her thoughts went to her windowsill of mementoes from her father back home. The shells, the wind chime from Mexico, the lotus blossom-painted fan from Japan, a hot-pink ink pen embossed with *Shangri-La, Thailand*. If she didn't have the memories she would lose the connection.

'Not all memories are happy ones,' Panos pointed out.

'No,' she agreed. 'They're not. But good or bad, memories and traditions shape who you are.'

He stopped and turned to her. 'You really believe this?'

'Yes,' she answered confidently. 'Don't you?'

He shook his head vigorously. 'Actually, I refuse to believe it.'

'Well, that's just silly.'

'Silly?'

'Yes,' she continued. 'Everything that happens to us changes us in some small way.' She paused for a second. 'Like that car journey we just had. I will never complain about the potholes in the UK ever again.'

She saw a smile begin at the corners of his mouth. 'Your life changed forever in a thirty-minute journey,' he said.

'Yes,' she said nodding.

'So,' he began. 'Are we both to be changed by our visit to the community market today?'

His eyes were on hers again and she could feel the flush heating up her cheeks. She smiled at him. 'I'm here with an open mind… and a need for candles and tablecloths.'

He returned her smile. 'Then let us see what happens.'

Panos watched her looking at everything in awe. He had forgotten how enchanting Arillas was and today, with these beautifully carved stalls weaving down the road towards the beachfront, filled with local wares and produce, it was as if it had been crafted for a movie set. This was traditional Greece in all its glory with the modern take Alejandro Kalas had talked about.

'*Kalimera!*' a Greek man greeted as they approached his stall.

'What is this?' Imogen asked, her question directed to the man and Panos at the same time.

Panos smiled at her and asked the stallholder in Greek if they could try some. The man nodded and Panos picked up one of the little glass bottles filled with orange liquid. He poured a measure into two small plastic shot glasses and offered one to Imogen. He watched her take it rather tentatively and put it to her nose.

'What is it?' she asked again.

'You need to know what this is before you try it?' he asked. 'Where is your sense of adventure?'

'Just tell me if it's alcoholic before I burn the lining of my throat.'

'Alcoholic, yes. It is kumquat,' Panos answered. 'In Chinese this means "little orange". In Corfu this is a traditional product. You will not find this in any other area of Greece.'

'*Traditional*,' Imogen said, smiling at him.

'I like this one,' Panos admitted.

'Ready?' Imogen asked, raising the glass to her mouth.

'No, no, stop,' Panos said, taking hold of her hand. 'It is not a shot,' he stated. 'Take a small sip, slowly... Let the flavour travel over your taste buds and then down your throat.'

Her eyes were on his and that sharp stab of lust was currently on guard and ready to start fencing in his gut. He watched her lips touch the rim, a small amount of the tangerine-coloured liquid spilling out into her mouth. He took a sip of his own drink, all the while watching for her reaction.

She took a healthy swig and her face lit up. 'That's gorgeous,' she announced. She put the cup to her mouth again, sipping more. 'It's like liquid sunshine.'

Liquid sunshine. His mother had called it 'sunshine in a bottle'. She'd loved the drink and had made flagons of it herself. It was a pity Christos had treated it like his own personal store of moonshine near the end. He shook away the memory.

'I love it,' Imogen said, smiling at the stallholder. 'What's this?' she asked. 'Is it jam?'

Panos translated her words to the Greek and the man nodded and said something in reply.

'He said it is more of a compote. To be served as part of a dessert or simply on bread.'

She dragged the strap of her handbag off her shoulder and began rifling through the contents.

'This is what Harry's menu was missing for the desserts,' she said. 'This is just what he needs.'

'What are you doing?' Panos asked her.

'Looking for my purse. I know I have it.'

'How many do you need?' Panos inquired.

'I guess it depends how many puddings we're going to sell.' She blinked, looking at the jars on the stall. 'We still have no idea if anyone is actually going to come.'

Panos spoke in Greek to the stallholder, who immediately began collating jars together, chatting excitedly.

'How many did you say?' Imogen asked.

'He said he has just over fifty jars left and about thirty bottles of liqueur,' Panos said. 'I said I would buy them all.'

'What? That's too many, isn't it? I mean, what if Harry doesn't like the idea? I was going to buy a couple and see how it went. I don't know if I have enough to pay for that much.'

He smiled, enjoying her animation, the flustered talking and the way a few stray strands of blonde hair were flying about her face.

'Imogen,' he spoke. 'I will pay for these.'

She stopped still. 'And why would you do that? Isn't it your hope that our restaurant doesn't do well so you can force Harry to sell?'

He didn't answer straight away.

'That isn't what I want,' he insisted softly, surprising himself. He recomposed. 'I thought we were putting our differences aside like eggs.' He looked directly at her. 'I want to buy them for you, no hidden agenda.' He smiled, then turned to the stallholder, speaking in Greek again before handing over a stash of Euro notes to the man.

He then took hold of Imogen's arm and manoeuvred her away from the stall. 'Things do not always have to be so clear cut,' he stated. 'There is more than right and wrong. There is "not right now" or "not quite yet".'

'You're reconsidering your assault on the seafront?' Imogen asked tentatively.

'I am always open to new directions,' he said, his eyes marking hers.

He watched her swallow, giving away her reaction. He wanted to slip his arms around her waist and pull her against him.

'Is that why you've brought me here? To explore a new direction?' she asked.

Was she being deliberately provocative? It was certainly having that effect. He was imagining just how a kiss would taste if he stole one now. The tender skin of her lips coupling with the sweetness of the kumquat liqueur.

'To explore something with you,' he whispered, his body leaning toward her instinctively. He reached out to touch her cheek.

The blast from a trumpet broke the atmosphere and a trio of musicians appeared in front of them, starting to play a jaunty tune. He put his hand down and stilled, continuing to look into her eyes. Smiling, he took a step forward. 'Come,' he encouraged. 'I can smell *gyros*.'

THIRTY-EIGHT

They wound their way down the long road, stopping at almost every stall to see what was for sale. To Imogen the whole ambience felt like a carnival. She sensed the same feeling of happiness and community spirit she'd experienced as a child. She and Harry had been part of the Amesbury Carnival when they'd lived in Wiltshire. Both on their school float dressed in outfits from the 1950s, their father was home for the weekend and her mum had made the costumes: a teddy-boy suit for Harry and a bright pink top and circular blue skirt with music notes stitched on it for her. She'd loved the way the skirt flared out when she danced. They'd travelled on the back of an Amesbury Transport trailer from the sports centre, jiving to Elvis and Bill Haley. A circuit around the town and they'd ended up at the recreation ground. The lush, green park had been covered in stalls – guess the name of the bear, tombolas, toys to buy, toffee apples and homemade cakes. She had saved her pocket money all year to spend at the carnival. Here, in Arillas' market, it was like reliving those joyous moments, when her family had been all together.

'There are candles,' she said, looking to Panos. 'I need to get some.'

She stepped across the street to the stall she'd spotted and began to look at what was on offer.

'*Kalimera*,' she greeted the lady behind the counter.

'*Kalimera*,' she replied. 'English, yes?'

Imogen smiled. 'Is it that obvious?'

The woman smiled. 'It is nice you try to speak Greek.'

Imogen picked up a pillar candle and held it to her nose. A heavy waft of mint and lavender hit her senses.

'That's nice,' she remarked, setting it down. 'What other fragrances do you do?'

'Cinnamon and apple, gingerbread, olive and camomile, honey and lemon...'

'Oh, honey and lemon,' Imogen said excitedly. 'Could I smell that one?'

'Of course,' the lady said. 'Would you like pillar candles, votives or tea lights?'

'Tea lights, I think.'

Imogen watched her fetch a box before offering it out to her. She lifted it to her nostrils and the scent filled her mind as well as her nose. It was a fresh hit of citrus coupled with the warm, comforting sweet smell of fresh honey.

'That's so...' Imogen stated. She didn't have the words for how good it smelled. She turned to Panos and gave the box over to him. 'Tell me what you think.'

She watched as he took the box and lifted its open flap to his nose. He closed his eyes and inhaled.

As the combination of honey and lemon hit him he was plunged back to a moment in time. His mother screaming for help, his father lying on the floor of the lounge. Pulled from the honey cake and fresh lemonade he was enjoying under the shade of the olive tree in their garden by his mother's cries. He'd dropped his plate and run but there was nothing he could do. It had been too late.

He opened his eyes and passed the box back to Imogen. 'How about the olive and camomile?' he suggested. 'Not too overpowering.'

'Don't you like this one?' she asked.

He shook his head but recovered quickly. 'It is not to my taste. But, remember, as you keep telling me, it is not my restaurant.'

She smiled then. 'No,' she agreed. 'It isn't.' She handed the box back to lady. 'Thank you. Can we come back a little later?'

'Of course. No problem.'

Had she caught his reaction to the scent? The last thing he wanted to do was talk about it. But that's what tradition and community did, wasn't it? Brought back memories. Good and bad. Just like Imogen had said.

'I think I'm ready for that *gyros* now,' she said, looking up at him.

Gyros was the ultimate kebab. Gorgeous strips of meat stuffed into a pitta bread with fresh lettuce, tomato and cucumber drizzled in chilli sauce or *tzatziki*.

Imogen had plumped for the *tzatziki* and it was drizzling down her chin as they walked along the promenade. She followed Panos' lead and stepped down onto the pine-coloured sand. The ocean, rumbling toward shore in hefty waves for a July day, was on their right, skirted by a craggy headland hanging out into the sea. Its crumbling, pale rocks, coated on top by a slice of greenery, reminded Imogen of a cake. Layers and layers of biscuit-coloured stone made up the sponge, topped with spinach-hued shrubbery as the icing. The flat terrain of the beach was the perfect contrast to the rugged rock jutting out across it.

'This is so good,' she remarked to Panos, a slight breeze blowing through her hair.

He had been quiet since he'd smelled the candles. She had watched his expression as he breathed in the lemon-and-honey scent and she had seen something shift. The movement of his eyes under heavy lids had been like he was reliving something. He'd calmly said he wasn't keen on the fragrance but she thought there was probably more to it than that.

'I miss this,' he admitted. 'Corfu still makes the best *gyros*.'

'Where do you usually live?' she asked. 'The address on that business card of yours?'

'Yes, Rethymnon, Crete,' he answered. 'I have a villa there.'

'You live alone?' She grimaced slightly at her own question and felt the need to say more. 'I mean, Greeks all have big families, right?'

'I live alone,' he said.

'You've been married?'

He shook his head. 'No.'

'So you don't have any children or anything?'

'No,' he answered. 'Do you? Have children?'

Imogen smiled. 'Only Harry. He's quite enough at the moment.'

'But one day you will,' Panos said with confidence.

She looked up at him, watching him eat his *gyros*. The chiselled jaw moving with every chewing motion, his dark hair falling forward a little. There was no denying the fact she found him ridiculously attractive, more attractive than she'd found anyone in… Had it really been years? She swallowed as a remnant of *tzatziki* soured her throat. This was why she was acting like this – letting a man she didn't know very well kiss her, coming here, high on the romance and beauty of this island. She was horribly out of practice.

'Do you think you will have children?' she asked him. 'You know, one day, in the future?' A blush hit her cheeks as she thought about *him* in the act of making children. *With her.*

'Children complicate things,' he stated.

She'd barely managed to imagine what their children might look like when the bubble burst. 'What do you mean?'

'I work hard running my business,' he reminded. 'There is no time for children.'

'But... you won't work forever. Will you?'

His eyes met hers. 'You have just bought a restaurant,' he said. 'To make this a success you are going to have to spend most of your life running it.'

'*I* haven't bought it,' she reminded. 'Harry has.'

'And you are here with him.'

'Only for a few weeks,' she stated. 'A little less than two actually.'

'What?'

She willed moisture into her mouth as reality hit. 'I have a job at home and a house. My mum and Janie wanted me to come here to make sure Harry realised what a mistake he was making and get him to come home,' she said.

'And now?' Panos asked.

'And now I know I'm going to help him open it up but beyond that... Corfu was never in my life plans.'

'What job do you have?'

Thoughts of gut-buster breakfasts, Old Joe coughing and Mrs Green's bag of wool flashed into her mind. 'I'm in catering.'

'A restaurant,' he said. 'So, it is *you* that plans a chain. UK, Greece, where next?'

She shook her head, laughing. 'No, it's not like that at all.' It was time to come clean about her food and catering knowledge. 'I'm just a waitress. I mean I *can* cook. I *used* to cook, for fun... for friends... but I haven't done anything for ages.'

'Just a waitress,' he said, shaking his head. 'Imogen, in my experience they are some of the hardest-working people there are.'

'I *do* work hard,' she admitted. 'And I'm studying for an NVQ, a qualification in hospitality.' She pulled a piece of meat from her pitta bread and slipped it into her mouth. 'I hoped a long time ago to get into the hotel business. I applied a few months ago to the Wyatt Hotel Group. For one of their training programmes, you know, starting at the bottom and working my way up.'

'Hotels,' Panos breathed, as if the word was dirty.

'My dad wasn't an entrepreneur like your father. But all his stories about the places he stayed, the Egyptian cotton and the stargazer lilies, the miniature soaps and room service… I thought working somewhere like that would be the best job in the world.' She smiled. 'Plus there's the pens.'

'The pens?' He looked quizzical.

'My dad used to bring me a hotel pen from every place he stayed. I have hundreds of them,' Imogen admitted. She scooped her free hand into her yellow handbag and began to filter through the contents. Within seconds she was pulling out ballpoint after ballpoint. 'This one's from Tunisia. See, it has the Tunisian flag and the coat of arms.' She passed it to Panos and delved in for another. 'This one is one of my favourites. The Metropole Hotel in Brussels, Belgium. It's chocolate-coloured with gold lettering. It makes me think of truffles,' she admitted. 'Sometimes I can even smell them.'

He smiled, shaking his head as he took the pen from her hand and looked at it.

'I know they're just pens and it's a bit silly to keep them all like trophies but… my dad worked all the time so we could have a better life and really all we wanted was more time with him.'

He nodded, passing back the pens to her. 'I can relate to that.'

'Which is why you can't think about sharing your life with children,' Imogen guessed. 'Because you don't want to put them in the position you were in, missing your father when he was running hotels.'

He sighed. 'It isn't about sharing my life with children. It's sharing anything with anybody.'

'I see,' she stated, nodding her head. 'So you think it would be easier to tear up the town and alienate everyone around you than try and make a reconnection?'

Panos stepped up onto the concrete groyne that protruded out into the ocean and held out his hand to her. She accepted it and, with a lunge forward, joined him on the structure. There were a few fisherman casting their rods out into the ocean, the sea lapping back and forth against the bricks.

'Tearing down the town was always on my mind,' he admitted. 'But I really came to see my grandmother.'

The fact that he had admitted there was sentiment involved weighed heavy. What was he doing sharing that fact with Imogen when he barely wanted to share it with his own conscience?

He walked on, looking into the water breaking at the base of the jetty. 'I haven't been back to Corfu for a while.' He inhaled the salty air. 'I did not know she had given up the restaurant.'

'You didn't even know it was for sale?' Imogen asked him.

'No.' His eyes went to the rocky islands out in the sea. 'But that was *my* fault, not hers. I am not good at keeping in touch.'

'You're too busy working,' Imogen said. 'I'm sensing a theme here.'

'Yes,' he agreed.

'So, what about your mother? Do you keep in touch with her at all? Or, what about brothers and sisters?'

It was an innocent question he should have known was coming. He shook his head again. 'No, no brothers or sisters.' Was that answer going to be enough for her?

'But you're close to Risto?'

'Yes, he was always like a brother to me.'

'Was?'

'I have not kept in touch with anyone, Imogen.' He sighed. 'And I should have. Risto has been out of work for a long time. I didn't realise Corfu was feeling the burn of the desperate times in Greece like on the mainland.'

A silence fell between them as they reached the bench at the end of the breakwater, a chunky wooden seat set into the stone, facing the water.

'So, when did you leave? How old were you when you started your business?' Imogen asked, moving to sit down.

'Twenty,' he stated. 'I left Corfu when I was seventeen, determined to make a success of my life.' He sat next to her, his eyes still directed at the sea and the sunlight making the crests of the waves look like strings of bright diamonds. 'I moved from Rhodes to Crete, working bars and clubs and going from barman to bookkeeper. Then one day I met a man who changed my life.'

'Who?'

'His name was Yiannis and he owned a property business in Crete. He taught me everything I know about business.'

Yiannis had been his mentor and father figure. He had taken Panos under his wing and given him the benefit of all his experience in a working masterclass. The man had opened up his business brain and his home to an eighteen-year-old looking to expand his horizons and make the best of himself.

'I worked with Yiannis for two years and then it was time for me to stand on my own two feet.' He let a hand rub at the wood of the bench. 'I set up my own business, using the skills Yiannis taught me.'

'He sounds like a lovely man who was very generous with his time.'

'He was. I owe him everything.'

'Do you keep in touch with him?' Imogen asked, a smile on her lips.

He smiled back. 'When we are both not too busy working.'

'You think you have forever,' Imogen said. 'That's the real problem. My mum went through a lot when my dad died. Suddenly working two jobs, making sure we had everything we needed for school, then college for Harry… I missed my dad terribly but practically, physically and emotionally, she was the one who always had to be there for us. And she was.'

He swallowed. He hadn't given his mother much of a chance to be there for him. He had run away. Perhaps he should have thought more about being there for her instead of leaving Elpida to pick up the pieces.

'Imogen, I have never been in this position before,' Panos said, reaching for her hand. Light as a feather, he spiralled a figure of eight over her skin. His touch delivered sensuous sparks of longing shooting around her body in every which way.

'What position?' She swallowed heavily, wondering what was coming next.

'A position where I do not know what I am doing or where I am going.'

She didn't answer, sensing there was more to come.

'I came back here to see my grandmother, rip up the restaurant and make my world work, in Acharavi.' He took his hand away from hers and swept it through his hair. 'Then I got here and nothing was how it should be.'

She watched him wet his lips, his brow showing frustration.

'Or rather, nothing was how I wanted it to be,' he finished.

She smiled. 'It sounds eerily similar to the situation I'm in.'

He didn't smile. He just carried on looking at her. Those dark sultana-coloured eyes like an intense double-hit espresso. 'And then there is you.'

Her heart and stomach moved in unison, like Tom Daley and his diving partner on the high board, leaping up before the plunge.

'What am I going to do about you?' he whispered eventually.

He made it sound both like a threat and a promise. She shivered, the nearness of their bodies, sitting close together on the wooden bench in the middle of the sea, suddenly became something she couldn't ignore.

'You are standing in my way over the development plans. You are someone I should be going up against, not someone I want to…'

The look he was giving her finished the sentence for him. Inside she quaked a little.

'You say you are leaving in a week or so,' he spoke softly. 'And I also, do not know how long I can stay here but…'

She thought she knew what he was saying. She felt it inside herself too

He was gazing at her, no words coming from him, just the warmth of his breath mixing with the humid air as their heads held still just centimetres away from touching.

She should say something. Words were there, swimming around in her brain. Words like *complication*, *inappropriate*, *Harry* and a Greek–Cypriot cheese – *Halloumi.* But before she could say anything his mouth was on hers and her hands were smoothing the rough bristle on his jaw as she pulled him deeper.

He tasted of the kumquat liqueur and smelled of a mix of sea salt, lemon and hot man and she just wanted more of it. Lacing her fingers through his thick black hair she pressed her body against his.

He broke the kiss, breathing hard, his eyes not leaving hers. 'What you do to me,' he whispered.

His accented voice made her shiver even with the hot sun on her back. 'I don't know what to say to that,' she admitted.

'Say you understand some of what is happening between us. That this is not just me.'

She smiled at this soft declaration. 'It isn't just you. But I'm not sure I understand it either.'

He leant a little forward, letting his forehead rest against hers, still matching her gaze. 'I understand only that I am here,' he said. 'Here on the island I have tried so hard to forget.' He put a finger to her lips. 'And there is nowhere else I would rather be.' He smoothed the skin of her bottom lip with his finger then lowered his mouth to hers again.

She broke away. 'Panos, let's make a promise not to talk about the beachfront here.' She gazed at him, hopeful.

He nodded. 'No beachfront talk… No words of war or any more business speak.' He took her face in his hands. 'Let us always have Arillas, Imogen. This afternoon,' he breathed. 'Just for us.'

She reached up, linking her arms around his neck and pulled him into her. 'Arillas,' she repeated. 'Just for us.'

THIRTY-NINE

'You should get the candles,' Panos stated.

He had been watching her for the last few minutes, bouncing a little on her feet as they listened to the quartet of musicians. The sun was shining and restaurants had small stalls outside their premises offering free samples to try to entice diners in for main meals. The fragrance of thyme, bay leaves and mint, Greek specialities of *dolmades*, *moussaka* and parcels of *tiropita* was all along the promenade, tourists and locals mingling together. The community atmosphere, collective joy and smiling faces were something he hadn't expected in a resort he had always considered a little sleepy.

'What?' Imogen asked above the music.

'The candles,' Panos repeated. 'The ones you liked.'

'The ones you didn't?'

She *had* noticed. It was just a smell. He shouldn't have let it provoke such a reaction. He wasn't the child watching his family crumble around him any longer. He had to try to stop focussing on the last few years of his father's life as if that was all there ever was. It might have been the part that hurt the most but it wasn't the whole story.

There was a lot to like about Arillas today. The lively market doing good business, the restaurants full, the spirit of Greece coming to the fore around every corner. *Imogen*. Holding her against him. Without thinking he draped his arm over her shoulder, drawing her back towards him.

He felt her weight tip back slightly and suddenly he re-alised what he was feeling. *Relaxation*. He was relaxed. More laid back than he'd been for… he wanted to say months but in reality it was probably years. A feeling stung him. A worry that in an hour or so he would have to leave this bubble. And what came after that? He needed to call his lawyer about the deal with Tomas' and he needed to speak to Lafi about the purchase of Avalon. Imogen would be back on the other side of the fence with his grandmother, both of them hating what he was doing.

Imogen could feel Panos' warm, firm chest against her back and she settled herself, loving the way she slotted into the space. His fingers were gently manipulating the skin at her clavicle, spreading tingles of heat over her shoulders and down through her whole torso. Here she was, in a foreign land, with a man she had been battling with since she got here, in his arms, wanting to be there and wishing never to leave. But, when reality bit and they returned to Acharavi, it couldn't be like this. Panos was going to become the hard, consummate businessman as soon as he was back in another expensive suit. And she was going to be on the opposing side, making sure his plans didn't ruin Harry's restaurant.

Imogen turned suddenly, spinning around, looking up at him and studying his features. As clichéd as it sounded, he was that sculpted Achilles statue she'd seen in Spiros the shopkeep-er's shop. Every line and curve was perfection. Her fingers flexed on the solidity of his chest wall, knowing what lay beneath felt equally appealing.

He took her face in his long-fingered hands and gave her a kiss that stole the air from her. How could she resist? How could she not want to taste him again, here, in this buzzing, vibrant village full of laughter and song against a backdrop of azure sky, pale sand and turquoise sea?

She dragged her lips away and spoke his name. 'Panos.'

'Pan*o*,' he corrected. 'We are intimate now.'

She swallowed at the way he said 'intimate'. He'd made it sound like she was standing naked in front of him.

'Pano, we can't go back to Acharavi and be...' She took a breath. 'Intimate.' She cursed herself for using that word again.

'Where *can* we go to be... intimate?' He was smiling now, his full, delicious lips curving up at the corners and one eyebrow raised as he teased her.

'I need to focus on the restaurant. I'm already distracted with fighting your plans, I can't also be distracted by your...' She struggled to find an appropriate word. 'By your...'

'By my what, Imogen?' he asked, still teasing.

'By you,' she finished simply.

'I was hoping for so much more.'

Was this what she wanted? To end this frisson of lust before it became something she craved? Already she was staring at those lips and wanting to feel them claim her mouth again.

'I understand,' he answered finally.

'You do,' Imogen said, her tone a mixture of pleased and disappointed.

He nodded. 'There is only one way to move forward.'

'Yes,' she agreed.

'We must be like eggs. Just like you said.' He looked at her seriously. 'We must keep us... this... completely separate from my tearing down of the town,' he stated.

'What?' That wasn't the answer she had been expecting.

'You will keep being with me and, when we are together, we will not discuss my plans for redevelopment in Acharavi. Just like we promised to do here today. A lot of people together do not discuss their business.'

'Like who?'

'Do you think my grandparents discussed everything they do?' He smiled. 'For many years my grandfather did not know Elpida smoked. And Elpida also did not know that my grandfather had an account at Ebo's Bar.'

Imogen smiled. 'What are you trying to demonstrate?'

'Just that every relationship has some secrets.'

'But smoking and drinking isn't big stuff like potentially ruining my brother's dream. And I don't like secrets between people.' Imogen sighed.

He smiled, grazing his fingers down her cheek before finally cupping her jaw. 'You think we have nothing else to talk about but the beachfront at Acharavi?' He looked into her eyes. 'I think you are wrong.'

'But what if I'm not wrong?'

'Then we will find out soon enough,' he stated.

She watched him take a deep breath. 'I only want you to be Imogen with me. Fiery… beautiful… good Imogen.'

'You've made me sound like a cross between a nun and a pole dancer.'

'I think I would like to see that.' He smiled. 'I've always had a curiosity about nuns.'

She laughed. 'A little too much information there I think.'

He stilled, his fingers still touching her cheek. 'After today…' His gaze went to the stalls and crowds around them. 'Well, it might not fit with my plans for the future… but I understand *why* Alejandro Kalas thinks a community market could work in Acharavi.'

Was he really able to think outside his box full of wrecking balls and nightclubs? She held in her joy and waited to see if he would continue.

'This is how Corfu used to be, Imogen,' he admitted. 'Only better.' He sighed. 'It is like everyone here has finally woken up to the financial crisis and decided to tackle it head on.'

She nodded. 'They are using the skills they already have, the products they already make and displaying it with a new unashamed joy and… passion.'

'And it is a little contagious, no?' he whispered, lowering his face to hers once more.

As his mouth neared hers she was powerless to resist. After everything she'd said about their inappropriate match she just couldn't seem to draw herself away from him, nor did she want to. She touched his lips first, wanting to leave him in no doubt of her feelings. Then she let him deepen the kiss, enjoying the smooth dance of his tongue. Finally he ended the connection, but held his mouth still close, dropping tiny kisses on her bottom lip. And then he smiled and whispered, 'I know just the place to get your tablecloths.'

FORTY

Perethia

Imogen had sent Janie another text from Arillas with two photo attachments. One was of the stalls full of Greek produce she knew would poke at Janie's shopping and craft addictions and one of the view from the beach – more clear water, cornflower-blue sky and sizzling sun. She had accompanied it with a simple 'wish you were here'.

She checked her phone as the car slowed. No reply from Janie and no new emails from the Wyatt Hotel Group or anyone else.

Panos finally stopped the car outside a low-rise building that, to Imogen, looked like nothing more than a pile of bricks. Grey, ancient bricks, all in different shapes and sizes, made up a dwelling that looked only habitable to animals. There was a patch of tough-looking grass at the front of the house on which a mix of a dozen or so chickens and black turkeys were roaming and surrounding the shack were olive trees heavy with fruit and goats who all seemed to have stopped what they were doing to survey the car.

'What is this place?' Imogen asked.

He smiled. 'This is where Mrs Pelekas lives.'

'Who's Mrs Pelekas?'

'Someone who is most likely to hit me with her rolling pin the second she sets her sights on me.'

'Why? Did you try and tear down her house too? Because as much as I hate the idea of ripping up the beachfront of Acharavi I think anything done here would be a vast improvement.'

'Come,' Panos encouraged. 'With some luck she will have been baking.' He opened the door of the car and stepped out.

The heat of the afternoon and a whole raft of memories hit him as he got out of the Mercedes and observed the Pelekas house. It hadn't changed a bit since he was seven or eight, stealing lemons and oranges, teasing the goats and chickens with Risto. The cousin he'd all but abandoned, left grief-stricken with a loss much greater than Panos' own. He owed Risto something. Much more than he'd given him since he'd arrived back in Corfu. The young man could do better than working at a restaurant Panos was intent on closing down. He needed to think a little harder about where he could fit in in Dimitriou Enterprises.

He looked over at Imogen stepping over the rocky ground to join him.

'I used to come here when I was a child,' he said, smiling. 'I used to steal the fruit. Then Mrs Pelekas would chase me with a broom or whatever was close to hand.'

Imogen shook her head. 'You bad, bad boy.'

He laughed. 'I more than paid for it when she caught me.'

'I'm pleased to hear it.'

The wooden door, red paint peeling from it, creaked ajar.

Emerging from the shadowy interior and into the bright sunlight came an old woman. Her back was bent over so much it looked like a table top and she leaned all her weight on a hefty-looking wooden stick. Thinning white hair, a black kerchief over half of it, wearing a grey and white geometric printed dress, a long black cardigan draped around her small body.

Panos swallowed. He had imagined Mrs Pelekas would look unchanged. Still the stern, upright, strong woman who had chased him across the hills of her land. She had aged so much she was almost unrecognisable.

She spoke in Greek, her eyes moving to Imogen then him, then back again. 'What do you want?'

'Mrs Pelekas, it is me, Panos Dimitriou,' he responded in his native tongue.

The woman began slowly hobbling forward, using her stick to gain ground. Finally, no more than a metre away from him, she stopped and craned her neck as if to get a better view. He maintained his stance, her gaze penetrating, making him feel like a small boy again.

She spoke, asking him if he had come back to be chased, her voice full of emotion. He laughed then, shaking his head as she took both his hands, the stick falling to the floor as she wobbled on her feet.

'What did she say?' Imogen whispered.

Panos looked to her then, smiling. 'She said she now sees who I am and asked if I'd come to be chased around the garden again.'

The gnarled fingers gripped his firmly and he gathered the woman into his arms, laughing as she patted him on the back with all the force he remembered from his youth. Then suddenly she pulled away, her focus going to Imogen. Panos retrieved her stick from the ground and gave it back to her.

Mrs Pelekas spoke. 'Is this your wife?'

His eyes went to Imogen, whose weight was shifting on her sandals in the dust of Mrs Pelekas' track, blue eyes moving back and forth, a little unease in her expression. She was so beautiful.

Mrs Pelekas repeated her question even louder until Panos was forced to make a response. He shook his head. 'No.'

The old lady made a frustrated noise then beckoned with her free hand, turning in a semi-circle and leading the way back towards her house.

'Come on, I can smell *baklava* at the very least,' Panos said to Imogen.

'What did she say to you?' she asked, stepping up to him.

Panos swallowed. 'She asked if you were my wife.'

Imogen smiled, taking a step away from him. 'She obviously remembers the boy,' she said. 'Otherwise she would know the man is married to his job.'

He nodded, smiling as he fell into step behind her. 'Bravo, Imogen. Very good.'

Mrs Pelekas' house was like Mary Poppins' carpet bag – small on the outside and cavernous within. The front door led into a snug with a wooden table and chairs, a rocking chair and a kitchen area dominated by a giant stove. But off this central atrium were three different corridors leading to assorted rooms. Two were bedrooms, one full of fabrics and a large old-fashioned sewing machine complete with spinning wheel, a fourth was a bathroom and a fifth seemed to be inhabited by some of the goats, chickens and turkeys. Mrs Pelekas insisted on giving her the tour while she set Panos to work on making Greek tea.

All the way round, the little old lady chatted away in Greek and Imogen hadn't understood a word.

Panos was just filling a floral teapot with hot water from a brass-bottomed traditional kettle when they re-entered. Imogen stood while Mrs Pelekas moved towards the oven and began opening the door, grabbing an oven glove then pulling out a tray of biscuits.

The woman looked to Imogen, speaking quickly.

'She says you need to eat at least two of these because to her you look too thin,' Panos translated.

Imogen smiled. 'Do all Greek ladies think everyone is thin? They do look lovely. What are they?'

'*Ergolavi*,' Panos answered. 'Greek cookies.'

Imogen pulled up a chair in front of the thick stone window-sill and looked out at the garden. From this position you could see right down the valley through wooded copses and Corfiot flowers, the promise of sea in the distance if she turned her head a little. The sun was hitting every section of the outside area but this room, with its thick, concrete walls, was a little piece of cool heaven.

Mrs Pelekas manoeuvred herself into the seat next to Imogen and slid the plate of cookies to her, speaking in Greek.

'Cookies and tea,' Panos said, pouring the liquid into cups. 'It's Greek mountain tea.'

'And how does that differ to tea that isn't from the Greek mountains?' Imogen asked.

'It's made from ironwort plants,' Panos explained. 'It has healing properties.'

Imogen laughed. 'It *claims* to have, you mean.'

'It is true,' he insisted. 'Colds, boosting your immune system, lessening the red of your bites.'

The hand that wasn't holding the cookie went to her face then. She had almost forgotten she still looked like Lemmy from Motorhead. Mrs Pelekas was watching her, her eyes darting back and forth from Imogen to the cookie in her hand. She took a bite and the biscuit just melted in her mouth. A divine mix of soft dough and honey hit her taste buds.

'Oh… my goodness, these are good,' Imogen said. 'Sorry, I shouldn't have spoken with my mouth full.'

Panos spoke to Mrs Pelekas in Greek and she began rocking backward and forward on her seat, laughing out loud before slamming a hand down onto the table.

'Tell her the biscuits are delicious,' Imogen urged.

After tea, Panos started bartering for tablecloths. Mrs Pelekas had disappeared down the corridor that led to her sewing room and come back with an arm piled high with fabric. She placed the cloths down on the cleared table and picked one up, showing the design to Imogen.

'She said this one has embroidered into it some of the flowers of Corfu. The flower of the fig, the anemone, honesty...' Panos translated. 'Love-in-a-mist.' He cleared his throat. 'The poppy.'

'She did this all herself? It must have taken hours.'

Panos conferred with Mrs Pelekas. 'Months, apparently, in the winter of 2005.' He smiled. 'She has a good memory.'

'It's so beautiful,' Imogen said, reaching out a hand and touching the delicate images all hand-sewn onto a cream-coloured fabric. Mrs Pelekas passed the whole cloth over to her and pulled up a second one, beginning to explain.

'This one she made in memory of her husband,' Panos spoke. 'He was a fisherman and it's sewn with the symbol of Corfu. It is on the island's flag, an ancient boat with three golden oars.'

Imogen looked at the intricate sailing boat, running a finger over the neat stitches. 'Did he die at sea?'

'Yes. I never knew him. Though *yiayia* always said he was a good man.'

'It's so lovely to see something made by hand,' Imogen said. 'Does she have any I can buy? I mean, these are too special to be sold. They must mean so much to her.'

Panos addressed the old woman with Imogen's question and she shook her head furiously.

'She wants you to have these,' Panos said. 'She has twelve, all different.'

'I can't do that. They're too nice. They should be framed on a wall not on restaurant tables.' She touched Mrs Pelekas' hand and spoke slowly. 'I-can't-take-these. They-are-too-nice… beautiful.'

'*Ochi*,' the woman stated forcefully.

'Did that mean OK?' Imogen asked, her eyes moving to Panos.

'No. *Ochi* means no, she does not accept this.'

Mrs Pelekas spoke again, her voice determined, even though Imogen could see other more sensitive emotions written on her face.

'She says she does not want them to be hidden away like they have been. They need to be enjoyed. She wants you to have them. She wants to think about people having meals on them, laughing, celebrating…' Panos broke off and said something else to the old lady. When their talk stopped Mrs Pelekas gave a nod.

'The deal is done,' Panos said, clapping his hands together. 'We have settled on something. An old debt is about to be repaid.'

'Don't be silly! This is Harry's restaurant. He has some funds,' Imogen exclaimed.

'Just say thank you,' Panos suggested. 'Say thank you, in Greek.'

'Is it like "OK" meaning "no"?'

'No.' He slipped his fingers in between hers and made her look at him. '*Efharistó*.'

'*Efharistó*,' she repeated.

Mrs Pelekas sat up in her chair, trying to straighten her crooked form, smiling with apparent delight at Imogen's Greek word.

'*Parakaló*,' she said.

'She said you're welcome,' Panos spoke, squeezing her hand.

FORTY-ONE

Acharavi beachfront

Panos pulled the car to a halt on the track next to Halloumi and turned off the engine. Neither of them had spoken a word on the road back from Mrs Pelekas' home and Imogen knew, on her side, it was because she was sensing the parting of ways. How could they possibly investigate their connection with all that was going on?

She sat still. It was as if they were both waiting for the other to make the first move.

'I should go,' Imogen said eventually. 'I've been out for hours.' She reached for the door handle.

'Wait,' Panos said, his hand catching her arm. 'There are boxes of kumquat liqueur and compote in the back of my car... and the tablecloths.'

'I can manage,' she said, avoiding his eyes. 'If you just set them down outside I'll get Harry to...'

Before she could finish Panos slipped his hand into her hair, his fingers gently massaging her scalp, his breath warm by her ear.

'Don't... please... it isn't fair,' she whispered. 'We can't do this.'

'I am not used to not getting what I want,' Panos reminded.

'Until you met me,' Imogen countered.

He smiled, his fingertips tip-toeing down her neck. His thumb circled the skin on her tanned shoulder. 'But *this* isn't about the restaurant, so...'

'So,' she repeated, finally meeting his eyes.

'So this decision is all yours, Imogen. It *is* about what *you* want.'

She opened her mouth to say something, when a knocking on the driver's window disturbed them both. She shunted away from Panos, her cheeks flaming, as a beautiful olive-skinned woman stared in through the glass.

Panos turned his head to the window, his mouth dropping open. *Rhea*. It couldn't be. He wet his lips, buying time, trying to think how to respond.

He watched her frown, her manicured eyebrows dipping in the middle, her hand, jangling bracelets hanging from her wrist, raised to tap on the window of the car again.

'Can you open the boot for me please?' Imogen asked, opening her car door. 'I don't want any more of the villagers seeing us together.'

'The villagers?' he remarked.

'She isn't someone you know from the village?' Imogen asked, her eyes going to the woman still on the other side of a pane of glass.

'No,' he replied. 'She isn't from the village. Imogen…'

'Please, Pano, just open the boot. Let me get my things.'

He watched her slide her legs out of the car and stand up, smiling at the woman outside. This was a nightmare. He pulled the lever to open the back of the car then opened his door, standing up and finally closing it behind him.

'Pano!' Rhea exclaimed. 'What are you wearing?' She let out a laugh, her French polished nails clasped over a perfectly lip-sticked mouth in coral.

He looked down at his t-shirt and jeans, suddenly feeling unsettled. Rhea was wearing a dress fit for a dinner party with high stiletto sandals, her hair set in a perfect chignon. She could easily have just stepped off the pages of a fashion magazine. He turned his head, searching for Imogen. She had half her body in the boot of the car, attempting to haul out the boxes.

'Rhea, why are you here?' he breathed. 'Just… give me a moment.' He stepped towards the back of the car.

'Give you a moment? I got on a plane early this morning for you, not really knowing where you were,' Rhea stated, gesticulating. 'I come to your family's restaurant and the man there says he owns this now.'

He moved around the car until he was at the boot. 'Imogen, they are too heavy for you. Put them down.'

'I can manage,' Imogen hissed into the dark of the boot interior. 'Why don't you make things right with your *girlfriend*?' She blinked her eyelids hard. 'She *is* your girlfriend, isn't she?'

'Don't do this,' Panos said. 'I can explain.'

'There's absolutely no need to do that.'

'There is a need because it is not how it seems. She is not my girlfriend anymore. She never was…'

'Pano!' Rhea called.

'Imogen, I did not know she was coming here,' Panos continued. 'We are over.'

'I think it takes two believing that for it to work, unless she's a stalker.' Imogen lifted one of the boxes and waddled away from the car, heading towards Rhea with a smile. 'Hello,' she greeted. 'I'm Imogen. My brother is probably who you spoke to. We're opening up the restaurant soon.'

'*Kalispera*,' Rhea greeted. 'You are English?'

'Yes,' Imogen replied. 'And I truly apologise for Boris Johnson.' Rhea looked blank.

'My brother? The blonde floppy hair?' Imogen shook her head. 'Sorry, bad joke.'

Rhea smiled again and offered her hands out for the box.

'Oh no, you don't have to help, honestly, I've got this,' Imogen insisted, heading down the track toward the restaurant.

'Imogen... wait,' Panos called.

'Thank you for the trip to Arillas, Mr Dimitriou,' Imogen shouted back. 'I'll send Harry out for the tablecloths.'

It wasn't the weight of the bottles of liqueur and compote in her hands that was making her shake, it was the situation she had just been about to take control of before it was whipped out of her hands. By Panos' girlfriend. She had had the measure of him from the very beginning. Smooth, not trustworthy, someone who manipulated situations to his advantage. And he had well and truly done that with her. Worse still, she had let him.

'Immy, are you alright? Where've you been? I tried to call and... Let me take that.' Harry made a grab for the box as she stepped onto the terrace. Looking up, she saw the pergola was secured, the new struts all in position.

'What is it?' Harry asked, eyes on the box.

'It's something that's going to complement your pudding menu like nothing else,' she said.

'Hello, Auntie Imogen! We've had ice cream.'

Imogen froze. Both Tristan and Olivia appeared from the restaurant building, ice cream around their grinning mouths.

'We went for a ride in the fish van and there was a goat,' Olivia added.

Harry put the box on one of the tables. 'I'm not sure it was the one that visited last night. This one had a white ear, didn't it, kids?'

'Harry... what's going on... is Janie...' Imogen started.

'Hello, Imogen,' Janie greeted.

'You're here! Gosh! You're really here!' She wanted to kiss her sister-in-law right now.

'Good old EasyJet,' Janie spoke, a tentative smile on her lips. 'Managed to get a last-minute flight and they didn't even flinch when Tristan was sick in the aisle.'

'Excuse me,' Panos' voice called. 'Where would you like me to put these?'

What was he doing here? She turned her head briefly, ready to dismiss him, but Harry beat her to it.

'Hello, Panos. Let me take this stuff that's going to transform my menu,' Harry said jovially. 'What is it anyway?'

'Kumquat compote and liqueur. It is an island speciality. Sweet, syrupy, heaven for your tongue,' Panos said, his eyes fixing on Imogen.

Her stomach was off again, prancing and dancing like an accomplished Lipizzan horse from the Spanish Riding School. *Heaven for your tongue* was a timely reminder of what they had shared with each other that day. She lurched but she directed her gaze behind Panos, searching for the woman he was attached to, the girlfriend he had been cheating on… with her.

'Can we have some, Dad?' Tristan asked. 'I've never had kumquats before. Can you get them in Tesco?'

Harry laughed. 'Panos, these are my children. Tristan and Olivia. Kids, say hello to Mr Dimitriou.'

'I'm sure Mr Dimitriou has lots of important business to attend to and no time to waste,' Imogen interrupted. She stepped toward Panos and pulled the bag of tablecloths out from under his arm in one swift action.

'Hello,' Olivia greeted politely. 'Are you Greek?'

'He's from Corfu,' Tristan interjected.

'That *is* Greece, dummy,' Olivia snapped back.

Panos smiled at the children. 'Corfu is the best part of Greece in my opinion.' He held his hand out for a high-five to which both of the children obliged. 'It is nice to meet you.'

'I'm Janie,' Janie said, quickstepping forward, her hand held out. 'Harry's wife.'

'It is nice to meet you.' He shook Janie's hand.

'You too,' Janie replied. 'Hopefully, being a local, you can direct us to a decent hotel, because I've just discovered there are no beds here.' She breathed in and delivered a slightly strained laugh. 'No beds!' Her eyes went to Imogen. 'You never told me there wasn't even a bed here!'

Imogen swallowed. She had been focussing on the good things. The sea and the progress on the downstairs room. It was sparkling, the furniture was almost all sanded down and re-varnished, the walls were freshly painted... They were usually so exhausted they fell asleep before they even thought about it not being on a bed.

'I want to sleep on the beach,' Tristan exclaimed. 'Even at Scout camp we didn't sleep on the beach.'

'Please,' Panos interrupted. 'I can get some beds for you.'

'No, you can't,' Imogen snapped, her head whipping up. 'We're fine. We don't want any beds.'

In protest at her statement her back contracted. But she was damned if she was going to accept something else from Panos. All the absolute joy she had experienced at the Arillas' community market was evaporating faster than a puddle in the heat of a July day. It was like the whole afternoon had never happened.

'Imogen,' Harry started. 'Come on, we definitely *do* need beds. I haven't been able to find anywhere that doesn't have a delay of eight weeks. If Panos has contacts, then...'

'Sure,' Panos answered. 'It is no problem. I will make a call.'

'No... you won't,' Imogen blasted.

All eyes were now on her. Olivia and Tristan were looking at her so hard, their mouths ajar like hungry chicks waiting for worms. She had to remember this wasn't about her, this was about soldering the family back together. It was time to swallow her pride.

'OK!' Imogen huffed. 'Get the beds.' She held her head high. 'But we're paying for them. We're not anyone's charity case.'

She held Panos' gaze as Olivia and Tristan began cheering, running around the room like heat-seeking missiles in a quest to lock onto a target.

Her barriers were up and fastened securely. Singleville was the safest place to reside and from now on that's where she was going to be living. Not even ebony eyes and a body like Iron Man was going to break down her defences.

FORTY-TWO

Avalon Bar, Acharavi

Panos cradled the short glass of cream-coloured liquid in his hands and looked out from the terrace onto the beach. It was his second glass of *ouzo* and water and he was seriously considering a third without dilution.

The heat was just starting to subside as early evening came and loungers that had been full of sun worshippers were now empty as prime tanning time came to an end. He liked this time of the day. The sky was still clear but the sun strength was less oppressive. There was air to breathe and a view of the mountains unobstructed by reclining tourists.

'… so I packed a case and I came to you. To support you like I know you want me to but, well, you are too stubborn to ask.' Rhea toyed with the olive on a stick in her Martini glass.

She had been talking for the past five minutes, since he had departed Halloumi and joined her where he had left her. He had called in a favour and five single beds were going to be delivered to the restaurant before sunset. Despite Imogen's best attempts at a front, he knew she was wounded by Rhea's appearance. And she had every right to be. In addition, she only knew how he had been with her. Manipulative, fast, hungry, like he was looking for a quick release. Only these actions had been different this time, *felt* different. The intensity had been emotional as well as physical. He had started to open up to Imogen, becoming more open than he had ever been. How ironic when they were on completely opposing paths.

He watched Rhea's chestnut-coloured eyes widen as he finally drew his eyes away from the sand and turned to her. He didn't want to be looking at her. He didn't want her to be here at all.

'I do not need support,' he responded coolly. He shifted in his chair, thoughts of everything he'd shared with Imogen today presenting opposition to his statement. He'd wanted to give something of himself to her today, wanted to hear her opinion even if he knew it would clash with his.

'I called Manilos,' Rhea continued.

Now the hairs on his arms stood and a cold feeling swept down his spine. She had called his office? She had spoken to his employee?

'What?' he said, the words like ice.

'I wanted to know what was on your mind,' Rhea continued. 'You have been distracted these last few weeks and—'

'And he told you?!' Anger was coursing through his limbs as he gripped the glass, threatening to shatter it. If Manilos had betrayed confidences there was no way he could keep him in the business. He didn't want the wider business community knowing the deal with Asp was off the table. Business circles were always quick to judge when they thought something had slipped through your fingers. Just like they had been with his father.

'No,' Rhea stated. 'He told me nothing. That is why I am here. To listen. To work out whatever is wrong.'

His body uncoiled slightly. He liked Manilos. He was smart. Young but intelligent and willing to learn. Rather like him when Yiannis had been his mentor. Perhaps he deserved a promotion. He could give him more responsibility and start Risto off at the company in his place, learning from the ground up.

'Pano,' Rhea bleated, touching his hand with hers.

Immediately he withdrew, his mind flooding with nothing but Imogen. Their kiss on the breakwater, the taste of sweet fruit on her lips, her body close to him. Her fire and passion.

'You should not have come here,' Panos stated.

'But I *am* here,' she answered.

'And it was a mistake,' he told her.

'Do not say that,' Rhea begged, reaching for his hand again.

He folded his arms across his chest, leaning back in the chair to increase the distance between them. On his side there was nothing between them. He had had her simply because he could. Looking across at her wobbling bottom lip he suddenly felt like a monster. *Cold. Empty. Shallow.*

'Rhea, did you think I did not mean what I said?' he asked gently.

She began shaking her head, the brown shape of hair moving in one solid form. 'I *know* you didn't mean it.'

'But I did,' Panos stated softly. 'I did mean it.' This time he reached for her hand. 'Because I am not good for you.' He squeezed her fingers in his, locking eyes with her. 'I am not good for anyone.'

Did he believe that? The answer was a resounding yes, no matter how much it suddenly hurt.

'You *are* good for me,' Rhea continued, her fingers curling around his, clinging on like he was a hand-hold on the side of a rocky mountain.

He shook his head. 'No.'

'But we can be… we *can* be good *together*. I can be…' She paused, tipping her head a little to the right and pressing the tip of her tongue to her top lip. 'Whoever you want me to be.'

'Rhea,' he breathed.

A plate of steaming hot parcels of pitta *gyros* carried by a waitress made its way into his line of sight. The spiced lamb brought back the carnival atmosphere of Arillas' community market, holding Imogen in his arms, tasting her on his lips. He couldn't do it. He *didn't want* to do it.

He shook his head. 'I am sorry, Rhea. My grandmother has a spare bedroom and you can stay the night… but tomorrow you are going to have to go home.'

She ripped her hand from his then, anger and hurt mixing with the beginnings of tears in her eyes. 'No, I won't.' She sniffed. 'I won't let you do this.' She got to her feet, snatching up her designer handbag.

He watched the tears dispel then, as she rushed into the restaurant heading in the direction of the toilets. Right now it was as if the beauty of the day had never existed.

FORTY-THREE

Halloumi, Acharavi beachfront

The large green truck blocked the sea view and the pinkish hue of the sky as the sun descended to the west. Three men in overalls were currently walking through the restaurant carrying the last of the brand-new single beds destined for the upstairs space.

Harry was navigating them around the bends in the staircase as well as keeping an eye on Olivia and Tristan, who seemed to have gone hyper on bottled water alone.

'It looks so different to how I imagined,' Janie spoke.

Imogen then looked to the bright, white walls, the tables and chairs still currently bare but looking clean, the tiled floor showing only a layer of sand where the delivery men had walked. It was a miracle it looked this way considering how it had looked the day they had arrived. Her eyes moved to the patch of land next to the restaurant. She needed to ask Elpida if she knew who owned it. There was no time to lose strengthening Harry's foothold on the seafront.

'It's on the verge of being beautiful,' Janie continued. 'Really beautiful.'

Imogen felt her body relax at Janie's words and she smiled. 'Yes,' she answered. 'It is.'

Janie picked up the glass and made to drink. Realising it was empty she put it down again. 'I mean, as you know, my first thoughts were a bit "Greece, for God's sake". Greece! A place the BBC haven't stopped going on about for months. Financial crisis, refugee crisis, hashtag Grexit…'

'But then you thought *My Family and Other Animals*?' Imogen offered.

'What? Do you mean that scrawny cat I saw sitting outside?'

'No.' Imogen sighed. 'It doesn't matter.'

'But then you started sending the photos,' Janie said. 'And I remembered.'

'Remembered?'

'Remembered all the gorgeous weeks Harry and I spent here.' Janie lifted her face up to the sun, closing her eyes to the heat. 'Sand, sea and souvlaki in pretty little tavernas just like this one. It was so relaxed, so utterly blissful.' Another breath left her. 'And then I had the children showing me emojis of prawns and all Harry's excited talk and I didn't really know what I was thinking. I think maybe I thought it would be the horror it was to begin with, but secretly I think I was hoping it was like this.' Janie opened her eyes again. 'I mean there aren't any curtains… and the bathroom upstairs is far from Victoria Plumb, but…'

'Well, we've been concentrating on the communal areas,' Imogen jumped in. 'The kitchen has been the priority and this main room of the restaurant. I've cleaned everything. I've made the upstairs as comfortable as possible and Harry has worked so hard, until late into the night. Then he's got up early and started all over again despite some difficult circumstances.'

'What difficult circumstances?' Janie asked, leaning forward, her elbows on the table. 'The language barrier? The fact Harry knows sod all about running a restaurant and is relying on you?'

'Yes, and… a bit of talk about some of the other businesses along the beach being sold and redeveloped.' She looked at Janie out of the corner of her eye, gauging her reaction.

'Clarify "a bit" and quickly. Tristan said something about a nightclub and I thought it was sunstroke so I put a hat on him.'

Imogen immediately regretting going down this track. She should have kept quiet while Janie was being bewitched by the landscape and her memories.

'One of the locals has designs on redeveloping the area next to the restaurant. Originally he wanted to buy Halloumi, but…'

'What?! You had someone make an offer on the place and you didn't bite his hand off like a famished alligator?'

Imogen let out a breath. 'No… we didn't.'

'Why not? That would have been the perfect way out.'

'Harry doesn't want a way out. And you just said it's evoking all these wonderful memories. That it's beautiful,' Imogen reminded.

'Harry doesn't really know what he wants,' Janie protested. 'It's only this nice because you're here guiding him.'

'That's where you're wrong,' Imogen said, sitting forward. 'Harry knows exactly what he wants and what he wants is you, Janie, and the children.' She watched for her sister-in-law's reaction. 'Here in Corfu.'

Janie didn't immediately respond.

'He misses you,' Imogen said. 'He's told me all about your holidays to Corfu. How happy you were.'

The delivery men reappeared, waving their goodbyes as they headed back to the lorry.

'It may be a lot better than I thought,' Janie began. 'But just because we holidayed here and it was lovely it doesn't mean the restaurant is Harry's destiny. Did you check his phone for horoscope apps? Because at one point he had five!'

'Janie, please, just give Harry a chance,' Imogen begged. 'That's why you're here, isn't it?' She swallowed. 'No one flies three hours with two children unless they really want something special at the end of it.'

She watched her sister-in-law's features soften, then Olivia and Tristan came thundering out onto the terrace followed by Harry roaring like a lion.

'What do you say we all go out and have some Greek dinner?' Harry asked everyone. 'Kids? Fancy more ice cream?'

Cheering erupted from the children and then a scream came from Janie.

'What is it?!' Janie stamped her feet. 'It's a snake, isn't it? Get it off me!'

Imogen bent down and picked up the speckled kitten. 'It's just the cat, Janie.'

'He's so cute,' Olivia said, bouncing up to Imogen and stroking the cat's head, much to its delight.

'Is he yours, Dad?' Tristan asked.

'Well, he certainly seems to have taken a liking to the place,' Harry responded.

'What's his name?' Olivia asked.

'Socks,' Harry announced.

'What?' Imogen asked. 'You gave him a name.'

'Short for Socrates. I thought Socks was very Greeklish.' Harry grinned.

'Hello, Socks. You're a lovely boy, aren't you?' Olivia said, tickling the animal under its chin.

Imogen's attention went back to Janie, who was looking more bewildered by the moment. With her free hand she rubbed the woman's shoulder. 'The red wine is a bit rustic but plentiful and Greeks do pork chops as big as Chris Hemsworth's guns.'

Janie sniffed. 'With chips?'

'As many as you can eat,' Imogen said, smiling. 'But personally I'd have the Greek roast potatoes. They're to die for.'

FORTY-FOUR

Elpida Dimitriou's home, Agios Martinos

'It is so nice to have another woman in my house again,' Elpida announced, raising a glass of *retsina* in the air towards Rhea.

They were sitting outside the front of the house at the stone table, slightly in the shade of the oldest olive tree in the grounds. Lamplight and candlelight provided enough brightness to see and although the sun had now gone down, the humid warmth meant there was no need for covering up.

'You have said this already,' Panos stated. 'Twice.'

'Always so grumpy! Have another glass,' Elpida suggested.

He watched Rhea smile and toy with the *stifado* his grandmother had made. There had been no time for explanation when he had pulled up to the house earlier with Rhea in the car. His grandmother, thigh-skimming floral frock on her body, had been clambering onto the back of Risto's moped, a pile of linen in her arms. She had waved and strapped a helmet to her head and he was left alone in the strained atmosphere with Rhea.

He had given her the tour of the house to occupy the time, his patter like an estate agent, pointing out the advantages of two bathrooms and the panoramic views over the mountains. He'd looked out at the back garden and recollected his mother and father dancing in the moonlight as he, Elpida and Risto sang together and used sticks and pots as instruments, but he'd turned to Rhea and simply told her the number of fruit trees that grew there. He could tell she was still angry with him now, still hurting as they ate together, but there was nothing he could do to change that. Tomorrow couldn't come soon enough.

'Harry's wife and his children are here,' Elpida piped up, topping up Rhea's glass.

Panos nodded. 'I know.'

'You know?' Elpida quizzed.

'I saw them,' he continued under his grandmother's inquisitive stare. 'At the restaurant earlier.'

'The man that owns the family restaurant now? This Boris?' Rhea asked, picking up her wine glass.

'Harry,' Panos corrected.

'I thought the woman you were with was his wife.'

'The woman you were with…' Elpida repeated.

'I simply gave Imogen a ride to Arillas to purchase some items for the restaurant,' Panos answered. Still Elpida stared at him, that all-seeing, all-knowing expression on her face as his temperature rose. He wasn't thinking about the candles or the tablecloths they had purchased, he was remembering Imogen's hair blowing in the breeze as they sat on the bench on the breakwater and how the saltwater tasted on her lips. He reached for his drink.

'You went to Arillas,' Elpida said. 'It is their community market day today, no?'

'Yes… she wanted to do the tourist thing. Look for a good deal. Drive a bargain.' He smiled, regaining his composure.

'So, she is not the man's wife,' Rhea said again, her eyes homing in on Panos.

'No,' Elpida said. 'Imogen is Harry's younger sister. A lovely girl. A little thin… not as thin as you but… well, both of you need to eat a little more.' Elpida picked up the bread basket and held it to Rhea.

'That was a compliment,' Panos assured Rhea. 'I got some beds for them.'

'*You* bought the beds!' Elpida exclaimed.

'Yes,' he replied.

'Well, that was a very nice thing to do, Pano. Very community-minded.'

He shrugged his shoulders. 'We do what we can.'

'Yes, we do,' Elpida agreed. 'So, how long are you staying with us, Rhea? And what can you tell me about what this boy has been up to in Crete for all this time?'

'*Yiayia,*' Panos said, a note of warning in his tone.

Rhea smiled at Elpida and sat a little straighter in her chair, bracelets jangling as she moved. 'It is OK, Pano, I can answer.' She dropped her eyes briefly to her plate before matching the older woman's gaze. 'The truth is, I can tell you nothing,' she said. 'Because that is always exactly what Pano shares.'

Underneath the tablecloth, a cream linen affair with black-and-sage-coloured olives embroidered on it by Mrs Pelekas, Panos clenched his hands together. He deserved that. He had treated Rhea badly even if he had never intended to. He should have stuck to one night, not pushed the boundaries to weeks. She had become involved and he hadn't seen it. This was his penance.

Suddenly Elpida let out a laugh, her breath blowing out one of the candles in the centre of the table. 'This is so true! This girl, Pano, she really knows you!'

He smiled, glad of the break in the tension, but deep down he knew Elpida couldn't be further from the mark.

'You must stay for the folklore show,' Elpida stated, banging her fist on the stone table.

'What?' Panos exclaimed.

'When is that?' Rhea asked.

'I am afraid Rhea has to go back to Crete very soon,' Panos objected.

'It is the day after tomorrow,' Elpida steamed on. 'Halloumi is going to have a stall. It is going to be a trial run of the recipes before the grand opening.'

'*Yiayia…*'

'It is a very special day in Acharavi. There are stalls and music and at night is the festival with dancing and fireworks and the sea with flaming boats… It really is something to see!'

'I told you, it is sad but Rhea must leave,' Panos insisted.

'I do not *have* to leave,' Rhea replied.

He lowered his voice. 'We discussed this.'

'No. *You* decided. Not me.'

Her brown eyes challenged him to contradict her. He should have paid for her to have a room in the village. Why had he brought her here, to Elpida's home? Because of guilt?

He got up from his seat and made a grab for the bottle they'd been sharing. 'I will get more wine.'

Fifteen minutes later he was still in the kitchen, his eyes on the moon-shaped clock above the range, the second hand ticking relentlessly but never really getting anywhere. He didn't want to go back to the table. It would mean facing up to the situation, when what he really wanted to do was run. But run where? Back to Crete? To his office to sink himself into some sort of familiarity? To Imogen? He let out a breath, his mind filling with her scent, the sound of her laughter, the blue crystal of her eyes. Like the moon-faced clock it was as if time had stood still in Arillas that day, a small snapshot of harmony amidst everything else.

'Have we run out of wine?'

Elpida's voice had him making a grab for the tea towel and wiping his hands in an improvised action that was fooling no one.

'No, I was just coming out.' He put the tea towel down, picked up another bottle of wine and turned to his grandmother, a smile of confidence rapidly restored.

Elpida shifted right, blocking his way like a grand move in chess. He stepped to the left to get past and she repeated the action in the opposite direction, halting his progress again.

'What are you doing?' he asked, standing still in front of her.

'What are *you* doing is more the question.'

Elpida had her eyes trained on him like an accomplished sniper staring down the sight of his weapon. There was no avoiding her unless he wanted to dance a *sirtaki* around her kitchen. Even then he suspected she would be far more adept than him. He put the bottle of wine down on the countertop.

'Rhea is…' Elpida said. She stopped and tilted her head as if expecting him to finish off the sentence.

He shook his head. 'A friend.'

Elpida's eyes widened, not accepting his response as a proper answer. 'A friend,' she repeated.

'Someone I was just spending time with in Crete.'

'Spending time with,' Elpida repeated.

'Will you stop doing that?'

'Doing what?'

'Just repeating everything I say.' He threw his arms up rather like his grandmother did when she was frustrated by something. 'What do you want me to say?'

'I am trying to understand, that is all.' Elpida continued to regard him closely. 'Is she someone you are close to with your heart or just when your trousers are down around your ankles?'

'*Yiayia!*' he exclaimed.

'What?! I have two children. I have an occasional date. I know how the world works in that department, whether you like it or not.'

'I do not like it,' Panos answered.

'You have not answered the question,' Elpida reminded. 'Heart or trousers?'

His grandmother knew him too well. It was as clear cut as that. His heart had never been involved, with Rhea or anyone else. He wasn't sure his heart worked in any way other than pumping the blood around his body.

'Well?' Elpida prompted.

'I do not know why you are asking me this. She is going home tomorrow. Back to Crete.'

'The girl cares for you, Pano,' Elpida stated.

'I know that!' he blasted. 'And I told her she should not.'

'And Imogen?'

The mere mention of her name should not have his body reacting like someone had just injected him with a high dose of caffeine. But it did. Everything moved inside him. He shifted his feet, trying to control his emotions.

'Now I see,' Elpida concluded with a nod.

He swallowed, trying to maintain his stance. 'Now you see what?'

She smiled. 'It is quite simple really.' She reached onto the counter for a packet of cigarettes. 'Imogen is heart and Rhea is trousers.'

'No,' Panos jumped in quickly. 'No one is heart.'

'Pfft!'

'I am telling you—'

'No, Pano, *I* am telling *you*,' she interrupted. 'And I am telling you only two things now.' She pulled a cigarette from the packet and rolled it between her thumb and forefinger. 'You need to be respectful to this girl here. I have a feeling there was not a lot of respect shown in Crete, huh?'

He shook his head in disagreement, folding his arms across his chest.

'And the second thing.' She put the cigarette into her mouth, slipped a lighter from the pocket of her dress and flicked it into a flame. Sucking on the filter, she held the smoke in her mouth for a long moment before dispelling it into the air with a satisfied breath. 'In life you can have many pairs of trousers, Pano… and they might not all fit like you wish them to.' She took another drag before settling her eyes on him. 'But you only have one heart.' She nodded. 'Remember that.'

FORTY-FIVE

Almyros Beach, Acharavi

Imogen lay back on the golden sand, letting its underlying coolness seep through her clothes and soothe away the heat of the
day on her skin. The sun was setting, its last rays of light just
clinging onto the sky before darkness claimed them. She closed
her eyes and pressed the phone a little closer to her ear, waiting
for her mum to pick up. As the tone rang she took a deep breath
and tried to quell the ugly feeling sitting in her gut like indiges-
tion. She shouldn't have got involved with Panos today… or any
other day for that matter. He had a girlfriend and that hurt. Had
all his talk about keeping passion and professionalism separate
just been that – talk? Was his motive like before – that first night
at Elpida's when she'd lamely swooned in his arms? How long
would he have kept that pretence up, she wondered?

'Hello?' Grace greeted cautiously.

'Hel—'

Her mother interjected viciously. 'If you're trying to sell solar
panels or loft insulation we don't want any, thank you, and if
you're going to say you're from Microsoft and there's something
wrong with my computer, think again or I'll call the police.'

'Mum, it's me,' Imogen said, swallowing away her niggles.

'Imogen, is Janie alright?' Grace questioned. 'She tried to call
me earlier but we got cut off. Are the children OK?'

'Yes, Mum,' Imogen said quickly. 'Everything's fine. They're
here safe and Harry's taken them out for some food.'

'And the restaurant?' Grace asked. 'You're not really opening it next week, are you?'

'Yes, Mum, we are.'

She heard her mother's breath, long and low down the phone receiver. Sitting up, she looked across the water to Albania, lights twinkling in the dusk.

'Imogen, I've got some news of my own,' Grace said calmly.

'News?' She swallowed. What sort of news could her mother have when she barely left the house? Had she *actually left* the house?

'Yes,' Grace continued. 'And it's all a bit overwhelming actually.'

'Overwhelming,' Imogen repeated nervously, her hand tightening on her phone again.

'Yes… it's April,' Grace said with a shaking breath. 'She's left me her house in her will.'

Imogen's body contracted then relaxed.

'Her great-niece came round…'

'The one with Martin Clunes' boots,' Imogen joked.

'She told me the money and shares April had are being split between her and the Cats Protection and… I get the house.' Grace drew in another breath. 'I mean, all these years we've been friends and she never said a word about it.'

'That's lovely though, isn't it? It shows just what your friendship meant to her.'

'I know but… it's got three bedrooms, a conservatory and a double garage,' Grace answered. 'What am I going to do with all that?'

'Well,' Imogen started. 'You don't have to keep the house. You could sell it.'

'Really?' Grace exclaimed. 'Do you think that's the right thing to do? I mean, April loved that house, I wouldn't want to, you know, do anything she might not want me to.'

'No, I know, Mum,' Imogen said. 'But she knew you were on your own. I don't think she would have expected you to keep on her house as well as your own unless…'

'What?'

'Well, April's house does have the view of the park.'

'And you can see the river from the master bedroom,' Grace added.

'Is that what you want, Mum? To move into April's house and sell ours?'

She hadn't meant to say 'ours' but it had just come out. It was still the family home, one of her dad's jackets still hanging in the hall. 'I mean, yours.'

'I couldn't, could I?' Grace stated. 'At my age! Moving across the road. It hardly seems worth it.'

'Don't be silly,' Imogen said. 'What's age got to do with it? If you can see yourself in April's conservatory then what's to stop you?'

'I don't know,' Grace said, sounding a little uncertain.

Imogen closed her eyes again, listening to the sea lapping onto the beach, the breeze still warm on her cheeks. 'Look at what Harry's done,' she said. 'He barely thought twice about jumping on a plane and opening a restaurant. What is there to worry about April's house? How to work the central heating and the dishwasher?'

'You make it sound easy.'

'It could be easy. If you wanted it to be. And of course, when I get back I can pitch in and help you.'

'You are coming back then?' Grace said.

The question shocked her. 'What?'

'Well, you seem so on board with this restaurant idea already. I thought maybe you'd get caught up with the Greek weather and the *ouzo* and what-not.'

She wasn't about to define 'what-not' or relate it to a handsome Greek cheat. She swallowed before replying. 'No… of course not… I mean Harry knows I have my job at home and my NVQ and… you, Mum.' Plus the absolute outside chance of a dream job with the Wyatt Hotel Group. She really should phone them again, even if it was just to put herself out of the waiting game misery.

'I worry about your brother much more than I've ever worried about you,' Grace admitted. 'You were always so capable, even when you were little.'

Imogen swallowed, blinking her eyes at the darkness. Capable was such a weak word. It really said 'you got by' but never did anything extraordinary. Did she want that to be the watchword she was likened to?

'Well, Janie's here now and once she's got over the flight I'm hoping she's going to be enchanted by the weather and the *ouzo* and our fresh, clean restaurant,' Imogen began. 'And maybe also by the new improved Harry.'

'*Is* he alright, Imogen?' Grace asked. 'I mean, really?'

She sat up, putting one hand down into the sand and swirling her fingers amongst the grains. She nodded even though Grace couldn't see it. 'Yes, Mum, he really is.'

'OK then,' Grace said, as if a weight had been lifted. 'I'll think about moving into April's house once all the paperwork's gone through.'

'Good.' Imogen smiled. Her mum sounded more enthusiastic than she had in months. Perhaps everything was coming together for all of them.

'Oh, Imogen, I almost forgot. That woman rang again. Laura, wasn't it? Or it might have been Lorraine. Anyway, she was from the Wyatt Hotel Group and she didn't want to sell me a spa package. She wanted to speak to you.'

Imogen stabbed a finger into the sand, hardly daring to take another breath. 'What… What did she say?'

'I said you were away in Greece at the moment and could I take a message…'

'And did you?' Imogen jumped in. 'Was there a message?' Her heart was racing like a sprinting greyhound.

'No,' Grace stated. 'She said not to worry and she would send you an email.'

She deflated. A rejection was coming her way.

'Did I do the wrong thing?' Grace asked. 'I did apologise for the mix-up the other day.'

'It's fine, Mum, nothing to worry about,' Imogen said, recovering quickly.

'So… have *you* won a mini-break or something?' Grace inquired.

'No,' Imogen said, sighing. 'I don't think so. She probably wanted to sell me gym membership.'

'Oh well,' Grace said. 'If I remember rightly, April has some free weights and a rowing machine in her garage.'

FORTY-SIX

Acharavi beachfront

Running had always come naturally to Panos, but today it was hard. Today, when he should have been letting the rise and fall of the undulating terrain soothe his mind and pound away the stress, his brain was working overtime churning up anything and everything. His business. The reason he'd returned to Corfu. Rhea. Imogen.

Like a bird following its familiar path to hibernation for the winter he ran the same route he'd always covered. Out of Agios Martinos, down towards Acharavi, then onto the beach heading along the coastline to the tracks through the arable land in the direction of Agios Spyridon. He'd stopped for a breath at the old abandoned church, expecting to see the worn-down surrounds he'd remembered from his last run here years before. Instead, the property was painted in a warm buttermilk, a sign outside written in Greek and English proclaiming it to be Yan's After School Club. Times had moved on, not everything was coated in cobwebs of the past here.

The sun was up now, soaring into the Greek flag blue of the sky in readiness for the day. Up ahead, as he jogged along the road, his trainers skirting the pebbles of the beach, business owners were putting out their blackboards, changing paper menus with updated special dishes and welcoming early risers in for breakfast.

There was still so much tradition here but there *were* also tourists. His home town was far from the run-down ghost town the media were depicting it as. The news said Greece was done, he had seen evidence of it in the capital. But here, as much as he would have hated to admit it when he'd arrived back on the island, there were definite signs of recovery.

He stopped running and just breathed, letting the familiar saltwater and sand air into his lungs as he closed his eyes. The community market had affected him. As well as harking back to simpler times, it had a feel that was as new and different as it was authentic. Despite his own plans for the beachfront there was a part of him whispering that he wanted to get involved.

Was that what he wanted? Really? He straightened his stance, grounding his soles into the tarmac. Was there much money in it? Not a big profit share for him perhaps, but a huge plus to local businesses. But liking the idea in principal was one thing… Was it something he wanted to help create *here*? Or was it an idea to take with him back to Crete?

'Go on! Shoo!'

Breaking out of his reverie, Panos looked over to Halloumi. Imogen jumped down from the edge of the terrace, a watering can in her hand and two terrified-looking cats leaping for their lives just ahead of her.

Immediately his heart rate picked up to a level it had been when he'd been sprinting along the road at the back of the Blue Vue Hotel, passing the Pyramid restaurant and Bo's Bar. He swallowed, wondering what to do. Right now he was probably the last person she wanted to see.

And then she turned, facing him. He was caught now. It was too late to turn in the other direction and pretend he hadn't seen her. He started to walk, all the while hoping she didn't backtrack and try to avoid him.

Panos was the last thing she needed right now but there he was, no more than a few yards away, making his running gear look like a David Gandy billboard campaign. She would act like a grown-up and be civil. She was blaming those moments of madness in Arillas on Greece. There should be inoculations against the romanticism before you were allowed to board the plane.

'Good morning!' she called like she was addressing Old Joe in the diner.

He waved a hand, drawing closer. She was not going to look at his thighs… or his eyes. She swallowed. Except he did have lovely eyes. And that firm chest had been holding her up in Arillas yesterday. *But he was a love rat who had duped her and his girlfriend.*

'*Yassas*,' he greeted, stopping just in front of her, his hands on his hips.

Every section of mocha-coloured skin was toned to perfection and slightly dewy from his workout. *Two-timer.*

'Where's your girlfriend?' she blurted out. 'Couldn't find a matching outfit?'

She sounded so pathetic she wanted to give herself a kicking.

'If you mean Rhea, she is at my grandmother's house.'

'Of course I mean Rhea. Or do you have more girlfriends?' She huffed a sigh. 'Is there a whole Greek harem currently boarding ships to visit you?'

'You sound upset.'

She knew she did and that was annoying her. She shook her head. 'Don't flatter yourself, Mr Dimitriou.'

'I liked it better when you called me Pano,' he replied.

'I liked it better when you didn't have a girlfriend.'

She realised her mistake the moment she said it. She had admitted what she was trying so badly to hide. Rhea's appearance had annoyed her, got under her skin, hurt her.

He swallowed, looking at her. 'Imogen, please listen… I promise—'

'You don't have to make any sort of promise to me,' Imogen interrupted. 'We had a few moments, but they no longer have a place here.'

He felt his stomach contracting. This was absolutely what he deserved. Imogen thought he had tried to claim her like she was one of the properties he wanted to purchase. She didn't know that he had told her things he had never admitted to anyone.

'So, as far as I'm concerned we're back to where we started,' Imogen continued. 'Me helping Harry and you wanting to take all that away.'

He nodded. 'Yes, I can see you would think that.'

'Well,' Imogen snapped. 'What else is there to think?'

He took a breath in, his eyes not leaving her. 'That Rhea is not my girlfriend. That everything I told you in Arillas is true,' he suggested. 'But perhaps that would make things more difficult for you.' He took a step closer to her. 'Because then you might have to admit you feel something other than loathing for the man building a nightclub next door.'

He watched her breathing, her chest moving in and out as her heart rate increased. He desperately wanted to take her in his arms and kiss her right there on the promenade despite what was right or wrong about this situation they were in.

'Imogen!' Harry called from the terrace.

'I have to go,' Imogen stated, her voice trembling. 'Apparently there's a folklore day to get ready for.'

He nodded, his heart thumping a beat of disappointment.

'*Antio*,' Imogen said, turning away from him.

He watched her walk away. Who was he trying to fool? There was only one option open to him now. Work. That was all he had. He was going to get Panos Enterprises signs up outside Tomas' Taverna by the end of the day.

FORTY-SEVEN

Halloumi, Acharavi Beachfront

'So this is the menu, is it?' Janie sniffed and picked up one of the pieces of paper from the table.

It was early afternoon now and Olivia and Tristan were in sight on the beach, sun-creamed to the max and enjoying chasing each other across the sand. Imogen knew Janie was still suffering from the effects of last night's wine.

'At the moment, yes. It's not quite finalised,' she answered.

Her eyes went to the sparkling aquamarine water and today's clear vista of the Albanian mountains. Corfu had worked its magic on her from the moment she had opened up enough to let it in. It wasn't just the blue sky and the effervescent sea, it was the stark contrasts at every turn. From the dark grey of Mount Pantokrator to the bright white pebbles at the edge of the beach through undulating hills of woodland, fields of crops and fragrant flowers – there was a new scene just waiting to be captured at every turn.

'Look around you, Janie,' Imogen said softly. 'It's breathtaking.'

Janie turned her head, pausing for a few moments before turning back. 'I have to admit that Panos is pretty eye-catching. Gave me the gift of a divan.'

Imogen sighed. There was no escaping the man. Even when he wasn't here he was being forced into her mind. She pressed her lime-green pen with the lotus flower motif onto her notepad – *Imperial Hotel, Osaka*.

'Don't forget he's the local that wants to redevelop everything,' Imogen said quickly. 'Looks can be deceiving.'

'Anyone who buys me and my children a bed can't be all bad.'

No, he wasn't all bad, Imogen had to admit. But he was best kept at a distance, where she wouldn't be tempted to inhale the manly aroma of him. Could sniffing someone be classed as adultery? She shook a mosquito off her arm and refocussed on her sister-in-law.

'So, how do you feel now you're here? Seeing all this.'

'Confused,' Janie admitted. 'Because I wanted to hate it. I wanted to see it as a ridiculous notion. One of Harry's mad whims, like buying that boat he always threatened us with.'

'And you don't?' Imogen asked.

'Despite what you've said about the nightclub proposal next door… I see potential,' Janie admitted.

Imogen clapped her hands together, excitement filling her up.

'But it's still a risky venture to undertake with little experience.'

'Well,' Imogen started. 'I'm brushing off my cooking skills and am going to do my very best to get it up and running. Elpida and Cooky are going to help Harry until he finds someone permanent.'

'So, what's left to do? How can I help if boarding it all up again and putting it back on Rightmove really isn't an option?' Janie asked.

'We've got to cook food for a folklore festival tomorrow.'

'Let me have another look at that,' Janie said, snatching up the menu and staring it down like it was a mortal enemy. 'I'm no Mary Berry but I've cooked for the odd school event. Admittedly it was more rock cakes than… I can't even pronounce this word.' Janie narrowed her eyes at the Greek on the page.

'*Spanakopitakia*,' Imogen helped out. 'It's cheese and spinach parcels.'

'And this one?' Janie pointed at another item.

'That is *stifado*,' Elpida announced, coming up behind the pair.

'Elpida!' Imogen announced. 'Thank goodness you're here. I was starting to think I was actually going to have to Greek cook alone.'

'Pfft! I would not let this happen just yet,' Elpida said, smiling at the two women.

'Hello,' Janie greeted.

'Oh, Janie, this is Elpida Dimitriou. She used to own the restaurant and she's been such a help to us. And she's the woman who came to the rescue with sheets and blankets for our beds last night.' Imogen smiled. 'Elpida, this is Janie, Harry's wife.'

'It is wonderful to meet you at last,' Elpida said, clasping Janie's hands in hers. 'I have heard so much about you and your beautiful children. Where are they? Let me see if they are too thin.'

For a moment Janie looked at Elpida like she was the witch from *Hansel and Gretel* set on fattening up Olivia and Tristan to serve on the menu. Imogen laughed. 'Elpida thinks everyone is too thin,' she reassured her.

'Hello,' another voice greeted.

It was only when she spoke that Imogen became aware of Rhea, moving past the palm tree on the road next to the terrace. The very palm Imogen had been flattened against and ravished by Panos only a short time ago. She swallowed. This felt awkward. The woman was dressed so immaculately, in a pale pink all-in-one short suit, her long hair down, her make-up perfect, lips glossed. With dust and dirt marks on her t-shirt and fingers wrinkled from over-wearing of Marigolds, Imogen felt like a vagrant in comparison.

'Hello,' Imogen said quickly. 'It's Rhea, isn't it?'

'Come on, come forward,' Elpida urged. 'Imogen doesn't bite and Janie looks too thin to hurt you.'

'I can't remember the last time someone called me thin,' Janie said, smiling.

'I ask Rhea to help us in the kitchen today. She tells me her mother teach her traditional Cretan cooking. We can put her to work with this menu,' Elpida stated, clapping her hands together.

Imogen swallowed. She was about to spend time in the kitchen with Panos' girlfriend. It had to be a recipe for disaster.

FORTY-EIGHT

Halloumi, Acharavi beachfront

Elpida made Greek cooking seem as easy as breathing. The woman's hands flew from pot to bowl to marble slab and back again like a frenzied mime artist. All of it seemed complex compared to just coating cheese with flour and knocking up a *saganaki*.

'Are you writing down all this step by step?' Imogen asked, her eyes searching the worktop for evidence of paper.

'You need me to write down?' Elpida queried.

'Yes! I'm not going to remember all these things. I haven't made anything like this in years, Elpida.'

'Is OK,' Elpida said. 'I have all this in my recipe book. I bring this here for you.'

'Is some of it written in English?'

'Pfft! Of course not.'

'I can't read Greek!'

A cloud of flour puffed up out of the bowl as Elpida shot her hands into it again. 'I am going to be here… whenever you need me.'

'But that isn't fair on you,' Imogen sighed. 'You sold this restaurant because you didn't want to own a restaurant anymore.'

'You let me decide what is fair,' Elpida answered. 'Look, Rhea is doing so well.'

Imogen looked at Rhea's large ball of elastic dough she had just placed on the work surface. The woman was beautiful *and* a good cook. Even with the dreaded pastry. She was also completely lovely. You couldn't feel any animosity towards someone who was so friendly and now helping create food for your restaurant. Imogen swallowed. Rhea wouldn't be so friendly if she knew Imogen had been stealing intimate time with her boyfriend. There was a layer of guilt mixing around in *her* pastry bowl. She hated herself for getting into that situation.

'That looks perfect,' Imogen said to Rhea. 'You obviously cook a lot.'

Rhea shook her head. 'Not much anymore. There is no one to really cook for.'

'Ah,' Elpida said. 'There is always someone to cook for. Most people do not know they need cooking for but they will always eat.'

Imogen smiled. 'We need to send you out to famine-stricken regions.'

'Like England?' Elpida joked.

'We just eat the wrong things because we're too busy.'

'That is what Pano does,' Rhea continued. 'Or he will not eat at all.'

'Pfft! His father was the same. Always too busy to find time to sit down. Be still. Relax. Take the moment.'

'I think we're all a little guilty of that,' Imogen admitted.

'So,' Elpida began. 'We are making this new version of *spanakopitakia* for Halloumi. And it is different because it has an English twist Harry wanted.'

'It's the absolutely only thing I'm letting him put an English twist on. I keep reminding him we're in Corfu, not Benidorm.'

'So,' Elpida said. 'We are going to use shortcrust pastry instead of the traditional filo.' Elpida smiled. 'This is good for you, Imogen, because shortcrust pastry is the easiest pastry to make. How are you getting along?'

'Terribly,' Imogen answered. 'It doesn't seem to be binding very well.' She lifted her goo-covered hands out of the mixing bowl as evidence.

'Pfft! I will not have failure in my old kitchen,' Elpida said. 'Rhea, let us wrap yours and put it in the fridge to cool. Imogen, keep working it together while I fetch the other ingredients. Come.' Elpida led Rhea and her perfect board of pastry out of the main room to the pantry area that housed the walk-in fridge behind.

Imogen's fingers felt like they were glued together. She shook the mixture off them before grappling with the flour, water and fat again, attempting to goad it into a shape… any shape that was solid. She really needed to get competent at this but nothing was transforming. The whole sorry mess looked like something found on the pavement outside a nightclub at four in the morning.

'How is it going?'

She flicked up her head to greet Panos, leaning on the doorjamb at the exit to the restaurant. He was wearing a business suit, the crisp white shirt open at the neck.

'Fine,' she answered stiffly. 'Pretty perfect actually. Shortcrust pastry Joe Wicks would definitely disapprove of.' She looked up from the bowl. 'What are you doing here?'

'Looking for my grandmother,' he said. 'So, can I see what you are making?' He took a step into the kitchen, indicating her work.

'Definitely not. It's still a work in progress. It needs complete privacy.' Couldn't he take a hint?

'The pastry needs privacy?'

'Please don't look,' she begged.

It was too late. He was beside her, his lemony scent soaring up her nose, his eyes on the semolina consistency in her bowl.

'*Skatá*,' Panos said.

'I know what that means,' Imogen answered. 'That's not nice. I'm sure it will taste OK.'

'If you can get this out of the bowl,' he said.

'That isn't funny. Go away,' she urged. 'It's none of your business how it looks. Don't you have some demolition to get on with?'

'I think I know what is wrong,' he stated.

'I'm no good with pastry? I could have told you that.'

He shook his head. 'No.' Suddenly, he sunk his hands into the mixture, his fingers around hers.

'What are you doing?' Imogen breathed.

'I know why your pastry is like this.'

'You needed to put your hands in my bowl to tell me.'

He nodded. 'Yes.'

His fingers were kneading more of her than the mixture. It felt like she was re-enacting the pottery scene in *Ghost* with a Greek Patrick Swayze.

'Your hands are too hot,' he offered.

A snake of perspiration trickled down her back. 'I've never heard anything so ridiculous in all my life.'

'It is true. The best pastry is made with cold hands,' he answered. His proximity was doing absolutely nothing to bring down the temperature of her hands or any other part of her body.

'We have herbs and halloumi cheese and… Well, well, well,' Elpida greeted as she and Rhea returned to the room. 'I never think this day will come. Cooking, twice in one week!'

Imogen shot her hands out of the bowl, bringing up the whole soggy mess of dough, the porcelain falling to the tiles with a smash.

'Gosh, I'm sorry,' Imogen exclaimed. Her cheeks were burning up as she bent down, trying to pick up the pieces of ceramic with her hands caked in mixture.

'Stop,' Panos said, bending down too. 'Remember what you did to yourself with the wine glass.'

He was looking at her intently, seemingly uncaring that his grandmother and girlfriend were witnesses to the scene. She wanted the floor to open up like a sink-hole and suck her into oblivion.

Panos got to his feet. 'I was just trying to help,' he explained. 'Imogen was having trouble with her pastry.'

Panos was having trouble keeping his cool. Sinking his hands into the moist dough, slipping his fingers between Imogen's and almost tasting her unique scent in the air between them had caused a stinging need. But it was wrong to feel that now, here, with Rhea looking on like a crushed mosquito just waiting for the final killer swat.

'I need to start from scratch,' Imogen said, getting up. 'With new mixture. Rhea's was brilliant. She's a wonderful cook.' Imogen faced the woman. 'You're so good. I already know that, just by the way you made that pastry… so much better than me.'

'Come,' Elpida said to Imogen. 'Let's wash off those hands and start from the beginning.'

'I don't know if I'm ever going to get the hang of it,' Imogen admitted.

'Pfft! You will not fail on my watches,' Elpida insisted, leading the way out of the room towards the pantry area again.

Panos grabbed the nearest cloth and began wiping his hands with it, all too aware that Rhea was still regarding him.

'It is her, isn't it?'

Rhea's words sent a pinch of hurt to his gut. He closed his eyes, still working the mixture off his hands before he looked up and faced her.

'No,' he responded. 'It is not like you think.'

Rhea shook her head. 'Liar.'

'Rhea, when I left Crete…'

'You don't have to explain it, Pano. I see it.' She blinked back tears. 'I see it with my own eyes. The way you look at her… You have never looked at me that way.'

'Rhea, don't,' he begged. 'It is not like that.' What did he mean? What wasn't it like? And who was he trying to convince?

'I should have left this morning,' Rhea said. 'You told me and I did not listen. I still hoped…'

'I have behaved badly. I should have known how you felt and been more considerate. This is all down to me.'

'No,' Rhea sighed. She shook her head. 'You told me when we first met you did not want complications.'

'It was not fair of me to expect you to be the same as I am.' He heaved a sigh. 'No one is like I am.'

'Not even Imogen?' Rhea asked.

He looked through to the other room. He could just see the back of his grandmother and Imogen, spraying water into the sink and trying to clean the pastry from Imogen's hands.

'No,' he answered. 'Not even Imogen.' He wiped at his hands again and threw down the cloth before meeting Rhea's gaze again. 'I want you to stay for the folklore festival,' he stated. 'If you would like to.' He paused. 'It *is* something special.'

She shook her head again. 'It is not my place.'

'Come,' Panos stated. 'There is dancing and great food and drink. It is exactly your place.' He smiled. 'It is maybe not like my clubs in Crete but…'

'This whole island is nothing like Crete,' Rhea answered. 'Nothing happens here.'

'You have only been here a day.'

'I do not know how you have survived all this time.'

He swallowed.

'And seriously, Pano, if you have no feelings for Imogen, I would be worried about your sudden interest in getting your hands covered in pastry mixture.'

He looked down at his hands, the goo hardening on his fingers. He raised his head. 'So, will you stay? For the festival day?'

'On one condition,' Rhea answered.

'Go on.'

'Your private plane to take me back home again?' She pouted, batting her extensive eyelashes.

'I am certain that can be arranged.'

'What can be arranged?' Elpida asked, marching back into the kitchen with Imogen behind her.

Rhea smiled, bracelets jangling as she wiped her fingers down the front of the apron she was wearing. 'I am going to stay for the festival tomorrow,' she stated.

'Wonderful! Another mouth to feed and another pair of hands to help here!' Elpida answered excitedly. 'Isn't that good news, Imogen?'

Panos looked to Imogen, who hurriedly nodded and smiled, all the while keep her eyes firmly away from him.

FORTY-NINE

Halloumi, Acharavi Beachfront

Dimitriou Enterprises signs had gone up outside Tomas' Taverna late that afternoon. At first the villagers had seemed to think the truck and the men with hammers were something to do with the folklore festival, but then the boards bearing the blue-and-white logo had appeared and everyone had begun gossiping, congregating around the side of Halloumi and looking to Imogen with something akin to pity in their eyes.

Panos' conversion of the beachfront was becoming a harsh reality.

'Ladies and gentlemen, boys and girls, I give to you… Halloumi's Greek biscuits with cream and a kumquat compote.' Harry pulled the cloth off the plate he was holding and slapped the platter and a small porcelain jug down into the middle of the table.

Imogen, Elpida, Janie, Olivia and Tristan sat in the middle of the restaurant area for a tasting session. It had also been a chance to dress the room in preparation for their opening in a few days. Mrs Pelekas' tablecloths adorned each table and in the middle of every setting was one of the candles Imogen had got in Arillas. Even though unlit, they were giving off a subtle fragrance that filled the room.

Tristan and Olivia clapped their hands together in applause, as they had done each time Harry, Imogen or Elpida brought out the next dish. Imogen smiled, looking around the room, glad that the essentials were all in place. They had plates, they had cutlery and glasses, they even had strings of fairy lights adorning the bar area. The one hitch had been the delivery of beer barrels. They were going to have to make do with selling bottled beer from the supermarket for a few days until it arrived. Outside, the new pergola was in place over the terrace, just a coat of creosote to go.

'They smell gorgeous,' Janie stated, looking at the food. She turned to Imogen. 'You made this?'

Imogen smiled. 'I might have... eventually... after several attempts to get them just right.'

'And these are very simple,' Elpida stated, toying with an unlit cigarette. 'Soon, children, your father and your auntie will be making much more complication things.'

'Can we help make something?' Tristan asked.

Visions of ketchup-festooned pastry and chocolate spread filled Imogen's mind and she opened her mouth to protest.

'Course,' Harry said, beating her to it. 'Elpida's recipe book is so thick it looks like something out of Dumbledore's office.'

'Who is this Dumbledora?' Elpida asked.

'He's from Harry Potter,' Olivia informed.

'Is this a place?' Elpida inquired.

'No,' Tristan said. 'Hogwarts is the place.'

'Pigs with warts?' Elpida said. 'I have some cream for this.'

'Can we have some of the biscuits now?' Tristan asked, the tips of his fingers inching the platter nearer to him.

She watched Harry serve up the biscuits, dolloping cream on everyone's plates. His eyes were alive, his body language open, full of energy.

'Immy has been brilliant,' Harry stated. His eyes went to his children. 'Did you know your Auntie Imogen can wrestle a goat?'

'What?!' Olivia exclaimed, mouth open wide.

'Really?!' Tristan said. 'I don't think even Darryn our scout leader can do that.'

'It's true,' Harry continued. 'I never saw anything like it before.'

'Harry...' Imogen started, a smirk on her face.

'No, Immy, you take the credit where it's due,' Harry insisted. 'And I have to say, the tablecloths, the candles and this kumquat stuff... it's just... I was just thinking for a better word than "brilliant". But I'll say it in Greek.' He cleared his throat. 'Éxochos.'

'Very good,' Elpida said, clapping her hands.

'I really want to learn Greek,' Olivia stated.

'Me too,' Tristan agreed, grabbing a spoon and beginning to eat.

'Well, if you spend lots more time in Corfu you're going to pick it up in no time,' Harry said, beaming.

'Harry,' Janie said, a warning note to her voice.

'What?' Harry said, nudging his wife's arm. 'I know how you feel about Corfu, don't hide it.' He put a hand over hers. 'I know you still remember that little pebble beach at Agni.'

Janie's eyes shone as a blush pinked her cheeks.

Imogen picked up the small jug of compote and spooned some on a plate before offering it to Harry for a plate of biscuits for Janie. 'So, these kumquats are a big thing here in Corfu,' she said. 'Apparently the hot summers and the amount of annual rainfall are perfect growing conditions.' She smiled, putting the plate down in front of Janie. 'Who knew?'

'Yes,' Elpida stated. 'Who knew that you know this?' She sniffed at her cigarette like it was smelling salts. 'It is amazing what you can find out from the town of Arillas, no?'

Imogen caught the woman's eye. Just how much did she know about Arillas?

'It's *really* nice,' Tristan said through a mouthful.

'Children eating fruit without complaints. I'm all for that,' Janie said, taking a sip of wine, her other hand unmoved under Harry's.

'This is *fruit*!' Olivia exclaimed.

'I won't tell you how much sugar also went into it,' Imogen whispered to Janie.

'Who's going to want seconds?' Harry asked them.

Two hands went up in the air, followed by muffled affirmations.

'We could have ice cream with it. I've got four flavours,' Harry reminded.

'Vanilla, please,' Olivia said.

'Chocolate for me, Dad,' Tristan answered.

'You were right, Imogen,' Janie whispered as Harry got up from the table and headed back towards the kitchen.

'About what?' she asked, turning slightly in her seat.

'He's a different man here.' Janie continued to watch him. 'Today I saw him shifting crates of drinks, painting a pergola, hanging fairy lights, talking to someone from the local council, driving a van… then running around in the sand with the children.' She fingered the stem of her wineglass. 'Here in Corfu he's so calm. So… at home.'

'Ah, soon you will feel this way too,' Elpida stated, eyes on Janie.

'Who, me?' Janie exclaimed, one hand on her chest. 'Oh no, I mean, I love Corfu for a holiday but my home's in England.'

'For now,' Elpida said, nodding.

'So,' Imogen began, sitting forward on her seat and changing the subject. 'Panos' signs went up today.'

'Pfft! Do not talk to me about signs. I hate signs. They are meant to tell everyone that he own this, like a statement of what a big parcel he has in his trousers.'

'Who has a parcel down their trousers?' Olivia asked, licking at her spoon.

Janie began choking on her biscuit.

'No one,' Imogen said quickly, her eyes darting to Elpida.

'That boy will be the death of me. He says he worries about me smoking too much. Pfft! I could smoke all the cigarettes in Greece and his stress will still be the nail in the coffin before the tar and nicotine can start to rot me.'

Imogen's vision moved to the green patch of wasteland. 'Elpida, do you know who owns that piece of land between here and Tomas' Taverna?'

The woman put the unlit cigarette between her lips and sucked as if hoping to get some relief. 'Why do you want to know this?'

'Well, it's right next to Halloumi and if Panos can buy it, it means his nightclub complex could be actually wall to wall with us. I can't envisage our diners wanting to hear the latest Flo Rida pumping through the cavity.'

'I'm worried about that too,' Janie admitted. 'I mean, if the restaurant doesn't go well and Harry does have to sell it again how much less will it be worth right next to something like Spearmint Rhino?'

Tristan pulled a face. 'I don't like spearmints. They taste funny.'

'I was thinking,' Imogen carried on. 'If Harry and I could buy it then we could maybe put a play area there.' She thought about the little dark-haired girl and her ball she'd seen the other day. 'Swings and a slide or a play house,' Imogen mused. 'It might encourage more families to Halloumi and later in the night, when the rave is really kicking off, the children won't be there to hear it because they'll be in bed and it will just give us a little breathing space.'

Elpida let out a breath. 'I am hoping it won't come to this. That Pano will see sense before any of this will happen.'

'Signs going up tends to mean people are serious,' Janie offered.

'So, could you find out?' Imogen said. 'Ask around?'

Elpida nodded. 'I will find out.'

'It's all go at the moment, isn't it? What with the restaurant and your mum getting April's house,' Janie spoke up.

Imogen nodded. It was true. Everything was changing around her but in some ways she felt like a bystander, close to the action but distanced. Just like how things were with Panos at the moment.

Unconsciously she picked up her phone and refreshed her inbox. She was still holding on to a last flicker of hope that the promised email from the Wyatt Hotel Group was going to be something other than a rejection. She watched the circle spiral around and three new emails arrived. Vistaprint, Amazon and a prince of Nigeria. That just about said everything.

FIFTY

Elpida Dimitriou's home, Agios Martinos

Panos looked at the papers laid out on the table before him.
He had been sitting in the early morning fingers of sunlight
since it was light enough to see his way to the garden from the
back door of the house. In front of him was a map of the area
and some workings Alejandro Kalas had passed to him in confidence. This was the rough outline of a community market for
the Acharavi region. Why he was looking at it now the signs
were up on Tomas' Taverna he didn't really know. He had another meeting scheduled with Lafi from Avalon but he was unsure
what the outcome was going to be. One business on the beachfront might not be enough unless... he acquired the strip of
land next to Halloumi. He just needed to find out who owned it
and make them an offer. The community market could perhaps
be something else. A pet project that might appease the locals
once the diggers moved in.

His phone rumbled next to the papers and he picked it up,
looking at the screen. A business news alert.

Fraser Limited buys up StoreCo

Tension invaded his jawline as he swiped to reveal the article.
His step-father had been busy. First awards, now his company
had just purchased one of the biggest businesses in the UK. Did

he really want to read the gory details? And why was he filled
with envy? John worked hard. He had built his company up
from nothing. He loved Panos' mother.

His eyes went to the article. There was John, finger-pointing
and looking like a politician, speaking at a conference last year.
He scrolled down the screen, his eyes skimming the details of
the billion-pound deal. And then he stopped as another photo
appeared.

John and Sophia. His mother looking so vibrant and beautiful. He swallowed, eyes fixed on her image. She was wearing a
sea-green-coloured cocktail dress, her red hair loose like a Titian
goddess. She was smiling, not just with her mouth for the camera, but with every single part of her body. He couldn't remember seeing her look quite like… not since he was a boy and she
had danced with his father on a Saturday night.

The last message she had left for him had been an invitation
to visit her in the UK. He had never responded. Why? How he
felt about family, how he had chosen to live his life wasn't down
to her. It was down to him… and because of Christos.

'Pano!' Elpida's voice called.

He put his phone back down and hurriedly folded up the
papers as he heard Elpida's steps coming across the decked
area. Standing up, he faced her with a smile. She looked almost
dressed for combat, wearing a rainbow-coloured knee-length
dress in a camouflage print and matching headscarf, black trainers on her feet.

'Good morning,' he greeted.

'What is this?' Elpida asked.

'What is what?' He had positioned himself to hide the paperwork. Unless she had developed X-ray vision there was nothing
to see here.

'You, up at dawn, in the garden.'

'I had work to do,' he stated.

'I have seen the signs, Pano, but today? Festival day?' Elpida exclaimed like he had committed an awful sin.

He smiled. 'I worked early so I could help you now.'

'Good,' she began. 'Because Rhea and I need a car to Halloumi to get things ready. Risto has taken my car.'

'I can do this.'

'*Kalós*,' she nodded.

'So, you saw the signs,' Panos said, hands on his hips.

'Yes, the name of your company in big letters. Very good. You would like me to do a *sirtaki* dance?' Elpida asked, lifting one foot off the floor.

He shook his head.

'Good, because I save my dancing for tonight.'

'But I do want to ask you something,' Panos stated.

'Go on,' Elpida said. 'As long as it is not to do with smoking then I listen.'

Panos pulled in a breath, already expecting resistance. 'Do you know who owns the piece of land next to our old restaurant?'

'Pfft!' Elpida shook her head violently. 'What is the matter with you? Is it not enough to buy one of my favourite restaurants and get ready to close it down? And I know Avalon is on your list too. Cooky told me. Now you want to buy up something right next to Harry and Imogen's place!'

'It is business, *yiayia*.'

'I don't like that sort of business.'

'Listen, it is confidential for now but… I hope also to be involved with the community market.'

'Pfft!' Elpida remarked. 'To try to make yourself look good?'

'I bet you do not say these things to John,' he said, immediately wishing he hadn't.

'Why do you speak of John?' Elpida asked, narrowing her eyes and focussing like a fly about to descend on a leftover meal.

He shook his head again, unwilling to reveal more.

'Should I dislike John because he is not my Christos?' Elpida asked. 'Pfft! That is no way to behave. Christos is gone and I will not wish for John to pay for my son's mistakes.'

He could see there were tears in his grandmother's eyes and he hated that he had caused that. Was that what he wanted to happen? For his step-father to fail because his own father had?

'Imogen also asked me who owned the land next to Halloumi,' Elpida admitted. 'She wants to build a play park for the children visiting the restaurant.' She sniffed. 'When I speak to the owner I know which offer I shall be recommending.'

'*Yiayia*…' he began, reaching out for her arm.

'Pfft! No more sentiment, Pano, there is much to do today,' she said, shifting out of his reach. 'Change into something old,' she said as she turned away. 'I have a lot of carrying for you to do.'

FIFTY-ONE

Halloumi, Acharavi beachfront

'Right!' Harry clapped his hands as he entered the kitchen. 'Let's get this show on the road.'

Imogen looked up from the bowl of mussels, fresh from one of the local fishermen this morning. She had soaked them in cold water, discarded the ones that had opened when she'd tapped them and she was now scrubbing any barnacles or imperfections from them. They were going to be steamed with shallots, garlic and rosemary and served in disposable pots at the folklore festival.

'Is Janie still asleep?' she asked.

'No, she's getting Olivia and Tristan ready.' Harry grinned. 'I ducked out when Tristan started moaning about his Southampton football shirt not being in his suitcase.'

'Oh dear,' she answered. 'It sounds like a heinous crime.'

'He thinks so,' Harry said with a laugh. 'So, Immy, today's the day.'

'I know,' she answered, dropping another handful of mussels into a dish. 'I'm making a dish I haven't made in years but I picked a simple one. One you can make when I'm back in the UK.' She looked up at her brother. 'Is everything ready?'

'I don't know,' Harry said. 'What do you think?'

Both of them gazed out of the kitchen and through the now open hatch into the main restaurant area. There were gauzy cream drapes at each window now, enough to give a little privacy but not enough to block out any light or the fabulous sea view. Imogen drew in a contented breath.

'So, you can admit it now,' Harry said, slipping an arm around her shoulders. 'You should have trusted your big brother.'

'Let's not go too far,' she answered with a smile.

'We're down to the final few hurdles.'

'Hurdles?'

'Hoops,' Harry said.

'To jump through? What sort of hoops?' Her heart kicked up a gear and she dropped the mussel she was holding.

'Nothing that can't be sorted,' he insisted. 'Breathe.' He pulled in a breath, his motion causing her chest to rise almost involuntarily.

'We know what food we're making today and we have enough ingredients to see us through opening night and the next week, yes?'

Harry closed his eyes, still breathing, and nodded. 'Yes.'

'And you're going to get the condiment pots for the tables today.'

'Yes.'

'This morning I'm picking up the flyers with the vouchers on to give away.'

'Yep.'

'The fire man is coming to inspect before noon and then he'll go to the fire station and get us the certificate,' Imogen reeled off.

'That's right.'

'Then...'

'I'm still waiting for one very small piece of paperwork,' Harry admitted.

'What sort of paperwork?'

'It's nothing for you to worry about.'

'Saying that only makes me worry more.' She shrugged off his arm. 'Tell me.'

'There was a problem getting my business permit.'

'I only heard the word "problem". Explain!' Imogen begged.

'We just need to have that in place before we open.'

'Before we open when, Harry?' she asked. 'Because although we're not *open* open we're going to be *open* today.' Her heart was pounding now, like she was running for a train that was about to leave. 'We're going to be serving food! What does this mean?!'

'I'm not sure,' Harry responded.

'What?!' Imogen exploded. 'Harry! How can you not know?!' So much for him being the epitome of calm. How could he be when there was a licence missing?

'There's a lot of red tape in Greece but they also seem to be sensible about things.'

'That isn't an answer!' She put her hands on her hips. 'Do we need to call someone? Go somewhere? Will Elpida know?'

'De-stress,' Harry said, putting his hands on Imogen's shoulders. 'Take another breath.'

'How can you be so relaxed about this? I don't understand it… You've been writing lists since we got here, I thought we had everything under control. How has this gone unnoticed?'

'It hasn't. I just needed to dot some Is and cross some Ts and after all the dotting and crossing… well, we've been busy,' Harry reminded her.

'I don't believe this. After everything we've done and all the hassle with… Panos.' She heaved a sigh, feeling her eyes filling with tears. This was stress but it wasn't just down to Harry's business permit, this was concern for Harry and Janie's marriage and the children and everything else hinging on this launch going well.

'Immy,' Harry said, attempting to put his arm around her again.

'I'm fine. It's the mussels… they're… mussely.' She sniffed. 'Tell me how we fix it?'

'I'll ring the permit guy as soon as they're open,' Harry promised. 'Because it's *my* restaurant and *I'm* taking responsibility.'

He nudged her arm with his elbow, forcing her to reconnect. 'What will you be doing without me when you get home, eh? Boredom central without a restaurant to open.'

She knew he had meant the comment in jest but it stung. What would she be doing? There was still nothing from the Wyatt Group. Home was going to be endless plates of egg and chips and the latest offering from ITV. A regular visit to her mum and her upcoming conservatory then something with David Tennant in it. She swallowed.

'Hey, come on, today's going to be great,' Harry said, swinging both arms around her and drawing her into a hug. 'Elpida said there's some group dance the whole village does. Something to do with asking the gods for a good olive harvest. I might need your help. You know how bad I am at dancing.'

Imogen stifled a laugh against his chest and looked up. 'Whatever you do, just don't embarrass Olivia and Tristan.'

FIFTY-TWO

Halloumi, Acharavi heachfront

'Shall I hang this one up over here?'

Olivia had one foot on the low wall of the terrace and another stretched out behind her like a ballerina's as she balanced tentatively, a string of bunting in her hands.

'Careful, Olivia. If you fall and break something it's an hour to the hospital,' Imogen said, moving to hold onto the girl's free arm.

'You sound like Mum,' Olivia moaned.

'Who wouldn't have even let you climb up on that wall,' Imogen added.

'There!' Olivia said, hooking the bunting over the outside of the pergola. 'We might need to get some sticky tape if it gets windy.'

'It *can* get windy in Corfu,' Imogen replied, helping the girl jump down.

'I like it here. It's always sunny,' Olivia said, using Imogen's hand to spin underneath her arm like a fork twirling spaghetti. 'And Daddy's happy.'

Imogen smiled. 'Yes, he is.'

'And Mummy's happy too. She even held Daddy's hand last night.'

'I know,' Imogen answered, smiling.

As Olivia span around her, squealing with delight as giddiness started to take hold, Imogen looked again at the view right outside their restaurant. White stones mixed with ecru sand, the turquoise water rolling gently in and lapping the shore. People sat on striped deckchairs, lay on sun loungers under blue and white striped parasols and further up the beach there was a flurry of activity around a makeshift stage.

Panos watched them from across the road on the edge of the beach. The little girl bobbing up and down decorating the front of the terrace area, Imogen with paperwork on a board, counting on her fingers then writing numbers down, looking at her phone, then back to the papers. He knew now, despite everything he kept trying to tell himself, what he felt wasn't just physical attraction. There was so much more. Something so deep it scared him to death. She was his match. But they were still two people at odds over beachfront property.

He took a breath of the sweet, humid air rolling off the sea and, through his sunglasses, his eyes went to the length of road skirting the sand. Restauranteurs, bar owners and residents were all out in force preparing for the afternoon and evening festivities. The fragrance of a cocktail of fruit invaded his nose – watermelon, guava and kiwi – all in abundance in the back of the van loading produce onto a stand. There were stalls going up all along the road, a buzz about the area that reminded him of the market at Arillas. It was life. Greek life. Corfu life. Alive, well and prospering. And there was his sign, outside Tomas' Taverna, heavily hinting at something else.

Walking across the road, Panos stepped up onto the terrace and paused, watching Olivia and Imogen dancing together on the tiles. Suddenly Imogen spotted him and stopped dancing. She stepped back and started brushing the wayward strands of blonde hair off her face.

'*Kalimera*,' Panos greeted them both, bowing towards Olivia.

'That means "good morning",' Oliva answered. She waved her hand. '*Yassou.*' She smiled. 'That means "hello".'

'That is very good,' Panos said, clapping his hands. 'You speak wonderful Greek already.'

Imogen jutted out her chin. 'If you're looking for Elpida and Rhea, they're in the kitchen with Harry and Janie.' She indicated the bunting above his head. 'Olivia and I are on decorating duty and Tristan is playing with Socks.'

Panos furrowed his brow. 'Socks?'

'It's our cat,' Olivia answered. 'It's short for Socrates.'

He smiled. 'Very good.'

'You're the man who bought us beds, aren't you?' Olivia continued. 'And the man who wants to build Peppermint Rhino.'

'Um, let's just talk about the beds shall we?' Imogen jumped in quickly.

'Are you sleeping well on these?' Panos asked Olivia.

'Mine's better than my bed at home,' Olivia admitted.

'And you?' Panos asked, his eyes on Imogen. 'How is your bed?'

She shuffled her feet. 'It's—'

'Immy,' Harry said, bouncing out onto the terrace. 'I've phoned the permit guy. His name's Spiros – what else! We need to pick up the permit today… Hello, Panos.'

'*Yassou.*'

'Today? Where from? Here in Acharavi?' Imogen asked.

'I'm afraid not,' Harry said. 'Corfu Town.'

'But… you can't… you've got so much to do here,' she answered. 'And I need to get back in the kitchen as soon as I've finished out here.'

'I was rather hoping *you* could pick it up. He doesn't need me in person and I've got the fire man coming soon. Elpida has the kitchen covered.'

'Oh, Harry! That awful drive up from the airport almost killed me,' she stated. 'And I need to be here, getting ready for this afternoon and tonight.'

'I could take you,' Panos interjected.

He felt every single set of eyes go to him and felt the need to qualify his statement. 'I have made deliveries for Elpida already. She does not need me to help set up for the party until later.' He swallowed, realising he really wanted to take Imogen to Corfu Town. 'And I know Spiros. If there is any problem I can deal with this.'

'That would be brilliant,' Harry said almost excitedly.

'It's OK,' Imogen said. 'I can drive the Micra... I mean I've done it once, I can do it again.'

'The Mercedes will be quicker,' Panos said.

'Speed around those bends? I *do* want to get there.'

'I have been on these roads since I was sixteen.'

'And was it donkey or moped?'

Imogen bit her lip. That was a low, horrible comment brought on by the fact her stomach was zinging down a zip wire at the thought of being alone with him again.

'I think it's a good idea Panos goes with you,' Harry said. 'Those roads *are* tricky and...' He looked sheepish. 'Spiros said he's only there until one o'clock.'

'Harry!' Imogen exclaimed. 'That's only an hour and a half. What if I get lost or... break down or...'

'I know where the office is,' Panos stated.

'That's settled then,' Harry concluded. 'Come on, Olivia, come and see what's happening in the kitchen.'

'Do you really have a donkey?' Olivia asked Panos.

'Not anymore,' Panos answered with a smile.

Olivia and Harry left them alone and Imogen turned her attention to the beach. Anything to stop herself from having to look at him.

'Are you ready to go?'

She turned back. 'Are you?'

'Come,' he said, leading the way off the terrace. 'The sooner we get there the sooner we can come back.'

Looking at his perfectly formed body in that near-transparent white shirt and black jeans, Imogen strengthened her resolve. *The sooner they got there the sooner they got back* was just fine with her.

'One kilometre over sixty and I'm out,' she said, hurrying behind Panos.

He turned, a smile on those ridiculously full lips. 'That is OK. I will find you the nearest donkey.'

FIFTY-THREE

Corfu Town

Imogen and Panos had reached Spiros' office just in time. She was in possession of the permit and Halloumi was good to take part in the festival and open its doors on launch night.

Imogen thought she had seen most of Corfu Town during the stressful drive from the airport en route to the north of the island a week ago. It was busy and noisy with hundreds of people and twice as many mopeds to navigate around. In her opinion, it wasn't somewhere to spend quality time. You got out as quickly as you could, to quiet roads – albeit, pothole-ridden roads with hairpin bends – and you only went back when you absolutely had to. Like for your return flight or… for a vital business permit. But now, as she walked along the Liston with Panos, the reality was nothing like she had expected.

Tall Venetian-influenced buildings in lemon, terracotta and peach lined narrow streets and alleyways. Wares spilled from doorways and hung from ropes and stands – tourists' fare of postcards, keyrings and multi-coloured sunhats sat alongside beautiful artwork, natural soaps and sponges and local lace. Nestled in between the riot of colour were the more muted tones of designer-branded stores – leather handbags, watches, high-end clothes. It was somewhere in between a shopping street and a Tunisian *souq*.

The very old mixed with new in a fusion of styles Imogen had never encountered before. Wooden shutters over windows of all shapes and sizes – standard rectangular, circular and arched – white wrought-iron Juliette balconies and rope rows of washing hanging across the maze of streets. Slender, sky-touching palms met pale, weeping willows and in the very centre of the town was a village green that wouldn't have looked out of place in the depths of the English countryside.

'Here they play cricket,' Panos stated, as if reading her thoughts.

'Really?' she asked.

He nodded. 'Really. Just like the English.'

'It's so beautiful,' Imogen remarked, her vision going to the arcade of arches to their left, white canopies shading some of the tables on the *piazza* from the intense heat of the midday sun.

'We should have a drink,' Panos suggested.

She shook her head. 'No, we have to get back. There's a lot to do.' She looked at her watch to emphasise the point. If she stopped, if she sat down in this picturesque setting with the sun on her back, the scent of citrus and bougainvillea, cooking coming from the numerous cafes, her guard would drop.

'I would like to talk to you,' he said softly.

Even his voice was beautiful. It wasn't fair. She looked up, focussing on the salmon-and-white tower ahead of them, a bird sitting on top of one of the two bells. It was like her right now. Poised to make a move should its situation become precarious.

'Please, Imogen, it's important.'

She turned to him then and stopped walking. Something about him was different. His eyes revealed a contrasting layer, nothing like she had seen before.

'Please,' he said again.

She swallowed, bringing up a hand to shield her eyes from the sun. 'One drink,' she agreed.

Panos led the way to the café bar at the edge of the water. It was one of his favourites in Corfu Town, a place that epitomised the beauty of the whole island. Under a large cream-coloured sun shade they sat at a table on the very edge of the terrace overlooking the cerulean water with the Old Fortress as a backdrop. To him it was one of the most serene, calming places on Earth.

He took a sip of his coffee, his eyes moving from the view and resting on Imogen. She sat back in her chair, face turned up to the sun, eyes closed. How he wanted to caress the soft skin of her cheek with his fingers, let his lips glide over hers again. He swallowed the coffee down. He didn't even know where to begin, or whether saying anything was going to do any good.

'Rhea and I…' he started. 'We really are not together anymore.'

He watched her open her eyes and look back at him.

'We were never wholly together at all,' he admitted. 'Well, obviously, we were… in some ways, but…'

She didn't speak, and he suddenly felt like he was giving an awkward talk to a committee where he hadn't quite done his homework properly. *Trousers* was the word he wanted to use and internally he cursed Elpida's damn analogy.

'For me,' he started again. 'The relationship was not serious.'

'And for her?' Imogen asked. 'I'm guessing if she flew over a few islands to come here the relationship was more serious in her opinion.'

He cradled his coffee cup. 'I think she wanted it to be. I think she thought I could be a different man. The man she wanted.'

Imogen sat a little further forward on her seat and picked up her tea cup. 'But you can't be?' She sipped at the drink.

He shook his head. 'No,' he said. 'I can't be the man she wants. I'm not quite sure that this man exists.'

'Rhea's nice,' Imogen replied. 'I like her.'

'I like her too,' he admitted. 'But not in the way she needs me to.' What did he want to say? 'Imogen, I want you to know that I am going to help Alejandro Kalas start up a community market in Acharavi.'

After mentioning it to his grandmother this morning he hadn't really made a final decision but, sitting here, his life in Crete felt a million miles away. He wasn't ready to back down on the complex along Acharavi seafront, but he was ready to make a commitment to the community in another way.

'Why?' Imogen asked. Her tone was full of suspicion and he could hardly blame her.

He let out a breath. 'It is a good scheme. I have been over the information. I think we can make it work in Acharavi just like it is working in Arillas and other areas.'

'And what about the beachfront?'

She fixed her eyes on him until he could feel the burn of her stare on his skin.

'It is my business, Imogen. I am always going to have to look at new opportunities,' he admitted. 'But, I would also like to try something different.' He paused. 'Like you helping Harry build a restaurant business.'

He watched her ease herself back into the chair, settling into the pale biscuit-coloured cushioning.

'I don't think Harry really needs me now,' she admitted. 'I'm not sure he ever did. I think I was more like a cooking comfort blanket for him. A bit of security from home to cling on to until he found his feet… or your grandmother.'

'I think you have been much more to him than that.'

'Do you?' she asked. 'Because Elpida cooks Greek food far better than I can. And he's ignored almost all of my business budgeting advice and you really don't need an NVQ to wrangle goats.'

He reached across the table for her hand and she moved it away.

'Don't, Pano,' she said.

'Why not?'

'Because.' She let a breath go. 'Because I like it too much and I *shouldn't* like it… and I'm leaving at the end of next week.' The humid air hung between them.

He didn't say anything. He didn't know what to say. He could offer her nothing but now. He had never been able to offer anything else.

'My mum needs my help. She's going to move house and she's playing it down but it's going to be a big wrench for her.' Her eyes moved to the line of yachts moored on the water underneath the fortress. 'It's the right thing to do but it's our family home and… things are still up in the air with Harry and Janie… It's my job to be there for my mum.' She turned back to him. 'Family's always been my thing. I'm not a career girl or a party girl, I'm the one who papers over the cracks and holds things together.'

'You said you wanted to be hotel girl,' he reminded her.

'Yes,' she sighed. 'When I dared to dream.'

'You mean you have stopped?'

She shrugged. 'Any day I'm going to get a rejection email from the Wyatt Group.'

'How do you know this?'

'Because I don't have the qualifications or the experience.'

'There are other companies you could try.' He moved the salt cellar on the table, picking it up and rolling it in his palm. 'To try and be rejected is not failure. But, to not even try is the very worst failure of all.'

He watched her reaction to his words. She was still looking into the mid-distance, perhaps the top of the Old Fortress, thoughts as layered as the stone walls.

He put the salt cellar down. 'Do you think Harry and Janie will be reconciled?'

'I don't know but I really hope so.' She paused. 'I don't really know why they broke up in the first place. There never seemed to be one solid reason, just a lot of little things happening all at once… Harry's accident and his depression…' She leant forward, picking up her tea cup. 'And as much as I love Tristan and Olivia, children are always trying.'

'You think there is still love there?' Panos asked her. He observed her again as she thought about her reply.

'I think there will always be some sort of love there. They have the children together so there's always going to be that connection.' She put her cup back down. 'But maybe that isn't enough. And, I suppose maybe it shouldn't be.'

He nodded. Was that what had happened to his parents? He hadn't been enough to keep them soldered together? His father had destroyed their lives when he'd got complacent and gambled with everything they had. Their love had burnt out, got too broken to be fixed, or could probably have been mended if only either of them had wanted to try.

'I am not sure I know what love is,' he stated.

Somewhere between the strong coffee, the memories he was restoring and the ambience of the setting, his thoughts had escaped and it was too late to take them back. It felt like the words were floating there, hovering above the table.

Imogen watched him, half present, half somewhere else. She could see he was thinking deeply.

'I don't think it's as simple as that,' she said. 'Emotion doesn't have to be put into a box and marked with a label.' She sat up in her seat. 'I really think you have to decide who you want in your life and why and start there.'

'And if some of the people you remove from your life are family?' Panos offered.

'I never said family are easy.'

'But *you* need them and want them.'

'Not everyone feels the same. Not everyone is lucky. I don't have a father any more, remember?' she said.

'And I wish I never had mine.'

He had answered quickly and she knew, from the sparse information he'd given her over the time they had known each other, speaking about his family didn't come easy. She seized on the opportunity.

'What exactly did he do, Pano?'

She watched the grills go up on the windows of his soul, his expression cloud and that firm jawline harden further. Was he still not ready to let anyone in? She maintained a silence, half-hoping he would start to talk, half-afraid she wouldn't know what to do if he did.

'He destroyed us,' he whispered, his voice strained with vehemence.

She kept quiet, her fingers winding around the arms of the wooden chair as she tried to remain still.

'He destroyed us and then... then he destroyed himself. And by then, I didn't care.' He picked up his coffee cup. 'Because he had gone from being my everything to being the man that tore us all apart.'

FIFTY-FOUR

The outskirts of Acharavi

Panos hadn't said a word on the drive back across the island. After they finished their drinks by the sea they had walked back to the car and he had made uneasy small talk about the patchwork plaster on the buildings they passed, the old and new forts that rose up like brick-built guardians and Vido, the wildlife sanctuary and previous island hospital for Serbian war soldiers, sitting in the mouth of the port of Corfu Town. He had been keen to give her a brief history lesson rather than talk about what was in the box of memories he had opened up.

Imogen settled back into her seat as the roads flattened out, recognising some of the signs and landmarks from her previous trip and knowing they were nearing Acharavi. She had the business permit. That's what she had gone to the capital for. Halloumi was her priority. If Panos couldn't open up it wasn't her concern.

But then he was pulling off the main road, up a dirt track that quickly turned into a steep incline. Imogen reached for the handle by the top of the door frame and clung on.

'Where are we going?' she asked. 'If this is a short cut I'd really rather stick to the main road.'

When Panos didn't answer she turned her head. He was focussed on the road and navigating the difficult terrain in the saloon. With the size of the rocks and rubble on the trail even a monster truck would have had difficulty.

Jerks and jumps had Imogen hanging on, until a building came into view and Panos swung the car left, pulling to a stop outside the site.

'What is this place?' Imogen asked, looking through the passenger window. It was a tall structure that looked completely out of place in the middle of an olive grove. Gnarly trunks with slender silvery-green branches swayed in the breeze around the concrete.

'It is nothing,' Panos snapped. 'Look at it.' He wrenched open his door, his shoes crunching the gravel beneath their soles.

Imogen hastened out of the vehicle too, closing the door after her and checking out the towering four-storey construction ahead of them.

The exterior of it was finished. Thick breeze-block walls with red brick over half of it; some of that work was even plastered. Inside, however, was a different story. It was dark, completely empty, no doors, no windows, just the basic shell like a few properties she'd seen around the area. But it wasn't just bereft of paintwork, fixtures and fittings, it was lacking any warmth. It was raw, hollowed out, a cave. It was as if someone had started the project with energy and enthusiasm and then run out of steam... or money.

'What *was* it going to be?' Imogen asked, watching Panos as he walked up to the entrance and placed a hand on the wall.

'A hotel,' he stated. 'It would have been one of the biggest hotels in this area.' He drew in a breath. 'And he wanted it to be the best, too.' He shook his head. 'Nothing but the best for Christos Dimitriou.'

Then she understood. 'This was one of your father's hotels.'

'Yes,' he breathed. 'This was the final property he built. This was what he had always wanted. This was going to be the icing on his cake. His flagship. His way of saying to all the doubters,

"Here I am. The son of a farmer. Rich. Successful. So much better than everyone I grew up with.".' He kicked a foot at the rocky ground. 'My mother owns this now. I tell her years ago she should sell this or just knock it down but she won't. It is like she wants this ugly reminder to stay here forever.'

Imogen swallowed as every ounce of his agony coiled in her chest. She needed to say the right thing now if she wanted him to carry on opening up. 'Tell me what happened?' she asked softly.

He shook his head. 'I really do not know where to start.'

She watched him hang his head, leaning his entire weight on that one hand flat against the wall of the building. He looked utterly deflated. The confident, self-assured businessman completely missing.

Taking tentative steps forward, Imogen moved closer to him. 'Just tell me what he did to you,' she whispered.

He threw his hands up to the sky then, as if someone or something was up there. 'He made me who I am. He has dictated my entire life. And I am starting to realise… I hate that.'

The words were spat out, angry and coated in hatred. He snapped his hands back down then shot them out again. 'Look at this place!' he exclaimed. 'Look at what it could have been!'

Imogen took in the structure again, then shifted her vision to the surrounding area. The gorse, olive and cypress trees, wild flowers, the mountain in the background. 'It's a little out of place.'

'Yes!' he agreed. 'Yes it is. And that is one of the things he got wrong.' He shook his head. 'But, by the time this place was built, he was already finished.'

She picked a long straw of grass and began to strip it slowly with her fingers, hoping he would continue. She saw so much pain in him it was possible he had been holding onto this burden for years. Carrying the weight of all that rage and hurt had to do something to a person.

'He dreamed too big, Imogen,' he said in quieter tones, the words drifting out of him on the mountain breeze. 'He set his sights on the top of Mount Pantokrator when really he should have started out trying to conquer the foothills.' He sunk down onto the ground, his back resting against the front wall of the hotel, shoes and trousers getting coated in dust. 'He had success with his very first deal, a hotel in Kavos, in the south of the island, and he built a very good business – buying up hotels, renovating them, running them for a few years then selling them on for a profit. But he got greedy. What he had was not enough. He wanted the moon. He wanted to be a business king.'

She stepped up until she was alongside Panos, then sunk down next to him, stones slipping into her sandals as she stretched out her bare legs. 'Is that what you want too?'

He cranked his head left, his eyes full of fire. 'I have done it already. I succeeded where he failed. He made that my destiny.'

Saying the words out loud had Panos sounding like a fool. But he knew. He had always known. He had followed his father's path, not out of some blood-tied loyalty but because he wanted to be the man his father had failed at being. He wanted to have the million-Euro business, the string of successful enterprises, be the king. Win for Dimitriou, be better than John.

'He was an alcoholic near the end,' Panos whispered. 'He used to come home hardly able to walk.' He shook his head, his dark hair moving with the motion. 'The last time… I heard him come in, there was the sound of smashing glasses or plates… I do not know… and then my mother, she is screaming.'

He pressed his finger and thumb to the bridge of his nose as the memories flooded his consciousness. 'He died right there. On the floor. In a pool of his own vomit. Forty-five years old.'

Tears welled in his eyes and he tried to temper his feelings. He felt Imogen's arm go around his shoulders and his instinct was to shrug it off, shift away. Showing that this had affected him was weak. You couldn't be weak in life. Weak people were losers and losers, well, they lost.

'Pano—'

'There is nothing you can say,' he interrupted.

'There is,' she answered.

'What? That I should not let his mistakes be a shadow over me?'

'Well… yes.'

'And I should grieve, let all this pain out?'

'Maybe that too, yes.'

He shook his head. She didn't understand. How could she? He focussed on her then, her beautiful elfin face, that determined expression set as default, the soft shape of her pink lips. 'You did not have a father like mine,' he whispered.

'No,' she said. 'I loved my father very much but he wasn't there either. He spent half his life in a plane, working to support us, when all I really wanted was him at home.' She kicked a toe at a stone. 'Everything he ever brought back for me I cherished but I would have gladly swapped it for more time with him.'

He exhaled. 'And now it is too late for everyone. Things cannot be changed.'

'Wait,' she said. 'I didn't mean with you.' Her tone was insistent. 'Following your business dream… your *father's* business dream… hasn't made you as fulfilled as you thought it would, but there's still time to do something else.' She paused. 'You're *doing* something else… with the community market.'

'I want to, yes,' he agreed.

'Then that's a new start,' she said. 'A change.'

He shook his head. 'There are parts of me I cannot change.'

'Like what?'

How could he tell her that he didn't think he was capable of love because of all he had seen and experienced? How could he tell her he didn't think he was brave enough to even try? He had already fallen for her and she was leaving soon.

He swallowed, his eyes picking out the undulating hills leading down to the coast, the sea a whisper of blueish silver in the distance. 'I do not know if either of the new projects here will be enough.'

He felt her body move against him and her hand sought his, her fingers lengthening as they closed every space between them.

'It will be a beginning,' she whispered. 'Once you have that, the rest is up to you.'

FIFTY-FIVE

Main Street, Acharavi

The afternoon of the festival had gone well. When Imogen and Panos returned to Halloumi it was to find Elpida in mid scurry with Cooky taking trays of garlic and herb mussels in pots with thick slabs of fresh bread to the beach stall just outside the restaurant where Harry, Janie, Rhea and the children were handing out food to the celebrating villagers.

The sound of lute, *bouzouki* and guitar filled the air, along with toots and drum beats from a marching brass band, all accompanying a team of Greek dancers leading *sirtaki* along the promenade.

Risto had handed out coupons for discounted meals on Halloumi's opening night and all of them were now gone. If even half the people made use of them and booked a table, the restaurant was going to be busy on its first evening.

Now, as the sun began to go down, the entertainment had moved to the very centre of the town, the main street, where another stage had been erected just in front of the pump 'roundabout'. Spiros the shopkeeper had told Imogen the old water pump was where the villagers all used to collect their water from in days gone by and, in honour of this, the restaurant directly opposite was called The Pumphouse.

Tonight the owners of all the restaurants on the main street were preparing a feast for the entire village. Goats, pigs and lambs were all turning on spits outside the various eateries and the fragrance of rosemary, bay leaves and other assorted spices filled the air.

For the duration of the night there would be no traffic down the road. Barricades had been placed at both ends, virtually cutting Acharavi off from the rest of the island, long trestle tables lined the street, all decorated simply with paper tablecloths and glowing tea lights in jam jars.

Imogen accepted a plastic glass of clear liquid from a passing man, a tray of drinks hanging around his neck. She took a sip and the harsh alcohol almost sizzled her tongue. She hung it out into the air and Risto touched her arm.

'You are OK?' he asked.

'What is this?' Imogen coughed.

Risto laughed. 'That is *tsipouroi*. It is made by the Lasko family.' He drank some from his plastic glass. 'Every year no one is quite sure they get the mixture right. But…' He finished the liquid in his cup. 'We drink this anyway.'

Imogen smiled as the team of dancers bobbed and swayed on the road in front of them. It was a real carnival atmosphere with nothing but happy, smiling faces and the noisy chatter and laughter almost as loud as the Greek music. Through the dancers she picked out a familiar face. Sitting with a group of other Greek women all dressed in black was Mrs Pelekas, bouncing her knee up and down in time to the beat of the drum.

Her eyes went to Harry, who was being persuaded into the line of Greek dancing, Olivia on one side of him, Tristan on the other and Janie clapping along as she watched. Her sister-in-law was smiling, her face glowing as she looked at Harry. Was Corfu working its magic on them?

And then there was Panos, standing with Alejandro Kalas, Vasilis and his daughters, Rhea next to him. Her stomach turned and she moved her eyes away, fixing on Elpida and Cooky, the two women standing on chairs, swaying in time to the music, singing at the top of their voices.

From across the road Panos watched Imogen. The last light was beginning to fade and the strings of bulbs like miniature fireflies flickered from the boughs of every tree. Under the glow, her blonde hair, for once not tied up, cascaded over her bare shoulders, a treacle-like contrast to the plain black bandeau dress she wore. Her sun-kissed skin was radiant and she had never looked more beautiful to him.

He shifted on his feet. What was he going to do about that? He had opened up to her today, shown her his fears, told her his story, but instead of feeling unburdened, he felt more tied up than ever. Because how he felt still hung there, swaying in the breeze like figs on a tree, cautious as to whether to fall or be picked.

'So, Pano...' Alejandro boomed, grease from a pitta *gyros* around his mouth. 'We are agreed about the community market, yes?'

He nodded, raising his plastic glass of *tsipouroi*. 'It is a sound idea.'

'*Poli kaló!*' Alejandro answered. 'You will help me show this to the council at the next meeting.'

'Wait... what?' This wasn't what he had planned. He had made the decision to help, but his ultimate priority was going to be the bars on the beachfront. He didn't want to be the figurehead of this campaign.

'We need to fix costs, show them how this will make money for the community, fuel solidarity between us and bring in even more tourism.'

'Alejandro, I will help all that I can but, as you no doubt know, I have bought Tomas' Taverna. We need to finalise my plans for the beachfront complex.'

'Rhea, you must come to dance with us!' Margot said, tugging at the woman's arm. 'Vasilis, you too!'

Panos was grateful for the interruption and took a swig of the highly intoxicating drink while the two Kalas women, Vasilis and Rhea departed for the circle that had formed around the pump roundabout.

'*Ochi*, Panos,' the man said, shaking his head. 'I tell you, the council will not pass plans like this anymore. Since the crisis they have concern about all new buildings like this.'

Panos' mouth dried up, his tongue hard and unmalleable. 'Alejandro, I am willing to work with you on the community market but I need the go-ahead on the plans for a Dimitriou Enterprises development.'

'That is a condition of your help, is it?' Alejandro asked, his eyes darkening. 'You wish for me to push this through the council?'

Panos swallowed, ducking into the older man's space and lowering his voice a little. 'I will make sure you are rewarded.'

Alejandro snorted. 'What would your father think?'

'My father was a failure. I am never going to be that.' He stood firm, keeping his head held high.

Alejandro shook his head. 'Your father got in over his head but he would never have tried to do what you want to.' He took a slug of his drink. 'Your father loved Acharavi just the way it is,' Alejandro continued. 'Why do you think he wanted to build the last Dimitriou Hotel outside of the village?'

'Because permission was turned down for that size of building in the centre,' Panos stated confidently.

'No,' Alejandro stated gruffly. 'Because he wanted to give tourists the five-star contemporary stays they were looking for *and* the real Greece too. The Greece he grew up in, the Greece he raised you in, the tradition that should still run deep inside you.' He paused. 'I saw his plans. He did not want to build something that would ruin the look of the village. That's why he chose the site a few kilometres away. He was going to run a minibus to the town several times a day to ensure his guests spent money in the village, at the local tavernas and bars. The heart of the community was always at the forefront of his mind when it came to home.'

His cheeks flushed at the councillor's words. He felt like he had been kicked in the stomach. Was this true? Had his father felt that way?

'But, he simply ran out of money. Took on too much,' Alejandro said. 'Panos, your father, he was a good man with a true heart.'

Panos took a swig of his drink and tried to maintain his cool. Had his father developed outside of the village because he *wanted to*, not because he *had to*? That small point could make a difference to everything he lived by.

'Pano, Corfu is your island and Acharavi is still your home. We are going to make a wonderful team.' Alejandro's meaty hand came down on Panos' back. 'The north of Corfu will be as vibrant as it used to be.'

He kept his expression neutral, gave a brief, non-committal nod he hoped was enough. He had no idea how to move forward now. He was lost, anchor up and drifting.

'OK, it is time for me to find my dance partner,' Vasilis announced, coming back to the group and putting his plastic glass down on the table next to them.

Alejandro laughed, shaking his head as Vasilis left again, weaving in between dancers as he crossed the street. 'He has taken to the English girl.'

Now Panos felt like someone had dropped a flagon of *tsipou-roi* in the middle of his chest. He watched, his body stiffening as he kept his eyes on Vasilis. Every inch of him, inside and out, was screaming at him to move, to do something, as he saw the younger Kalas offer his hand to Imogen. But what should he do? It was the festival, everyone danced, why shouldn't Vasilis dance with Imogen? She was single. She wasn't his. *He wanted her to be.* But why? So he didn't feel like he'd lost again? Everything seemed to be slipping through his fingers like sand on Almyros beach.

'She is a very pretty girl,' Alejandro remarked, jamming the remains of the pitta *gyros* into his mouth.

He couldn't speak. All he could do was look while his stomach dropped down to his shoes.

'Imogen! Come up onto the table!' Elpida called from her precarious vantage point, the table rocking like it was about to collapse at any moment.

'Come on, Imogen!' Cooky encouraged. 'Come up and dance right here!'

She shook her head. 'No thank you. If I break my leg EasyJet aren't going to let me fly home.'

'Pfft!' Elpida said. 'Good. Then you have to stay here for more time.'

'You would hate it. I'd be making terrible pastry in the kitchen,' Imogen called back over the music.

'But you make wonderful mussels,' Elpida replied. 'And Harry says you can do amazing things with salmon.'

Imogen smiled. 'He's my brother. He's being kind. You'll notice salmon isn't on the menu.'

'That is where you are not right,' Elpida said. 'It is going to be a special.'

Imogen balked, a heavy mix of surprise, worry and excitement invading at once.

'Imogen.' She quickly turned her head to see Vasilis Kalas standing in front of her, his hand held out.

'Oh, *yassas*, Vasilis,' she greeted.

'You look very beautiful tonight,' he said, smiling at her.

'Thank you.' She couldn't help a blush hitting her cheeks.

'Would you like to dance?'

She hesitated. Panos was looking directly at her, his hands in the pockets of his black jeans, the top two buttons of his white shirt unfastened. Dancing with Vasilis had been enjoyable before but the strongest memory she had of that night was falling hard into Panos and feeling that her heart was going to burst from her body.

She shook her head. 'Thank you, but... I'm OK,' she said. 'I was just about to get some more drinks with Risto.' She took hold of Risto's arm, feeling she needed a prop.

Vasilis bowed politely. 'Another time?' he asked.

'Yes.' She nodded. 'Another time.'

FIFTY-SIX

'Oh! It is time!' Elpida exclaimed, swaying into Imogen as they stood in the dancing circle after a lively traditional Corfiot dance rejoicing the gods and asking for a good harvest. There had been left and right and sashaying this way and that and Imogen had spent more time trying not to tread on Janie or Elpida's toes.

Her sister-in-law looked happier than she had seen her in some time and Olivia and Tristan were also caught up in the atmosphere, forming friendships over home-made lemonade and jumping games with the village children.

'Time for what?' Imogen asked, moving backwards as all the people encouraged the circle to widen.

'This dance excite her every year,' Cooky chipped in, her bosoms almost falling out of the low-cut jade dress she was wearing.

'If it's complicated I'll have to sit down,' Imogen said. She unwound her arm from behind Elpida's shoulder.

'No, you stay,' Elpida said.

'I'm almost better at making pastry than I am at dancing,' Imogen stated.

'Hush, this is where you get the gossip,' Cooky informed.

'I'm lost,' Imogen answered.

'This is dance of lovers,' Elpida stated. 'Only people that dance are people in love.'

'You get the married couples, bound to each other for all eternity and it is very sweet, but...' Cooky giggled. 'We like to watch the ones we have been watching all year come out!'

'*Come out*,' Imogen said. 'It's just a dance. What if these people don't know it's a "dance of lovers".'

'Pfft,' Elpida exclaimed. 'Everybody know. Besides, you only have to listen to the music.' She closed her eyes and sucked in a lung-filling breath. 'The Greek *bouzouki*… the trumpet… the heady, passionate rhythm of the tango.'

A fizz of sensation shot up Imogen's spine as the first wail of the trumpet started to play. Straightaway, couples began to slip out of the wall of the circle and dance in twosomes in the centre, some a little apart, dancing formal, stately movements, others pinned together with not even a gasp of air between them.

'Look, there is new girl from the post office,' Cooky remarked. 'And Zico from Versus Club. I tell you there is something going on there!'

Imogen felt like a voyeur looking into the souls of these dancers. Were they really being bewitched by the music to come out and show the town their feelings towards one another? Was she really starting to believe in Elpida's Greek wives' tales?

'It is like a statement,' Elpida said, as if reading her mind. 'Like putting a ring onto someone's hand and pledging life-long love.'

Imogen shook her head. 'So that's it, is it? The girl from the post office and this Zico are destined for a lifetime together?'

Elpida looked at her as if the very idea of it not being true was madness. 'You are still too English,' the Greek woman said. 'You only believe what you see on YouTube.'

'Zoella's hair tips maybe,' Imogen answered. 'Apart from that…'

'Ai!' Cooky exclaimed. 'Your brother is out there!'

'What?' Imogen stared hard across the circle, trying to pick out Harry.

There he was, dancing so close to Janie, not even a cocktail stick's width apart. Their eyes on each other, moving perfectly in time to the music.

Imogen shook her head. 'Harry won't know what this dance means… I mean, what it's supposed to represent, according to Greek ancient history.'

Elpida smiled at her. 'Look at them, Imogen. They do not need to know the history. They are busy making their own story.'

She couldn't keep her eyes from them. Her brother, leading Janie around the road, leaning her back and forth, copying the moves of the other couples around them. Olivia and Tristan were sat at a table next to their parents, picking at a *meze* in between clapping their hands together and avidly watching. It seemed that almost the whole of Acharavi was in love tonight.

'You are not dancing?' Rhea asked Panos.

He shook his head slowly, unable to draw his eyes away from Imogen. She was stood in the line, next to his grandmother and Cooky, watching the couples take their places in the centre of the circle, moving to the hypnotic beat of the tango.

'Pano,' Rhea breathed. 'You should dance.'

He turned and looked at her, wondering if things between them were still unclear. 'You know what this song is.'

'Yes, Pano, it is the same all over Greece.' Rhea let go of a wistful sigh. 'It is the song of lovers.'

'Then it would not be right for us to…' he started.

She smiled at him. 'I did not mean with me.' She hitched her head across the street. 'You have not been able to take your eyes from her.'

He blinked, his vision blurring for a second then focussing right back where it *had* been for the majority of the evening.

Imogen, her cheeks flushed from the Greek dancing, an intense look on her face as her eyes concentrated on the couples swaying in front of her. His whole business world was falling apart. The last thing he should do was get caught up in the Greek tradition he always seemed to be battling against. Wasn't it?

'Go and ask her to dance, Pano,' Rhea urged. 'If you feel even half of what is written on your face then… you must.'

Could he? The song was part of his family history. His grandparents had danced to it every year, holding each other close, looking into each other's eyes as if they were the only ones in the world. His mother and father had danced to it too. The thought stamped on his heart. Was every memory he had so tainted by his father's demise that he couldn't remember how things really were? Had he been letting the tumultuous end of his parents' relationship take over *all* his thinking? What about the time they had loved? They *had* loved once. Deeply. Taking a breath he put one foot forward, stepping into the road.

The music *was* hypnotic and as Imogen stood and watched the number of couples grow with every bar of the song, she felt like she was a witness to something special. It was like the first dance at a wedding – intimate looks, two people frozen in time, seeing and feeling nothing but each other.

A familiar scent of lemon and sandalwood twisted her attention away from the scene and she looked up to see Panos in front of her. She swallowed, feeling self-conscious, almost bare, as his dark eyes appraised her.

'Will you…' he began tentatively. He stopped talking, held out his hand to her. 'Imogen, will you dance with me?'

It felt like mosquitoes had taken flight in her belly and were busy spearing her with their probes, each jab injecting a new slightly terrifying sensation. She looked at his hand, then over his shoulder at the couples in the circle.

'Elpida said...' she began hesitantly.

His eyes seemed to enlarge, holding hers hostage. 'It is the dance of lovers, yes,' he answered.

Now her heart was hammering faster than the *bouzouki* players fingers were moving over the strings. Elpida had said it was a statement akin to someone putting a ring on your finger...

'Please,' he whispered. 'Dance with me.'

With her mouth as dry as the Corfu sand and her stomach still dealing with the equivalent of a plague of locusts – or Asian hornets – she lifted her hand, letting it glide into his.

The heat from his skin did nothing to play down her emotions and Imogen tensed as Panos walked them to a space in the centre of the circle right next to the grey stonework of the ancient pump. Positioning her hand in his and setting her other on his shoulder, she stilled, looking only at him.

'I can't dance,' she whispered, her lips trembling.

He smiled then, pulling her in close, and a gasp left her as their bodies connected together. Re-clasping her hand tight in his, he then latently slipped his other hand down the bare skin of her arm. It felt like a whisper of satin, making each fine hair shift upwards in anticipation. His arm snaked around her waist until nothing could separate them, heads close, eyes locked together.

He put his mouth close to her ear. 'Just listen to the music,' he said. 'Then.' He paused. 'You will begin to feel it.'

Imogen closed her eyes, letting the sounds of the band wash over her, until the music and the tension in her torso was all there was. Letting Panos move her slowly back then forward, she started to step with more confidence, following the rhythm of the musicians.

'Look at me,' he whispered.

She very slowly opened her eyes, the lights from the bulbs swinging from the trees and along the frontage of the tavernas dazzling her for a moment. He swayed her backwards, leaning into her, stepping in time to the tango beat and she let herself be led, following his footwork as best she could.

Everything else melted away except him and his irresistible inky eyes. She was now the one fastened to this moment in time, showing her soul to the villagers of Acharavi – and that really *was* what she was doing. Whatever she felt for this man, it had an unparalleled intensity and here, on this night, there was no other place on Earth she wanted to be.

She shifted her hand, taking it off his shoulder and letting her fingers explore. As they continued to dance at a slow tango tempo, she let her hand glide across his chest, her fingers seeking out every subtle dip and curve of his pectorals then lower, smoothing her way down over his tight core.

And then his hands were slipping down her body, from her shoulders, descending past the sides of her chest wall until he had her waist. He picked her up, spinning her around before catching her and bending her back in his arms as the music came to an end.

Her breath was catching in her throat as she looked up at him, his hand at her back, holding her up, his other hand entwined with hers again. She felt giddy, overcome with a heady sensation she had never experienced before. He gently lifted her up until they were back on level terms again and the rush of blood to her head began to dissipate.

'I have never danced to that song before,' he spoke softly, connecting his other hand with hers.

'Pano,' she breathed, his name almost not making it past her lips.

He took her face in his palms and drew her towards him, his mouth covering hers in an instant. And she clung to him, desperately pressing her mouth to his and not caring that the whole town was watching.

FIFTY-SEVEN

'Where are we going?' Imogen asked as Panos pulled her away from the main street.

'You want Elpida to start talking about big, fat Greek weddings?' he asked her. 'Cooky to begin designing a cake?'

She stopped moving with him and snatched back her hand. Crossing her arms over her chest she gave him a hard stare. 'So, what, you're ashamed of me now? You don't want to be seen with me?'

'No,' he said immediately. 'No, nothing like that.' He took her hand back, softly caressing both sides between his. 'I just…' He kissed her lips tenderly. 'I don't want this moment to end. I want to hide… from everything… and to keep you for myself just a little bit longer. Separate the eggs for just a little more.'

Imogen kissed him back, her hands sliding into his dark hair as he held her. Quickly she broke herself away. 'Elpida's coming!' she hissed, her eyes picking out Panos' grandmother heading towards them.

'Run!' Panos urged, pulling her towards the nearest side road.

Walking with Imogen, her hand in his, felt like the most natural thing in the world. But hand-holding, taking someone in his arms for anything other than sex, letting someone in emotionally, was all completely new to him. And it scared him. Terrified him.

'Where are we going?' Imogen asked into the darkness, the mountain range still just visible against the midnight-blue of the sky.

'We are almost there,' he answered.

'Isn't this the road to Elpida's house?' she asked.

'Yes.'

'You're taking me home for coffee?' she queried.

'Not quite that.' He started the walk up the incline which led to his grandmother's home.

'*Ouzo*?' Imogen guessed again.

'If that is what you would like.'

'I don't want that grape stuff made by the Lasko family. My mouth is still recovering.'

'I might have a cure for that,' he answered, smothering her mouth with his and savouring the taste of her lips.

She broke the kiss. 'Is our tango going to be the talk of the village tomorrow?'

He could tell she was grinning, even in the dark. 'Absolutely. Spiros from the shop on the corner, Zico from Versus Club…'

'The girl from the post office,' Imogen added.

'What?'

'Nothing.'

He tightened his grip on her hand as they rounded the hill and he came to a stop just before Elpida's property. 'We are here.'

'Where's here?' She looked around, her head twisting. 'I don't see anything.'

He watched her looking right and left in the dark, searching for something that wasn't there. He smiled. He could see the outline of the treehouse but only because he knew it was there and every line of its make-up was ingrained in him.

'Up there,' he said, moving close behind her and pointing up into the boughs of the olive tree.

'What is it?' she asked. 'A treehouse?'

'Yes. *My* treehouse. One of the most important buildings I have ever been involved in constructing.'

'You're serious, aren't you?' she whispered. 'This means something to you.'

He nodded. 'Yes... and I want to share it with you.'

Panos made her climb up first while he waited behind, perhaps a little afraid that she might fall. But with her flat sandals and a dress that was elasticated in all the right places she made light work of the lower boughs before a make-shift ladder appeared and she was able to climb into the wooden house among the foliage.

It was maybe two metres square and tall enough for her to stand up in without fear of bumping her head on the roof. She walked over to the window opening and leant against the frame, looking out. Even in the blackness of the night the view was incredible. Trees of all shapes and sizes made a dark thicket, dots of individual light picked out rural homes, clumps of gold signified small hamlets and then bigger groups of villages all cascaded down to the orange, yellow and mix of colour that was Acharavi. Beyond that was the ocean, almost mingling with the sky, the glow from towns across the water in Albania the only thing marking the border between earth and air.

She heard Panos climb into the room and she turned her head from the scene. 'It's a beautiful view.'

Panos stood behind her, circling his hands around her waist, his body tight to hers, his head nuzzling her neck until she could feel his breath on her skin. 'I wanted you to see it.'

'You used to play here? When you were small?'

She felt him nod. 'Yes.' Then a sigh left him. 'Out of all the memories I have of family life when I was a child, this house in the tree is one of the good ones, perhaps…' He took a moment. 'Perhaps the best one.'

She turned to face him, taking his hands in hers. 'Tell me.'

He hesitated for a second, then grabbed for something on the shelf to his right. He shook out a blanket, laying it on the floor. Slipping off her sandals she sat down, curling her legs up underneath her and watching as he did the same just opposite, their knees almost touching.

'We built it together,' he began. 'Me and my father. In one weekend. Early morning until late at night until it was ready.' His eyes went to the window and the view. 'I was six and it was the happiest few days of my entire life. How must that sound to you, Imogen?'

She shrugged. 'Some times are just made more perfect than others.' She smiled. 'I have one day that makes me feel happier than the rest.'

'With your husband?' he asked.

She shook her head. 'No… nothing with him.' She smiled. 'Mum, Dad, Harry and me spent a day on the beach in Bournemouth. I was ten and Harry would have been fourteen. There was nothing remarkable about it except we laughed the whole day long. We swam in the sea, Harry made a sand aeroplane Airbus would have commissioned… I admired the lifeguards and Mum and Dad held hands and collected shells.' She smiled again, recalling that perfect sunshine summer in August when everything had been simple and she was just a girl with her life stretching out in front of her. 'Mum made so many egg sandwiches we were still eating them three days after that trip.'

Panos reached for her hand. 'I don't know what to do, Imogen.'

'What do you mean?'

He sighed, dropping his eyes for a moment. 'I do not think I can develop the beachfront now.'

A gasp left her and she quickly swallowed it down.

He let go of her hand and put his fingers to his eyes, closing the lids and pressing the skin as if they hurt. 'I do not know what I am doing any more,' he admitted.

'Where has this come from?' she asked, studying his expression.

He shook his head. 'I came back here conflicted and I thought if I could just put my mark on the town, make it *my* place again, then everything would be… right.' He sighed. 'But then the restaurant was gone and my grandmother was so much older and all these memories just started haunting me like ghosts in Greek traditional clothing.' He shook his head again. 'And I hated it as much as I craved it.'

She didn't know what to say. She reached for his hand again, taking it in hers and smoothing her fingers over his.

'I think I got it wrong,' he stated. 'I think I came looking for something that wasn't there.' He looked to the window. 'I think I wanted justification for staying away all these years, for keeping out of touch with my mother, for distancing myself from this place.' He squeezed her hand. 'I think I wanted to believe that my father was this hard-hearted monster, who put deals and business ahead of me and my mother and… in part that was right but… it was not the whole of the story.' He adjusted his position slightly. 'He did not fail because he could not adapt to modern business. He did not even fail because he ran out of money. I think he failed because ultimately he cared and he loved. Because he tried to juggle too many balls at once, keep everyone happy. And, in doing that, he made no one happy. And it ended up killing him.'

'Pano…' Imogen began.

'My father twisted himself up so much trying to *be* somebody, that when it came down to it he ended up being a somebody nobody wanted.' He took a breath. 'When all we wanted him to be was the man we loved before everything else took over.' He sighed. 'A simple man who built a treehouse with his son.'

The urge to put her arms around him was so strong but she sensed to move now would be the wrong thing to do.

He looked deep into her eyes. 'I know you have to go, Imogen,' he whispered.

She nodded. 'Yes… yes I do.'

'And, although I want to commit to the community market plans… I still don't know where my home lies.'

She smiled. 'A little over a week ago I'd never even been to Greece before.' She reached up, her palm finding the fine bristle on his jaw. 'Now I somehow feel like I'm swimming in the middle of it.'

He put his hands over hers. 'Is this a good or a bad thing?'

'It's a complicated thing.' She sighed. 'Before Halloumi, my family were all together in the UK. Now Harry's here and my mum's moving house and after tonight I don't know how Janie is going to feel… It's going to be a little bit different that's all.'

Panos smoothed his free hand over her hair. 'You told me earlier today that making a change is a good thing.'

'I know I did.'

'But *different* is not right for you?'

His words made her smile. 'Different just takes a bit of getting used to.'

'And me?' he whispered. 'Do you think you could get used to me?' He held her face in his hands and his breath mixed with the humidity of the night, warm currents of air caressing her cheeks.

'You said you're not sure where your life lies,' she answered, her tone delicate.

He shook his head then. 'No.' He padded his thumb against her bottom lip. 'I said I am not sure where my *home* lies.' He swallowed. 'Wherever I am… I was hoping that you would be part of it.'

Imogen kept her eyes fixed on his and saw the depth of meaning seeping out from underneath those long, dusky lashes. He was truly exposing his soul to her now. He was ready to face his demons, confront his issues with relationships and he wanted to take those first steps with her.

'What I feel for you, Imogen… I cannot begin to express,' he started, his every syllable like a pounding heartbeat.

'I know,' she replied, placing her hands on his. 'I know, Pano, because I feel it too.'

He saw her visibly shiver as she spoke and it sent a shockwave of lust rippling through him. He wanted her so much in every way – physically, sexually – but knowing his heart was alive and *leading* this made every pull of need double in intensity.

She was quaking now underneath his hands as he held her face, but he wasn't going to rush. He wanted to savour every second of each moment. The expression in her eyes mirrored everything he was feeling and he held her gaze, looking, feeling, soaking it all up and letting the weight of their shared passion fill him.

Her breaths were coming thick and fast like his, and as she finally blinked, breaking the visual contact for a brief second, he couldn't hold off any longer. He kissed her, his mouth claiming hers with such force she fell, taking him with her onto the blanket. He broke from her, his breathing out of control. 'You are OK?'

She responded by reaching up, her hands in his hair, dragging him back down towards her, *her* mouth taking his this time and her fingers clawing at the buttons on his shirt. He ended the

kiss, sitting up on his knees, astride her, removing his shirt, all
the while holding her eyes with his. He threw the shirt to one
side, leaning forward, palms flat on the wooden boards either
side of the blanket she lay on, just looking at her looking up at
him.

Reaching up, her index finger trailed over his skin and he
closed his eyes, letting each tiny sensation spark its way into his
consciousness. He shifted slightly as her fingers grazed his navel,
slipping lower, centimetre by centimetre towards his waist. He
opened his eyes, wanting to see her.

Under his gaze she slithered, as if he had cast a cold spell
around her bare shoulders. He leaned in, his mouth dropping to
the skin around her collarbone, his tongue delivering hot, moist
circles as he worked across the breadth of her chest.

'Pano,' she called into the dark.

His name on her lips had his arousal stinging hard and, as
patience began to leave him, he pulled at the fabric of her black
dress, wanting more and more inches of her exposed to him.

Panos pulled at her dress, rolling the material down her body
and discarding it. Naked from the neck down, the only barriers between them were her knickers and his trousers. Imogen
watched him appraising her, his deep plum eyes languishing on
her breasts until they tightened too much to bear, aching for his
touch.

As his mouth descended on her once more she sent her fingers to the waistband of his trousers, squirming as he nipped at
her breasts, shudders of longing weaving through her body. She
unfastened the fly and pushed the fabric apart, inching it down
over his hips until he had no choice but to assist. With one hand
he wriggled free of his trousers and underwear until every part

of him was bare to her. The sight of him took her breath and as he relieved her of the last scrap of cotton and lace she shivered in anticipation of what was to come.

'Imogen,' he spoke, his whole weight on his palms as his eyes roved over her. 'My Imogen.'

It was a declaration of possession but one that didn't hold any fear for her. She *wanted* to be his. She wanted him to be *hers*. More than she had ever wanted anyone to be part of her life before.

She reached up, both her hands on his muscular shoulders. 'Be mine,' she whispered.

He needed no other words. She could see he was ready, just like she was, to join together in something that had been creeping up on them both over the past week. What had started out as a brute chemistry had grown into something so much stronger, something that now couldn't be halted even if they wanted to.

Bucking her hips towards him, she felt his full thickness surge inside her and she gasped, digging her fingernails into his back, aching, wanting more. She clung to him, pushing, pressing, needing to envelop herself around him until they reached that beautiful place together.

He rocked her, moving to her pace, each gliding motion reaching a part of her that craved this heat, this ultimate closeness. She pulled him nearer still, her breath in his ear, the hammering of his heart against her chest. Every movement was swamping her internal sensory board with delicious, sweet agony as she yearned for a divine release.

And then it was there. Building slowly, like someone had just ignited a sparkler, increasing in intensity, getting hotter, fizzing rapidly, ascending dramatically until she was no longer in control. Her body told her to let go while her head and her heart shouted to hold on, prolong this special moment, cling to him and every sentiment they were sharing.

'Imogen,' he said, his voice rich with desire.

'Pano, I can't stop…'

'Do not stop,' he ordered. 'Let go.'

'Not yet,' she breathed.

'With me,' he whispered. 'With me… *theé mou!*'

Suddenly she was lost, being swept away like a boat unhitched from harbour, caught up in a storm that was as exhilarating as it was dangerous, surging up onto a crest of a wave then plunging down into the depths of the ocean, wild, fast surf fizzing over every inch of skin. She cried out, dragging Panos in close, the vibrations of his body echoing hers.

He lifted his face to look at her, his hair dewy with perspiration, his eyes darker than ever, and she put her lips to his, wanting him to know how she was feeling. Breaking the kiss, he pushed her hair back from her face before cupping her cheek with his palm and locking their gaze.

'I think, Imogen,' he began. 'I think that *you* might be my home.'

FIFTY-EIGHT

Halloumi, Acharavi beachfront

'Imogen Charlton! The walk of shame!'

Janie's exclamation was almost loud enough for walkers to hear on Mount Pantokrator but, even though it was slightly embarrassing, Imogen couldn't keep the smile off her face. She avoided her sister-in-law for a moment, regarding the sea view. Above, a few white fluffy clouds speckled the perfect blue sky and the water calmly lulled backwards and forwards, not a breath of wind to create a wave. Her skin attested that the temperature was already rocketing and the sun was busy warming the loungers on the beach ready for the first worshippers of the day.

The humming of the cicadas had woken her up an hour ago and when she'd opened her eyes sunlight had streamed through the large glassless window of the treehouse. She'd stretched out her body ensuring tension in every part of her torso and then had quickly realised she was alone. For a second she had wondered if Panos had had a change of heart. Last night had been so intense, the dancing, the heart-to-heart… the making love, perhaps when reality had dawned with the new day he had thought better of everything he'd said. But then his head had appeared through the round hole in the floorboards and he'd climbed through carrying travel cups of coffee brought down from Elpida's home. They'd drunk the coffee first and then he'd ripped away the blanket she'd been covering herself with and made love to her again.

She stepped up onto the terrace. 'Don't let the children hear you say that,' she said to Janie. 'They will want a full and detailed explanation.'

'Which is exactly what *I* want,' Janie replied, pulling out a chair from under the terrace table she was sitting at.

'I'm pretty sure Harry will be up to his eyes in last-minute things we need to get sorted before opening night,' Imogen said, about to walk by.

'Oh no you don't,' Janie stated. 'Sit!'

Imogen stopped and, sensing no escape, she pulled up the offered chair and sank down into it, suddenly realising every limb she owned ached. She grimaced as her bottom refused to get comfortable on the seat. Putting her handbag down on the floor, she removed her phone and set it on the table.

'You're stiff!' Janie exclaimed. 'What on Earth did you do last night?'

'Slept on the floor of a treehouse,' she answered.

'Ooo, rustic! But something tells me you're pushing the word "slept" to the very limits of believability.'

Imogen laughed. 'Is that so?'

'Imogen, the way you two were with each other last night. Well! It was like watching an episode of *The Affair* without any of the weird time-lapse bits… or the deeply annoying problem children… or the drugs… I think.'

'Well, I could say the same about you… and Harry.' Imogen raised an eyebrow and watched for Janie's response.

A long, low sigh came from her sister-in-law's body and she smiled. 'You've got me there.'

'So, I'll share with you if you tell me what exactly is going on with you and my brother,' Imogen offered, swiping a finger down the screen of her phone to refresh her inbox now she had 3G.

Janie leaned across the table, excitement in her eyes. 'Deal. You first... Just how good does he look with no clothes on?' She propped her head up with her hand.

'You do realise you're talking about someone I have feelings for and not a piece of meat?'

'Ooo, "someone you have feelings for".'

'Stop it.'

'I have to admit, I was getting concerned you were still pining over Daniel.'

Imogen shook her head. 'I was never pining over Daniel.'

'I didn't really gel with him. He thought far too much of his Playstation in my opinion.'

'Janie!'

'I bet Panos doesn't have a Playstation.' She grinned. 'I bet Panos knows much better ways of exercising his fingers.'

'And presses all the right buttons,' Imogen added with a raise of her eyebrows.

Janie shrieked with laughter and rocked back on her chair. 'Stop it!'

'You started it.' She took a breath. 'So... you and Harry?'

'But you haven't told me anything!' Janie moaned.

A twinge in her lower back brought back a delicious memory of holding onto a naked Panos as he turned her into a trembling wreck. She wasn't about to give up details.

'We like each other,' Imogen stated. 'We like each other a lot. That's all I'm saying.'

Janie clapped her hands together in excitement. 'You'll have beautiful children. One blonde like you, one dark like him. Have you seen those eyelashes and those eyes? What am I saying?' She paused as if for dramatic effect. 'You spent the whole night contorted into different positions looking into them!'

'And did you spend the night looking into my brother's eyes?' Imogen asked. 'Because you know you danced to the dance of lovers.'

'Yes, I know,' Janie said, a sigh on her breath. 'Elpida told me and her friend with the crazy hair.'

'Well?'

'We might have… shared a moment when the children finally came down from the sugar high and got to sleep.'

'Oh, Janie!' Imogen exclaimed happily. She tempered down her enthusiasm as she picked up on the other woman's lack of buoyancy. Could Harry's hopes be coming true?

'It scared me a little bit,' Janie admitted.

'Scared you?'

'Yes.' Janie picked up her bottle of water from the table and took a swig from it. 'I mean, we separated because things weren't working out and… nothing's changed.'

'Oh, Janie, everything's changed,' Imogen stated.

'Has it, though?'

'Yes,' Imogen insisted. 'Look how Harry is here. I mean, I know we both thought what another fine mess he's got himself into with this restaurant but… well… it's becoming the making of him.'

Janie looked up, her eyes watery. 'I still love him, Imogen. I never stopped loving him, but is that enough? I don't want to say we should maybe try again if I'm not two hundred percent sure. I couldn't do that to him or the children.'

Imogen nodded. 'I know you couldn't and that's absolutely right.'

Janie sniffed again. 'And if we tried again… he's here in Greece. There's so much to think about.'

'But you could think about it. It isn't impossible.'

Janie nodded. 'I don't know whether it was the music or the wine but, last night… I think last night, if he'd asked me to marry him again I would have.'

'Oh, Janie.' Imogen squeezed her hands and watched the tears slip from her sister-in-law's eyes. The dance of lovers had a lot to answer for.

The phone on the table began to quake and Imogen sat forward, looking to the screen.

'Is that lover boy? Wanting another rustic rhumba?' Janie asked, grinning.

Imogen held her breath and looked at the screen. *Louanne Bartlett – Wyatt Hotel Group*. Here it was. Confirmation that when she returned to the UK it would be to Old Joe coughing over hash browns and griddled mushrooms and helping Grace pick out soft furnishings. Which was fine. Absolutely fine.

Speed-reading over the first couple of lines, her jaw dropped.

'What is it?' Janie asked. 'He hasn't dumped you, has he?'

Imogen looked up, wide-eyed and exhilarated, her heart racing. 'It's…' She stopped. She couldn't tell Janie. Janie would tell Harry and Harry was just about to open a restaurant. He didn't need anything else to think about. She quickly changed her expression. 'I won… the lottery.'

'What?!' Janie exclaimed.

'Yes,' Imogen carried on. 'Four numbers. Almost sixty pounds.'

'Oh,' Janie said, deflating. 'The way you looked I was thinking it was at least enough to buy a boat.'

Imogen smiled and dipped her head back to her phone and the email. She had an interview for the intern programme. And she was down to the final five.

FIFTY-NINE

Elpida Dimitriou's home, Agios Martinos

'I have made omelettes,' Elpida said, swinging around in the kitchen, a plate in each hand. She deposited one in front of Panos and another in front of Rhea. 'After the amount of grapes we consume last night we all need a good breakfast.'

Panos wasn't feeling hungover but he was feeling different, liberated. Last night with Imogen had been something he thought he would never experience. He had given himself totally, utterly, body and soul and the seismic shift was vast.

'Oh, I couldn't,' Rhea stated. 'I ate so much last night.'

'Pfft! You will waste away,' Elpida said.

'My taxi will be here soon,' the woman responded.

Panos looked at her. 'You have ordered a taxi?'

Rhea nodded. 'It was enough that you arranged the plane. I called them and we are leaving at midday.'

'Pano can drive you,' Elpida stated, bringing her food to the table and pulling up a chair.

'No, it is OK,' Rhea insisted. 'You... did not expect me to turn up here and you have been so nice...'

'I can take you,' Panos said. 'It is no trouble.' It was the very least he could do.

She shook her head. 'No, honestly, Pano, you do not have to.' She smiled. 'I think there is somewhere else you should be spending your time now.'

He shifted in his chair, saying nothing.

'Ah,' Elpida said through a mouthful of egg. 'The dance of lovers.'

Panos pushed his plate away, reluctant for his personal life to be discussed over breakfast. 'I will make some coffee,' he said, rising from his chair.

'Pfft! Sit down,' Elpida ordered. 'We need to make plans.'

His grandmother's tone worried him but he sat back in his chair and prepared to listen.

'What is your intention with Imogen? Because you know you cannot dance with someone to the song of lovers unless you are committed to them.'

Rhea let out a laugh. 'Is that really true? In Crete we have the same old tradition but no one really takes it that seriously now.'

'In Corfu we do,' the older woman responded. 'So,' Elpida continued, looking again to Panos. 'What are you going to do?'

'I am going to take Rhea to the airport.'

'That was not what I asked,' his grandmother said. 'Imogen lives in the UK. You live... You live where, Pano? Crete? Rhodes?' She lowered her voice. 'Here in Corfu?'

'I cannot give you the answer you want yet,' he said, standing to leave.

'I just want to know that you are going to do the right thing this time,' Elpida said, looking to Rhea.

The young woman shook her hands, bangles shaking. 'You leave me out of this.'

He sighed. 'It is not my intention to ever hurt Imogen.'

'Not good enough,' Elpida snapped in reply.

'*Yiayia*, this is new for me...'

'And she is a good person.'

'I know this.'

'And he is going to do his best. Aren't you, Pano?' Rhea chipped in, a smile on her face. 'Because it is time for a new start. For all of us.'

'You sound like *you* have plans,' Elpida said, forking omelette into her mouth and turning her attention to Rhea.

'I do,' Rhea answered. 'I called my sister last night. I am going to stay with her for a while. She lives in Chania and has a holiday property business. I thought I might help her a little, see a bit more of my home island, concentrate on me.'

'I think that sounds like a wonderful idea,' Elpida said. 'But if you ever want a job in a kitchen, I'm sure Harry and Imogen would be very grateful to have you. I know *I* would.'

'Thank you, Elpida. Will you say goodbye to them for me?' Rhea asked. 'And to Janie and the children.'

'Of course,' Elpida said.

'I am glad I got to see where you were raised,' Rhea said, her eyes going to Panos.

'Me too,' he answered with sincerity.

The taxi arrived on time. All that was left to say was goodbye and Panos felt so much sadder than he could ever have envisaged. Taking her hands in his, he looked at her, admiring the beauty he had always seen and the true person inside he had never really been open to knowing.

'You have to stop looking at people like that, Pano,' Rhea stated. 'You have no idea what those eyes do to a woman.' She smiled. 'Thank you for letting me stay.'

He shook his head. 'No, thank *you* for staying. For helping Elpida at the restaurant and… for helping me too.'

'Don't mess this up, Pano,' she said, her eyes welling up. 'If you feel what I think you feel for Imogen, don't waste a second.'

She threw herself into his arms, hands pulling him close as her usually nauseating scent somehow surrounded him with comfort. He wasn't sure he deserved her understanding after being so absent from the relationship they'd had but parting on good terms would mean they could both move forward.

Rhea stepped back, quick to press her hair into place before bending to pick up her large handbag. '*Antio*,' she said softly.

Panos opened the car door for her and she pushed in her handbag before slipping her body down onto the seat. '*Antio*, Rhea,' he replied.

He closed the door and stepped back as the taxi driver started the engine. From inside, Rhea waved a hand and he waved back, standing still and watching as the vehicle moved down the track and onward, out of the village. He sighed as the taxi disappeared, leaving him with the view down over the green of the mountain. He reached up, leaning back and stretching his hands in the air, releasing the tension in his spine. Today was going to be a new start. He had a different plan and it started with getting an answer today about who owned the piece of land next to Halloumi.

SIXTY

Acharavi beachfront

'*Antio*, Manilos,' Panos spoke into the phone. He ended the call and sucked in what he hoped was a decision-affirming breath. He had just decided on something that might just be the most crazy business move he had ever made. It had certainly felt that way when he was explaining the bare bones of it to Manilos. Could it work? There were no guarantees. It would also involve getting the business owners of Acharavi completely behind him. The idea had sprung from the community market plan but this was more personal. It was about giving something back.

'What am I doing here?' Elpida asked, appearing behind him and setting her eyes on the Dimitriou Enterprises sign outside Tomas' Taverna. 'If you are cutting a ribbon before the earthmovers come I really do not need to see it.'

He smiled at his grandmother. 'No earthmovers,' he stated.

'They are running late already?' she asked, raising her eyes to Heaven. 'Only in Greece, huh?'

'They are not coming,' he said. He straightened his body, lifting his face to the sun. 'They are not coming at all.'

He watched Elpida's lips disappear into her face like she was sucking out the stone from an olive. 'Do not make jokes about this, Pano. Joking around the heart of an old woman is worse than her smoking herself into an early grave.'

He shook his head. 'I am not joking.'

She looked even more confused, the lines etched into the swarthy skin on her forehead creasing. All the pain her sons had put her through and both dying too young. Him resenting everything and everyone. How was Elpida still standing eternally strong?

'I am not going to create an entertainment complex here, *yiayia*,' Panos clarified.

'But... the signs and... you have bought Tomas' Taverna...' Elpida spluttered, as if still trying to make sense of his words.

'I know,' he answered. 'And I still hope to buy Avalon and the other three restaurants on this section of Beach Road.'

Elpida shook her head. 'Then I still do not understand.'

He smiled. He wasn't sure he had quite got his head around it himself yet but suddenly it all seemed to be making sense.

'I am going to offer to buy the restaurants. And then I will lease them back to the restauranteurs at a minimal rent,' he stated.

Elpida blinked, then blinked again, as if the words were foreign to her. She patted the pockets on the front of her green leopard-print dress. 'Where are my cigarettes? I need to smoke.'

'No, *yiayia*, you do not.'

'This sound very much like a trickety trap,' she stated. 'How would you be making your millions grow by doing that?'

'I would not,' he said. 'This would not be about me making any more money.' He took a breath. 'It would be about me giving something back to Acharavi.'

'I need to smoke,' Elpida repeated.

'I know these restaurants are still going through troubled times. Tomas had re-mortgaged. Lafi at Avalon is doing a little better, but I suspect the other restaurants are running on empty.' He looked straight at his grandmother. 'By giving them a lump sum they would be able to be debt free and keep their businesses, paying me a small amount each month they can afford, re-establishing themselves. By buying the properties I can ensure that no other developer can ever decide to rip up the beachfront. Because…' He paused. 'That would be a stupid idea.'

'Pftt!' Elpida exclaimed. 'And what if you change your mind? You will own everything. What is to stop you getting bored in a few years' time and demolishing it then?'

'Alejandro Kalas has made it quite clear that developments such as mine would not be welcomed by the council. But,' he said. 'I am going to try and make sure the whole area is protected from people like me in the future.'

He swallowed. He realised it was a complete about turn, but over the past week Corfu had slowly seeped its way back into his heart and the blinkers that had been so permanently fixed in place had started to shift. All the women in his life had had a hand in it. Elpida, Imogen, even Rhea. The next thing on his list was reconnecting with his mother. If she would accept the offered olive branch.

'This sounds a little too good to be true,' Elpida responded.

'There's more,' Panos said, wetting his lips. 'I want the restaurants on the front to work together. They will not be my businesses, I will just be the landlord, but I hope they will take on board an idea I have had.'

'What idea?' Elpida asked with a sniff.

He sucked in a breath of the sea air and gazed out in the direction of Roda.

'Vouchers,' he said. 'I remember seeing Risto giving out vouchers for money off meals at Halloumi for opening night.'

'Go on,' Elpida urged, her eyes still monitoring him.

'Each restaurant along the strip will give out vouchers for one of the other restaurants.'

'Their competitors? Pfft!'

'No, their *colleagues*. Businesses all with the same aim. Making a living,' Panos countered. 'The very best way in business now is to work alongside one another, gain new business as a group, help to promote the sea-front restaurants as a whole.'

'Are you talking about community, Pano?' Elpida asked, looking a little suspicious of his motives.

'Yes,' he said. 'I am.'

She shook her head, tears in her eyes. 'Now, finally, you begin to understand,' she whispered.

Her expression cut him to the quick and he looked from her to the beach where Spiros the doughnut man was beginning his afternoon walk along the sand. He had come here intent on making his mark on the village but he had come at it from entirely the wrong angle, from the same direction he had been coming at everything since he had left the island all those years ago. It had been about wanting to be better than his father, to be better than John, to prove the Dimitriou name was about success not failure. Except all he had proved was success in that form meant nothing if you were alienating everyone around you.

'The hotels were not Christo's dream in the beginning,' Elpida said wistfully.

Panos raised his head, his eyes meeting hers. 'What?'

She shook her head. 'I do not think you remember how close Christo was to his brother Spiro. The hotels were always something Spiro talked about. Spiro wanted them to go into business together but Christo was not sure about the change.'

Panos swallowed. Risto's parents had died when Risto was only two, he a few years older. It was just after that Christos would have purchased his first hotel.

'I think your father's grief played a very big part in shaping the man he was to become. It was like he was on a missionary to be the best... but not for him... for his brother.'

Panos shook his head, inhaling deep. It sounded such a familiar tale, trying to better his father but by making the same selfish choices. And now he was being told they weren't really his father's desires but his Uncle Spiro's. 'All of us Dimitrious have made many mistakes.'

Elpida nodded. 'But it is not too late for you.'

'That is what Imogen says and I hope she is right,' he admitted, slipping his hands into his pockets. 'Because there is one more thing I need to ask you.'

'Pfft!' Elpida exclaimed. 'You think this is enough to make me stop smoking? I think this is a wonderful idea but Harry's attempt at grilling the cheese his restaurant is named after is enough to make me need a packet a day.'

He smiled, settling his eyes on his grandmother again. 'It is not to do with smoking this time.' He moved his vision to the patch of land they were stood next to, the crop of grass gleaming in the sunlight. '*Yiayia*, I got Manilos to find out who owned this piece of land.' He paused. 'With the mapping how it is in Greece it took him a while, but today he gave me the answer.'

He watched Elpida study the rough tarmac on the ground.

'*You* own it, *yiayia*,' he said.

She shrugged her shoulders, finally lifting her head to face him. 'And it seems to be the piece of land that everybody wants to buy around here.'

'Why did you not build on it? Make the restaurant bigger?' Panos asked.

'I get Nico to cut the grass,' she said, stepping onto the lush oasis of the turf. 'To keep it green like the trees in the mountains.'

He watched Elpida slide off her shoes and embed her feet into the lawn. She sighed, tipping her head back and rubbing her bare soles against the grass. 'I do this every time I go past here, Pano,' she informed. 'This is where your grandfather and I had our first date. Right here, before all of the beachfront was built. On this patch of grass.' She smiled. 'Olives and Cooky's father's bread never tasted so good.' She smacked her lips and let out a laugh.

He nodded, finally understanding.

'You want to buy this from me?' Elpida asked, dabbing her feet up and down like she was treading grapes.

'Not now I know how much it means to you,' he responded.

'What do you want it for?' she asked.

He sighed. 'It does not matter.'

'Pfft! Take off your business shoes,' Elpida ordered.

'What? No, do not be crazy.'

'Pfft! Awful things that make your toes sweat. Take them off!'

He shook his head. '*Yiayia...*'

'Off!' Elpida ordered. 'Or I will smoke twice as much as soon as you are out of sight.'

She was staring him down with that age-old expression he knew there was no escaping from. He used the heel of one shoe to pull down the side of the other and slipped it from his foot. He then bent, pulling off the second shoe with his hands, before dragging the dark socks loose and leaving himself barefoot.

'Now come,' Elpida beckoned. 'Come onto the grass.'

He strode off the stony road, ignoring the jab of gravel on his soles and sunk down into the green layer, letting the coolness soak into his skin.

He felt Elpida take his hand in hers, squeezing it tight.

'Now close your eyes,' she ordered.

'I really do not want to be thinking about you and my grandfather sharing olives, bread and Zeus knows what else,' he stated, his eyes closing.

'We do not share anything more than that the first time. Your grandfather was a gentleman,' Elpida reminded him. She breathed in, her hand tightening in his. 'Do you feel it?' she asked. 'The very roots of the island moving underneath you?'

He concentrated hard, trying to let go of everything but his feet on the Earth and his grandmother's hand in his. He didn't know about the roots of Corfu but he did know he had never felt freer.

'Now,' Elpida whispered. 'You tell me why you want to buy this land.'

'For Imogen,' he said. 'For her play area for the children.'

He felt Elpida breathe even deeper, then he watched her open her eyes, regarding the picture-postcard scene in front of them like it was the best sight in the world. He opened his mouth to say something else – that now he knew how much the plot meant to her he didn't want to pursue the idea.

'Then you can have it,' she said. 'For a fair price.' She turned her eyes to him. 'On one condition.'

'What?' he asked.

She smiled. 'That it stays a green space, just like this… forever.' Her eyes went back to the beach – fishing boats bobbing far out, children splashing nearer to shore, holidaymakers with their drinks and books on loungers under parasols. 'When I am long gone,' she said. 'I want to know that children will be here, playing barefoot, laughing like goats.' She chuckled. 'Promise me this, Pano.'

He was quite certain goats didn't laugh but he understood. 'I promise, *yiayia*.' He squeezed her hand. 'A green space, forever.'

SIXTY-ONE

Halloumi, Acharavi Beachfront

Halloumi Restaurant

Starters
Keftedes – lamb meatballs with tzatziki
*Spanakopitakia – Halloumi and Feta cheeses with spinach, garlic
and herbs wrapped in a parcel of shortcrust pastry*
Saganaki – traditional Greek fried cheese
Ouzo Prawns

Mains
*Grilled swordfish served with crushed new potatoes, Greek salad
and a mustard dressing*
Corfiot inspired pot-roast chicken with orzo
*Stifado – traditional Greek beef and bean stew served with fresh
bread and a homemade garlic butter*
*Moussaka – layered aubergine, minced meat, tomato, potato,
onion and garlic with a béchamel sauce*

Desserts
Panna Cotta served with a honey and blackberry jus
Greek biscuits with cream and a kumquat compote
Baklava
Lemon Meringue Pie
A Filo of Fig
Ice cream by the scoop (Chocolate, strawberry, vanilla or all three!)

<u>*Chef's Specials*</u>

Fresh mussels with chilli, garlic and coriander
Salmon fillets with olives, onion and houmous served with green
beans and Dauphinoise potatoes
Ox cheeks with a Greek relish
Stewed octopus with a herb tabbouleh

'Well?' Harry asked.

Imogen looked up from the revised menu, tears in her eyes.

'Say something,' Harry begged.

'Yes!' Elpida chipped in. 'Say something! Anything!'

'It's perfect,' Imogen breathed. 'Just perfect.'

Harry howled like a werewolf and Elpida said something in Greek and clapped her hands together in delight.

'It looks like a menu for a restaurant,' Imogen said, her eyes going back to the paper she was holding. 'Like, I don't know, something for a Greek Rick Stein.'

'That's because it is,' Harry stated, laughing.

'It all feels real now.'

'I've been trying to tell her this since we got here,' Harry said to Elpida. 'But seeing this… I'm really feeling like the king of my new culinary castle.'

'Do not say that after house red wine,' Imogen told him.

'And tonight the king will be served,' Elpida stated.

'What?' Harry asked.

'Tonight, we will do a full test run, a rehearsal of dresses… is that how you say it?' Elpida asked.

Imogen looked at the little woman, confused. 'A dress rehearsal?' she guessed.

'Yes… for Harry and Janie and the children. You, me, Pano and Risto. We will open up the restaurant and we will serve them like it is opening night,' Elpida informed.

'Elpida, you don't need to—' Harry started.

'Pfft! You have not put your feet down for a moment since you arrive here. Instead of making these beans on grilled bread every night or giving money to Lafi down the beach, you will eat your own food, here, and we will cook for you.' Elpida looked at Harry like refusal was not an option. 'Pano and Risto will be the waiters. Imogen, you will run the kitchen with me. Harry, you go and get Janie and the children and I will make the calls.'

Harry looked to Imogen and she shrugged helplessly. No one dared argue with Elpida when she was on a mission.

When Panos arrived at the back door of Halloumi that evening it was to be greeted by his grandmother's voice yelling instructions.

'Seven minutes, Imogen. If the vegetables have longer than seven minutes they will be like the weed from the sea.'

'Some people don't like to lose their teeth when they have dinner out,' he heard Imogen answer. 'No one wants carrots like bullets.'

'I tell you, seven minutes and they will be perfect.'

'Perfect for what? Rabbits?'

He smiled, pushing open the door and being enveloped by steam and the scent of steaming fresh produce. '*Kalispera*,' he greeted. 'Is it safe to come in?'

'You are late,' Elpida stated. 'Risto is serving the wine, and the starters are almost ready.'

Imogen turned from the griddle pan she was cooking meatballs in, her face red, her hair covered by a net. She smiled at him. '*Kalispera*.'

Straightaway he wanted to drag her out of the kitchen and take her home with him.

'Where have you been?' Elpida asked.

'Not far,' he answered. 'Kassiopi… for a meeting.'

'I do not want to know any more now. We have dinner to serve.' Elpida whipped up a saucepan and pointed to the work-top across the kitchen. 'Take the bread and oils out before the children start to eat the candles that smell like lemons.'

Panos moved into the room but headed for the range not the food. He pulled Imogen away from the cooker, turning her around to face him before pressing his lips on hers.

'Oh, for the love of Zeus!' Elpida exclaimed. 'There is a rea-son we have hair nets and clean hands in the kitchen. It stops the spread of germs. Tongues and lips are not welcome unless they belong to the ox on the specials board.'

'I have something to tell you later,' Panos said softly, tucking in the stray hair that had escaped from Imogen's net.

'Elpida told me Rhea went back to Crete today.'

He nodded. 'Yes, she said to say goodbye to you.'

'Very nice girl,' Elpida remarked. 'But too thin and too many bracelets.'

'I have something to tell you too,' Imogen said.

'Pano!' Elpida stated. 'The bread.'

He kissed Imogen once more, then, picking up the tray of bread and oil, he headed out into the restaurant.

Working in the Southampton diner back home and her previ-ous adventures in food seemed so simple now Imogen had spent an evening in the kitchen with Elpida, cooking Greek dishes she wasn't familiar with and wanting to make it all perfect for Harry.

While Elpida put the finishing touches to the desserts she slipped out of the back door for some much-needed fresh air and a chance to catch her mum before it got too late. She wanted to tell her about the Wyatt Hotel Group email. She hadn't shared it

with anyone because, in truth, it was churning her up. She didn't
want to distract Harry before the opening of the restaurant and,
although she was going to tell Panos, she was dreading it. When
she first arrived on Corfu she almost couldn't wait for the two
weeks to pass, but now it was a completely different story. So
much had happened and so much had changed. And now she
also had the dream job opportunity within her grasp.

She took a breath, fanning a hand over her face to move the
humid air, and put her phone to her ear, eyes noting the first
stars beginning to appear in the dusky sky.

'Hello,' Grace answered.

'Hello, Mum,' Imogen replied.

'Oh, hello, you just caught me,' Grace said.

'Were you off to bed?' Imogen asked, checking her watch
again.

'Bed? It's only seven o'clock here.'

'I know, I just… well, were you going out?' She couldn't remember the last time her mum had ventured out of the house
in the evening since April had passed away and they'd gone to
shows at the Mayflower.

'Yes, I'm going across the road… to the new house,' Grace
stated proudly.

The way her mum had said 'new house' made it sound like a
prize from the upper end of the Win the Ads segment from *Ant
and Dec's Saturday Night Takeaway*. She was glad this windfall
was giving her mum a new lease of life.

'That's lovely,' Imogen said.

'Yes, Fionnula, that's April's great-niece, has given me a key.
Someone has to keep an eye on the property for insurance pur-
poses until the probate goes through and as I'm here and it's
going to be mine, she's left keys with me.'

'You sound excited, Mum.'

'I am… a little bit… and apprehensive of course. I mean it is much bigger than this place so I need to be mindful of the fuel bills.' She sighed. 'And I'm not entirely sure how to operate the wood-burning stove.'

'We'll work it out together.'

'So, how are things there with the restaurant?' Grace asked.

'They're good,' she admitted, smiling. 'Really good. It's the grand opening tomorrow night. We've got a *bouzouki* player coming and a hundred balloons to blow up and lots of preparation to do but… it's exciting.'

She really *was* excited. At the beginning, watching Harry had been compelling, her brother growing in stature and confidence with every passing moment on the road to restaurantville. But now it almost felt like she owned it too. Planning the menu, cleaning the floors, restoring the old furniture, placing the new sofas, settling in Mrs Pelekas' tablecloths and the candles from Arillas – she was at the centre of it too now, heart and soul.

'And how are Janie and the children?' Grace asked.

Imogen turned towards the terrace. Janie and Harry were sat opposite each other, one child on either side, hand-holding, sharing smiles, conversation, home-made lemonade and red wine, the bulbs strung across the pergola above their heads and the candle on their table creating an atmospheric glow. Panos and Risto appeared from inside, each carrying plates. Her stomach clenched at the sight of the complex man she had fallen for.

'They're really well here, Mum. Corfu is just the most wonderful place.' She inhaled the humid air, turning her gaze to the darkness, the street lamps flickering against the night sky, the faint shush of the water rolling up to the beach. 'I wish you could see it.'

There was silence from the other end of the line, until…

'You sound really happy, Imogen. I don't think I've heard you sound this happy since... since you got all those hotel pens out your dad used to bring back for you and we counted them.'

She smiled to herself, nuzzling her head closer to the phone in her hand. 'One hundred and three.'

'Was it really?'

She nodded, dipping her hand into the yellow bag on her shoulder and pulling out the first pen-like object she found. It was black-and-white-striped like a zebra and she knew without even looking it was from a hotel in South Africa. 'I am happy, Mum,' she said, rolling the pen between her fingers.

'I'm glad,' Grace said. 'And I'm glad Harry and Janie are getting along and Corfu... well, it does sound lovely.'

'It is,' she breathed.

'I bet you'll miss the weather when you come home.'

She swiped at a mosquito in the air, a rush of humidity running over her. Then she jumped a little as something brushed up against her legs. It was Socks, his tail winding around her calf like a snake. She bent to stroke him and he arched his back with pleasure. The weather wasn't the only thing she was going to miss about the place. Her eyes went across the night to Panos.

'We had rain today,' Grace continued. 'Gallons of it, and there's still a hosepipe ban, can you believe it? Oh!' Grace exclaimed suddenly. 'Did you ever hear back from that...? Lydia, wasn't it? From the hotel?'

Imogen's heart started to race as she watched Panos serving wine to her brother, those inky eyes just visible in the half-light, tendrils of his sexy dark hair touching his forehead as he poured from the bottle. She swallowed, dropping the zebra pen back into her bag.

'No,' she said quickly. 'I didn't ever hear back.'

She had a decision to make.

SIXTY-TWO

Halloumi, Acharavi Beachfront

'I don't believe I've just had dinner served to me in my own restaurant,' Harry exclaimed, leaning back into his chair when he had finished all three courses and had coffee and chocolate mints.

'It was absolutely lovely,' Janie said. 'Thank you.'

'I liked the ice cream best,' Tristan said.

'That was the only bit Elpida and I didn't make!' Imogen remarked, picking up the final plates.

'I liked the moo… What was it again?' Olivia asked.

'*Moussaka*,' Janie said.

'I liked the pastry parcels,' Imogen whispered to her niece. 'But I don't think I was meant to eat any.'

'I heard that!' Elpida chipped in, bustling about with the coffee pot, refreshing cups.

'A round of applause for our wonderful cooks and our equally fantastic waiters!' Harry said, looking to Risto and Panos and starting to clap. 'You're all dismissed. We can do the clearing up.'

'Pfft! You think I will make a kitchen a mess and not clean up!' Elpida exclaimed. 'I tell you, how you find this place when you come is not how I leave it.'

Imogen moved to carry the dishes back to the kitchen when Panos caught her, pulling her close. 'I want to take you somewhere,' he whispered.

'Where?' she answered with a smile. 'Another treehouse?'

'It is a surprise.'

'Now I'm intrigued.'

Harry cleared his throat. 'Please, take my sister out, Panos.'

'Harry, I'm not leaving Elpida to clear up.'

'She won't be,' Janie interrupted. 'Harry and I...' Her eyes went to her husband, a smile on her lips as if she wasn't used to saying the phrase. 'We'll sort everything after we've put the children to bed.'

Groans came from Olivia and Tristan.

'One more bowl of ice cream?' Harry bargained.

Cheers ensued and Harry winked at Imogen. 'Go!'

'Close your eyes,' Panos whispered in her ear.

Imogen shivered as he placed his hands on the bare skin of her shoulders. She was still a little hot from the cooking but here, outside the restaurant, the temperature finally starting to drop, goosebumps prickled her arms. She did as he had instructed then felt him guide her slowly forwards along the road.

'Where are we going?' she asked, small stones slipping into her sandals as she shuffled, a little off balance.

'Not far,' he answered.

'Good, because I would make a terrible blind person and my navigation when I *can* see isn't that good either.'

'Stop.'

'We're here? Already?'

'Open your eyes,' he told her.

She opened her eyes and blinked, looking but not seeing. She wrinkled her nose then turned around slightly, gazing up at Panos. 'I don't see anything.'

He opened his arms, palms to the sky, as if that held the answer.

Imogen turned back, looking at the whitewashed wall of Tomas' Taverna, a few customers sitting on the rectangular terrace, sharing carafes of *retsina*. What was there to see? Then, suddenly, it all clicked into place. She put her hands to her mouth. 'The sign has gone,' she stated, turning to look at him again. 'The Dimitriou Enterprises sign.'

He nodded. 'Yes.'

'But… what does that mean? That you're not buying Tomas' anymore? That you're not going to redevelop?' The last sentence came out no louder than a whisper.

'I am still buying Tomas',' he stated. 'And, with luck, the rest of the strip.'

She listened intently as he went on to tell her his plan to buy the buildings, charge a minimal rent and then, if the business owners agreed, to implement the mutual benefit strategy with coupons and joint advertising.

When he had finished she shook her head, her eyes wet with unshed tears. 'This is all so…' She didn't quite know what to say. 'Unexpected and… I just…'

'You were right, Imogen, about so many things,' he told her.

'Was I?'

'Yes,' he said, taking her hand. 'But most of all about it never being too late for a second chance.' He inhaled deeply, his eyes matching hers. 'And that is what I am wanting,' he stated. 'To begin again here. To live my own life.'

She squeezed his fingers, wanting to connect a little tighter, the warmth of his palm radiating its heat into hers.

'But there is more,' he said.

He pulled her slightly, making her face the patch of ground between the two restaurants, his hand still entwined with hers.

'I have bought this land,' he said.

'You have?' Imogen said.

He nodded. 'Yes.'

She thought about the girl with her wayward ball and the plan she had to buy it and make it a play area before he could snap it up and turn it into an extension of his planned complex. Now she was at a real loss as to why he wanted it.

'Do you know who it belonged to?' Panos asked.

'No, I…' Should she admit she'd had designs on it to halt his progress? She shook her head. 'No.'

He smiled then. 'My grandmother.'

'What?' She looked up at him in shock. She had specifically asked Elpida to find out who the land belonged to.

'Yes, she says this piece of land is where she and my grandfather had their first date together, sharing olives and… other things we should not think about too much.'

Imogen smiled. And the woman had kept it, even though she had sold the restaurant. She had wanted to hold on to her memories of her husband. It was so romantic and beautiful… but why had Elpida now given it up?

'I bought it for you,' Panos told her.

'For me?' she said, her tone unsure.

He nodded, enjoying her reaction. 'Elpida told me you thought Halloumi might benefit from a play area for the children.'

She gasped, putting her hands to her mouth for the second time since they'd stopped walking, mouth agape, eyes large and bright.

'I thought swings and a slide… Maybe we can choose the rest together,' he suggested.

'Oh, Pano,' she exclaimed, rushing at him.

He caught her as her arms wrapped around him, drawing his body in line with hers. Tendrils of her hair touched his face, the scents of the night – jasmine, lavender and bougainvillea – coating his senses. He realised then, he wanted to hold this woman forever.

And then she drew away, her eyes still sparking but this time with something other than the joy he'd just witnessed.

'There's something I have to tell you,' she said, her voice weak. 'I haven't told Harry yet or Janie and I chickened out of telling my mum earlier.' She met his eyes. 'I've got an interview. The Wyatt Group sent me an email.'

He smiled hurriedly, trying to decide how to react. He had always known she was leaving. This news made no difference to their situation but all the difference in the world to Imogen. This was her dream. 'That is amazing,' he said, grabbing both her hands. 'It is what you wanted.'

'I know. But… I'd have to leave the day after Halloumi's opening night and it just feels… too soon.'

He bit the inside of his lip. It was too soon for him too. He thought they had more time, even if it was just another week. To know they only had a couple of days…

Squeezing her hands, he smiled. 'It is the opportunity you were looking for, no? You think they would say no. They have said yes.'

She nodded. 'Yes.'

'Then you must go, Imogen,' he said confidently. 'You must go and get your place and follow your dream.' He tried to maintain the smile but inside him something very different was happening, a small landslip of emotion he didn't want to acknowledge. 'This means you do not have to be just a waitress any more. Like you said.'

He watched her expression change a little.

'I know I said that… but… it isn't so bad.' Her eyes went to the beach. 'We have a lot of regulars. Old Joe and Brian the Biker and Mrs Green… she might even know what her grandchild is by now.'

'You are not sure about the hotels?' he asked.

'No… I mean, yes.' She smiled. 'I am sure… it's just a shock to get a reply. I don't have any experience and I'm only half way through my qualification and… it's come at a funny time.'

He nodded. 'You are concerned about your brother.'

'Not like I was when we first arrived. Then I thought he was completely out of his mind. I mean, thinking he could open a restaurant when most of his food knowledge was obtained from watching Dean Edwards on *Lorraine*.'

'But now he has done this.'

'*Almost* done it,' she answered. 'There's a little thing like a launch night tomorrow. And there's Janie and the children.' She sighed. 'Getting the Charlton family reunited isn't a done deal yet.'

He put his arms around her then, drawing her into his body. 'Did they not dance to the song of lovers?'

'Yes,' she replied. 'And maybe in Greek custom that's enough, but us Brits need a little more than the Lakas family hooch and dancing in the moonlight.'

He drew away, looking at her quizzically. 'Really? This is true?'

She laughed. 'Yes.'

'I do not believe it,' he answered. 'Come. Come with me.' He pulled her hands, directing her towards the grassland he had purchased from his grandmother.

'What are you doing?' she laughed.

'Take off your shoes,' he ordered.

'What?'

'Do this,' he said. He let go of her hand to remove his shoes, ripping off his socks and standing barefoot just as he had earlier with Elpida.

'Don't tell me this is a Greek custom too,' Imogen said.

'It is a Dimitriou custom,' he answered. 'As of today.' He watched her slip off her sandals and put down her slender feet onto the lawn. He reconnected their hands and took a long inward breath. 'Now look at me.'

She met his eyes with those pure aquamarine irises he could look into for a lifetime and held his gaze.

'Do you feel it?' he whispered. What he was feeling was not the grounding of himself in Greece but the fiery, intense connection with her.

'Yes,' she answered. 'I've been feeling it almost ever since we met.'

He moved his head a little closer into the space between them, the humid night air still dense. 'Dance with me. Here, in the moonlight.' He connected their bodies just as he had on the main street of Acharavi the night of the folklore festival, one hand on her hip, the other holding hers.

He felt her tremble underneath his touch as he slowly began to sway her over the grass in a latent tango.

'There isn't any music,' Imogen said, her eyes still caught up with his.

'No?' he asked her. 'Listen.'

He watched her close her eyes then, her body hot against his as they moved as one. From high up in the hills came the sound of crickets and cicadas, mixing with the delicate lute and *bouzouki* from Tomas' Taverna, interspersed with the soft sound of the sea slipping up on the sand.

It was one perfect summer night he would hold on to when he had to let her go.

SIXTY-THREE

Halloumi, Acharavi beachfront

A hot, wet tongue met her lips and, half-asleep, Imogen shifted a little, widening her mouth into a smile.

'Is it morning?' she whispered.

She kept her eyes closed, knowing she was laying naked on the floor of the restaurant, covered only by one of Mrs Pelekas' tablecloths that didn't have a home yet. After she and Panos had danced on the grass they had bought kumquat liqueur from Tomas and taken it down onto the beach. By the time they had arrived back at Halloumi everyone else had been in bed and neither of them had wanted the night to end. Panos had suggested a hotel, but the thought of the opulence and chocolates on pillows she'd always hankered after hadn't seemed right. She had locked the door and had his shirt off before she'd even said no to the idea.

There was the tongue again, warm and moist, making its way over her lips. She smiled again, her hand reaching out for him.

'Imogen.'

It was Panos' voice but it was a little too far away. She flicked open her eyes and came face to face with fur and whiskers, a pink tongue ready to kiss again.

'Argh! Ugh! Socks!' she screamed, sitting up and wiping at her face with her hands. The cat had the good grace to skit across the floor and settle under one of the tables.

She looked up at Panos, holding two steaming cups of coffee, wearing nothing but his underwear. Her eyes couldn't help roving all over the washboard stomach and firm chest, trailing up to that David Gandy jaw and cheekbones and the thick dark hair, tousled from where she had run her fingers through it.

'The cat has good taste,' he remarked, handing a cup to her.

She took it. 'The cat is going to get us shut down before we are even open.'

He shook his head, smiling as he sat down next to her, folding long, lean, athletic limbs. 'Cats are as essential to Greece as...'

'Olives?' Imogen suggested. '*Ouzo*? Metaxa? Feeding people up?'

'I was going to say tourism, but I like your suggestions.'

She smiled and took a sip of her coffee. Panos made good coffee. She would miss it as she would miss a lot of things about Corfu: the gorgeous views, the sunshine weather and, most of all, Halloumi. Her gaze went to the interior of the restaurant, the restaurant they were about to open for business that night. How could a place she had likened to Sleeping Beauty's time-eroded castle just a short time ago mean so much to her now? So much that the thought of leaving it, even with the job opportunity she had always wanted in her sights, was filling her with apprehension?

She looked at the tables, Mrs Pelekas' hand-crafted cloths on each of them, waiting for shining silverware and glasses. The bright white-washed walls, acrylic paintings of scenes of Corfu hanging in appropriate spaces, old earthenware jugs and plates from the original Dimitriou restaurant washed and polished for display and the two sofas in the 'chill-out' area Harry had ordered almost from the outset. It was beautiful.

'What are you thinking?'

She turned her attention back to Panos. 'Nothing,' she answered immediately. She paused. 'Actually, everything.'

He reached out, slipping his long, tanned fingers in between hers. 'The restaurant looks…' He stopped as if he were searching for the right words to say. 'It looks right,' he finished.

'It does, doesn't it?' she agreed with a nod. 'Harry's done a great job.'

'And you too, Imogen. I seem to remember how good you are with paint.' He smiled. 'And going head-to-head with a developer who had very different plans for the beachfront.'

'Hmm,' she mused. 'He was a tricky customer but, in the end, he succumbed to my English charms.'

'Is that so?' Panos asked, shifting forward, his bare parts back in her sightline.

'Isn't it so? Mr Dimitriou?'

His lips met hers and she allowed herself to fall, elbow snagging the leg of a chair as her back met the tiles. She touched the rough bristle of his cheek, fingers wanting to memorise the feel and ingrain it into their tips like Braille. She felt him cup her hips with his hands and she drew his body closer to hers just like she had several times last night.

Suddenly there was a knocking on the glass of the front door. Imogen dragged her mouth from Panos', eyes wide. 'Oh my God! There's someone at the door! Pano… I'm naked!'

He smiled wolfishly. 'I know.'

'It's not funny! We only have drapes, not blinds… you can see through drapes!'

'Hello! Is anybody alive in there?' The voice came through the door as if a mouth had been put to the letterbox.

'Oh, Pano, it's Cooky. I forgot she was coming early with the bread!' Imogen pulled Mrs Pelekas' cloth up over her again and used her free hand to start locating her items of clothing.

'I will let her in,' Panos said, getting to his feet and seemingly unconcerned about his half-nude appearance.

'Wait! Not yet! Let me get something on!' Imogen flapped around for her dress but all she could find was Panos' shirt and her sandals.

Panos parted the gauze drapes at the window of the door and saw Cooky outside, her wild hair scraped back by a flamingo-patterned cotton hairband. He unlocked the door and pulled it open. 'Good morning,' he greeted.

Cooky's arms went up in the air. 'Praise be! The Lord has listened after all these years!' Her eyes roamed from Panos' bare feet up to the breadth of his shoulders. 'If they have this well-matured steak on the menu I will be eating here every night!'

He shook his head. 'I am not sure how I feel about the word "mature", Cooky. Are you certain of the translation?'

Before he could stop her, Cooky had poked a head around the door. 'Is that Imogen?'

Panos took a look back and saw Imogen fighting to pull his shirt over her head but failing miserably. Some hair, two floppy sleeves of cotton and a yelp signalled some kind of acknowledgement to their visitor.

'The song of lovers is still working its magic I see,' Cooky announced with a crusty laugh.

'Have you come with something?' Panos asked. 'Or is this just an early morning visit to provide gossip for the *kafeneio*?'

'I have bread,' she announced. 'In the back of my car.' Cooky made no move to collect it, still watching Imogen.

'Then I will get this,' he stated. 'And you will help me.' He directed Cooky backwards as he stepped out onto the sunlit terrace and closed the door behind him.

'Dressed like this?' Cooky asked, her gaze roving all over him again.

'I am wearing more clothes than most of the statues in Achillion Palace and nobody complains about them.' He led the way off the terrace and stopped at Cooky's battered red Renault 5. He opened up the back and picked out a tray of perfectly browned baps.

'Until this day I never think I could ever feel envy for a bread roll,' Cooky said, smacking her lips.

'Ai!' The familiar scream had Panos' eyes diverting left and there was Elpida, clambering down from the back of Risto's scooter, candy-striped dress ridden up past her knees. 'I know Harry and Imogen book a *bouzouki* player for tonight's entertainment. I do not realise they also book stripper!'

Panos shook his head. 'What are you all doing here so early?'

'Early?' Cooky exclaimed. 'If you think this is early how do you think bread ever gets made?'

'We are here to help with the preparations,' Risto said. 'The restaurant is fully booked for tonight but Harry wants it to be full every night, so I have more flyers to hand out this morning.'

'Planning, Panos. Harry is good at planning,' Elpida stated.

'Nobody is awake yet,' Panos countered. 'Not even the children.'

'I think someone was awake,' Cooky said. 'Although they did not seem keen to get out of bed… or should that be… off the floor.'

'Where is Imogen?' Elpida asked, taking a step up onto the terrace.

'Halfway out of a shirt that is too big for her,' Cooky said.

'Risto!' Elpida called, marching on. 'Come! You will make the coffee.'

SIXTY-FOUR

Halloumi, Acharavi beachfront

Imogen had never felt this nervous in her entire life. This feeling was topping the morning of her driving test, the morning of her wedding and the afternoon she knew she had to tell Daniel their marriage was over. She had never wanted anything to be as perfect as much as she wanted this night to be for Harry... for the whole family... for her.

As she laid silverware on the beautifully set tables she breathed in the fragrant aroma of Corfu, Greece. There were her perfumed candles, burning brightly in jars she'd polished and filled with sand from the beach and some carefully selected shells, her and Elpida's cooking – rich onion, tomato and garlic, lighter notes of bay leaf and rosemary and the creamy scent of halloumi cheese – and closer to her that indescribable hue of freshly-showered Adonis. She settled the final fork down and looked to Panos, who was rubbing at the wineglasses with a soft cloth. He had worked so hard for them today and it seemed like the most unlikely scenario. The man who had wanted to snatch the business from them, tear down the rest of the tavernas, was here now, helping launch the restaurant. And she loved that. Loved him? The question in her mind gave a kick to her already nervous stomach.

'Did you manage to deliver all the leaflets? I thought Harry was a little bit cheeky suggesting you took some to Roda,' she said. 'I'm not sure the restaurant owners there will be too keen on us trying to take a bit of their business.'

He placed the glass down and looked at her. 'Relax, Imogen. Tonight is going to be a great success and you underestimate the spirit of community in Greece.'

She laughed out loud. 'You're definitely not the same man I met at Tomas' Taverna.'

'No,' he agreed. 'I am not.'

They shared a look of understanding and then it was broken by a loud shriek as Socks came speeding into the room, almost on two paws.

'Auntie Imogen!' Tristan called, running in almost as fast as the cat. 'Socks has knocked over something.'

Shouting in Greek ensued from the kitchen area and the only word Imogen recognised was *skatá*. 'What has he knocked over, Tristan?' Imogen asked, going over to her nephew as Panos collared Socks.

'Those crispy cakey things that taste like honey,' he answered, eyes wide.

'*Baklava*,' Imogen and Panos said together.

Panos passed Socks to Tristan, making sure the boy had a tight hold. 'Tristan, take Socks onto the beach just outside. I will get your sister and Risto. You need to do one of the most important jobs tonight.'

'I do?' Tristan said, as if a cloak of responsibility had been slipped around his shoulders.

'Yes… In Greece, what is more important than the food and the candles and the *ouzo* is hospitality,' Panos said, resting a hand on his shoulder.

'Hospital what?'

'It means the warm welcome,' he explained. 'We need to make people feel so welcome at your father's restaurant that they never want to leave it.'

Imogen's gut flinched as she watched this gorgeous man with her nephew. That was how Corfu was making *her* feel. That, barring a few teething problems, she'd been made so welcome she never wanted to leave it. But she *was* leaving it. She *had* to leave it. To chase her dream. The very next day.

'And how can I do that?' Tristan asked. 'Use the knots I know from Scouts?'

Panos laughed. 'That would be one way to keep everybody here. But no… we give them a big smile, we say "a very warm welcome to Acharavi's new restaurant on the beach" and we give them a free aperitif.'

'A pair of teeth?' Tristan said, looking completely outraged.

'It's a drink,' Imogen stepped in, moving closer to them. 'We're giving out small measures of kumquat liqueur.'

'Can I have some?' Tristan asked.

'No,' Panos and Imogen said together. Now Tristan looked a little scared.

'It has alcohol in it, Tristan. I'll get you some orange juice.'

Socks started to wriggle in Tristan's arms, kicking its legs for release.

'Come,' Panos said, leading the way to the front door. 'Let us get you ready to be the best maitre d' in Corfu.'

'I said that cat was nothing but trouble. Didn't I? Pfft!'

Imogen smiled as she bound together the ingredients for more *baklava*. The kitchen was almost at boiling point in all respects. The oven was on full bore, the stove was boiling up pans of water for reasons she didn't dare question and the outside temperature was still over twenty-five. Elpida was readying the courses for that night's menu while she and Janie were making another batch of *baklava*. Having done all the food preparation earlier, Harry was getting showered and changed ready to be the face of Halloumi when it opened its doors.

'He's outside now with Tristan and Olivia. Risto and Pano are giving lessons in welcoming our first diners.'

'We have half an hour,' Janie exclaimed, wiping the sweat from her brow with the sleeve of her shirt. 'Can I just say it now and then I won't say it again for the rest of the night?'

'Say what?' Imogen asked.

'What the fuck are we doing?'

The ferocious air seemed to still, the volume of the bubbling water decreasing as if it wanted to listen in to the conversation. Imogen wet her lips and looked at Janie. Her hair was pinned back from her face with one of Olivia's elaborate hairclips – pink and glittery – in the shape of a swan.

'Pfft!' Elpida exclaimed. 'We are fucking running a restaurant!'

Imogen put a hand to her chest, shocked and then Elpida let out a loud, rasping laugh. 'You English! A little hard work and you are scared! In Greece we work this hard every day and… we would not have this any other way.'

'I didn't say it was too hard,' Janie countered. 'I was just pointing out…'

'I think it's a bit late for wondering what we're doing here,' Imogen admitted. 'We're in the middle of it. Hands in the halloumi… or the *baklava*,' she said, holding up her sticky fingers.

'Pass me that spoon,' Janie said, gently easing the pastry she was taming off the board.

'So, Imogen, tomorrow I will show you how to cook the perfect *stifado*,' Elpida said, hands flying from one saucepan to the other, sprinkling in one, sifting into another. 'It takes a long time but it is worth it for the most tender meat.'

Imogen focussed her eyes into the bowl. She hadn't wanted to say anything to anybody until after they had delivered a successful opening night, when they were hopefully on a high, sharing a bottle of celebratory *retsina* and toasting Halloumi's future. But now she was on the spot there was no avoiding it.

'Actually, Elpida, you'll have to show Janie or Harry.' She swallowed. 'I have to go home tomorrow.'

'What?' said Elpida and Janie together, both moving their eyes from their respective cooking and setting them on her.

Imogen set down her spoon and wiped her hands down the front of her apron. 'I've got an interview,' she admitted. 'For an internship at a really big hotel group back in England.'

'Oh, Imogen, that's what you've always wanted,' Janie said immediately.

'Yes,' she replied. 'It is.'

'Hotels,' Elpida said, her voice flat.

'Yes… I mean it's just a start and I might not even get on the programme yet… but they have so many applications and I'm down to the final five they're interviewing.'

'It's great news,' Janie said.

Imogen's eyes went to Elpida, who had now turned back to stirring the largest pot on the hob. It was quite obvious the Greek woman didn't think this was great news at all. And after all she had done for her and Harry, she suddenly felt riddled with guilt, like she was going to be deserting them at the first opportunity.

'I probably won't get it,' Imogen said. 'And, if I do, I'm sure I'll get plenty of time off to visit.'

'Pfft!' Elpida snorted. 'In the hotel industry there is never time off.' She looked directly at Imogen. 'I should know. One of my sons was killed by it.'

'Elpida…' Imogen started. 'I was always going home.'

'Janie… keep your eyes on the pots. Do not let them boil dry,' Elpida said. 'I am going to smoke.'

'Elpida,' Imogen said as the woman disappeared out of the kitchen and headed towards the back door.

'Leave her,' Janie said. 'She'll calm down. It's that Greek temperament, isn't it? All fiery and hot-blooded… You should know all about that now you're sleeping with one of them.'

Imogen shook her head. She didn't want to fall out with Elpida. She adored her. She had become like a second mother.

'Does Adonis know you're going?' Janie asked.

'His name's Panos,' Imogen said. 'And yes, he does.'

'And what did he say?'

Imogen sighed, the memory of him holding her, dancing with her on the patch of land he'd bought for her play area. 'He told me to follow my dreams.'

'Wow,' Janie said. 'That's a keeper right there.'

She swallowed. Yes, Panos was one of a kind. Complex and complicated but with a deep, true heart she wanted to get to know even more.

'I'm taking it Harry doesn't know you're going tomorrow.'

Imogen shook her head. 'This is his big night, Janie. I know he'll panic and I don't want him to panic. Not now he's done all this and he's about to open it up to everyone, showing it off for the first time. It's a special night. Please, Janie, don't tell Harry yet.'

Imogen didn't hear the creak of the door until it was too late. 'What's going on here then? Keeping girlie secrets are we?' Harry asked, standing tall in his tuxedo. 'What can't Janie tell me?'

SIXTY-FIVE

'Welcome to Halloumi,' Olivia greeted, dropping a curtsey at the arriving group of diners. 'This is the best restaurant on the beach and I recommend everything.'

Imogen smiled at her niece and nephew as they performed under Risto's watchful eye at the entrance to the terrace. The sun was spreading tendrils of light across the pebbled paving stones and the furniture on the patio area had been arranged so that each seat had a view of the sea and what a view it was this evening. Not a cloud in the cornflower-blue sky, Albania clear across the millpond of an ocean, palms and the revived and new Halloumi potted plants fluttering their pinks, purples and reds.

'Cheer up,' Harry said, nudging her elbow with his. 'It could be worse. Your brother could have just told you he'd bought a restaurant in Corfu.'

Imogen smiled, turning her attention to him. 'Are you angry with me for not telling you about the interview?'

'Angry with you?' Harry said. 'How could I be angry with you?' He grinned. 'You travelled a thousand miles with me and drove us down a mountain to get here. Then you went up against a fearsome property developer… someone I think you're still up against now but in a very different way… you scrubbed and you cleaned and you supported me even when you thought I was mad as a goat.'

She smiled. 'You've been listening to too many of Elpida's Greek analogies.'

'I'm over the moon you've got that interview, Immy. They'd be crackers to turn you down.'

'Thanks, Harry.' She straightened up as the first guests made their way towards them. 'I feel terribly guilty about leaving you in the lurch though. Will you be able to manage?'

Harry waved a hand at the entering customers. 'I'm hoping to get a more permanent member of the kitchen staff a little later.' He winked before stepping forward, hand outstretched. 'Roger… Ann… lovely to see you. Welcome to Halloumi!'

Panos placed two bottles of Mythos on the bar and accepted the money from the walk-in customer. The night was going so well. All the tables were full, customers were happy, plates were empty and the skeleton staff were working like Trojans. The best *bouzouki* player in Corfu, Vangelis, was just beginning his second set of the evening and he knew, within a couple of songs, there would be dancing.

Risto approached the bar, curls a little slick with perspiration. 'Another bottle of Merlot for table nine.'

'No problem,' Panos said, taking a bottle from the shelf and reaching for the corkscrew. 'So, how is tonight going for you?'

'Good,' Risto said, observing the restaurant scene in front of him, taking a little time and resting his arm on the bar.

'You like working here?' Panos inquired.

'Oh yes,' Risto said. 'For so long I do not have any job. Here, Halloumi, it is the best thing that has happened.'

Panos nodded. 'So, if I were to offer you a job working for me…'

Risto's eyes lit up. 'Really?'

'Do not get the wrong idea, Risto. I do not want to take you away from here.' He popped the cork on the bottle of wine. 'But

I am going to be involved with business in Acharavi and I will need some help. I would like to keep this in the family.'

Risto nodded. 'I would like that.'

'Good,' Panos said. He put the wine onto a tray and passed it to Risto. 'Here… And when you come back I will have the two Metaxas for table seven.'

He looked to his next customer, an older lady who had just entered the restaurant, a heavy-looking holdall on her arm. '*Kalispera*, I am afraid we are fully booked for tables tonight but would you like a drink for the terrace or the chill-out area?'

The woman let out a gasp, settling herself on one of the stools in front of the bar. 'Water… not from the tap, and then a large whisky, no ice.'

'Very good, madam,' Panos said. 'You are from England, yes?'

'Yes.'

'On holiday?'

'Yes,' she said, taking a grip of the water bottle Panos had just placed on the bar and unscrewing the cap from it. 'I'm here to visit my children.' She guzzled the water greedily, droplets speckling her lips.

'They live here?' Panos asked. 'In Acharavi?'

'One of them plans to, I know that much,' she answered, taking a revived breath.

'Granny?' Olivia queried, stopping in front of the bar and staring at the woman on the stool.

Panos balked. What had Olivia said?

'Livvy, dear, look at you!'

'Granny, what are you doing here?' Olivia asked.

'I've come to visit you, of course, and your brother and your mum and dad and Imogen. Where are they?'

'Excuse me, madam,' Panos said. 'You are Imogen and Harry's mother?'

'Yes, dear,' she extended her hand. 'I'm Grace.' She smiled. 'Calamari.'

Imogen had to be seeing things. Bursting out of the kitchen, her hands full of *meze*, and there was her mum sitting at the bar, talking to Panos. She felt the porcelain slipping through her fingers.

'Auntie Imogen! Granny's here!' Olivia announced, jumping up and down just in front of her.

Her mother was in Greece. Her mother, who was supposed to be measuring up curtains and cushion covers back in Hampshire, England, was sitting only a few metres away clutching a whisky glass. It didn't seem possible.

'Yes,' was all she could manage to say.

'Auntie Imogen, your meatballs are going to fall on the floor,' Olivia said.

Startled, Imogen quickly tipped the plates level and shifted back into action, navigating her way to the table in the corner to deliver the starters. Wiping her hands on her apron, she made her way over to the bar, still completely taken aback.

'Mum, what are you doing here?' she asked, her fingers pushing back stray wisps of hair from her face.

'Recovering,' Grace answered. 'From an awful taxi ride from the airport.' She took a sip of her whisky. 'No one said anything on the phone about Corfu being so mountainous.'

'Granny, I had an octopus sandwich earlier,' Olivia stated, grinning.

'Don't be silly, dear, you don't have octopus sandwiches. It was probably prawn,' Grace said.

'No,' Olivia said. 'It was octopus. Elpida gave it to me.'

'We have octopus on special,' Imogen said, her eyes going to Panos.

'Listen to you,' Grace said, a smile on her lips. 'You sound like you're running a restaurant.'

Imogen didn't know whether to laugh or cry. Her mum was here. She had travelled on her own, all this way, when she hadn't left the house in weeks.

'You have come a long way,' Panos said. 'Would you like me to get you something to eat?'

Grace shook her head. 'Not if it's octopus.'

'We have lots of other things, Mum,' Imogen said. 'How about some *baklava*? Janie and I made it.'

'Socks knocked the other trays on the floor,' Olivia stated with a giggle. 'He's naughty.'

'Come, Olivia,' Panos encouraged. 'Let us find something for your grandmother to eat.'

Olivia looked to Panos as he took hold of her hand. 'She mainly likes things from *Slimming World*.'

Imogen stood still, watching her mum look around the restaurant, taking it all in. The chatter was competing with Vangelis' *bouzouki* music and on the patrons' faces were contented expressions. The whole fusion was one of joy, laughter and lots of half-full wine glasses.

'I can't really believe it,' Grace said, her words wrapped up with so much emotion. 'This is Harry's restaurant.' She had said it like it was her first proper realisation of the project.

'Yes, Mum,' Imogen replied. 'It is.'

Grace shook her head. 'It isn't anything like you said.' She took another sip from the whisky glass. 'You said it was run-down, fit for nothing but demolition by dynamite.'

'I don't think I was that harsh.' Had she been? It all seemed so much more than just over a week ago. 'But it wasn't in a good state when we got here. *We* did this,' Imogen said proudly. 'Harry mostly. He had the vision of what it could be and it's…'

'Gorgeous,' Grace answered.

'Yes,' Imogen agreed. 'It is.' And she really felt that. It was like those little tavernas by the sea you saw on dream destination programmes, but somehow so much better. Tonight's ambience, the Greek music and that stunning sea view from each and every front window was a perfect mix.

Imogen refocussed on her mum. 'But, Mum, I don't understand. Why didn't you tell us you were coming? I thought you were busy with April's house.'

Grace managed a nod, but behind that subtle movement Imogen saw so much uncertainty. She watched her mum pick up a serviette from the bar and dab the beads of sweat on her head. A heavy and resigned sigh left her body. 'It wasn't for me,' she sighed.

'What d'you mean, Mum?'

'The house. April's house.' She sighed again. 'It wasn't for me.'

'But you were excited,' Imogen said. 'About the conservatory and the view of the river and… the free weights.'

'Things,' Grace said. 'Those are just things.'

'I know, but it did have an extra bedroom too.'

'And what would I need an extra bedroom for when Harry's here and Janie and the children are here and you're here.' She shook her head. 'Things aren't what make people happy, Imogen. People… family… loved ones, that's what makes a life.'

Imogen swallowed. Her mother was having some sort of reckoning. She slipped her hand into the pocket of her apron and toyed with the pen she had been taking orders with. *Gibraltar.*

'So, I decided,' Grace said with a sniff. 'I'm going to sell April's house.'

'You are?'

'Yes, and I'm going to take a holiday. Starting with here, in Corfu, at my son's restaurant and then… who knows? I might start visiting all those hotels I never got to go to with your father. Or I might invest.'

'Invest?' Imogen queried.

'I've been watching a bit of Jonnie Irwin of an evening. He finds bargain properties for people like me all over the world. I might even find something in Corfu.'

'Mum…'

'As long as you promise me there are no Asian hornets here.'

Imogen smiled. 'I promise.'

'Good,' Grace answered. 'Now, how about a hug for your new adventure-seeking mother before you go and find that brother of yours?' Grace opened her arms and Imogen stepped into the embrace, closing her eyes and relishing the comforting reassurance only a parent's love could embody.

'Mrs Charlton?'

Imogen broke the connection, looking up to see Panos and a platter of mixed *meze*. She smiled, then, taking her mother's hand, she directed Grace to look to him. 'Mum, I want you to meet someone,' she said. 'This is Panos Dimitriou.'

'It is a pleasure to meet you,' Panos said.

'And you,' Grace replied, shaking his hand. 'May I say that you are an excellent barman, knowing just what a weary traveller needs, and the whisky is exquisite.'

Imogen opened her mouth to correct her mother, but Panos beat her to it.

'Thank you, Mrs Charlton.'

'Oh please, do call me Grace.'

'Grace,' he repeated.

'Now, what have we got here?' Grace asked, hungry eyes moving to the *meze*.

SIXTY-SIX

Imogen had never felt so completely exhausted and exhilarated all at the same time. She had cooked, served and danced with customers and she was perspiring in places she didn't even know existed, watching the diners of Halloumi perform a group *sirtaki* dance around the restaurant. And her mum was at the centre of it. Arm entwined with Harry's on one side and Elpida's on the other, her mother was almost unrecognisable from the grief-ridden shell of a person back in England. Whether it was the enormity of April's house or just the realisation that life was short, Imogen wasn't complaining. She had her whole family here for this night, celebrating Harry's success.

'You do not want to dance?'

It was Panos' voice, low and sultry. She turned to him. 'Not tonight,' she admitted. 'I'm happy just watching.'

If she was honest, she was standing back and observing from a distance so she could capture the whole scene and memorise it. When she spoke to Janie on the phone or FaceTimed with Harry she would be able to replay this perfect summer night in her head and remember just how special it really was.

'I was thinking,' Panos began again. 'Your mother will need somewhere to sleep tonight.'

Imogen smiled at him. 'And you were thinking perhaps she could have my bed and we might spend some more time with Mrs Pelekas' tablecloths?'

He laughed. 'What sort of millionaire would I be if I always had you on the floor?'

A sting of arousal buzzed through her and she bit her bottom lip. 'I think Elpida is still cross with me. I'm not sure I'll be welcome in Agios Martinos.'

He shook his head again. 'I have other plans,' he admitted.

She whispered. 'The treehouse?'

He moved his head closer to hers, his mouth at her ear. 'Somewhere with an actual bed,' he whispered. 'Come on. We will dance.'

'Pano,' she said, about to protest.

'Risto!' he called to his cousin. 'Come!' He looked back to Imogen. 'Dance is very important in Greece. I thought I had taught you this on Acharavi main street.'

He squeezed her hand, drawing her into the crowd to the jaunty rhythm of the *bouzouki*. It was all happening so quickly, this wonderful, triumphant night disappearing so fast, tomorrow nearly upon them. It was going to be so hard to pack her case the following day and get on a plane.

'Imogen,' Panos said. 'We move first to the left,' he instructed, swaying so naturally in time to the music. 'And then to the right.'

She nodded, moving her feet in time to the music. Left and right were easy. It was backwards and forwards she was having trouble with.

Vangelis' strumming brought Zorba the Greek to its dramatic conclusion and the throngs of people dancing all put their hands together with shouts of *opa!* and other exclamations of delight. Out of breath, with her face flushed, her hair damp and a gorgeous man holding her hand, Imogen had never felt happier.

'Excuse me, ladies and gentleman!' It was Harry's voice, breaking over the hubbub of excitement and *ouzo* fumes. He moved to the front, beside Vangelis, and took ownership of the microphone. 'Excuse me!'

Risto put his fingers to his lips and let out a loud whistle which immediately silenced the room.

'He is making a speech?' Panos asked, looking to Imogen.

'It looks that way… although…he usually writes things down.'

Harry continued. 'I just wanted to say, thank you all so much for coming tonight and making it such a memorable evening for me and for all my family.' He swallowed. 'Even my mum is here and that was a total surprise.'

There was a collective 'aah' and Elpida raised Grace's hand in the air.

'I just wanted to say that I really appreciate your support.' He paused. 'My sister and I arrived here only a short time ago and she thought I was completely crackers for wanting to open a restaurant here and there were moments… moments I kept to myself I might add… whoops, sorry Immy.' He laughed. 'There were moments I did wonder whether I had bitten off more than I could chew.'

Imogen shook her head, tears pricking her eyes. Panos squeezed her hand.

'But here we are… in my restaurant… in Halloumi with… so many friends and family… my children speaking Greek and dancing like mini Zorbas.'

Imogen could tell he was starting to get really emotional and her heart was swelling with such pride for everything he had achieved and how fiercely determined he had been from the very beginning.

'And now there's someone special I'd like you to meet.' His eyes looked out into the crowd. 'Janie… will you come up here?'

Imogen put her hands to her face, deeply worried. The restaurant being a hit wasn't going to be enough for Harry. He'd always wanted to be reunited with Janie and the children. She was terrified this was way too soon.

'This is my wife, Janie… who fell in love with me in Corfu many moons ago… someone who has been with me through everything and has put up with far more than anyone could be expected to put up with…'

'I have to go up there,' she hissed to Panos, trying to squeeze herself past Roger and Ann.

'What? Why?' Panos asked, holding onto her hand.

'Janie… I know things have been tough but… I adore you and I never, ever stopped loving you.' Harry dropped down onto one knee. 'Will you marry me?' He blinked. 'Again.'

Imogen closed her eyes tight, unable to look or barely breathe.

'Yes, Harry! Yes I will! I love you! And I've missed you! I've missed you so much!'

Imogen snapped open her eyes just in time to see Janie throwing her arms around Harry, Tristan and Olivia circling around them, chasing Socks and a stray meatball.

'Imogen,' Panos said, pulling her back to him. 'You should have a little faith, no?'

She smiled, tears filling her eyes, and then she hooked her arms around him, holding him close.

SIXTY-SEVEN

Roda

As Panos drove along the coast from Acharavi towards the village of Roda his heart was swimming in his chest. He looked across at Imogen, her hair loose now, her face still flushed from the monumental cooking efforts and the dancing and a dart of emotion hit him square in the chest. This was what he thought he could never have. How he felt about her… it was love. He was certain of that now.

'Where are we going?' she asked, turning to face him just as he set his eyes back on the road.

'Roda,' he responded. 'Just a few miles.'

'Are you taking me to a club, Mr Dimitriou? Like one of your chrome monsters in Crete?'

'No,' he answered. 'But I will take you to one one day and you will see how much fun they are.'

She smiled. 'It's a deal.'

He pulled off the road, slowing the car down and creeping up a smaller road until it narrowed at the top and he swung into a driveway. As the car came to a halt on the drive, a security light flicked on, illuminating the grey and biscuit-coloured stone house. It looked different in the dark, but he still felt the same connection to it as he had earlier that day. He hadn't gone with Risto to deliver flyers for Halloumi. He had met an estate agent.

He stepped out of the car, eyes going to Imogen as she too got out and looked towards the swimming pool, shimmering in the glow of the lamplight, two wooden loungers beside it.

The house wasn't vast inside but it was in the very centre of some of the lush vegetation that gave Corfu its title: the Emerald Isle.

'Do you like it?' he asked. 'It has views to the sea.'

'It's lovely,' Imogen answered. 'It looks very traditional.'

'It is more modern inside.' He offered her his hand. 'Let me show you.'

'Pano, what is this place?'

He had hoped to have a little longer, perhaps to get inside the house and show her the mix of contemporary and Greek charm the estate agent had introduced him to earlier. What he'd done was fast. But it hadn't been done without consideration. He was grounded here again. Of that he was sure.

'It is mine,' he breathed into the night.

'Yours?' she answered.

He watched her in the pool of light, her eyes moving over the terrace to the water and the tall cypress trees at the outer boundary of the property's land.

'Yes, Imogen. I am going to live here.'

The house was stunning on the inside and furnished simply – a perfect mix of sleek lines and traditional Greek architecture. There was a large open-plan kitchen diner, the units in a cream Shaker style, a pine table with benches on the marbled floor. An archway led to a living area with two two-seater tobacco-coloured sofas, sliding doors at the far end of the room leading out to the terrace and the pool. Upstairs was a family bathroom and two bedrooms – a guest twin and a large master suite with a balcony that looked out onto the mountain and woodland views.

Standing on the balcony now, Imogen gazed out into the black, the only light coming from a small exterior lamp on the wall, around which a moth was flapping furiously.

She felt Panos before he appeared, like they were connected with an invisible thread. He moved close to her.

'What do you think?' he asked.

She looked at him. The house was incredible but its simplicity had also surprised her. Given that Panos had a very successful business and Google, she'd found out, claimed him to be one of the wealthiest men in Greece, the property didn't shout 'rich man's palace'. It wasn't the dwelling of someone showing off their off-shore bank accounts and mass of assets… It was cosy.

'Are you really going to live here?' Imogen asked. 'Full time?'

'Yes.'

'You're not going back to Crete?'

'No,' he said. 'I will be managing my business from Corfu, as well as helping set up Acharavi's community market and, hopefully, helping establish a more mutual networking approach to promotion for the beachfront restaurants.'

'And will that make you as much money as the nightclubs and go-karting?'

'I tell you this is not about the money, Imogen. My whole life has never really been about the money. It was always about the succeeding.' He sighed. 'Other people might measure success by monetary terms. I tended to measure it by how busy I was.' He clasped his hands to the rail of the balcony. 'If I was too busy to think then I was winning.'

'And that, you feel, has changed?'

'Yes,' he agreed. 'Being back in Corfu… meeting you… confronting… my ghosts…' He swallowed. 'I have been hiding from so much and it has stopped me seeing things clearly.'

Imogen breathed deeply. 'Me too,' she responded wistfully. 'I almost didn't let myself care for you.'

'Care for me?' Panos asked.

Was that enough? To say she cared for him? In reality it was much more but she was worried it was too soon.

She nodded. 'Very much.'

He placed a hand over hers. 'I was hoping you would say something like this.' He smoothed the skin of her fingers. 'Because, when I bought this house today, I hoped… well… I saw us together here.' He looked at her. 'When you visit Harry I thought maybe… you could stay here.'

Imogen smiled. 'Mr Dimitriou, are you asking me to make this my permanent holiday home?'

'Yes, I am,' Panos stated. 'Starting now… Tonight.'

'That's quick work,' she said.

'Well, we *did* dance to the song of lovers. I have to commit.'

'*Have* to?' she queried, an eyebrow raising.

'Want to,' he answered, leaning into her. 'Need to.' He pressed his lips to hers. 'Cannot wait a moment longer.' He scooped her up into his arms then and she squealed as he turned in the direction of the bedroom.

SIXTY-EIGHT

'Imogen.'

She smiled, keeping her eyes closed. His voice was like smooth, dark Arabica coffee with a swirl of rich, sweet cream.

'Imogen,' Panos said again.

She held onto the sound, letting it rove through her ear canal and slip down into her mind, determined to imbed it into the memory section before she truly gave into consciousness.

Finally Imogen began to open her eyes, a few millimetres at a time, small pieces of the man she'd fallen for coming into focus. Honed abdominal muscles, solid pecs, all covered by taut skin the colour of almonds. She'd had every fabulous inch of him all over her all night.

'*Kalimera*,' she greeted, hands walking up his stomach to his chest.

'It is past nine,' he said, taking her hand in his and bringing her fingers to his mouth. She let him kiss her thumb and index finger before she acknowledged what he'd said.

'Is it really?'

He nodded. 'I have to get you back to Halloumi… to pack your things,' he reminded her, before moving his mouth to her third finger.

'I know,' she sighed, enjoying the erotic stroke of his tongue. 'My mother has just got here and I'm leaving.'

He leant over her, olive-skinned perfection gazing down with a look of adoration in his eyes. Had she ever been looked at like that before? Like she was the only girl in the world? She reached up, sleeking her hands into his thick, black hair, pushing it back from his face, highlighting his cheekbones.

'It is going to be hard to let you go,' he whispered. 'Even for a short while.'

And there was the issue. She couldn't even tell him how long it would be. She didn't even know herself. If the interview went well, if she got the place, it could be months before she had any time off. She would want to do her very best, to concentrate hard, to learn all there was to learn. And if the interview didn't go well and she didn't get a place? What then? Would she go back to working at the diner? With Harry and Janie back together and planning to be in Corfu if schooling for the children allowed, with Grace keen for new experiences, what was left for her in the UK? What did she truly want? She sucked in a breath. It was definitely the Wyatt Hotel Group. This was her dream. Travel, good pay, new experiences, seeing the world her father had seen… this was her chance and she was going to grab it with everything she had. She had made the final five. Now it was up to her to make sure she was the last woman standing.

She closed her eyes for a beat, letting her fingers trace the contours of his jawline, before reconnecting their vision. 'I *will* come back, Pano,' she promised.

'To me?' he asked, as if it wasn't a foregone conclusion.

'Of course to you,' she whispered. 'To here… to us.'

He moved forward then, his mouth claiming hers in a kiss that set her head spinning as it moulded into the pillow behind her. She held onto the emotion coursing through her veins, knowing it needed to fill her completely if it was to be called upon when she was on her own in England. Neither of them knew how this was going to turn out, but, for now, as Panos' lips delivered sensual kisses that scorched her skin and branded her heart, Imogen knew what they had together was worth fighting the distance for.

SIXTY-NINE

Halloumi, Acharavi beachfront

With her case packed and beside her, Imogen stood on the terrace she'd got down on her hands and knees to scrub when she'd first arrived, staring out over the beach. It was tranquil today, almost subdued. The sun-worshippers quietly reading or just snoozing as they topped up their tans, children made silent sandcastles, even the constant hum of the mopeds wasn't as prominent as usual. She sighed, her gaze going to the palm tree at the side of the restaurant. That's almost where it had first started. The first time Panos had kissed her.

A furry tail curled around her bare calf and she looked down to see Socks' fluffy face gazing up at her. Even he was out of sorts, no chasing or sprinting, just mewing and looking for attention. She scooped him up, rubbing his head with her hand.

'Imogen.'

It was Elpida's voice and Imogen turned with a nervous swallow, expecting to receive the sharper side of the woman's tongue. She cuddled Socks close as if he could protect her.

'I have to say I am sorry and I hate to say this,' Elpida admitted, looking contrite.

'No, I should be the one saying sorry. I should have told you I was leaving sooner and I've made Pano promise not to do anything with the play area without me.'

'Pfft! Come here!' Elpida opened her arms and both Imogen and Socks landed in Elpida's hug, accepting the squeezing with relish.

When she thought her air supply was truly going to be compromised Imogen stepped back. 'I care for Pano, Elpida, so much, and if I didn't have this great possibility then...'

'Pfft! You are doing the right thing,' Elpida said. 'You are a strong woman who is striking out on her own, making a good life for herself. That is to be admired.'

'I know. I think I just have to go to this interview and see and then...' She shrugged. 'Who knows?'

'Yes,' Elpida agreed. 'And you have left me a replacement. I like this Grace, your mother.'

Imogen smiled. 'You do? I'm glad.'

'I think she come here for a holiday but she already talks of making apples that crumble for the menu.'

'Apple crumble is Harry's favourite,' Imogen said.

'And we have a wedding to plan soon, huh?' Elpida grinned. 'The song of lovers strike again.'

Last night Harry and Janie had been like newlyweds already, before Panos had whisked her off to Roda. The couple were going to renew their vows where it had all started for them and, where it seemed, their future lay... in Corfu.

'You and Risto will look after Pano, Elpida, won't you?' Imogen said, as Panos' Mercedes pulled up outside the restaurant.

'He is a different person now,' Elpida said, following Imogen's eyes. 'He has better priorities.'

Imogen smiled and waved at him.

'Don't think you're going to sneak off without giving your brother a hug,' Harry's voice boomed.

She put Socks down as she turned around to see Harry, Janie, Grace, Risto, Tristan and Olivia peeling out of the restaurant doors, smiles on all of their faces. They all looked like they could advertise the benefits of a Mediterranean lifestyle.

'I'm only going back to England. It's three hours on the plane,' Imogen said. 'Mum did it all by herself yesterday and I have Pano's personal jet,' she reminded them.

'Pano?' Grace queried. 'I thought he said his name was Panos.'

Imogen couldn't bring herself to explain the shift in intimacy now. She was sure Janie would fill her mother in later.

'I'm going to miss you so much, Immy,' Harry declared, his arms folding around her.

She closed her eyes, breathing in the scent of … was that kumquat or fig? She sighed. Her brother was turning Greek and she was going to miss it all.

'But this is an amazing chance and we are all rooting for you,' Janie chipped in. 'That's what he was meant to say. The non-selfish version, not the what am I going to do with a wife who can only cook cupcakes, two children who just want to *eat* the food and a cat who wants to *play* with the food version.'

Imogen turned to Janie. 'You made great *baklava* yesterday.'

'I did, didn't I?' Janie replied.

'And you two,' Imogen said, addressing the children. 'I want you two to be in charge of two people while I'm not here.'

'Who?' Olivia asked.

'Firstly, Socks,' Imogen said, indicating the cat who was belly up, eyes closed, stretching his body towards the sun. 'He isn't allowed in the kitchen.' She lowered her voice. 'But you can feed him leftovers when everyone has gone home.'

'Who else?' Tristan enquired.

'I want you to listen to Risto a lot,' Imogen said, looking to Panos' cousin. 'He is our head waiter and he can teach you two a lot about how a restaurant is run. Then, maybe when you're older, you can run Halloumi.'

The horn of the Mercedes blasted and Imogen checked her watch. It was time to go. She looked to her mum last of all.

'I'm so glad you're here, Mum, even if I'm going back for a bit.' She swallowed the knot of emotion in her throat. 'Corfu is beautiful and it is time you had a few adventures of your own.'

Grace dabbed at the corner of her eyes with her fingers. 'Remember what you said, it's only three hours away... plus the car-mountaineering of course.'

Imogen forced a laugh and took one last look at her Greeklish family lined up before her. 'I'm going to miss all of you,' she stated. 'So much.'

'Pfft! Enough of this goodbye-ing,' Elpida said, waving a hand over her face as if stemming her own tears. 'We have an evening service to get ready for.'

'Bye, Auntie Imogen,' Olivia said, pigtails shaking.

'See ya! Wouldn't want to be ya!' Tristan shouted, waving a hand.

'Bye,' Imogen said, pulling on her case. She turned away before the first tear began to fall.

SEVENTY

Ioannis Kapodistrias Airport

Imogen looked out at the planes sitting on the tarmac, passengers disembarking in the plus thirty temperature, coming to this beautiful island for a week or a fortnight's holiday. She had been one of them. Perhaps not looking forward to an all-inclusive break, but someone knowing nothing about this Greek island and wondering what she might find. She had never expected what had ended up being there for her.

There was the mountain range that dominated the island's landscape and the green cypress trees, tall and slender, rising up as if they might touch the sky. Waves of heat seemed to bend everything in her sightline or perhaps that was the tears still congregating in her eyes.

'Imogen.'

Panos' voice broke into her thoughts and she drew her eyes away from the runway. The private aircraft that had taken Rhea just a short hop down to Crete was now taking her home to England.

'The plane is ready. You will make a stop for fuel,' Panos said. 'But it should not take too long.'

She nodded. 'Thank you for this.'

'For what?'

'That plane… Arranging it at short notice and getting me back for the interview.'

'Of course I would do this. It is what you have been waiting to do for so long.'

'Yes,' she said, looking back to the planes but not moving.

'I have something for you,' Panos said.

She turned back to him, breathing in his now familiar scent, sucking up how utterly hot he looked in a slim-fit shirt and casual blue jeans.

He held something out to her and she took it. It was a pen. She twisted it between her thumb and forefinger, looking at the embossed letters. *Dimitriou Hotels.*

'It was my father's,' Panos explained. 'Back then he did not have pens for promotion like hotels do now but he had a small number. Like this one.'

It was an ink pen. A proper fountain pen with a heavy silver barrel and a blue body. But it wasn't what it was, it was what it meant, to him, and what he knew it would mean to her.

She burst into tears, clutching the pen in her fist and putting that fist to her mouth.

'Sshh,' he said quickly, drawing her to his body, his hands in her hair. 'I do not mean to make you sad.'

She shook her head. 'You haven't. You've made me happy. So happy. And leaving is so hard.'

He held her a little way away from him, gazing into her eyes. 'You must do this, Imogen. Follow your heart, remember?'

She nodded, trying to bolster her resolve. 'I remember.' She sniffed. 'So, while I'm away I want you to throw yourself into the community market project,' she began. 'I'll never forget that perfect day in Arillas.' She swallowed. 'Make that happen in Acharavi.'

'Imogen,' he started, touching her arm.

She shook her head. 'Don't… Let me finish.'

He dropped his hand, but his gaze remained with her.

'Call your mother,' she whispered.

He dropped his eyes to the floor.

'No, don't look away. You need to do this properly,' she told him. 'If you're going to move on from the past. You need to build bridges or you'll lose the connection forever.' She offered him a weak smile. 'I know you know this but I also know that you haven't called her yet and you're terribly stubborn.'

He kissed her then, pressing his mouth to hers then gathering her body up in his arms, holding her tight, as if letting go would be the end of him. She broke off, stepping back as the tears welled up in her eyes.

'Goodbye, Pano,' she whispered. 'I'll see you soon.'

'*Antio*,' he replied.

He watched her walk to the gate, showing her passport to the woman on the desk before the double glass doors opened. She stopped, waving a hand before heading through and down the steps to the waiting bus.

Moving then, he positioned himself at the glass, looking out over the planes on the tarmac, his jet the nearest. He could see Imogen approaching the bus down the incline to the concrete, her small case behind her, steps slow. He watched her get on board ready for the rather ridiculous one minute ride to the planes.

He slipped out his mobile phone, pressing the display and searching through his contacts until he found what he was looking for. *Mama*. He would call her, like Imogen asked. He *wanted* to call her and make things right again.

Looking to the window again he watched the bus stop by his plane and the doors open. Any second now he would be watching the woman he loved get on a jet that was going to take her away from him. But it wasn't forever. He had to remember that.

The bus doors closed again and he pressed his face against the glass, looking for Imogen as the vehicle turned in an arc and headed back to the terminal. Where was she? Had he missed her? The engines of his jet started turning. And then he looked back to the bus. The doors whooshed open and there she was, bolting off the step of the bus, case flying behind her as she sprinted back across the ground.

He moved then, unconcerned for anything but her.

'Sir, you cannot go through there,' the woman at the desk said, stepping sideways to try and detain him. He brushed past her, forcing the doors to open, and running, taking the steps two at a time.

Imogen felt sick and her heart was racing but she was certain of only one thing. She couldn't get on the plane. She couldn't leave. She didn't want to. She ran up the incline, hair flying in the breeze, everything sticky with the heat and then she stopped. Because he was there, running towards her. She dropped her case and flew into his arms, holding on with everything she had.

'I couldn't leave, Pano. I don't want to leave,' she rushed out. 'The Wyatt Group isn't what I want any more. It's here. It's Corfu. It's my family. It's you,' she gabbled.

He held her, his skin pressed tight to hers, and then he parted them, looking at her with those charcoal eyes under thick lashes. 'I love you, Imogen.'

'Oh God, Pano, I love you too. So much!'

He kissed her then, to the hum of an Airbus engine, and she knew without any shadow of a doubt that her future lay here, serving up Greek magic under azure skies with the man she loved. And, as Panos deepened their kiss and promised never to let her go, she was sure, from somewhere high on the mountain, she heard a goat laugh.

EPILOGUE

Halloumi, Acharavi beachfront

'Ladies and Gentleman, if I could have your attention for just one minute,' Harry announced.

Imogen, two dessert bowls in her hands, stopped moving and looked around at the full restaurant, customers in the middle of dining.

'I don't want to interrupt you for too long but today is a special day for us here at Halloumi and I thought it would be nice if you would share it with us.' Harry held up a shot glass filled with kumquat liqueur. 'Today is mine and Janie's wedding anniversary,' he said. 'And in just a few weeks' time we're going to be renewing our wedding vows right here on the beach. So, I'd just like you all to raise your glasses in a toast to my beautiful wife.' Harry raised his glass in the air. 'To Janie.'

'To Janie.'

Imogen quickly dispatched the bowls to the table that had ordered them and clapped her hands in applause. She headed back towards the kitchen and as she swung through the doors she almost bumped into Panos carrying two plates of swordfish.

'*Kalispera,* Miss Charlton, but try and be a little more careful, huh?' Panos said, stopping in his tracks and setting his dark, delectable eyes on her.

'I think you'll find it's you who ought to be more careful. I almost ended up wearing that meal you're carrying,' she replied.

'And what would have happened then?' he asked. 'Your shirt would have been ruined.'

'And I would have had to take it off.' She smiled, her eyes challenging him for a response.

'You win,' he breathed. 'You must stop this or I will not be able to carry on working here.'

'Two panna cotta! I have two panna cotta here! Cooky! Where is the compote for table nine?' Elpida's voice came from the kitchen. 'Grace, we need pie!'

'Your swordfish is getting cold,' Imogen remarked, trying to move past him.

'Everything else is getting hot, I promise you,' he whispered.

'Not in front of your mother,' Imogen said, hitching her head over to one of the tables.

'Sophia, will you teach me how to get my hair like yours?' Olivia asked Panos' mother.

'Of course,' Sophia replied. 'But it will involve lots of brushing, Olivia.'

Panos brought the meals over to Janie, Olivia, Tristan and his mother. 'How is everything for you?'

'It's all lovely and it's still going so well, isn't it?' Janie remarked, eyes roving over the room full of customers.

'And now, my mother comes to help us out.' He looked at Sophia, smiling.

'It is so nice to be spending time with you all,' Sophia said.

That first phone contact with his mother was the day he had taken Imogen back to Acharavi after she had fled the airport bus, and it had been the start of the walls between them tumbling down. A tentative beginning had resulted in Panos crying his heart out over everything he had endured in his childhood followed by his admission of guilt in his failings – running away, isolating himself and cutting off one of the people who *had* been there for him until *he* had chosen for her not to be.

'We can't stay long,' Janie said. 'These two have to be at school next week. Then it's the vow renewal and then we need to look at things properly.'

'We don't want to go,' Olivia said. 'We want to stay here.'

'I'm very aware of that, thank you, but these things are very complicated,' Janie said.

'I can count to three in Greek,' Tristan announced.

'Well, I can say the word for delicious,' Olivia bragged. '*Nóstimo*.'

'Very good,' Panos said, topping up everyone's water glass.

'How long are you able to stay, Sophia?' Janie asked.

Panos looked to his mother, waiting to hear the inevitable.

'Actually, John is going to be joining me here for a few weeks.' She ran a finger around the rim of her water glass. 'We've never really spent very much time on Corfu for… for a variety of reasons… and we both thought it would be nice to reconnect with the island… and spend some more time with family.'

Panos met her eyes then, seeing her obvious affection for him.

'That is OK with you, Pano?' Sophia asked him tentatively.

He nodded, swallowing away the building emotion. 'I would like that very much.'

Imogen entered the kitchen, scooping up another two plates destined for table six. Elpida was stirring a giant silver pot with the biggest wooden spoon she had ever seen. Her mum was beside the Greek, furiously mashing up potatoes.

'This octopus!' Elpida exclaimed. 'It does not want to be mixed.'

'Are you sure it's dead?' Imogen asked, looking into the pot.

'If it is not dead from the boiling water it will be dead from that spoon,' Cooky remarked with a crusty laugh.

Harry burst through the door, red-faced and out of breath but looking insanely happy. 'Another three octopus specials for table nine and a swordfish.'

'Raw food is all the rage now, isn't it?' Imogen remarked.

'Not in Greece if you want to keep your health and hygiene certificate,' Harry stated. 'Is something wrong?'

'He is relenting,' Elpida said, bashing the spoon into the pan and smiling at Harry.

'I'm glad I have the potatoes,' Grace remarked.

Imogen picked up another order and ushered her brother out of the kitchen. She stopped walking just before they got to the restaurant area. The lilt of *bouzouki* and lute from the musicians in the corner of the room filtered up into the wooden-beamed ceiling, the lemon scent of the candles on each table as well as Elpida, Cooky and Grace's cooking filled the space and Imogen breathed it all in deep. It was home.

'Look, Harry,' she whispered. 'You did it. Your own Greek restaurant, busy, successful… perfect.' She turned to her brother. 'Is it still how you imagined it?'

Harry shook his head. 'No,' he responded. 'It's nothing like I imagined it.' He took a deep breath, more colour and pride coating his cheeks. 'It's so much better.'

'Harry!' Elpida's voice screamed. 'Get this cat out of the kitchen or I will sell it on a stall at the first Acharavi community market!'

'Oh dear,' Harry said. 'Socks still doesn't seem to like being told what to do.'

'I wonder where he gets that from,' Imogen said, smiling.

Harry looked back to the full-to-capacity restaurant, hands on his hips. 'I tell you what, Immy, if business keeps going like this I might have enough spare cash to buy that boat I always wanted… or another restaurant, you know, when this one is under control.' His eyes lit up. 'Maybe we could start a chain… a small chain… here in Corfu.' He looked to Imogen. 'What do you think?'

Imogen smiled before linking her arm through her brother's. 'Oh, Harry, I think you should definitely buy a boat.'

GREEK RECIPES

The restaurant Halloumi was inspired by a real restaurant called Lavender on Beach Road Three, Acharavi, Corfu, run by Mandy's friends Michelle and Lee Chapman and Melinda Jacobs. They have kindly shared some of Lavender's usually top secret, special recipes for you to try at home!

Ouzo Prawns

Ingredients

- 3 tablespoons olive oil
- 4 garlic cloves, crushed
- 1 small onion, finely chopped
- ¼ teaspoon crushed dried chillies
- 1 x 400g and 1 x 200g can chopped tomatoes
- 3 tablespoons *ouzo*, plus extra for sprinkling
- 1kg large, raw, shell-on prawns
- A little olive oil, for brushing
- 175g feta cheese, crumbled
- Small handful of wild fennel tops, roughly chopped
- Salt and freshly ground pepper
- Wild fennel tops, to garnish

Method

1. Pour the olive oil and garlic into a frying pan and place over a medium-high heat.

2. As soon as the garlic begins to sizzle around the edges, add the onion and crushed dried chillies and cook gently until soft but not browned.

3. Add the tomatoes and 2 tablespoons of the *ouzo* and simmer for 7-10 minutes until thickened slightly. Season well with salt & pepper and keep hot.

4. Peel the prawns, leaving the last tail segment of the shell in place. Put them into a bowl and toss with the remaining *ouzo*, ½ teaspoon salt and some freshly ground pepper. Set aside for 5 minutes.

5. Turn grill on 10 minutes before you are ready to grill the prawns. Thread the prawns onto pairs of parallel thin skewers – this will stop them from spinning round when you come to turn them. Brush them lightly with olive oil and grill for 1½ minutes on each side until cooked through.

6. Stir half of the feta cheese into the tomato sauce with the chopped wild fennel tops and spoon it over the base of 1 large or 4 individual warmed serving dishes.

7. Push the prawns off the skewers onto the top of the sauce and sprinkle with the remaining feta. Garnish with the fennel tops and serve hot.

Corfiot-inspired Pot Roast Chicken

Ingredients
Serves 4

- 1 x 2kg chicken (portion the chicken into 2 breasts and 2 legs/thighs to brown in the pan)
- 4 tablespoons olive oil
- 1 large onion, halved and thinly sliced
- 4 garlic cloves, thinly sliced
- 60g sun-dried tomatoes
- 400g tin of chopped tomatoes
- 1 cinnamon stick
- 1 tsp dried oregano
- A generous pinch of crushed dried chillies
- 150ml of chicken stock
- 400g orzo pasta
- 25g butter
- 50g finely grated *kefalotyri* (Greek hard cheese) or, if not available, Parmesan
- A small handful of flat-leaf parsley leaves, roughly chopped
- Salt and pepper

Method

1. Preheat the oven to 180°C.

2. Heat 3 tablespoons of the olive oil in a large casserole dish and add the chicken and brown on all sides over a medium heat.

3. Remove the chicken to a plate and add the remaining oil and the onion to the casserole and cook until soft and lightly browned.

4. Add the garlic, sun-dried tomatoes and tin of tomatoes, cinnamon, oregano, dried chilli flakes, chicken stock, 1 teaspoon of salt and some black pepper.

5. Bring to a simmer, replace the chicken and cover the casserole with a tight-fitting lid. Transfer the casserole to the oven and bake for 1½ hours until the chicken is tender.

6. Bring a large pan of salted boiling water to the boil in a large saucepan.

7. When the chicken is cooked, lift it onto a carving board and leave it to rest covered in foil for 10 minutes.

8. Skim the excess fat from the surface of the sauce, place the casserole over a medium heat and simmer until the sauce is reduced and thickened.

9. Cook the orzo for 7 minutes until *al dente*.

10. Drain and return to the pan with the butter and grated cheese and toss together well.

11. Remove the cinnamon stick from the sauce, stir in the parsley and season to taste.

12. Carve the chicken.

13. Spoon the sauce onto warmed plates and place the chicken on top.

14. Spoon the orzo alongside and serve.

Lemon Meringue Pie

Ingredients

For the pastry

- 225g/8oz plain flour
- 175g/6oz butter
- 45g/1¾oz icing sugar
- 1 large free-range egg, beaten

For the lemon filling

- 6 lemons, zest and juice
- 65g/2¼oz cornflour
- 250g/9oz caster sugar
- 6 free-range egg yolks

For the meringue topping

- 4 free-range egg whites
- 225g/8oz caster sugar
- 2 tsp cornflour

Method

1. Pre-heat the oven to 180°C/350°F/Gas 4.
2. First make the pastry. Measure the flour and butter into a food processor and blend together until the mixture resembles fine breadcrumbs.
3. Add the icing sugar, egg and 1 tablespoon of water and whizz again until combined to a ball.

4. Tip the pastry onto a work surface and roll out to a 3mm thickness.

5. Use the rolling pin to lift the pastry up and transfer it to line a 23cm/9in loose-bottomed flan tin. Be careful not to stretch the pastry as you tuck it into the corners.

6. Cover in cling film and place in the refrigerator to chill for 30 minutes.

7. Take the pastry-lined tin out of the fridge and trim the excess pastry.

8. Press the top edge of the pastry so that it stands slightly higher than the top of the tin.

9. Line the pastry case with parchment and fill with baking beans.

10. Bake for about 15 minutes then remove the beans and parchment and return to the oven for a further 5 minutes.

11. Remove from the oven and reduce the temperature to 170°C/340°F/Gas 3½.

12. For the filling, mix the lemon zest and juice with the cornflour and stir to form a smooth paste.

13. Measure 450ml/16fl oz of water into a pan and bring to the boil.

14. Add the lemon cornflour mixture to the hot water and stir over the heat until the mixture has thickened, then remove from the heat.

15. In a bowl, mix together the sugar and egg yolks and carefully whisk into the lemon mixture in the pan. Stir over a medium heat until thickened.

16. Set aside for a few minutes, then pour into the baked pastry case.

17. For the meringue, whisk the egg whites in a free-standing mixer until soft peaks form when the whisk is removed.

18. Add the caster sugar a little at a time, still whisking until the meringue is stiff and glossy.
19. Add the cornflour and whisk again.
20. Spoon on top of the filled pastry case and spread the meringue to completely cover the lemon filling. Then create a swirl on the top of the meringue.
21. Bake in the oven for about 15 minutes until the filling is completely set and the meringue is lightly golden and crisp.
22. Serve warm or cold.

LETTER FROM MANDY

I really hope you're smiling after your holiday with Imogen, Panos, Elpida, Harry and all the gang at Halloumi on the beautiful Greek island of Corfu! With this book I wanted to give you all another feel-good beach read that also captured the wonderful spirit of Greece and its people. I love Corfu – that's why I holiday there and get so inspired!

THANK YOU SO MUCH for buying *Those Summer Nights*! If you enjoyed the book I would LOVE you to leave me a review. Reviews really do mean the world to us authors.

Who was your favourite character? Did you laugh at Elpida? Did you want to be a diner at Halloumi? Did the story make you want to book your next holiday to Greece? Let me and the rest of the world know how you felt about it!

And, if you liked this book, perhaps you want to read more! I love connecting with readers on Twitter, Facebook and Goodreads. Come and join me!

To keep right up-to-date with the latest news on my new releases just sign up at the webpage below:

www.bookouture.com/mandy-baggot

Here's to more feel-good fiction and hot heroes!

Mandy xx

@mandybaggot
mandybaggotauthor
www.mandybaggot.com

ACKNOWLEDGEMENTS

A huge THANK YOU to my FABULOUS agent, Kate Nash, who works tirelessly answering all kinds of mad requests at all times of day and never seems to be fazed! I am so grateful for all your support!

Thank you to my best supportive writing buddies who are so invaluable to me for all sorts of reasons, some of which involve wine and food! Rachel Lyndhurst, Zara Stoneley, Linn B Halton and Sue Fortin – love you ladies!

To my street team – the Bagg Ladies - who are an amazing band of bookworms who seem to love all things Team Baggot. We've got another amazing year ahead!

A BIG thank you to Michelle and Lee Chapman and Melinda Jacobs for gifting me their restaurant – in a literary sense! Lavender Restaurant and Tea Rooms, Beach Road 3, Acharavi, Corfu was the inspiration behind Harry's restaurant, Halloumi. If you guys hadn't invited me for a book signing there this book would never have been written. I can't wait to spend more of the summer with you eating your FABULOUS food!

To all my readers, Facebook and Twitter followers – without your fantastic support I wouldn't be on this journey. Every purchase, every review, every share and supportive comment means so much! Thank you!

And finally, to my husband, Mr Big and my two daughters – thank you for putting up with me! Who knew living with an author was so hard?! Love you three to bits!

Made in the
USA
Columbia, SC